The Patricians Book Two

BITTERSWEET REV

R.G. ANGEL

Bittersweet Revenge – Patricians book 2

By R.G Angel

Cover: Red Leaf Book Design
Editing: Writing Evolution

Dedication:

To my lovely Readers, thank you for the kind words and sweet reviews. I'm so happy you are enjoying Esmeralda journey as much as I enjoyed writing it.

To my betas and in particular Miranda and Amber. Your enthusiasm and love of the story and characters helped me go through with this version of the story and your invaluable suggestions helped me shape this story.

To all bloggers who are helping me and supporting me through any new releases. You guys are fantastic and I'm forever in your debt.

To all the members of my readers group 'RG's Angels' – You guys are amazing and your love of Bittersweet Legacy and its characters is the reason why this book came to light earlier. Your eagerness motivated me to write better and faster.

To Nicole, who helped me brainstorm the plot of Bittersweet Revenge. Thank you for your twisted mind!

To the amazing Christina S who supported me and helped me promote my book when I had no clue how to do things. Your kindness matters more than you think.

To my fellow authors and in particular Siobhan Davis and LJ Shen for a) writing engrossing stories that kept me entertained during my meltdowns and b) for being very supportive and helping me get my story out there. You are both amazing and I can only hope to one day be as talented as you are.

And last but not least thank you to my family and friends for always being in my corner even when I'm an Emo fool. I love you.

Contents

Chapter 1- Caleb

I wasn't sure how long I'd been sitting in the car, but it was long enough for my ass to go numb. I sighed, keeping my eyes locked on to the bay windows of Seashell Diner.

"Seashell Diner," I said, and snorted at the stupidity of the name. It was so unoriginal for a diner located by the seafront… Small town, small people, small minds, and–

I lost my train of thought as my eyes followed the waitress exiting the kitchen. Her wavy ponytail moved from side to side as she carried an impressive amount of plates to a table full of jocks I wanted to kill, just for the smile she gave them.

I closed my eyes. Pinching the bridge of my nose, I tried to keep my feelings in check, tried to bury them so deep inside I'd forget them. I wanted to go back to the man I'd been before - unfeeling, but functioning at least. Before her I had never felt like a bipolar man without his lithium. Before her I'd never felt out of control.

I hated myself for all these feelings and it made me hate her even more. I opened my eyes and looked at her as she cleaned a table close to the entrance. I could see the necklace I'd given her shine around her neck and this caused a lot of complicated and contradictory feelings to settle in my treacherous heart.

Esmeralda Forbes… I had known from the moment our eyes had connected that first day when I'd driven to Archibald's home that she was trouble – with her pinup, unassuming beauty.

I had thought it was an act before; no girl that looked like that could be so kind, so humble and yet she was…or was she?

A new wave of anger filled me. She had played me. I looked down at my hand and the engagement ring resting in my palm. For all I knew it might have all been an act.

I clenched my hand around the ring and squeezed, squeezed with all the rage, betrayal and shame I felt – rage at the whole situation and reason behind her slip-up, betrayal by her and Archibald who'd plotted against me, and shame for not seeing it coming.

Archibald was smart. I couldn't prove his involvement, but she'd disappeared so well, leaving breadcrumbs leading in the wrong direction. As far as I could see Esmeralda was smart, but she was not calculating. She was not a mastermind, not like Archibald and I were. She was much more controlled by her feelings, as her slip-up a week ago had proved, and this disappointed me in some strange way.

If she hadn't called him, that stupid insignificant jock, she would still be at bay, any trace of her existence hidden so well – suspiciously, professionally so.

For a month William and my father had spent thousands of dollars trying to find her to no avail, nothing at all except this stupid wild goose chase around New York where her ring was found.

I had almost lost all hope of finding her, punishing her, lost the hope of getting my revenge for making me feel like a fool, for letting her see the small chink in my armor and using it against me. Maybe I should thank her for that, for pointing out that chink, because it had allowed me to seal it, cover it and make myself stronger and angrier than I had ever been. It had allowed me to plot and organize a revenge of biblical proportions. I was going to make her feel what she'd made me feel tenfold.

Feelings were a liability, a weakness, something that were used against you, even by the people you cared for. My mother had told me that time and time again and I'd thought I'd learned…until her.

And Esmeralda had fallen in the same stupid trap when she'd called the insignificant Ben Deluca, that pauper idiot. So here I was about to bring her home, back to a cage so secure she'd never escape again - at least until I had considered my revenge complete.

My phone vibrated on the passenger seat. I rolled my eyes at the name flashing up – *W. Forbes.* I had to pick up if I wanted to prevent him from jumping in his other jet. I'd barely managed to have him agree to let me come here by myself.

"Have you found her?" He demanded as soon as I picked up the phone.

Good morning to you too, I thought sarcastically. "Yes sir, I have just found her." *Lies.* "She is working and there are a lot of people around her. I need to find an opportunity to get her alone. I need time."

He sighed with frustration. "Why? You can just carry her away. Drug her if you have to."

I rolled my eyes again. This man was just so basic. "In this day and age, sir, with social media, I would strongly advise against a public tantrum and attempted kidnapping unless you want the videos to hit the web. Then everybody will know that Esmeralda Forbes didn't take a sabbatical in Paris like we said, but ran away from you."

"From *us*," he corrected, and I knew he enjoyed my demise much more than he cared to admit.

I pursed my lips, taking a deep breath to calm my nerves. "Maybe so. I agree that it wouldn't look good on me to have a runaway bride, but having a daughter disrespect the all-powerful William Forbes…" I trailed off, letting him interpret it the way he wanted to.

"Just–" he growled. "Just bring her back. I don't care how. I want her home - tonight. If you can't I'll dispatch a team and–"

"That won't be necessary, sir."

"One can hope. Call me when you are on your way to the airstrip or if you're failing."

"I can handle it!" I barked, letting go of my fake patience. Who did he think he was? By claiming Esmeralda, I was saving him from an impending scandal. He owed me! I wasn't one of his lackeys he could bully. He would have to learn to respect me too.

He hung up without another word.

I scowled at the phone in my hand. I could handle Esmeralda. It hadn't taken me long to find her once I'd made it to Carmel – less than six hours in fact. I'd planned to grab her at the end of her last shift, but had hesitated when I'd seen her exit, the silver necklace I'd given her proudly around her neck. I'd realized that I'd missed my opportunity when she was engulfed by the crowd on the pier.

I'd followed her, hidden under my baseball cap. She'd stopped by a hot chocolate cart and ordered one; it might have been January, but it was California. Then she'd walked further down and sat on a bench, looking up at the temporary Ferris wheel, set up for what I presume was the holidays. I'd seen her face quite well from my spot, half-hidden behind a newsstand. She'd looked up wistfully, almost pained. Was she conflicted? Was she thinking about the day I never should have given her? A day that made me look and feel weak and foolish?

My will had wavered in that moment and it'd angered me to realize that, willingly or not, she still had power over me. I had tried to reason with myself, pretending that I just needed to see the life she'd built in case she wanted to leave again; the more you knew about your prey, the more leverage you had.

I had followed her to the three-story apartment building and stayed there, in the parking lot, for over an hour before going back to my bed & breakfast. It had been risky to do that. What if she'd actually noticed me and disappeared into the night?

But I was relieved in the morning when I'd parked in front of the diner and saw her waiting tables. This was where I had been for the last two hours, just observing.

You're turning into a fucking stalker, Astor. I could hear Archibald's voice in the back of my mind, taunting me.

I growled, reaching for the Yankees cap on the passenger seat. It had been one of Theo's favorites, along with his Iron Man one. I wasn't sure why I kept the memento, but even now, I couldn't let it go completely.

But now was not the time. Now I had to bring home a more-than-reluctant bride.

I waited for Esmeralda to disappear into the kitchen before walking into the diner and grabbing a menu. Sitting at the back, I opened the menu to hide my face.

"Do you need anything else?" I heard her ask on my left. Just her voice caused unwanted emotions to arise - mainly anger, but even that was too much. She shouldn't be able to affect me this much. Any feelings she caused, positive or negative, were a weakness - a weakness I couldn't afford.

"Your number," one of the jocks sniggered.

I gripped the yellow laminated menu tighter in my hands, using all my willpower not to jump from my seat on an overused brown leather bench and smash his head on the table for daring to covet what was mine.

She sighed. "I already said I was not interested, but thank you."

"Ah, come on. He's been forcing us to come for greasy breakfasts for the past ten days just because of you," another one whined, his voice even more aggravating than the other.

"You think insulting my place of work will help you?"

These guys don't think, Esmeralda. They're idiots... Driven by lust, not logic.

One of them sighed. "Come on Vicky, look at him. He is a catch in college and well off."

Esmeralda snorted. "If you're such a fan, why don't you date him yourself? I assume you don't need anything else, so if you'll excuse me, I have other tables to attend to."

"What can I get you?" She asked much closer now and whilst I knew it was impossible, it was like I could feel her.

I placed her engagement ring in the middle of the table. "What can I get for that?" I asked before sliding the menu down.

She paled. "Why are *you* here?" She whispered, looking around the room.

I frowned at her question. She seemed surprised that I was there, but not that she'd been found.

I arched an eyebrow. "Not really the question I'd expected," I admitted

She gave a guarded look, resting her hand on her chest, trying to hide her necklace. *Too late, little girl.*

"Where are the others?"

I cocked my head to the side, running my thumb back and forth over my bottom lip - a sort of compromise to stop me from doing this to her own rose petal plump lip.

"Who? Your father? Your brother? Whichever traitor helped you escape?"

"Nobody helped me."

She'd answered too fast for it to be true. *I'll find the traitor…traitors…and they'll pay just as she will.* I sighed, reaching for the ring again.

"Why did you come?" she asked, taking a step back.

I'm not certain, I thought as I showed her the ring. "I came to remind you that you made a commitment which you have to uphold."

"But–" She pursed her lips and once again she seemed puzzled by the wrong things.

"Aren't you going to ask how we found you? Where did you fail?"

She shrugged. "It doesn't matter anymore, does it?"

"No, I guess not." I stood up, putting the ring back in my pants pocket. "Let's go."

"Caleb, I–"

I shook my head. "No, you lost the right to make demands the moment you left." I gripped her wrist before she had a chance to take another step back.

"I think you should let her go," one of the jocks from the nearby table interjected.

I rolled my eyes as irritation overshadowed my feeling of betrayal.

I pointed at him, not even bothering to look in his direction. This boy didn't deserve my full attention. "And I think you should sit down and eat your cholesterol-ridden breakfast. This has nothing to do with you."

I could see from the corner of my eye that he was still standing, looking for trouble. If only I had the time or the care to deal with the backlash of social media.

"What now?" I growled, finally looking at him while keeping my grip on Esmeralda's delicate wrist.

"I think the lady doesn't want to go with you," the jock said, tilting his chin up.

"Doesn't she? You didn't seem to be that bothered about her consent when you were harassing her to get her number. Also, not that it has anything to do with you, but she is my fiancée." I squeezed her wrist almost involuntarily.

"I–" He looked at Esmeralda. "Vicky?"

I snorted. "We don't have time for this Esmeralda…" I tried to put as much threat as I could into this statement. I would not be humiliated any more than I already had been.

She nodded. "Okay, let's go."

I let go of her wrist, her soft skin too tempting. I narrowed my eyes with suspicion. She'd gone to extreme lengths to disappear, risking so much, and yet after a single request, she was giving in? It made no sense.

"Esmeralda…" I warned. "If this is one of your tricks, I–"

She shook her head, taking my hand. "No, no tricks. Let's go."

I nodded once, shaking her hand off before gesturing her toward the door.

She rushed behind the counter, apologized to the owner, grabbed her handbag, calmly followed me outside, and got into the car without a fight.

I wasn't sure why, but it felt like I was following her plan instead of mine. We'd tracked her here and yet she sat beside me in the car as if she was the predator instead of the prey.

I didn't want to engage more with her in the state of anger I was in. She'd turned out to be more conniving than I'd thought and I realized that I had a tendency to give her more than I wanted to.

"You know I'm taking you back to Stonewood, right?" *Give me fear. Beg. Anything*, I willed her.

She nodded, aloof enough to infuriate me even more.

"Do you think you'll get away again?" I snorted. "Because let me tell you, you won't – not unless I will it."

She turned toward me, looking at me with the thoughtful gaze I'd come to both cherish and hate. There was so much going through her head but she was so different, such an anomaly. I couldn't anticipate her, which made me uncomfortable and I hated that feeling.

I was Caleb Astor. Nothing got to me… at least nothing had until *her*.

Chapter 2 - Esme

I kept glancing at Caleb as we flew back to Stonewood. He seemed to be doing his best to avoid looking at me.

Of all the people I'd expected to walk into the diner, Caleb would have made the bottom of the list.

My plan was working the way I'd expected it to. I'd needed them to find me but… I looked at Caleb again as he typed away on his MacBook.

Why him? I sighed. There was no point asking him. He had always had a cold edge, but now it ran deeper than before, so much deeper, and I couldn't help but think it was somehow caused by me.

Betrayal isn't something Caleb will take lightly, Archie had warned me before I'd left and I could see the Caleb in front of me now was not the Caleb I'd left behind. He was not even the Caleb from the beginning. He was a colder version, seemingly unaffected by me and I found that somehow scarier than his anger.

He didn't speak a word to me when the plane landed. He just stood up and left me sitting there as if he couldn't care less if I followed him down to the waiting car or not. The silence was oppressive; it felt so ominous, so final. On the ride to my father's house, he kept looking out of the window as if he was fascinated by the landscape. I was sure he'd seen it a million times.

"I gave you your freedom back," I blurted when I couldn't take it anymore.

He turned slowly toward me, his face as expressionless as ever. "Did you?" He nodded. "Is this why you slept with me? To free me?" His words, even if said placidly, had a little bite in them.

I simply looked at him. Saying 'yes' would be a lie. It had served a purpose in the end, but at the time it was not the reason I'd done it, no matter how much I tried to convince myself to the contrary. I'd wanted to connect with Caleb at that level. I'd wanted to be with him. It was only after the fact, that

I'd thought about using it to free him. It had been more than a gift to him. It had meant something to me, but I knew he wouldn't listen to me – not yet, not now.

He nodded as if my silence gave him his answer. "Ah, it's good to know that you were not just being a basic whore, but one with a purpose. I respect you a little more."

I recoiled at the word. "Whore?" I repeated as if I'd misheard him.

He chuckled. "Well, you did give up your virginity awfully fast, Esmeralda. It took one fake date and your panties dropped, especially when you were supposedly in love with that Ken guy."

"Do you mean Ben?"

"Ken, Ben, whatever." He shrugged. "Even Aleksandra took two dates."

I couldn't help but gasp at the pain his assessment brought. He held my eyes a little longer to show me that my hurt didn't affect him in the slightest.

"Then why come for me?" I asked, angry at the slight tremor in my voice.

"You've made a commitment. You need to honor it."

"A commitment you don't want," I insisted.

"A commitment you want even less," he replied with a smile. It was a horrible smile, a smile mirroring my father's – cold, hateful, with a promise of pain that sent shivers down my spine.

He turned toward the window again and I looked at him with my mouth hanging open. It was his vengeance; he was ready to sacrifice his freedom to make me pay.

"You know what Confucius said about revenge, Caleb – '*Before you embark on a journey of revenge, dig two graves*'."

Caleb didn't reply or even acknowledge my comment until we reached the house and the butler opened the car door. "You better start digging too, Esmeralda, because you started along this path. I'm just joining you for the ride."

"Mr. Forbes is expecting you in his office," the butler announced formally. "Miss Esmeralda," he bowed slightly toward me. "I trust you enjoyed your trip to Paris."

I frowned with confusion. *What trip to Paris?* But I didn't get a chance to ask what he was talking about as Caleb rested his hand on the small of my back and nudged me up the stairs.

"Paris?" I whispered as I looked around for Sophia's friendly face, but she wasn't here. Was she mad at me for escaping and leaving her behind?

"Ask your father," Caleb replied through gritted teeth and I could tell he was not happy being here either.

Caleb knocked, which was so different from the air of defiance he'd had when we'd gotten engaged.

"Come in."

Caleb pushed me into the room and I was surprised to see Archie there, leaning against the bookshelf. He looked so stoic, but I knew better now.

"Esmeralda…" My father trailed off and my name itself sounded like a threat; the man was skilled. He walked toward me slowly and once his back was to Archie, Archie let his mask slip for a second looking at me with both concern and puzzlement.

My vision of Archie was blocked by my father's shoulder. "Did you really think you could run?"

Yes, I did, and you only caught me because I wanted you to, I thought, but looked down. I was scared he would see too much. He needed to think I had fallen into his trap.

"LOOK AT ME WHEN I'M TALKING TO YOU, ESMERALDA!" His voice lashed like a whip.

I looked up, not needing to fake the fear I was feeling. This man had never been shy with his chastisements and I could feel one coming my way. I also knew that Archie couldn't stop it. He couldn't blow his cover. I'd never allow it.

"Did you think, even for a minute, that you would get out unscathed?"

Ah, there it was. I recognized it well, the sadistic glimmer in his eyes preceding every time he hurt anyone.

He raised his hand and I closed my eyes, tensing, bracing for impact.

Nothing happened. I opened an eye and was surprised to see Caleb's hand circling my father's wrist, preventing his slap.

I think my incredulity and surprise were matched on my father's face. I was certain nobody had ever challenged him in this way before.

"How–" my father started as I took a step back out of reach. He threw daggers at Caleb with his eyes. "How dare you?" He finally uttered, the shock in his voice still overshadowing the anger at Caleb's disrespect.

Caleb's nostrils flared, his back ramrod. "I don't mean to disrespect you, but I think you wouldn't appreciate anybody damaging what's yours and as I have claimed her, her punishment is mine to give."

My father turned to me, his eyes narrowing in anger as he briskly removed his wrist from Caleb's hold. "I won't accept this type of behavior again from her, Caleb," he told him while keeping his eyes on me.

I was not even worthy of his words now? If he thought he had offended me, he had another thing coming.

My father resumed his lecture. "As long as she lives under my roof, she will–"

"She is coming with me," Caleb announced.

I gasped, turning toward him. That was not something I wanted. At least while I was here I had Archie and Sophia to protect me from moody-psycho Dad. But sharing a living space with this version of Caleb? I shuddered at the idea.

"The fu–" Archie stopped, clearing his throat. "Father, surely you can't agree to this!" He scoffed. "This is preposterous! We barely managed to avoid the scandal she caused when she ran by inventing a social trip to Paris!"

Thanks, Archie, I thought. He was sharing information the only way he could.

"How are we going to justify the wayward daughter moving in with her fiancé prenuptial? What about her virtue?" He grimaced. "Even the powerful William Forbes won't be able to avoid the scandal."

My father turned to Archie, his face thoughtful. Archie shrugged like it didn't matter to him, but my heart swelled with love at my brother's attempt to keep me close. So much had changed between him and me in so little time.

"I officially claimed her, Archibald," Caleb seethed before turning toward my father. "The world has known since the announcement that your innocent little girl is not so innocent anymore. We're basically married as far as our peers are concerned – as for the rest of the world, why should we even care?"

My father hesitated; it was clearly not because of my wellbeing so I didn't really understand. "She's wild, untrained and clearly not receptive to training," he said.

"Are you talking about me or a poodle?" I let slip and Archie rolled his eyes at me with frustration.

My father's nostrils flared in anger as Caleb's hold on my bicep tightened painfully.

"See!" My father gestured to me. "She is too unruly. I don't believe a boy can–"

"Are you calling me a boy?" Caleb cut in, raising an eyebrow. Well in my father's eyes that was clearly the case. "Are you doubting my ability to keep my future wife in line?"

"That is not the point," my father shot back.

"Actually, sir, it is. Let me prove you wrong. Let me show you I'm capable of the responsibilities to be incumbent upon me after the wedding."

What responsibilities? I thought, but I'd have to wait and ask Archie because I was positive that neither my father nor Caleb would be forthcoming.

My father sighed, throwing his hands up in surrender. "You want the hellion? Take her, but don't forget that her behavior will still reflect on me, at least until you are legally married. Should this get out of control, should she step out of line… I'll get her back here. Are we clear?"

"Crystal, sir."

I didn't need to be a Caleb expert to see it had cost him to grovel like that. Good! *Now you know how it feels, King Caleb, to be at someone else's mercy.*

"I presume she has no belongings," my father said.

"No, I do not," I replied firmly. No matter what, I hated being treated like a doll.

My father glared at me. "I'll call Sophia to take her upstairs for some things. Caleb, you stay here; we have things to discuss," he added, leaving no room for dissent.

Archie took a step toward me. "I don't think Sophia is the best choice, father. I'm still not convinced she hadn't played a role in Esmeralda's escape."

It took all my willpower to keep my face smooth. Since Archie and I had made up, I seemed to have forgotten he could be as ruthless as the rest of them, and throwing poor Sophia under the bus when he knew she had no hand in this was as cold as it came – especially in the environment we lived in. My father was an evil man who treated her like dirt at the best of times. How he would treat her if he thought she was involved, didn't bear thinking about, and it seemed that Archie could not care less.

"No she didn't. Nobody did," I finally choked out once the shock wore off, but I was yet again ignored.

"So what do you suggest Archibald?" My father's voice lashed like a whip.

Archie shrugged, ignoring the tone. "I can do it if you want. You know with me she won't be going anywhere."

I was impressed and a little worried about my brother's ability to twist the situation to his advantage and make it as if he was doing them a favor and not the other way around. He really was a master manipulator, but at least he was working for me in this case…or was he?

I shook my head, willing the doubt away. *Don't be silly, Esme. He risked a lot to get you out. Don't start doubting him now.*

"Esmeralda?"

I focused on my brother now standing before me. *How long did I zone out?* "Sorry?"

"I said you need to move; I don't have all day." He gestured toward the door.

"Archie, what–"

"I don't have time for this," he barked, but his face was gentle, his eyes worried. He rested his forefinger against his mouth in a 'shh' gesture.

We walked silently to my bedroom, my mind still reeling from everything that was happening, especially me moving into the Astor mansion. That was such a step back in my plan to find my– our mother's killer.

As soon as Archie closed the door to my bedroom, he pulled me into a bear hug and for a minute I let myself forget about all the insanity and enjoyed the comfort of my brother's arms. He really gave the best hugs – it was like being in a cocoon of warmth. He really should give them more often.

He reached for my shoulders and gently forced me out of the hug. I let go reluctantly.

"Why are you here, Esme?" he whispered with urgency. He detailed my face. "Why did you come back?"

"Ah, you don't think I was stupid enough to get caught?" I asked, somehow glad that he thought higher of me.

He snorted. "Of course I don't. If you got caught it's because you wanted to be caught. The question is why?"

I pulled him into the closet. "I came back because of this," I said, passing him the folded note.

He unfolded it to read, but kept his eyes trained on the paper much longer than reading 'YOUR MOTHER'S DEATH WAS NOT AN ACCIDENT' warranted.

"Archie?"

He looked up at me with incredulity. "Please tell me you didn't come back just because of this," he said, waving the piece of paper.

I frowned in confusion. Why didn't he look more shocked? Why didn't he take it for the bombshell it was? "I…What?"

He sighed. "Esme, you just gave up your freedom for something you're not even sure is real. We don't know who wrote this. It could be a hoax. You should have told me, let me deal with it."

"And let you take all the risks?" I shook my head. "No, if we do this, we do this together. And why would it be a hoax? This person had mom's journal, didn't they? Mom called this person her ally. Why would they lie?"

Archie shook his head in defeat, running a hand over his weary face. "Because they might just think so? We don't even know who this person is! Why didn't they make themselves known when they gave you the journal? It might be some delusional wacko who–"

"Who's a delusional wacko?" Caleb asked as he stepped into the wardrobe.

Archie slipped his hand into his pocket, hiding the note. He detailed Caleb up and down. "If the shoe fits."

Caleb's nostrils flared, the only outside sign that the jab had landed. He pointed between Archie and me, the closeness of our bodies, my hand resting on his arm.

"You seem awfully close for siblings who supposedly hate each other. I guess helping somebody escape can create bonds."

I expected Archie to deny it, to call Caleb delusional, but instead, he stood straighter. "Prove it," he challenged him.

I groaned at the testosterone battle happening in my closet. It was neither the time nor the place.

Archie glanced at me before turning to Caleb again. "As you can see, she's not packed. Go wait downstairs."

"Are *you* ordering *me*?" Caleb asked, pointing at his chest in disbelief. It was another clear indicator that Archie had never bothered to stand up to Caleb before, but I also realized it was because he never really cared enough before to fight.

"My house, my rules…"

"Your father's house."

Archie shrugged. "Then go complain."

They glared at each other for a few seconds, the tension almost choking me.

Finally, Caleb broke eye contact and concentrated on me, granting Archie a small victory but I could see in his eyes I was the one who was going to pay for this. "Fifteen minutes, Esmeralda, or I'll be back up and so help me God…" He trailed off, turned around stiffly, and slammed the door hard behind him.

"You shouldn't have done that. He knows now," I told Archie. I couldn't help but worry about him.

He gave me a gentle smile, removed some hair from my forehead, and kissed it gently. "It's nice to be cared for, nice but terrifying." He sighed. "And believe me, Caleb is a lot of things, but he is extremely smart, scarily so – more than he even lets people see. He already knows I'm part of it. I don't care. Anyway, come on. Get that suitcase ready. We don't want him to get his panties in a bunch. "

"You can't keep me out of this investigation, Archie," I countered. "One way or another I'll do it. I think it'd be safer if we do it together."

He crossed his arms over his chest and I knew I was spot on; he intended to keep me out of it. "I want to keep you safe."

"Then keep me involved because you know I'm stubborn enough to do it by myself if I have to."

He looked heavenward, probably begging for patience and that made me smile, the simple sibling relationship.

"Also stop blaming Sophia for shit," I added. "I don't want her to get into trouble for me. She's always been kind."

Archie's expression sobered. "She might look kind to you, but she's not innocent. She–"

I raised my hand to stop him. "Just don't please. She's been nothing but supportive to me. She's been a saving grace; without her I'm not sure I would have survived. I can't have that guilt on my conscience."

"You're stronger than you give yourself credit for. You would have been just fine and it's not on your conscience, it's on mine and there's no guilt. I don't mind destroying anyone if it means keeping you safe – innocent bystanders included."

"You're ruthless," I breathed, still not comfortable with this side of him even if it was to my benefit.

"Yes I am, and maybe you should be too."

I took his hand in mine. "I read a quote from Morrissey once and it said that 'It takes strength to be gentle and kind' and it does, it really does."

Archie brought my hand to his lips. "Not in this world, Esme, and you know that, but you know what? You can be the good twin." He grinned. "I'll be the evil one. I enjoy it anyway."

I chuckled. "Ah, I'm glad I have you."

He sighed. "I am too, even if you're now a weakness I'm not sure I can afford."

"What–"

He shook his head. "Not now, just pack things for a few days. I'll bring you some more soon. As for this–" he took the piece of paper from his pocket and gave it back to me. "Swear you won't do anything without me. I'll help you 100%, just please don't put yourself in danger. I don't think I could bear it."

I nodded. "Yes, I swear. She was your mom too. We're in this together."

He detailed my face for a few seconds and nodded. "Oh, now hurry up!"

Chapter 3 - Caleb

I didn't know why I'd done this – why I'd had the impulse to take her home with me. I glanced her way quickly, still trying to understand what had pulled me into defying her father and my own resolve.

I couldn't really say what she felt right now as she looked down at her hand, trying to remove the chipping lilac nail varnish from her thumbnail.

She looked so innocent and frail here, but what did it mean? Nothing as far as I was concerned. She was just so good at pretending.

And yet we were on the way to my home, which I now had to share with her. I needed to reassess my revenge plan, most of it at least. Now that she was moving in, there would be no speculation as far as her virginity was concerned, but it didn't really matter. She was claimed. She'd become more than my fiancée when I'd opened my mouth that night and now this part of my revenge plan, the blackmail over her lost virtue, was gone.

I let out a sigh and she glanced at me curiously, her eyes a mixture of wariness and fear. I gave her my darkest scowl until she looked down again, shoulders sagging a bit more.

Good! I thought, feeding on her feelings. *You should be scared. Nothing good will come your way now, traitorous siren.*

Now, on top of sharing my space with her, I'd have to deal with the drama her presence in my home would cause. I had a small reprieve - my parents were in Italy for a month, but they'd be back soon enough and then what?

My mother despised the girl. Why? I wasn't completely sure, but she wasn't the most stable woman on the best of days… My back tingled as it did every time I thought about my mother's mental stability. She was going to be beyond furious to have her here, especially since my father always cut her meds in half when they had trips planned. I guessed that having a lobotomized wife at garden parties tended to scratch through the veneer of a perfect family.

I shrugged mentally. She'd be back on her cocktail of Xanax, Aripiprazole, and whatever else my father was feeding her 'for her own good' soon enough and she'd be too high to care.

As for my father, I wasn't sure how he would take it to be honest. I was not sure how I felt about having these two under the same roof. I was not overly enamored with my father's weird fascination with the girl…. 'Weird fascination,' that was a nice way to put it. 'Fucking messed-up obsession' would be more accurate. He seemed to be living this relationship through me. What would happen when she'd be so readily available under our roof? Would he try his luck? Was she conniving enough to let him think he has a shot to get what she wanted? I glanced toward her again as the car stopped in front of the estate. Yes, of course, she was. She wasn't innocent. She was like every other girl. She just hid it better.

I opened the door, ordered the driver to take her suitcase into the house, and gestured her to precede me in. It was not something I did to be a gentleman; it was not in my nature. I was doing it because I hated having people behind me; when I couldn't see, I couldn't control. And besides, it gave me a premium view of her amazing ass molded to perfection in her faded blue jeans. I might be angry, but I was still a man.

"Where are your parents?" she asked as she stepped into the hall.

"In Italy for a while." She didn't deserve more detail.

"It will only be…you and I?" She swallowed with apprehension. Maybe she was smarter than I thought.

"Mostly you – I've got school tomorrow and Friday; you're not expected before Monday... Jetlag, you know."

"Okay." She nodded, looking around.

"You'd better behave, Esmeralda," I warned her. "The guards have been ordered not to let you go and if you slip, you'll end up at your father's. At least you won't get physically hurt here."

"I'll get hurt in other ways, though." She seemed resigned.

I shrugged. "As long as you do what I say, when I say it, it should be fine."

"I won't be treated this way!" she shouted, jutting out her chin, and once again I hated that she'd found a way to impress me. Everybody was scared of me... Or at least wary. Even the Oppenheimer girl who I suspected was scared of nothing, not even Satan himself, was cautious around me. It was the natural human survival instinct, but this foolish girl seemed to be defective because she enjoyed challenging me, her father…anybody with enough power to effectively destroy her.

"I might have accepted to come back to King Caleb, to become his queen, but I will not be a shadow queen, do you understand me? I will not be in the background of my own life."

I let out a bitter laugh. The fact she thought there was a way for it to be true was beyond laughable. I couldn't make that happen, even if I wanted to. Not that I'd ever mention it to her. "You are right Esmeralda, you are not a shadow queen. You're no queen at all. You're merely a pawn on the chessboard. You're a sacrifice – less than insignificant."

"If I'm that insignificant, why are you keeping me here with you? Why lock me in?" she asked challengingly, crossing her arms on her chest.

Ah, that was the million-dollar question wasn't it? "Just to prove to your father I can tame the hellion, that I'm better than him and that I deserve the place on his board." Before she had a chance to question me again and cause my last thread of patience to vanish, I waved my hand dismissively. "Other than that, you can do whatever you want. I don't want you anymore. I can't touch someone like you." I wrinkled my nose in disgust except I wasn't completely sure it was directed at her.

She took a step back, visibly hurt by my words even if she was trying to hide it. *Good. Hurt, Esmeralda. There's so much more where that came from.*

"In public, you will behave and be a good fiancée. In private you do your thing and I do mine. I wash my hands of you, just be discreet."

"You... Don't care anymore?"

Was it disappointment that I could hear in her voice? I nodded. "No, I really don't. I've requested from your father your old phone and computer; they're being brought into your room now. Call your boyfriend for all I care." I was impressed with myself and my ability to hide the jealousy caused by my own words. I didn't want her to misinterpret my jealousy. I was not jealous because I cared, not anymore. No, I was just never good at sharing my toys.

I sighed looking at my watch. "Benjamin will show you to your room. I have to go; don't wait up," I added and left the house. I'd let her puppy eyes get the best of me.

I drove to the Stonewood Club - 'Our gentlemen's club' as my father had proudly announced on my induction when I was thirteen. A club that was created by the Astor and Forbes families back in 1852.

It was a stuffy, old-fashioned place that I only visited on rare occasions, but today I was running away from my home. I needed an outlet for my frustration and the club was the best available now because fucking Esmeralda was out of the question and Aleksandra was too clingy to give it another shot.

The valet rushed to open my door, completely disregarding the car before mine, another plus of being of the bloodline of the club's founding members. I threw him my keys and walked into the club.

"Mr. Astor, what a pleasure to have you here today," said the club Majordomo as he helped me out of my jacket.

"Is there anybody available for fencing?" I replied. I needed to take my frustration away and nothing could quite take the edge off than pretend-stabbing an adversary multiple times. As an expert swordsman, I rarely lost a match.

"I believe Mr. McAllister is here, sir. I can enquire if you wish."

"Which McAllister? Stuart is a decent opponent, but if it is Leopold, don't bother asking. I'd get a better bout from the training dummy."

The Majordomo's lips tipped up in a half-smile. "Stuart, sir, I would never offer Sir Leopold."

"Very well I'll go get ready. Tell Stuart I'll be in the Blue Room."

"Very good, sir," the Majordomo said before turning on his heel and striding away.

And for the next hour I fenced, winning every point and never conceding one. I knew I was lethal both in life and on the piste. I was aggressive, conniving, strategic and athletic. Stuart hadn't held a chance, but at least I was now sore and tired enough to go home and let Esmeralda's presence go.

I took my time to relax, bathed in the hammam, even grabbed dinner in my family's private salon, before going home quite late into the night.

"Did she give you a hard time?" I asked Benjamin as he met me in the corridor to take my jacket. I wondered if this man ever slept at all. It didn't matter what time I came back, he was always there to tend to my needs.

"No Sir, I haven't seen Miss Forbes since I showed her to her room."

I frowned, turning toward him. "What do you mean?"

He straightened, giving me a wary look. "I'm not sure I understand your question, sir."

"Did she stay in her room the whole time? What did she have for dinner?"

"The windows and door alerts are on, sir, and they remained silent, so yes, she stayed in her room. As for dinner, she didn't."

My frown deepened. "Have you offered her food?"

"Of course!" Benjamin scoffed, clearly offended. It was rare for him to lose his perfect composure, but he'd been working for my family since before I was born and he was better than perfect. I decided to let his lack of decorum slide. "I enquired to her room twice, sir, but she politely refused the first time and didn't respond the second time."

I nodded, grinding my teeth so hard I was surprised they didn't shatter in my mouth. I tightened my hands into fists. The anger and frustration I thought I'd left at the club was back with a vengeance.

I took the stairs two at the time and by the time I reached her room my anger had grown further, almost blinding every coherent thought I could have. I pounded my fist against the door with all I had. "Esmeralda, open the door!" I roared, pounding on the door again. "I swear Esmeralda if you don't open…"

"You what?"

I sighed with relief at the sound of her voice which annoyed me even more. *No Caleb, don't feel relief. You don't care, remember?*

"You'll have dinner with me now!" I ordered, not sure why. I'd already had dinner and spending time with her was the last thing I should want…and yet.

"No."

"No? No?!" I glared at the door, wishing it to burn away. I had a master key to open it but I didn't want to have to use that trick now.

"No."

"Esmeralda, if you don't come now and stop acting like a spoiled brat, I swear I will treat you like the temperamental child you seem to be. You will not be allowed outside of this house. I will take your WiFi away and alter the mobile signal to your room. You will be cut off from the world." My chest was heaving under the rapid breathing my anger caused.

"Do what you need to do," she replied, so coolly I wanted to break the door down.

"Fine! Starve! See if I care," I shouted, rushing back downstairs. "She is not to leave this house!" I ordered Benjamin pointing at the stairs.

"Sir, I'm not sure this–"

"Nothing, Benjamin! If she wants to act like a victim, I'll treat her as such!"

How was it she was turning the tables on me? I wanted to unsettle her, grate on her nerves and she managed to get me to unravel.

I needed to distance myself; she was my kryptonite.

Chapter 4 - Esme

The funny thing about hunger is you get hungry and then you reach a level where you are so hungry you don't even feel it anymore.

It'd been two days since I'd moved in with Caleb and I had yet to exit the room. He'd kept his word though, and I'd lost internet connection and phone signal impressively fast.

It wasn't a big deal. I was busy rereading my mom's journal anyway. I'd been lucky it was in my bag when Caleb had appeared at the café. I'd been expecting them – it had been the reason I'd called Ben. Why Ben though? I feared I'd got him on Caleb's hit list given he was being territorial as shit. He clearly didn't want me anymore and yet he hated the idea of anyone else having me. This was Spoiled Child 101: I don't want my toy, but it doesn't mean you can have it either.

I'd thought that calling him would make the slip-up more believable. A young woman in *like* with a boy is more likely to make mistakes. I knew I had made lots of them with Caleb… Ben, I had no choice other than to say 'like' because it was not love. It couldn't have been love – not when Caleb unraveled me with a look much more than Ben ever could.

I rolled my eyes at the thought of Caleb. It had to be the lack of food making me confused... Yeah that was it.

I closed my eyes and turned to the side, ready for another snooze. At least when I was sleeping, I was not thinking too much.

I opened my eyes as my door opened. How did that happen? I was sure I'd locked it.

"You need to get up, sister of mine," Archie ordered, but the deep affection in his voice and loving smile made my heart constrict in my chest.

I shook my head. Wasn't it too early in the starvation process to be suffering hallucinations?

Archie walked to the window and opened the heavy blackout curtain, letting the unforgiving winter sun enter my room and making me hiss like a pissed-off vampire. No, it was definitely real.

He chuckled. "You need to chill, Lestat; it's only a little light."

I glared. "I'm not Lestat. I'm a girl."

He leaned against one of the carved posts at the foot of the bed. "With the way you look right now? I'm not sure."

I rolled my eyes, nestling more comfortably into the feather pillow from heaven.

"Why so sullen, sourpuss?"

"I went from Lestat to sourpuss? Damn brother, I love you too."

He grabbed my foot and nudged me. "Come on, twin. Talk to me."

"I came back to deal with…" I looked around, not sure there wasn't a bug in the room.

"I know why you came back."

"And I'm stuck in this room. I need to do something, solve this. Caleb forbade me to go out."

"Maybe it's because you are refusing to eat and stay locked in your room."

I frowned. How did he know that? And how did he even manage to–

"How did you manage to come here anyway? If Father or Caleb think you're an ally…"

He shook his head. "Caleb doesn't care."

That hurt me more than I cared to admit. Caleb told me he was done with me and it seemed that was true.

Archie shook his head. "I don't mean it like that." He could so easily read me. It was no wonder he'd suspected my desire to escape from the start.

"Yes you do. Caleb told me he was done with me."

Archie rolled his eyes. "Whatever you say, Esme… But he is the one asking me and Oppenheimer to come and 'knock some sense into her and stop her childish temper tantrum'."

"Are you siding with him?" I asked, feeling both incredulous and betrayed.

"The day I side with an Astor will be the day Hell freezes over, but you do need to shake it off, okay? You catch more flies with honey than vinegar. I'm not sure where the investigation is going to take us, but antagonizing Caleb might not be the most productive way to deal with things."

I crossed my arms on my chest and pouted. I hated that his words made sense.

He chuckled. "That's the spirit."

"What if father finds out you're here? You'll be blowing your cover."

He grinned. "No, he knows I am here. He encouraged it, at least he thinks he did. I'm a double…" he cocked his head to the side. "Triple? Ah, I'm not sure… Triple agent?"

"I think I'm having a stroke," I said.

He stuck his tongue out. "What I'm saying is that I explained to Father my doubts at Caleb's ability to rein in such an unruly girl." He ignored the glare I was giving as he continued. "And Caleb disrespected father quite significantly when he took your side."

"He never took my side!"

Archie sighed. "Yes he did, consciously or not, he did… When he stopped father from hitting you, that was an act of rebellion." He raised his hand on seeing I was about to argue. "No matter what Caleb's reason was, it is not something Father will easily forget. His power comes from a place of fear and Caleb showed he did not fear him, at least not enough." He sat at the foot of my bed. "Anyway, Father would love for Caleb to fail so he can put him back in his place. So that's why I'm here to spy on you and report back."

"I see…"

He grinned. "But I will be working for *us* – you and I – and give him the information we need him to believe."

"So you're a double agent."

"Basically."

I nodded. "You're good at this."

"Thanks for the compliment."

I cocked my head to the side. "To be fair, I'm not sure it was meant to be one."

He rolled his eyes, stood up, and laid across from me, turning to face me. "I think part of me always knew."

"Knew what?"

He let his hand slide across the silky bedspread and rested it on top of mine. "That you were alive."

I frowned. "How?"

He sighed, shaking his head. "I don't know. It makes no sense. I can't explain it to myself, so explaining to you would be close to impossible. But it felt like this part of me was missing somewhere. I thought it was because mom had died, but no, it was you… It was always you. When you pulled me into your arms that day it was like the dull pain I didn't even notice anymore faded completely, like a band just snapped into place and it terrified me. I hated it."

"You hated feeling complete?"

"I hated for my pain, or lack of it, to be so intrinsically linked to someone so hell-bent on leaving me. I'd loved one person before and she'd left me behind… I didn't think I'd be strong enough to go through this again."

I turned my hand in order to hold his. "I'm not going to leave you again. Even after we find out who killed her, I'll find a way to stay."

He smiled. "Yes, we'll find a way."

"I've reread her journal and made a list of potential suspects… Father's in it."

Archie sighed and nodded. "Yes, I expected him to be. I just hope it isn't him."

"Why?" I asked, somehow taken aback by this. Did he want Father to remain on the throne?

"Because he already took so much from me, much more than I'm ready to admit. If he did that – took away the one ray of light I had in my life…" He turned on his back, staring at the ceiling. "I'm not sure how I'd deal with it."

"It might be someone not in the journal."

Archie shrugged. "Maybe." He took a deep breath. "Is there any clue about who gave you the journal in there?"

I shook my head. That would have been so great. "No, Mom only refers to that person a couple of times and calls him 'her ally'."

Archie nodded. "Could I–" He stopped and the emotion in his eyes hurt me too. "Could I read it?"

"Of course! It's your mother's too."

"Yes, but she wrote it for you."

I shook my head. "She wrote it for us, you were her 'beautiful boy'."

He took a shaky breath, turning his head toward me, his silver eyes shining with unshed tears.

"You know, she was always happier when he was gone. She was a real mom then – happy, carefree. Even though I knew I shouldn't, I found myself looking forward to every business trip of his. She would always make me the best peanut butter and chocolate pancakes. I miss those so much."

I stood up and swayed, probably due to my hunger. I grabbed the post.

His sad look morphed into concern. "You need to eat, Esme. Even if only for me, please do."

I nodded, reaching under the mattress. "Here, take the journal, and I'll make you the pancakes. I've got the recipe."

"Yeah, but…" He wrinkled his nose "Take a shower before, okay?"

I sniffed under my arms. "Asshole!" I muttered, heading toward the bathroom.

"I'll be right here, reading."

I was already feeling better after I'd showered and dressed, but now the hunger was back with a vengeance.

"Let's see if they have the ingredients we need."

"Okay and maybe you can just give me your list too while you cook for me."

"It's a short list really," I replied as we arrived downstairs under the butler's wary eyes. Was he worried I was going to leave and get him in trouble?

"We're just going to cook something. Is it allowed?" I asked him.

He seemed surprised by my request. "Yes, Miss. Please feel free to use this house's amenities as you wish. This is your home."

Ah, my home. What a joke!

"So, the list?". Archie asked sitting on a stool at the kitchen island.

I shrugged before going to the pantry, trying to find the ingredients I needed. "It's really short, pathetically so. Our father and the Astors."

"Ah, that's short."

"I know," I grimaced, resting all the ingredients on the counter before rummaging in the cupboards trying to find what I needed. "I don't know the people here."

"But I do," he said.

I nodded. "Exactly." I looked around. I wasn't sure if Caleb was around listening to our conversation. He was so angry at me, I wouldn't put it past him to sell me out just for revenge.

"He won't be back for a while. He has Class President shit to deal with," Archie said.

"He is Class President?" I asked with surprise, and yet somehow it made sense. That guy had crazy high expectations. I wouldn't be surprised if one day he ended up running for the White House.

"Do you even know anything about him at all?"

Yes, the things that matter, I thought. I know his heart, at least part of it…or I thought I did. Instead I replied: "No, not much."

Archie shook his head with a sigh. "This is an issue for another time. Opening Caleb Astor's Pandora's Box will take weeks and only cause you unnecessary trauma." He waved the journal. "I think what we need to figure out first is who gave this to you."

"I have no idea. I told you before, I just left my things for like ten minutes and it was there when I went back."

"That didn't leave that person a wide window. They had to be studying you. Didn't you notice someone following you or staring at you?"

I snorted. "I was the long-lost daughter of William Forbes. No offense brother, but I was headline news; everybody was staring." I extended the spoon full of batter. "Want to try?"

"Salmonella?" He raised an eyebrow. "I'll pass."

I licked the spoon before putting it in the dishwasher. "That's an urban legend, you scaredy cat."

"Did you notice anybody in the library when you went?"

"Except for Ms. White." I shook my head, concentrating on cooking my pancake. "No, no one."

"Who?"

I glanced at him before looking at my pan again. He seemed genuinely confused.

"Ms. White? The librarian?"

"The Amish weirdo with glasses?"

I scowled at him, flipping the pancake over. "Don't be an ass."

"What? I didn't know her name."

"You've been in this school for what, five years and you don't even know the name of your librarian?"

"Don't be like that, Esme. Don't make me say it because we both know you won't like it." He waved his hand dismissively. "Mom has been gone thirteen years and this Ms. White is not really part of the same scene as us."

I shrugged. "She is nice. I like her." I placed a plate full of pancakes in front of Archie just as Caleb entered the house and came into the kitchen, probably informed by Benjamin of our whereabouts.

He stopped on the threshold, detailing me, then Archie, and finally the plate of pancakes.

"Esmeralda," he said, his voice and face devoid of emotion which always drove me crazy. "Archibald," he greeted before turning around and walking away down the corridor.

"Offer him some," Archie whispered, looking at the plate of pancakes. "Honey remember, not vinegar."

I rolled my eyes, but did as Archie suggested. "Caleb!"

Within a few seconds, he was back at the threshold, his eyebrow cocked in an invitation to continue.

"Why don't you join us for pancakes? I've made way too much and I still have lots of batter."

"Why would I?" He asked, crossing his arms on his chest. "I'm not four and I wouldn't want to interrupt the sibling bonding time."

I grabbed a plate and put some pancakes on it. "First, try it before you diss it, my pancakes are awesome even if you're not four, and secondly, what is stopping us from bonding with you around?" I shrugged. "I've got nothing to hide."

Archie looked at me with pride and a sort of admiration I wasn't sure I liked. That lie had come out too well, too fast. I didn't want to become like them.

"Come on, Astor. Don't make it so difficult," Archie insisted.

Caleb sighed, but uncrossed his arms and took a seat two stools away from Archie. These two…

"So why did Tay not come with you?" I asked before putting way too big of a bite in my mouth.

"Classy," Archie teased. "She was busy, I guess. I'm not Oppenheimer's keeper, you know."

The cold edge in his voice surprised me. It seemed it was containing so much unsaid. She couldn't be mad at me; that wasn't it. I'd spoken with her since I'd left. She had said that things were changing, but our friendship was intact. That much I knew.

Caleb threw Archie a surprised look before concentrating on his pancakes again. What was he not telling me?

I couldn't doubt Archie, not when I was already questioning so many things. I needed to trust one person at least.

"You should talk to her," Archie added, "And thank you for the pancakes. They do taste just like Mom's. I didn't realize how much I needed them."

Caleb looked up, his fork halfway to his mouth, his face betraying the surprise at Archie's emotional confession, especially in his presence.

I only smiled, squeezing his hand. There was nothing to say; it was all there on his face.

"I, umm," Caleb rubbed his neck, visibly uncomfortable now. "I have to go. I have a call with my father. The pancakes were okay," he added before nodding toward me, leaving the room again.

"Okay?" I asked Archie, twisting my mouth.

"Coming from him?" Archie pointed his thumb to the direction Caleb had just taken. "It's like a five-star review."

"So… Taylor," I started again.

Archie stood up like his butt was on fire. "Nope. I'm not doing that with you, not now, not ever. I've got to go anyway. I'll read the stuff-" he patted his jacket - "and look into those people. I'll tell you on Monday."

"But–"

He leaned over the island and kissed my forehead before grabbing a pancake from the plate. "One for the road. See you soon and remember to eat!"

Chapter 5 - Caleb

I hung up the phone and leaned back in my father's office chair, frustrated at the fact that he would still treat me like a child when he felt it was necessary, and at having Esmeralda living under my roof.

I'd avoided her today. I'm not sure why, but seeing her smile in the kitchen with Archibald yesterday wasn't sitting well with me.

I hated this jealousy, this weakness, and I hated that, despite the anger and betrayal, I'd been relieved to see her eat in the kitchen when I should have felt nothing but contempt.

I closed my eyes and let out a sigh of frustration. I wasn't sure why I couldn't hate her as much as I should.

I still had not told my father about Esmeralda living here. Why? I wasn't sure. He was always commenting on my decisions and I was sure this one wouldn't please him…or maybe I feared it'd please him too much. I'd seen the lurid way he looked at her when he thought no one was looking, and it made me want to murder him.

I looked down at my cell, tapping my forefinger on the mahogany desk. I needed to get her out of my mind.

Aleksandra was clingy, but she sucked like a vacuum and she was the perfect distraction from Esmeralda. Maybe after finally releasing my pent-up sexual frustration things would be okay. I hadn't had sex since that day with Esmeralda and it had been the longest dry period since I was fourteen; maybe this was why I couldn't get her out of my mind. Yes, it had to be that, and it was nothing that Aleksandra's magical mouth couldn't fix.

I stood up, grabbing my car keys and my phone. *We'll establish ground rules,* I thought. *My father does this all the time. It's–* I was interrupted by a knock on the door.

"Come in."

Benjamin walked in and took in the keys in my hand. He never missed a thing. He'd been in the background since before I was born. To have seen all the things he'd seen and still be around was rather astonishing.

"I'm guessing you're going out, sir."

"What do you need?"

"Miss Esmeralda expressed the wish to dine with you tonight, sir, but I shall inform her of your unavailability."

"No, I'll go out later. Dinner is fine." I didn't like the elation I felt at the idea of having dinner with her. I also didn't like how easily I'd set aside a chance at mind-blowing sex with a woman much too eager to please me for dinner with a traitor who would end up giving me the cold shoulder at best.

I thought I saw disapproval on Ben's wrinkled face, but it was gone as soon as it'd appeared. "Very well, sir. It will be served in the main dining room at eight as usual."

I looked at my watch. That gave me thirty minutes to get ready. Why should I even care and yet – I rubbed my jaw, feeling the sprinkle of my five o'clock shadow.

I decided not to dwell on the reasons why my chest was lighter when I went to my room to take a shower I didn't need and shave my face clean.

When I walked into the dining room, I was taken aback to find Esmeralda already standing there, looking at the flames crackling in the grate of the oversized fireplace. She was wearing a beautiful blue dress and flat shoes, showing how tiny she really was. Did she know blue was my favorite color? Was she trying to look small? Defenseless?

"There is something strangely soothing about looking at a fire burn," she said, keeping her back to me. Her hair was up in her trademark messy bun, revealing her delicate, graceful neck and the small mole resting at its base. I looked at it every time she had her back to me. It was almost hypnotic and every time I had to fight my instinct to brush my lips against it. I could almost see her shiver, as if she could feel that phantom kiss.

"It is mesmerizing because it is a perfect contradiction," I replied, walking to her with my hands in my pockets. "It looks so beautiful, but if you get too close it will destroy you…" *Just like you,* I added to myself.

"Why did you decide to join me for dinner tonight?" I asked as I stood beside her, looking at the flames. She was right; it was strangely soothing.

"Because you gave me the WiFi and phone back." She shrugged. "I called Taylor and it was nice, so thank you."

"And you thought that gracing me with your presence would be the right way to thank me? A little presumptuous, don't you think?"

Her complexion turned the loveliest shade of pink at my comment. I would rather remove my own tongue than let her know what was already so infuriating to acknowledge myself – that looking at her and her alone, provided me with a sense of peace that my soul didn't deserve.

"I- No, that's not it. I thought–"

"Sir, madam, dinner is served," Benjamin announced, breaking her flustered response, and it frustrated me. I enjoyed seeing her squirm.

I was surprised that the table was set in a more intimate fashion than was customary. When there were only my parents, usually they'd be sitting at both ends of the table which was built for twelve. Even that though was rare as they avoided each other beautifully well when there were no witnesses to their downfall except for me, their useful-yet-insignificant son.

But this time the plates were set across from each other. I threw a look toward old Benjamin as he set the warm bread rolls on the side plate. I wasn't sure what his endgame was, but we needed to discuss this.

"This looks delicious," Esme said to Benjamin with a small smile. She was always just so…kind to them, when she didn't need to be.

Benjamin bowed. "I will let the chef know. He will be pleased."

"The fact that he has a job is a testament that he is adequate," I replied firmly. "Compliments are not necessary." This was not the type of household to recognize talent. It was best for them not to expect recognition. I never did and I was better for it.

Benjamin left the room as Esmeralda sighed. "That was unnecessary."

"I'll deal with my staff the way I see fit."

The lightness of her face started to fade and the living, breathing contradiction I had become since she'd walked into my life was apparent again. It annoyed me that she reacted so negatively to my presence even if I was causing that reaction on purpose, but I was also somehow pleased to at least have an effect on her, just as she had an undesired effect on me.

"When are your parents coming back?" She asked, changing the subject. She didn't want to fight tonight that much was clear, and that too was a little disappointing. I enjoyed seeing the angry Esmeralda, the fire in her eyes, the red on her cheeks. It was when she was the most beautiful… Well, if you didn't count her drunk with desire in my bed – at that moment she'd been a goddess.

"Why does it matter?" I asked back, resting my cutlery on the table, detailing her face, trying to find her tell. Once I had the key to decipher her, she would stop being such a mystery to me and I was sure that her appeal would lessen.

Her eyes sparked with frustration. "It matters because I live here, because I deserve to know, because I'm down here trying to make polite conversation, and you're doing your utmost to be the biggest asshole in the world. Congratulations, you are succeeding."

Ah, finally, she was letting go of her mask of cool indifference. I liked the untamed Esmeralda, even if I'd take death before admitting that fact.

She removed her golden napkin from her lap and threw it on the table. "If your dinner request was just an optic to bully me, I think I'll pass. You do that enough in every unfortunate encounter. Now if you'll excuse me," she added, standing up and turning around to leave the room.

I should have let her leave. I'd thrown a few good punches. I had made her try only to be pushed away. I just needed to take the car keys and go to Aleksandra, and yet I found myself standing up.

"They're back in two weeks, on Tuesday to be exact."

She turned around, remaining by the door, her face full of suspicion and foreboding.

"I've got a present for you," I blurted out. *What the actual f–* I thought as I looked down at my glass. Was the water drugged? It really seemed like it when she was in the room. When her eyes were on me, I had minimal control of my thoughts.

"With the way you've been acting, I'm not sure I want it," she replied suspiciously.

I chuckled at that. I really enjoyed the spunk. I couldn't deny it. She was one of the first people I'd met who didn't tiptoe around me, who wasn't scared. The issue I had was with her ability to lie so well.

I gestured to Benjamin to clear the table. "It's a good one. I promise. Come, I'll show you."

"Uh-huh," she said noncommittally as she followed me back to the multi-car garage we had.

I pointed to the red and black Bugatti Chiron. "I bought you this."

"You bought me…a car?" She turned to me, confusion written all over her face.

I couldn't blame her after the way I'd treated her since I'd retrieved her from California, but truth be told I'd bought her this car before she'd escaped. I had ordered it after our day together… T*hat fake day she used to cheat me,* I thought as the bile of deception rose in my throat. I took a deep breath, forcing the anger down. It was not the time, at least not yet.

I'd bought it for her because I'd started to care a bit too much, because I hadn't liked the idea of her depending on anyone else for rides, because I'd known about the trick Archibald had pulled on her the day of her introduction party. He had laughed about it, but I hadn't really approved, knowing their father. I hadn't even known at the time about his tendency to hit his own daughter. If I had known at the time...

If you HAD known, then what? A part of my brain taunted. *You like the power too much, you never would have said anything to get on the bad side of William Forbes.*

There was no point dwelling on it now. It was clear that even then Archibald was playing me. He had probably planned this with his sister – hoping that I or Antoine would rescue her and gain some leverage.

"Caleb, you bought me a car?" She asked again, bringing me back to the here and now.

I nodded, entering the code of the key safe and getting the keys of the Bugatti out, extending them to her.

"Yes, I did," I replied as she took the key tentatively. The only thing that I had added this week was a tracker under the car, which I could use to disable the car at distance and one that would automatically disable should she try to exit Stonewood. "It even has custom plates." Again, something I did when I'd mistakenly cared for who I thought she was.

She circled the car and her face softened as she took in the plates. It was so stupid. In retrospect I now wished I'd changed that before giving it to her. My state of mind was different now. The feelings were gone.

Are they? The taunting voice was back. *Fuck you!* "I've got a lot of obligations and I won't be able to take you to and from school every day and I'd rather you didn't spend too much time plotting."

She ignored my last comment as she was frozen to the spot looking at the license plate – 'ANG3L5' surrounded by wings. I'd done that as a gesture before she'd betrayed me.

She looked up at me, her hand on her mouth, her eyes expressing a tenderness I hated, hated because I didn't know if it was fake or not and also because it still managed to get through to me in seconds when I thought I'd repaired my impenetrable emotional armor. She looked at me like that and those feelings slipped through again, like a sword through a gap in chainmail.

"You remembered…" she whispered as if it meant something.

She took a couple of steps toward me and took me by surprise when she kissed my cheek and hugged me.

"Thank you," she whispered.

No, it wouldn't work I couldn't cope with her attention. I hated how my heart reacted to her despite everything. I needed her to stay away. I needed her to want to stay away. I needed her to hate me too and if she cared even a little, I needed her to keep it to herself. I was not strong enough to resist. I needed her to do it for me.

"You like it enough to give me a blowjob?"

She jerked back, looking at me with uncertainty. "What?" Her voice trembled.

I jerked my head toward the car. "I took care of your need; you should take care of mine," I added with a smirk, resting my hand on her shoulder and pressing down, not hard enough to make her bend, but enough to show her I meant business.

I tried to keep my poker face at the surprise I felt seeing her sink to her knees in front of me on the hard concrete floor.

"Is that what you want? To see me beaten and broken on my knees? Giving you favors just because you order it, because you buy them?"

She looked angry. The fire was there, but there was also disappointment and sadness – something that I didn't expect from someone as calculating as she was. Was it all an act too?

She kept her eyes on me as I reached for my belt, the sound of the metal buckle echoing ominously in the eerily quiet room. I couldn't cave, not now, and my body was responding only too well to her position on her knees, my dick so hard that it had passed the point of being uncomfortable to just plain painful. I needed her to back away before I did – *or maybe you don't!!* The part of my brain that was controlled by my libido shouted in frustration. What if I made her please me? She couldn't mind that much, could she? She'd given up her virginity without a second thought on a powerplay – why would a blowjob matter? Was it even her first one? My jaw tightened, my teeth almost shattering in my mouth at the idea of her on her knees for that dark-haired idiot, Ben Deluca. He was too addicted to her for it to be a simple crush – or was it? This woman was addictive. She had me tangled before I'd even kissed her. She was not a good addiction though. In retrospect no addictions were good. They were all destructive on different levels and she was the type to annihilate everything you were.

I liked seeing her like that, on her knees, powerless. I could almost feel her silky hair tightly wrapped around my fist, but the problem was that I didn't want her to surrender by force. I wanted it to be her choice. I wanted her to surrender her power to me willingly and I didn't want her helpless for anyone else... Ever... Just me… Only me.

"Have you done this before?" I asked, my voice as cold as could be, hiding the treacherous tremor of desire the anticipation caused. "I wouldn't want to waste a hard-on on your inexperience like I did taking your virginity," I added mockingly.

Pain flashed in her eyes, pain that affected me in ways I refused to acknowledge, but then it was replaced by anger, her grey eyes turning to steel. Ah, finally the reaction I wanted, the one I was rooting for. Her hate, her anger I could deal with, even thrive on. The pretend affection, the fake care… I had no time for that.

She stood up, shoving me back. She was no match for me physically, but the force of her anger made me stumble.

"You can suck your own dick and choke on it, Caleb Astor!" she shouted, throwing the keys at me. "It will be a cold day in Hell before I willingly sink on my knees in front of you again, and if you ever try to force your way into my mouth," she snarled, snapping her pearly white teeth, "I'll bite it right off."

I felt that snap, right down to my now-fully-erect cock. I really was a sick bastard, getting aroused by her anger even more than her softness.

"We'll see," I replied with a cocky smile, burying my hands in my pockets with my belt still undone.

She threw me a look full of venom, "Who broke you?" She asked and walked away without a look back.

"So many things, so many people, Esmeralda… You included," I whispered after she was long gone.

Chapter 6 - Esme

When I woke up on Monday, I was excited to go to school to see Tay and Archie, as well as to start the investigation, but I was also dreading being alone in a car with Caleb.

I couldn't believe the horrible things he'd said to me on Saturday. His mood swings were giving me whiplash; it was like he didn't know himself how he was supposed to feel. It was like he was trying to make me hate him again. Well if so, he was on the right path. I had avoided him like the plague since the incident in the garage, although I hadn't had to try too hard as his car had been gone most of the day on Sunday. He had probably been getting the blowjob I hadn't given him.

As I got ready, I started rethinking my decision of not asking Archie to pick me up. He was already so worried about me; I didn't want to add to his burden. I would tell him the truth, that life here wasn't great, but I couldn't drive him and Caleb more against each other; that wouldn't be right.

I prepared myself for a few more minutes, building up the courage to face my devil of a fiancé. I didn't want him to see how much his low opinion of me and my role in his life, had hurt me. I was also angry at myself for expecting anything different. He was the worthy heir of all the hateful fathers.

My eyes wandered in the mirror until they connected with the small blue box on my bed. I'd found it in front of my door this morning with a simple card. '*Your engagement ring; wear it proudly. C*'. I sneered at the note. Even in one sentence he could taunt me.

I sighed and slipped the ostentatiously gigantic ring I'd hated from day one onto my finger. I suspected he knew how much I hated it and made me wear it as a punishment.

I walked downstairs to find Benjamin expecting me.

"Breakfast is served," he announced, gesturing me toward the salon.

I preceded him and was surprised to find a table set for one. I turned around, throwing a questioning look at him.

"Mr. Astor left early this morning; he had business to attend to."

What kind of business would an eighteen-year-old high school senior have to attend to? In my world not much, but in this one? Who the hell knew?

I nodded. "It's fine. I'll call Archie for a ride."

Benjamin shook his head and reached in his suit pocket. "There is no need Miss. Mr. Astor said to take your car," he added, setting the key to the Bugatti on the table.

I looked down at the large gaudy fob as if it was a scorpion ready to strike. Why was he giving in after what had unfolded on Saturday? Was it his way of apologizing? I doubted it. His way to make a point that I owed him? More likely.

I had half a mind to throw the key in a hole somewhere as a major 'fuck you', but on the other hand, what other chance would I ever have to drive a car like that? Plus, it would stick it to Aleksandra, the she-devil, who had probably spent all of yesterday providing the services I'd refused.

Don't be dumb, I chastised myself. I didn't need to pile more issues onto my plate. I had a murder to solve. I could deal with whatever else later.

"Is there a problem, madam?" Benjamin asked, cutting into my thoughts.

I shook my head. "No, Benjamin. Nothing." I grabbed a crispy croissant. "I'll go now. Thank you for everything."

"It's my pleasure, Miss. Truly."

I smiled at him and walked to the garage. I let my hand stroke the bodywork of the car before sitting on the beautiful black leather seats. I sat there for a few minutes just reeling over the luxury of this car, from the comfortable seat to the wooden dashboard full of electronics. I'd driven Luke's old truck many times, but this was on a whole new level. I looked at myself in the rear-view mirror and despite the determination in my eyes, there was sadness there too – a sadness that had never been there before I'd left my poor life, a sadness that now seemed to be a permanent feature, a part of me.

I shook my head, then sent a quick text to Taylor telling her I was on my way and to wait for me at our usual place. I was actually pleased to see my friend again. I missed her and her sunny attitude. If anyone could get me out of the gloom it was her.

The drive to school was a dream and if it had been up to me, I would have driven it forever.

Taylor was waiting for me by the steps as I parked the car, her usual grin on her face, and even though she couldn't see me through the tinted glass, I found myself grinning back.

"Damn girl, the psycho husband is generous," she teased, walking toward me as I climbed out of the car.

"Psycho fiancé please," I teased back. I looked around the lot, but Caleb's car was not here. Archie's Maserati was though.

"Archie is here?" I asked, already taking my phone out of my bag.

She rolled her eyes, hooking her arm with mine. "Yeah, he and Antoine are busy with King matters that nobody cares about – School Council and stuff."

"Seems fascinating," I replied with a small smile.

"I missed you." She squeezed my arm, all humor now gone.

"I missed you too."

"I need to tell you some stuff." She grimaced. "We couldn't really discuss this on the phone. I did something and–"

"Ah, the pauper princess is back from her trip to Paris. How did the attempt to make you a bit less trashy work out?"

I rolled my eyes at the aggravating voice of the girl who was quickly becoming my nemesis. I adjusted my hold on the leather strap of my bag and smoothed my face before turning around.

"Aleksandra. It was perfect. Thank you for asking."

"Don't worry, I kept your fiancé occupied while you were gone."

I smiled. Caleb might have slept with her while I'd been away, but this was confirmation that he hadn't gone to her yesterday and somehow it made me feel better.

She frowned, visibly displeased by my reaction. Flipping her hair over her shoulder, she asked, "Why are you smiling, freak?"

"Because you were not good enough company." I pointed to the Bugatti. "He missed me so much, he bought me this car after he asked me to move in with him." I shrugged. "Maybe I should thank you."

Aleksandra reddened with anger, her nostrils flaring as her two lapdogs did their best not to laugh at her.

I sighed. Turning around, I grabbed Taylor's arm again. "So, where were we?" I asked, resuming our walk into the school.

Taylor threw me a side look, full of approval. "Damn girl, that was amazing. I think you'll be just fine here."

I waved my hand dismissively. "I have bigger things to deal with."

She nodded, her face somber. "The reason for your return."

I was scared to tell her everything, but not because I didn't trust her. After everything she had done for me, all the risks she had taken, I trusted her with my life, but if my mom's murderer was still around here somewhere, I was terrified to put Taylor in harm's way. However, at the same time, I knew she would try to find out what the issue was and put herself at more risk.

There was safety in numbers and all that.

"Yes, I need to explain it to you, but I'm not sure now is the time and place," I added as the corridors started to slowly fill with students and I met my brother's eyes as he and Antoine exited a room.

Archie looked so serious, his face tight. It made him look so much older. He might have been the prince of a dynasty, but the worry on his shoulders was so far beyond his years, and I couldn't help but feel guilty about it as most of it was involuntarily my fault.

Taylor turned around to follow my eyes and Antoine smiled brightly. Seriously how could a man be that pretty?

"Ah, ma Belle! I missed you," he beamed.

I was about to tell him off, ask him to tone down on the flirting. I didn't need to anger Caleb any more than he already was.

But before I even had a chance to say anything, Antoine wrapped a possessive arm around Taylor's waist, pulled her against him, and placed a tender kiss on her button nose.

She smiled back at him, her cheeks tinted pink.

My mouth hung open with surprise.

"Ah, I guess she didn't tell you either," Archie stated, his lips pursed tight, a deep scowl of disapproval on his face.

I brought my hand up, smoothing the deep line between his eyebrows. I understood now why his tone had been cold and dismissive when I'd mentioned Taylor. This was a story worth listening to for sure!

"Maybe we should take this somewhere else," Antoine suggested, already pulling Taylor into an empty classroom.

I threw Taylor a cautious look. I didn't know Antoine well, and even though I knew his secret, I couldn't count on his loyalty.

Archie looked around before closing the classroom door. Leaning his back against it, he crossed his arms on his chest in a wannabe cool, devil-may-care position, but the furrow of his brow and the thickness of his jaw were clear indicators of how much he hated seeing them together.

"He knows everything," Taylor started as soon as I turned toward her again. "Well most of it. I had no choice, Esme. You've–"

I raised my hand to stop her. "I trust your judgment, Tay. If you told Antoine, you had your reasons, and he won't say anything, will he?"

Antoine flashed me his usual flirty smile. "You know it, sweetheart."

Taylor rolled her eyes. "We've discussed this. Please don't lay the flirting on so thick."

Antoine had the decency to look sheepish. "It's hard to switch off." He leaned in and gave Taylor a kiss on the forehead, and it was genuine affection, plain as day. I could see it was clear for Archie too from the taut lines on his face. Seeing Taylor and Antoine together hurt him and I hated that, but I knew she had her reasons and she would tell me soon.

"Antoine caught a conversation between his father and yours a few weeks ago. Your father believed I helped you escape and wanted Antoine's father to give him the tech to listen to any phone conversations happening within my house, the phone being registered or not."

"We can do that?" I asked in awe. Technology was both helpful and terrifying.

Antoine nodded. "There is so much more than what you think. Not all is known to the public, but my father is working with your country's military and…" He winced.

I didn't need him to continue to know it wasn't pretty.

"Your father's com company depends a lot on mine," Antoine continued. "My father is at the top of technology and your father keeps a lot of his market share by selling phones built with our tech."

"This is why you said you and I were supposed to be matched." I remembered his words from the introduction party.

"Oh, I see, you tried to get Esmeralda and because you didn't, you settled for Taylor?" Archie snorted. "You deserve better than to be the second choice, Oppenheimer."

She glared at Archie, but I could see the pain under the anger. He'd hurt her badly and I knew neither of them would open up to me about it. Her because the recollection would cause her obvious pain and him because of his shame at whatever had happened. "Yes, I deserve a lot, Archibald, a lot more than some people gave me. This is why I cut loose ends."

"Anyway," I cut in. I needed to redirect the conversation before we had a full-blown drama in an empty classroom. The four of us in a room were bound to be suspicious and I wasn't sure how long we had before Caleb found us. I also couldn't help but feel guilty for plotting behind his back, engaging his friends in it. He was bound to be beyond furious when - if, he ever found out.

I explained everything to them by giving the quickest summary in history - the journal, the note, the reason behind my return, and my desire for justice.

Archie sighed, leaving his position. "I will give Antoine the list of people so he can look into their backgrounds."

"You can do that?"

Antoine smirked. "With my dad's system? There isn't much I can't do."

I nodded. "Impressive."

Antoine chuckled. "Ah! That's exactly what Tay said last night."

Archie growled as Taylor swatted Antoine in the stomach, making him gasp.

"Careful, babe. I'm fragile," Antoine said.

"And you're an ass!" She glared at him. "Cut the crap."

I rolled my eyes. No, we couldn't afford a battle of testosterone now, not with this much at stake. "We need to hurry; the bell will go soon."

Archie sighed. Reaching into his pocket, he extended a folded piece of paper to Antoine. "This is our list for you to look into." He turned to me. "I added your librarian, even if it is a long shot."

Antoine whistled, looking at the list. "Damn, that's not just anyone on this list!" He looked up at us, his eyes widening with surprise. "The Astors?" I nodded. "Your father?" I nodded again. "Sheriff Whiteman?"

I looked at Archie, surprised to see the name on the list.

Archie shrugged. "If it was murder, it was covered up really well. The Sheriff, coroner... Anyone and everyone who touched the case."

Antoine slipped the note into his pocket. "It might take a little while to go through the names on the list. I need to be extra careful and do it all myself."

"It's not like she is going anywhere, is she?" The bitterness in Archie's voice was not surprising. He had lived with our mother.

I extended my hand to him and he took a couple of steps forward. He was reaching for my hand when he was nudged forward as the door was opened by Caleb.

"Ah, the Scooby Gang is in session. Sorry to interrupt." He crossed his arms on his chest. "Anything I'm missing?"

"Where were you this morning? You missed the council meeting." Archie turned toward him, blocking my line of vision.

"So what?"

"It was critical."

Caleb scoffed. "What could be so critical at a High School meeting, huh? What will the prom theme be? Sorry to break it to you Archibald, but some of us deal with more important things."

This intrigued me, especially since both Antoine and Archie looked surprised. I took it that this wasn't Caleb's normal behavior with them.

"What are we talking about?" Caleb asked, and the smirk that appeared on his face showed me he was about to inflict pain. I just didn't know who the recipient was going to be. How sad was it that I could recognize his moods just by the type of smile he was sharing?

"Maybe we should do a couple's evening. What do you say? Oh no, wait." He turned his icy gaze to Archie, locking onto his prey. "We can't, Archibald Forbes is all alone," he added before looking at Taylor.

Caleb knew, that much was clear. He knew that Archie loved Taylor even if that idiot refused to admit it and I would bet everything I owned that he had played a part in whatever had gone down between them.

Caleb was a gifted puppeteer, one who thrived on people's misery especially when he was in pain, and I suspected that he was always in pain now that he'd lost Theo, now that I'd betrayed him after he'd dared showed me a little softness. I prayed for us all.

He extended his hand to me as the bell rang. "Let's go."

I looked at his hand, which was, I knew, just as soft as it looked. Why did he want to hold my hand?

"Come on, sweetheart." The word in his mouth sounding anything but endearing.

When I didn't make a move, he grabbed my hand and pulled me to the door.

"My fiancée just came back after a month in Paris. I missed her dearly," he added with such a flat voice that he could've very well been reading a science manual. But then, I realized, it was all about appearances yet again.

I sighed with resignation and squeezed his hand. It would always be about appearances – forever.

The morning classes went by painfully slowly. I just couldn't wait for lunch and hearing all about Taylor and Antoine.

I half-expected Caleb to demand I sit with him when we entered the cafeteria, but he didn't. Was it because I needed alone time with my friend? I shook my head at the thought. No, of course not. It was probably because he needed to deal with some Kings stuff.

"So how did that happen?" I asked Taylor as soon as we set our tray on our usual table.

She looked around ensuring we were out of earshot. "Why are you so surprised? You suggested it."

I snorted." As a joke, yeah. I didn't think it would happen."

She shrugged. "It almost happened... naturally." She cocked her head to the side, taking a drink of her Coke. "Archie was becoming a bit too present in my life after you were gone, you know for messages and stuff."

I nodded. I'd been grateful when she'd offered to relay messages to my brother while I'd been away, knowing all the bad blood between them.

"Yeah and I thought I was emotionally equipped to deal with him. Turned out I was not as strong as I thought I was." She looked away and I was way too familiar with the shine I could see in her eyes.

"Then one day I was just getting in my car after school and out of nowhere Antoine hopped in. He told me about the conversation he had caught between your father and his and... I'm not sure what happened really. I missed you. Archie was messing with my head again and then…" She shrugged again, her cheeks turning red.

"There is no shame in breaking down every once in a while, Taylor. We're human."

"Yeah…" she gave me a side smile. "Anyway, I broke down, telling him I knew the truth about him and he gave me a hug and it felt so good – so comforting. People saw us and the next day, the rumor mill was going full force." She sighed. "Anyway, that night he took me out for dinner and we just connected, you know? Him dating me made his father ecstatic, as you can imagine."

I snorted, shaking my head. This society was so backward.

"It was a way for him to protect me too. His father would never do anything which might hurt our relationship."

"Smart move," I conceded.

"And in the end this relationship is one of the best and truest I have ever had."

I frowned. Was Antoine bi?

"It's not what you think," she quickly added, probably seeing the confusion on my face. "The thing is," she leaned closer, almost whispering. "Because sex is off the table, we can be completely ourselves, you know, and we do have an intimacy which I think is greater. I just…" she shrugged. "I don't hate it."

I nodded, not really sure how that all worked, but if she was happy...

"I'm happy if you're happy," I said. "But I fear it is just a way to keep Archie at bay."

"It is, in a way," she admitted. "I'll tell you one day." She reached for my hand across the table and squeezed it. "I missed you, truly, and I'm sorry about the circumstances that brought you back here, but we'll figure it out and then you'll be free to leave again."

"Yeah." I smiled, but I wasn't sure I'd leave again. The terrifying part was that it was not because they would prevent me, but because I wasn't sure I wanted to.

Chapter 7 - Esme

"Antoine needs to see you in the student council room about that French assignment," Taylor announced as she came to stand beside me.

Suddenly, all the weariness I'd felt over the last week of living with Caleb and being thoroughly ignored, lifted, and the excitement at having a lead – any lead at this point – felt like a gift.

I looked around and met Caleb's eyes at the end of the corridor. It felt like he was always spying on me, trying to find anything wrong. I lifted my gaze and quickly met my brother's; he rolled his eyes, and that made me smile.

Caleb's scowl deepened as he looked from Archie to me. We should have been more careful about displaying the extent of our attachment, but my father thought it was a trick played by Archie to fool me. As for Caleb, Archie said he was too smart to be fooled.

Caleb said something to my brother before walking toward me. "Esmeralda, I've been informed by Saint-Vincent that he is tutoring you in French. When were you planning on telling me?"

Why did he have to be so formal all of the time?

I was about to snap that he was not my guardian and that I didn't have to tell him everything, but Archie threw me a warning look, so I swallowed my pride. I wondered how long I could keep doing this before I snapped or choked.

"I'm sorry, but it is during school hours and therefore doesn't affect our schedule, and it's not like I see you much around the house to exchange pleasantries."

Sorry Archie, I just couldn't contain that jab.

Caleb's nostrils flared. "Even so, this is the kind of thing I must be informed of."

"Well, maybe you should have chosen a location other than Paris for my… 'sabbatical'," I whispered angrily, using quoting fingers. I wasn't sure why, but even when I was committed to keeping the peace, I just couldn't stop myself from fighting back.

Caleb leaned toward me, grinding his jaw. "And maybe you shouldn't have run away like a little girl with a temper. You started all–"

"Come on, bro," Archie clapped his hand on Caleb's shoulder in what seemed to be a friendly gesture, but I knew better. My brother was fiercely protective.

Caleb turned his head and looked at Archie's hand on his shoulder with a cocked eyebrow as if he couldn't believe my brother, or anyone for that matter, had dared touch him without his consent. He looked up from Archie's hand to his face. "If I were you, I'd remove my hand this second, Archibald," he murmured, so eerily calm it was terrifying.

Archie conceded with a sigh. I knew he was not afraid of Caleb, at least not really. I was pretty sure he was giving in to avoid Caleb taking it out on me later. "You'll have enough on your plate with your parents coming back tonight. Why does it matter that–"

That caught my attention. "Your parents are coming back *tonight*?" I all but shrieked. I was not ready. "You said two weeks!"

"And it has been a week. What does it change for you?" He asked, looking at me challengingly.

"I–" What could I say? That, depending on what Antoine was going to tell me, I was planning on snooping around his house? Something I would have a hard time doing with his parents back home. "I would have liked to know. I live there too." I turned toward my locker to fill my bag; Caleb was too perceptive and I was too transparent. "Have you told them you moved me in?"

He stood there silently and I turned to look at him. His glare was a clear indication he hadn't.

"Maybe you should tell them. Your mom's clearly not my biggest fan. She deserves to know I'll be sharing her space." *Maybe she can force you to send me back to the Forbes Estate,* I added to myself.

"How I deal with my parents is none of your concern." He looked down at his watch. "Aren't you going to be late for your tutoring session?" he asked tauntingly.

"I am. I'll see you later." The elation of having news couldn't be tempered.

I found Antoine sitting on a stool facing the door, a French textbook in front of him.

I grimaced. "Okay…"

He chuckled, opening it to a random page. "Props." He patted the stool beside him. "If you care to join me."

I sat beside him. "So, what's new?"

He chuckled. "Hello to you too, sunshine. I'm doing well, thank you. How about you?"

I blushed at my rudeness, but the teasing look in his eyes showed he hadn't taken offense.

"I'm sorry, Antoine. It's just– I want to solve this so much."

"I know." He nodded, looking so serious that I was taken aback. "Anyways, so here is what I've found so far. The sheriff? Squeaky clean. Seriously, always has been. He is aggravating to our fathers which I enjoy very much. However, there was a deputy at the time - David Phang." He tapped the piece of paper. "The guy quit six months after your mother's death and bought himself a Chinese restaurant in New York City, cash. Do you know how much a low-ranking officer makes in such a small town?" He snorted. "He smells fishy."

"Maybe we can go and ask questions? A road trip or something?"

He shook his head. "No, we need to be smart about it. If there was foul play, it happened thirteen years ago. Their guard is down now, and if any evidence exists, it will be easier to find. However, if anyone suspects we're poking around… They will protect themselves again."

I sighed. "You're right. Do you know anyone who can help?"

He grimaced. "That's the problem. All the detectives, technicians, and IT experts I know are on my dad's payroll. I'm not sure they would be discreet."

The bell rang. "We're going to be late for homeroom," I offered when Antoine remained seated.

He shook his head. "No, I've got it covered with the admin. You and I have French tutoring once every two weeks to keep you posted."

"Oh," I sat back down. These guys could really do whatever the hell they wanted here. "So, your dad…" He has nothing to do with this, I reminded myself. Taylor had told me Antoine had moved here the summer before he'd entered high school. "Do you think he will talk?"

Antoine cocked his head to the side with uncertainty. "My father is very business-driven. He moved us here to be closer to his business associates. He has no loyalty other than money and his family. So no, I don't think we can trust him if it might cost him a deal."

"I see…" I trailed off, looking down at the French book and the text I couldn't understand. "Meaning, if my father ended up in jail…" I added as a subtext.

He nodded. "I've ensured Taylor's protection for as long as we are together."

"Talking about Taylor…"

His back turned rigid, his posture clearly defensive. The happy-go-lucky flirt was suddenly gone. "I'm not sure this is relevant here."

"It is. I understand it came from a good place, I do, but you can't miss the extra tension it is adding to our…" I twisted my mouth to the side, not sure how to define our relationship. "Our weird little circle of trust." I ran my hand along my chin. "We've already had so many challenges to face, I'm not sure a love rivalry, even a made-up one, would be productive."

He chuckled, but it lacked humor. "Pot, meet kettle." I frowned in confusion. I was about to ask what he meant when he raised his hand. "You were not there. You didn't see. You wouldn't be so quick to defend your brother's tender feelings if you knew."

"Then tell me!" I let out, throwing my hands up in frustration. "Fucking hell, it's like Watergate! Everyone is alluding and nobody's talking."

"I have no dog in this fight, Esmeralda, and it is not my place to say. But what I can tell you is that when it all unfolded, I'd been here a week, and it was that same week I realized your brother is as cruel as Caleb Astor, maybe even more so… I will not be the one changing your views of your brother. He might have changed; *you* might have changed him, but I know who he was then, who he was until recently. I don't feel bad for him and his poor bleeding heart. He deserves this, just as Caleb deserves to be tormented by his unwanted obsession and not-so-unrequited destructive feelings."

"What do you mean?"

He sighed, throwing a quick look at his watch. "This is a conversation for another time, with a lot of alcohol, but I've been closeted for way too long to miss the signs. A faker can't fool a faker and all I'm saying is that before looking into Taylor, Archie, and me you'll have to accept your feelings, just as he will have to accept his because if neither of you does you'll destroy each other and everyone around you in the process."

He shook his head, opening the folder again.

"For the deputy guy," I started. He was right, there was no good reason to dwell on what was and what should be. I had to deal with my mother's death first. The rest would have to wait.

"We can't go. Any of us getting too close to him would ring alarm bells."

I nodded. "What if I knew someone that could go undetected?"

"Someone you trust enough with this?"

I nodded, thinking about Ben. Before being a crush, he was first and foremost a friend- one who always came through for me, even when I couldn't explain why I needed him.

"Yes, I do."

"Okay, I'll get you the bugs to give your friend so he can plant them on Phang's phone and car."

"Okay." I bet Ben would have a field day with that. He loved all the stupid spy movies.

"I haven't investigated the parents yet, but will do that next," said Antoine. "As for your librarian, I didn't find anything."

"Yeah, I expected as much."

"No, you don't understand – I couldn't find *anything* – good or bad. It's like Anna White didn't exist before she attended Oklahoma Panhandle State University."

"Maybe there is nothing. It was before social media."

He looked at me like I was a mentally challenged child. "There is always a trace, Esmeralda. Social Security number, driving license, high school diploma… Always something, but here? *Rien du tout.* I'm not saying it has something to do with this. I mean, the woman is quite a bit older than your mother, so I don't think it is linked, but she is not as clean and innocent as she seems to be."

I shrugged. "Everybody has a past. It doesn't mean she is bad."

"No," he agreed, "it doesn't, but it intrigued me to look deeper, and also, I don't mean to brag, but Brentwood Academy is one of the best schools in the country. Four out of the six most recent Presidents have graduated from here. All the staff, academic, administrative or otherwise, are paid three to four times the average salaries for their respective roles. This has been done to ensure we attract the best of the best, but also so they keep their mouths shut and remain loyal."

"Okay…" I didn't know all that, but I still didn't see how it mattered here.

"She graduated from a state university. A state..." The corners of his mouth curled deep down in disdain.

I frowned, angry at his reaction. "I didn't peg you as an elitist pig."

It was his turn to frown. "Why? Because I'm gay? I assure you, Esmeralda, I'm just as entitled, and my sexuality has nothing to do with it."

"No, I just thought you were better because you're funny and a hedonist and also because you don't seem to mind sticking your tongue down the help's throat."

His eyes lit up with mirth, and I knew I had managed to diffuse the existing tension. "Guilty as charged." He shook his head, his bronze hair so perfectly styled, it didn't even move. "But all I'm saying is that this school is even more elitist than I'll ever be, and they'd never hire an average librarian from a state university. She would have to have graduated from the Ivy League."

"What are you saying?"

"That she's got well-connected people in her corner." He let out a breath, looking at his watch again, and I realized by looking at the clock on the wall that our hour was almost up.

"Anyway, let me know if your friend can do it," Antoine said. "I'll get everything ready, and I'll keep on looking into the librarian."

I nodded, standing up to exit the room.

"And for what it's worth, I do love her," he added as I reached the door.

I turned around, arching an eyebrow.

He sighed, closing the book. "I do. Maybe not in a Romeo-and-Juliet kind of way, not with that kind of destructive passion, but I love her in a Freddie-and-Mary way, the real way. The way that counts."

"I just don't want her to get hurt."

"She won't. Well, not because of me at least."

I understood the message. Archie was the arrow in Taylor's chest.

I texted Ben to tell him I needed to talk to him, then ended up skipping lunch when he texted right back to say he was available now.

I went to my car and dialed his number, shaking a little with apprehension. I was apprehensive because I was about to ask him something that could be dangerous. Something that he didn't owe me. Something that could backfire greatly.

"So how is life back in Snob Town?" he asked with humor in his voice as he picked up the phone.

The last time I'd seen him in person, it hadn't ended well, but things had gotten better with time. He'd helped before, and when I'd called him from California, I'd told him a lot of things.

"Interesting, to say the least," I replied. After everything Antoine had said about tapping phones, I didn't want to say too much. "Tell me, when are you getting your bike again? I liked the black one you had last time. What's the make again?"

"The bike?" He was clearly confused.

I bit my bottom lip. *Please get the message.* "You know the black one you rode when you visited?"

"Oh… oh! That one? It's a Yamaha R1."

"How nice…" *Is it?* I thought, sitting in my over-the-top Bugatti.

"I– hmmm." He stopped, probably trying to piece everything together. I couldn't blame him. "I will probably get it back soon."

I sighed with relief; he'd gotten the message. "Text me when you get it?"

"Of course. How is life treating you?"

"Not bad, all things considered… I'm long overdue for a trip to Port Harbor. I'll go soon with my brother on a shopping trip. There is a little store there I like."

"Ah, it's nice that you're settling in."

"Yeah," I knew he understand where I wanted to meet him. There we would discuss everything I couldn't say over the phone. "How come you can talk now? Aren't you supposed to be in class?"

"It's teacher training day and the football season is over for us."

"I'm sorry." Luke leaving had hurt the team and I felt a little responsible.

"Yeah, well, when two players get injured and we lose our coach, we're lucky to even hit the playoffs."

I winced. Luke had informed me of the rumors swirling around about the drama unfolding between him, William and me. He had wanted to start afresh and had left for a job in Maryland. I suspected he'd taken any job just to be closer to me.

"I miss you," Ben whispered on a sigh.

"I miss you too." My heart constricted, but not for the same reasons it had before. This life had changed me, but a part of me was still longing for what I had back then. It seemed like a lifetime ago, but wasn't more than six months... Six months. The realization hit me like a ton of bricks. How could such a brief period change someone so intrinsically? I wasn't completely certain it was him I missed so much or what he represented. A simpler time, a simpler life, when the worries were, in retrospect, so mundane… There'd been no murder, no betrayal, no lies, nor hidden agendas.

Ben and I talked a bit longer about everything and anything. It was good to feel like I was back in Missouri.

The rest of the day was quite uneventful, but as the day progressed, so did my stress level at the thought of being around Caleb's mother tonight. She had never made a secret of how much she disliked me. It would be a true nightmare; I would feel even more in prison now.

****

"Benjamin, could you please tell me where the swimming pool is?" I asked as soon as I walked into the Astor mansion, leaving my bag by the console at the entrance. I always left it there and always found it in my bedroom when I decided to do my homework. It was the little house fairies, I was sure.

I had loved swimming since I was a little girl, and the public pool had pretty much been all my father could offer me in the summer. I'd not swum here yet because I didn't feel comfortable and because I had no swimsuit, but I was now tense and apprehensive. When the Astors came back, I'd never dare swim again. I wouldn't put it past my future mother-in-law to put piranhas in the pool.... Or maybe even my future husband.

Benjamin stepped behind me to grab my jacket. "It is one level down, Miss. Turn to your left and just follow the corridor. You can't miss it."

"Thank you. Do you know where I could find a swimsuit?"

He nodded. "Yes, there are changing rooms at the pool and I believe there are a few items for you to choose from. Would you like me to show you?"

Lord, no. I shook my head. "No, it'll be alright. Thank you."

He bowed slightly before retreating... God knows where.

I went downstairs and looked around, somewhat intrigued. I didn't even know there was more to the house. I took the left turn and the smell of chlorine guided me from then on. I couldn't help but gasp as I passed through the door. The swimming pool here was even more majestic than the one at the Forbes mansion. It was seriously ridiculous! The pool was longer than the Olympic pool they had back home, and it was modeled to look tropical with fake trees, chairs, and a bar made out of bamboo. The changing rooms at the back looked like huts with palm roofs. The ceiling was made concave and cut to look like a cave, and at the end, there was an actual waterfall!

I shook my head, still in a daze. They'd hidden a flipping secret oasis in a Connecticut mansion.

"Who does that?" I whispered, taking it all in, trying to memorize the details that were appearing around me the more I looked. The citrus and coconut smell mixing with the chlorine. The grainy tiles which I presumed were designed to mimic sand.

I ogled at the ostentation of the room, but I was way too tempted to swim to stand marveling at it for long. I opened the bamboo chest by the huts and looked through the bathing suits. All the women's suits were skimpy bikinis, each smaller than the one before.

I picked up a red one which seemed to be the least suggestive and changed into it.

"Oh, this is not going to work," I whispered, detailing myself in the changing room mirror. The pieces of fabric barely covered me. I grimaced. I knew I had curves and sizeable breasts, but I was not big at all. Either these suits were made for the stick-thin models you saw on the runway or they were purchased like that on purpose so the lascivious men of this house could get a good look.

I grimaced, reconsidering the idea of a swim. Maybe I should just go buy my own swimsuit first?

I sighed, rolling my neck. I was alone here. I could swim a few lengths and then change back before going upstairs. Nobody needed to know, and I could buy a swimsuit another time, not that I'd swim here again anytime soon unless Jacklyn and James Astor were gone.

I looked out of the changing room. No way would I let others see me dressed like this. The room was empty though, and there was no sound except for the waterfall.

I sighed in relief. Stepping out of the hut, I adjusted the tiny triangles of fabric barely containing my heavy breasts. I rolled my eyes. I was prone to a flashing incident for sure.

"Oh, what the hell. It's just a few lengths," I muttered, hurrying to the pool. My worries quickly faded as my foot slid into the warm water.

I sighed with contentment once fully immersed, then started my lengths. The more I swam, the more I could feel the tension in my muscles fade. I pushed harder, enjoying the feel, the slight burn of exertion. I wanted to swim until I was too tired to think, too tired to get mad, just too tired…

When I felt my leg muscles starting to quiver and my arms feeling like dead weight, I decided to stop. I felt strangely better as I swam to the pool ladder, but froze as soon as I stepped out. Caleb was leaning against the bamboo bar with his arms crossed over his chest.

He detailed me from head to toe, making me shiver under the heat of his eyes. "Are you planning on taking a page from your mother's playbook, huh? Hook the father and the son? Don't bother." He took a step toward me, shaking his head.

"The son can see right through you and the father can't give you as much as you want him to." He threw me the bath towel. "Cover yourself; it's pathetic."

Anger spiked over the jab at my mother. It was enough to overtake the self-consciousness of my semi-nudity. "Stop soiling my mother's memory!" I pointed an accusing finger at him. "You know as well as I do she wasn't like that!"

"And how would I know?" He asked challengingly.

The journal extracts I'd left him were so clear. I'd even sent him the pages where my mother had said that James had come in the middle of the night after one of the horrible fights she'd had with my father, that he had offered to take her and Archie and leave his wife and Caleb to start a new life. She'd told him then that it would never happen, that she might have been attracted to him at first, but it had been a lifetime ago and that this attraction was long dead, never to be rekindled.

"The journal pages say it all!" I shouted.

He frowned with obvious confusion. "What pages?"

I scowled, wrapping the towel around me. "The journal–" I repeated.

He rolled his eyes. "What journal?" He sighed, throwing his hands up as if it didn't matter, and maybe it didn't. "I've got to get ready. Just stop being so pathetic," he added before walking away, leaving me still reeling about the revelation he'd just made.

He'd never gotten my letter. It had been intercepted, and now I knew for a fact that someone in this house knew more than they were letting on. I just needed to figure out if it was his mother or his father…

I needed to tell Archie and Antoine about this. It was not much. I knew Archie would be angry that I'd tried to share the pages with Caleb, but I'd just wanted him to hate us less. Now that those pages were out...someone knew I knew more than they wanted me to. It was a potential added liability, but I'd thought I'd done something good, something that would help him gain some peace. But he was never going to cut me any slack, was he? How dare he talk to me like that anyway?

I was getting angrier the more I thought about it and even the steaming hot shower didn't help calm my rage. I'd never done anything to warrant this, except claim back freedom I more than deserved.

I changed into my pajamas and opened my bedroom door, glaring at his end of the corridor, considering if challenging him was even worth it.

"It's enough," I muttered, walking to his room. I had nothing left to lose with him. Our pseudo-relationship had been annihilated and he wouldn't try to make it better. Archie's advice had been utter crap. This fly would not be caught with honey but with flipping cyanide!

I opened his bedroom door without knocking just as he was putting on his dress shirt. I frowned at the hint of the tattoo peeking out at the top of his spine as he did.

I was taken aback for a second. I, for some reason, hadn't expected Caleb Astor to be the tattoo type, and I was now dying to see what was under his shirt.

"Esmeralda," he enunciated, keeping his back to me as he buttoned his shirt. He turned around as his shirt was closed. "We're not respecting each other's privacy, I see. Good to know."

I didn't miss the underlying threat in his voice.

I shook my head. That was a discussion for another time. I followed him with my eyes as he scanned a box of cufflinks. He was taking a lot of time to figure out which ones he wanted to wear.

"How dare you disrespect me like that?" I said, my words dripping with anger. The shame and pain I'd felt at his words before had unleashed my tongue. I didn't think anything I could say or not say would be able to salvage our relationship at this point. I had broken the little trust, or faith, or whatever he'd felt for me when I'd left. I just had to learn to live with the consequences.

He glanced my way and detailed my pajamas. "I see you've put some clothes on. Good call. It would have been a wasted effort as my parents are actually not coming back until the end of the week."

That stopped the tirade I was about to give him. "Then why are *you* dressing up?" I asked as he tucked his shirt into his dress pants.

"Because I have a date with Aleks and I need to pretend to make an effort." He gestured for me to move out of the doorway.

I took a couple of steps back as he walked toward me. He passed by so close that I could feel the heat of his body on mine.

"Please don't go," I begged as he started down the corridor. I wasn't sure why it distressed me so much. I tried to convince myself that it was because it was Aleksandra and I knew that she would gloat tomorrow, even if I knew deep down it was more, that even if we were together in appearances only, it was more... At least for me.

"Why?"

"Because it's her, because I told you I won't stand being disrespected like that. I won't be made a joke of, Caleb."

I noticed his expression darken and I knew my answer had been wrong. He straightened. "Ah well, it's a good thing then that I don't care about what you think, isn't it? You belong to me and I do what I want. I don't think there is anything to add."

You belong *to* me...not *with* me. The difference spoke volumes and once again reminded me about how angry he'd made me and how frustrating he really was.

I shook my head. Begging was not worth it. He would not give in and was enjoying my downfall way too much.

"Fine, just go." I threw my hands up in surrender. "You actually deserve each other. You're both cold-hearted bastards."

His face morphed into a hard, soulless grin. "Yes, we are, and you'd better remember that, no matter what." He straightened his jacket. "The little part of humanity you think you'd witnessed, never existed, and even if it did, it died with Theo."

"I won't forget." Even if I didn't entirely believe that, I let it go. I was too hurt and angry to fight him.

"Good!" He turned around briskly and I followed him with my eyes. A small and yet exceedingly naïve part of me wished he would not go through with it. Yet, within a few minutes I heard the main door close. I walked back to my bedroom just in time to see his Aston Martin speed down the driveway.

I sighed, shaking my head. I knew better, didn't I? And yet... I turned around, letting out another sigh. I'd just won another reprieve. I wasn't sure when Caleb's parents would be back now, but I knew my window to explore the place undetected was closing. I decided to look around tonight, if only to keep my mind occupied with something other than what Caleb would be doing in the next few minutes with that girl.

I growled, rolling my eyes. *He made no promises to you, Esme. Quite the contrary,* I repeated to myself, somehow hoping that this statement would finally sink in, that I would finally forget the Caleb I'd seen before I'd left, that I would finally let my heart go back to the way it was before I'd set foot in this town.

I padded barefoot around the huge, impersonal house, my steps silent on the cold, tiled floor. The house seemed so empty even though I knew old Benjamin and a couple of staff were around. They were so good at being invisible, only appearing when you needed them. It was still so creepy to me. It felt like they appeared out of nowhere, like ghosts. I shivered, rubbing down my arms over my red Henley. It seemed that this house was haunted anyway and not only by staff with ninja skills, but by all the secrets, lies, and animosity seeping from every wall.

Walking into the kitchen, I found a bottle of white wine and a small card resting against it. '*A little present to take the edge off,*' it read.

I glared at the offending bottle before closing my hand around the card, crushing it as I wished I could crush Caleb right now.

This was beyond taunting. This was cruel. He knew how I felt about alcohol due to my uncle Luke's history, and yet... I threw the card in the trash and grabbed the bottle, reading the label as if it mattered.

I grimaced, not even able to pronounce the name in my mind. What did it even mean? *Gewurztraminer…* I shrugged. "Ah, you want me to drink? I'll drink and then I'll vomit all over your bed, you cold-hearted bastard. Wait until you come back to the stringent smell all over your carpet," I chuckled, rummaging through the kitchen for a corkscrew. "We'll see who'll laugh then."

I opened the bottle and didn't even bother with a glass. I might as well be the classless girl he was always accusing me of being.

After only a couple of sips, warmth started to spread across my chest. I looked at the bottle again. Was it because I'd never really had a drink before or was wine really that potent?

I shrugged, taking another sip. At least now I didn't care that much. I chuckled to myself. *Cheese!* My eyes widened at the realization as I slapped my hand against the countertop. I needed cheese… I needed cheese more than my next breath.

"Cheese is life." I nodded, agreeing with myself.

I opened the fridge, grabbed what I presumed was Brie, and took a big bite of it before taking another sip of wine.

Yep, best decision ever! I pulled at my shirt. Why was it so hot in here? I huffed, blowing some hair out of my face.

I took another sip of wine and glared at the bottle. Was this a normal reaction after only a quarter bottle? No wonder Luke enjoyed it. "Oh, it's too hot!"

I rested the bottle on the counter with a loud thump. I needed a swim. I chuckled. *Yep, Esmerima, the Little Mermaid.*

I sang songs from The Little Mermaid on my way to the pool, but stopped as soon as I walked in, a wide smile spreading across my lips.

"Mom!"

She smiled from her spot in the middle of the pool, the water at her waist, dressed in a pale peach-pink lacy gossamer nightgown. She looked beautiful with her wavy hair down her back, floating slowly, with a kind, loving smile on her face.

"I knew you'd come." I marveled, standing at the edge of the pool.

"Of course I did, my beautiful daughter," she said with a voice even more melodic than I'd ever imagined as she opened her arms invitingly. "Why don't you come closer? I've missed you so much."

I followed her into the pool and swam toward her as she kept smiling at me.

"Why don't you come with me?" she asked. "I'm so alone."

I nodded. "Of course. Where?"

She went deep under the water, gesturing me down, and I followed her to the bottom. She opened her arms and I let her embrace me until I fell asleep peacefully in the safety of her arms.

Chapter 8 - Caleb

I punched the steering wheel in frustration as I sat in the car, praying Aleksandra wouldn't check if I were gone.

'It happens to every guy,' Aleks had cooed with her syrupy voice like I was a child. *'Let me try harder.'*

No, it didn't happen to everyone, especially not hormone-riddled eighteen-year-olds and especially not to me. That girl was open to literally anything. I could have fucked my frustration away and taken whatever pleasure I wanted without any regard for her own, and she would have pretended to love it, like she always did. But I hadn't been able to. My dick was on fucking life support. Even the images of Esmeralda I'd tried to conjure had been hijacked. I usually saw her lying invitingly on my bed, her wavy bronze hair flowing on my pillows, her face flushed after the orgasm I'd given her with just my mouth - just like that day I'd felt like Superman. But no, today the only image I could conjure was her sad face when I'd walked away, the glistering of tears in her eyes when I'd turned my back on her after she'd begged me not to go to Aleksandra.

I wanted her to ask me to stay because she cared and not because it was Aleks. Would I have stayed if she'd said that? I growled.

I drove like a mad man back home. I'd taken her back to get revenge, to make her pay, but she was a virus spreading in my blood, invading the little bit of peace I had left.

She needed to stop whatever game she was playing. She didn't need to play the innocent, kind-hearted girl she pretended to be to get me to drop my defenses. I wouldn't be fooled twice. She needed to stop that charade as that only infuriated me even more. I needed her to be the conniving double-faced traitor I knew she was. That, I could respect.

I'd wanted to hurt her, humiliate her today – like I'd been humiliated when William had called me after school this afternoon. I had heard in his voice how glad he'd been to announce that he'd 'forgotten' to stop his tracking of Esme's calls. He'd claimed to be 'helpful' by letting me know that Esme had spent over twenty-seven minutes on the phone with Ben Deluca today. I had pretended to know they were in contact, that I couldn't care less, and yet even though I'd told her she could, I couldn't help but feel it had been a betrayal, a betrayal she needed to pay for.

This was going to be our life, each of us trying to get the upper hand, avenging ourselves, making each other crazy until one of us snapped. It'd be her, of course. She was much weaker, unprepared for this misery whereas I was born in it, built in it, thrived in it. She didn't stand a chance.

I took the direction of the club. No way I was going to go home and let her know that nothing had happened with Aleks. I couldn't show her that she had destabilized me. I should have just taken my freedom back when I had the chance. I'd been asking myself if this revenge was worth it, and right now, it felt like my revenge on her was also revenge on myself.

I growled at the memory of her stupid Confucius quote. It was like she knew, had cursed me. I scowled, swerving the car in the direction of the house. She'd caused the damage. She had to fix it! She'd give me what I needed, whether she liked it or not.

When I made it to the house, I didn't even bother to park the car. I simply stopped it by the stairs and rushed in, holding on to my anger and indignation before I changed my mind.

"Where is she?" I asked Benjamin as soon as I walked in.

"I'm not sure, sir. I was doing the inventory in the wine cellar for your mother's return. I just came back."

I waved my hand dismissively. I was pretty sure old Benji there had a soft spot for Esmeralda and wouldn't tell me where she was even if he knew. I sighed, taking the steps up two at a time. The old man needed a lesson in loyalty, but I was not sure I could blame him. I had started to suspect that she was a sorceress with her innocent smiles, fake solicitude, and pure beauty.

I knocked on the door. "Esmeralda." I wasn't sure what I expected after the way we had left things, but it wasn't her staying silent. "Esmeralda," I repeated louder. "Open the door now." I tried the handle and was surprised to find it unlocked. I walked in and got hit by her sweet scent of rose and lilac. I couldn't help but inhale deeply. I looked at her made bed and had to fight every instinct I had to lie there and take in her essence. I rolled my eyes. What the hell did this girl do to me?

I took a look around. The boxes we'd retrieved from her house were still in a corner unopened. There was nothing personal. It looked as if she was expecting this stay to be temporary. I tightened my hands into fists as a fresh wave of betrayal engulfed me. She was clearly planning on running again.

I turned around briskly, leaving before the impulse to destroy everything in her room became overwhelming.

I went back downstairs and to the swimming pool. I knew she would be there and it both angered and enticed me. I hadn't expected seeing her in a swimsuit would affect me the way it had. I'd seen many women in them, some actual models, but I had always controlled my body, mind over matter. Always. And yet when I'd seen her step out of the pool in that poor excuse of a swimsuit, my body had reacted in the most visceral way, my cock hardening so painfully against the restraint of my pants. I was grateful I'd been half-hidden in the darkness and by the side of the wooden bar. I could pretend only so much. My body was constantly, infuriatingly betraying me.

What angered me the most was the poison of doubt in my mind. How everything she did had an ulterior motive. How I kept being reminded of how she had fooled me with her fake feelings and contrition. How she'd made me believe she cared, acted like she could love me. And how she'd pulled the rug by disappearing and–

My step faltered as my eyes locked on the swimming pool and the sight of Esmeralda face down, floating lifelessly.

"Esme? ESME!" I shouted. "Benjamin! Help!" I jumped into the pool fully dressed.

I turned her over and felt a wave of nausea at the sickly white hue of her skin, the blue of her lips. "Don't do this," I huffed, pulling her as well as I could to the poolside, my soaked clothes and Oxford shoes feeling like a hundred pounds.

"Oh dear. Sir!" Benjamin took her hand as I helped her up. After laying her carefully on the floor, I started CPR.

"Call Blue Arrow and Dr. Willis now!" I huffed, doing the chest compressions to the horrible mental tone of *Stayin' Alive*.

I leaned in. "Come on, don't be a coward. Fight! Don't fucking give up!" I growled before giving her mouth-to-mouth.

I restarted the chest compressions, huffing with exertion as I glanced toward the door and cursed the useless Blue Arrow.

I didn't realize how arduous it was to do chest compressions until now. They made it look so effortless in films, but this was nothing like the inanimate doll from the mandatory CPR class I'd taken last year.

I was the only line between the life or death of a person - and not just any person. Even if I hated to admit it, having her life in my hands mattered so much more than a stranger's.

"Just, please..." For once I was not above begging, and this terrified me once more.

Finally, her body jerked, and she started coughing up water as I turned her onto her side.

I let out a sigh of relief as my eyes started to burn with what I decided was the chlorine and nothing else.

"Mom," she whispered in between coughs and heaves. It clearly hurt.

Good! At least she would not go and do anything this stupid again.

Just as I was about to turn her onto her back, two medics from Blue Arrow came in and rushed to her. I stood up, letting them get to work.

"It took you long enough!" I barked, walking around them with my darkest scowl as they worked on Esmeralda.

"You saved her life," one of the paramedics said after checking the numbers from the clip he'd put on her finger.

"No thanks to you! When I think of the price we pay you for being incompetent!"

"It took them seven minutes to come here, Caleb. I would hardly call that incompetent."

I turned around as the greying, bearded man made his way toward me, adjusting his glasses.

"Dr. Willis," I greeted. I guess a man who had brought you into this world and saved your life under more than miraculous circumstances, could take some liberty with decorum. Had it only been seven minutes? It felt like it had been seven hours.

"How is she faring?" he asked a paramedic as he came to stand beside me.

"Her pulse is weak, but constant. Her SAT is at 75% which is not unexpected after a drowning."

"Why is she so unresponsive?" I asked, not able to hide the worry in my voice. She was still scarily pale, but her lips were not sickly blue anymore. She still looked like a wax doll though.

"It took incredible effort for her body to fight to stay alive. She is exhausted and her body is concentrating oxygen to mandatory functions such as the lungs, brain, and heart. A body tends to shut down and make you sleepy in such circumstances in order to concentrate on the healing part."

I nodded like I understood it all, but all that mattered was her. "Is she going to be okay?"

"We can't be sure until we run a full panel of tests. How long was she underwater?"

I shook my head as the two paramedics put her on the stretcher.

Dr. Willis sighed. "We'll know more once we're at the hospital and–"

"No hospital. Her room." I gestured to Benjamin standing by the door, whose worry was making him look even older. "Show them to her room."

Benjamin nodded and exited, closely followed by the paramedics.

"Are you sure it is–"

"Will it risk her health any further?" I asked, interrupting him.

He removed his glasses, wiping them with the tissue in his pocket, shaking his head. "No, it shouldn't."

"Then she stays."

"What happened?"

"I'm not sure." And I was not sure I wanted to find out.

He nodded. "I see…"

Do you though? Do you? I wanted to ask, but kept my cool. I was an Astor, detachment was required.

"I will run the tests."

"Please." I grabbed his arm as he took the direction of the door.

He turned around, looking at me with expectation.

"I know you have to notify the incident to the Blue Arrow Board," I said, knowing full well that the head of the board was none other than my darling father.

"Yes, I have to do this immediately after stabilizing Ms. Forbes. It is the procedure. I cannot deviate from it."

"Fine, but no matter what you find, your assessment will be that she slipped and hit her head. Are we in agreement?"

He frowned. "Caleb, son, if you've got anything–"

"I'm not your son, Dr. Willis, and I'm not a child anymore. I've not done anything, and I don't appreciate being questioned. I might not have my father's power yet, but I am powerful enough to destroy you if there is a need."

He looked at me, almost pained. Seriously, what did he expect? "Very well, sir. She fell and hit her head."

I nodded. "Glad we understand each other." I gestured toward the exit, following him silently, reeling as I thought about all the situations that I'd caused which had led to her being face-down in the pool.

When we walked into the room, my stupid dead heart squeezed painfully in my chest. Seeing her sickly pale, lying motionless in the bed...

I leaned against the closed door as Dr. Willis worked on Esmeralda with the two paramedics. I watched as they attached a mini-heart monitor and put an IV in her arm. It was like they'd brought a hospital room to our house. Seeing all of this brought back some uncomfortable and unwanted images from a past I'd thought was long buried under meters of concrete.

This was something great about America. Money could buy you the health system, giving you access to private paramedics, ambulances, and hospitals. You could get the best of everything... But there was a price.

After a further twenty minutes, Dr. Willis dismissed the paramedics. He waited for them to leave before starting his assessment.

"Truth be told, Mr. Astor." Ah, the 'Caleb' was finally forgotten; he had learned his place. "There is no concussion or any other head trauma suggesting an accident."

I nodded.

"Her vitals are still weak but stable, which is good," he continued, pointing at the screen. "We've set her up with an IV just as a precaution in case her system is compromised by any…"

I ground my teeth, understanding only too well what he was saying. My mother was a pill-popping addict.

"When will you know for sure?"

"I'll do a full tox-screen when I get back to the hospital."

"The results will only be shared with me and then they will disappear. Are we clear on that as well?"

Dr. Willis studied me silently.

"Are. We. Clear?" I repeated, my voice as firm and cold as I could make it. "And don't start serving me your license and Hippocratic Oath! We both know for a fact that you've done things like this and much worse over the years," I added, my scars suddenly itching as a physical reminder of my memories.

At least he had the decency to look away, his face reflecting the shame of my words. "Yes, we are," he replied with a clipped tone that radiated disapproval. Not that I cared for his judgment. He was too far down the same path to have any legitimacy in that regard. He looked at his watch. "I will go now. I believe she will sleep most of the night; her body suffered quite a trauma and needs the rest. As we don't know how long she was underwater, I fear I can't say what the damage will be, if any, and there is also the risk of secondary drowning. I will come when she is up to do a full cognitive assessment, but for the time being, I will have a nurse come and–"

"No, I'll do it."

"You'll…do it?"

I couldn't deny that it was uncharacteristic to have an Astor do something like this, and yet, I felt like I had to. "I can take an IV out. I've done it before."

Dr. Willis pursed his lips in clear displeasure before letting out a sigh of resignation. "Very well, please call me directly on my cell when she wakes so I can do the assessment."

It was late. I couldn't contain my yawn as soon as the door closed behind the old man. I didn't have to look so controlled anymore. With him now gone and the adrenaline having dropped, I finally realized my clothes were still soaked. Shivering, I rushed to my room, discarding clothes on the way. I toweled myself dry, then slipped into a pair of pajama bottoms. I looked at my bed almost wistfully, but I'd said I would keep an eye on her. Maybe I could just… I thought about her king-sized bed before rolling my eyes at the consideration. I would just be lying there beside her to ensure she was okay, nothing else.

Walking back into her room, I was grateful once more that my parents had decided not to come back today. I knew I was showing a lot of weakness right now, even if I didn't want to.

I lay beside her, staring at the ceiling and wondering how I could even consider sleep after all that had happened. I closed my eyes, not realizing I'd dozed off until I was jerked awake by Esmeralda mumbling in her sleep.

I looked at the alarm clock. It was after seven in the morning. I'd slept almost five hours. I turned towards her. Despite the lack of light, I could see some of her color had returned and a little bit of the tightness in my chest eased. How could this little woman, this traitor, have such an unwanted effect on me? Was it life's sick joke? Karma punishing me for the tricks I'd played in my past?

I sighed, got out of bed, and rang for the maid.

I waited just outside of the door. When she rushed over, her cheeks were flushed.

"I will be gone for thirty minutes. You will go into this room and keep an eye on Miss Forbes as if she was the most important thing in your life. Do you understand?"

She nodded briskly.

"If anything, and I mean *anything*, changes, fetch me from my room immediately."

She nodded again, but remained in front of me. Was this girl mentally challenged? She was only a maid after all.

"Do you understand the words coming out of my mouth? Hablas Ingles?"

She frowned, apparently taken aback by my question. "I…I understand, sir," she stuttered.

"Then go!" I clipped with exasperation, pointing at the door.

I rang for a quick breakfast, then showered and shaved in record time. I didn't like leaving Esmeralda alone with the slow maid.

I was back in her room within twenty minutes. I was relieved to see that her vitals had remained as strong as they'd been when I'd left her.

I sat on the armchair by the door in the darkened room. There was just enough light coming through the gap in the heavy curtains for me to see Esmeralda. My eyes focused on her chest and the slow and regular movement made by her breathing.

Seeing her chest move was almost therapeutic, almost soothing. My heart squeezed painfully when I relived, for the hundredth time in the past couple of hours, the moment I'd walked into the pool room to find her face down, lifeless. Thinking about her gone permanently had scared me in an incapacitating way.

This was a fear I couldn't afford, not in the world we lived in and not in a world where I knew she'd never fully be mine. Not when she was longing for another life I was not, and never could be, a part of. She was a liability I'd thought I was strong enough to avoid.

Dr. Willis wasn't sure how long she was going to sleep. He'd just said her body needed to heal, but I almost wanted to wake her up to check she was still the same infuriating, bullheaded girl she had been before all of this. I growled, running my hand over my face. I didn't realize how I just needed her to *be* her until today.

I shook my head as a soft knock brought me out of my dark thoughts. Benjamin opened the door just a little, throwing a concerned look toward the bed.

The cool, phlegmatic Benjamin was showing feelings for a tiny girl? He was clearly smitten with her. How could he not be though?

She was just Esmeralda, impossible not to like.

"What is it?" I asked when he remained silent.

"Mister Archibald Forbes is here."

I gritted my teeth, pursing my lips in frustration. I could only deal with one problem at a time. I'd already received an email from my father saying that he had heard from Dr. Willis about the unfortunate incident and would, therefore, be coming home earlier to help me care for Esmeralda. What a joke that all was. I was sure the man just wanted to enjoy the misery that my life was becoming. Or maybe, even worse, he just expected her to be weak enough to take what I knew he contemplated in the dark corner of his sick mind.

"I said no visitors, Benjamin," I snapped a bit louder than I'd intended.

"I know, sir, but he heard about Miss Esmeralda's accident and is refusing to leave without either seeing her or speaking to you."

Accident. I sighed, "Now is really not a good time."

"I know sir, but–"

I raised my hand, stopping him in his tracks. I was a second away from losing my shit and breaking anything in view, the poor old majordomo included. “I don't care what you do with him. Just tell him to wait.”

Benjamin opened his mouth, but the look I gave him was enough to stop him. “Very well, sir. I will have him wait for you in the small library.”

I waved my hand dismissively; he could set him up on the roof for all I cared as long as it was not in this room.

As soon as he closed the door behind him, I locked it. I wouldn’t put it past Forbes to force his way in.

As if on cue, my phone vibrated with an email from Dr. Willis. Finally, the results were in.

I opened the email. Despite having expected it, seeing the results still affected me. I read the email again and again, tightening my hand so firmly around the phone that I couldn’t believe it was not crumpling in my hand.

As if on cue, Esmeralda stirred and hissed, probably pulling on her IV.

I stood up and turned on the lamp on her desk.

She blinked, looking at me silently as if she was confused.

Again, I didn't want to acknowledge how seeing her grey eyes made me feel. I prayed to God she remembered who I was. I needed her to be okay so that I could kill her with my bare hands for the test results in that email.

“Caleb?” she asked as I reached for the IV machine and turned it off.

I couldn't help the sigh of relief; at least she remembered me.

“What are you doing here?” She looked at the IV in her arm and winced. “What happened?”

“You tell me,” I replied, my voice sharper than I’d intended. Now was not the time to settle the accounts.

She shook her head, wincing again. “I don't remember. We fought and then…” She shook her head again.

I raised an eyebrow, taking a step back. Did she try to kill herself because I was going to see Aleks?

"Is that why you tried to kill yourself?"

She jerked on her pillow. "What? I'm no… I didn't."

"I thought you didn't remember what happened?" I asked, not able to contain the edge in my voice.

"It doesn't matter if I remember or not, I would never. No."

Despite the evidence in my hand, I wanted to believe her. I wanted her words to be true. It was hard to accept that someone, anyone, especially someone I once thought cared, would rather end her life than contemplate her life with me.

"How did you get access to my mother's meds cabinet?"

"I didn't."

I sighed; I was too tired to play games. "Stop it, Esmeralda. Let go of the fake person you're pretending to be." I extended my phone to her, showing her the tox-screen result. "You had Haldol and Klonopin in your blood. Now I repeat, how did you get access to my mother's medicine cabinet?"

"I didn't, Caleb." She tried to pull on her IV, but I reached for her hand, stopping her. "I have too much to do."

I frowned. "What do you have to do?"

"I…" She stopped, trying to pull herself up on the bed.

Now that she was awake and apparently okay, my frustration at her actions was back in full force. But even I wouldn't unleash my anger on a bedridden woman.

I threw my hands up in exasperation. "I'll call the doctor. When you're ready to finally tell the truth, we'll talk."

"Caleb, please," she begged. Her voice was still so thin and uncertain. It was too fresh a reminder for when she'd begged me not to go last night. This brought on a wave of new feelings I'd never experienced befo - guilt.

I shook my head, exiting the room and already calling Dr. Willis. I then decided to go confront Archibald. Maybe he could shed some light on what she'd done last night, and perhaps I could pass him some of the unwelcome guilt I was feeling.

I found him walking back and forth in the small library, his back straight, his hands tightened into fists behind his back. Archibald and I were very similar, which had helped our thin truce to sprout. We were cool, never letting anything get the better of us. But right now, he looked at me like he could murder me. It was clear to see that Esmeralda had gone through all his walls and pretenses, as she had with me. How ironic.

"How dare you keep me away from my sister, Astor?" he roared, charging toward me.

I tried to keep my cool, resting in front of the door. I knew he would hit me if he wanted to, but he also knew I fought dirty and wouldn't mind crossing lines he wouldn't get within ten feet of.

"Let me see her," he hissed through clenched teeth, standing almost chest to chest with me.

I shook my head. "No. She is resting. The doctor is on his way."

He raised an eyebrow as if he couldn't understand me. Well, that made two of us. "No, she needs me. I need to make sure she is safe."

Ah, I saw it now. He believed I'd hurt her. My mouth morphed into a humorless rictus. I wanted to shut him up more than keep the secret of what had happened to her. "Oh, you are an expert on your sister? Could you please tell me then why she tried to kill herself?"

Archibald took a step back, allowing me to slip past him and walk into the library. "What did you say?"

"Your sister, the girl you know so well, she tried to end her life."

Archibald scoffed, shaking his head. "This is ludicrous. Esmeralda would never do that."

He was so confident in his words, as if he'd known her his whole life, and that small and aggravating part of me hung on to this belief harder than it should have.

I threw him my phone. "Then explain this."

He looked up after a minute and threw it back at me. "I'm not sure how to explain that, but I can tell you with absolute certainty that my sister would never do that."

"Oh yeah?" I crossed my arms on my chest, looking at him mockingly. Did Esmeralda fool him as she'd fooled me? "What makes you so sure?"

"Because she is my sister and because I know her."

It was my turn to snort. "Oh, do you now? What makes you an expert in Esmeralda? The few months she shared your roof? When you plotted together to make us believe you were enemies? Sorry to break it to you, Forbes, but it takes more to know a person."

Archibald rolled his eyes. "Are we still on this?" He sighed. "Yes, I helped her escape. Was that what you wanted to hear?"

Was it? I wasn't sure. "It's a start."

"But what you need to know is that *we* didn't plan that, *I* did."

I raised an eyebrow in disbelief. It'd been clear from the start that Esmeralda's only goal had been to disappear. I'd only started to believe she could change her mind after our day in Port Harbor.

Archibald looked heavenward before glancing at the door almost wistfully. He wanted to go to her, but he knew that I would have security stop him before he ever reached the top floor.

"I know you won't believe it, but everything that transpired between us in the beginning was the absolute truth. I hated her being here, making me worry and care. I wanted her to hate our lives, but she was always so damned good all the time, so caring." He growled softly as if the memories caused him pain, and maybe they did. Good! It was the least he deserved for what he'd done to me.

"Despite everything she went through, she wasn't damaged or broken. I hated her for this. When the engagement happened, I realized that I didn't want her to suffer that badly. I didn't want her to become the broken doll Sophia is or the shadow of a woman your mother has always been."

"Is that what you think I will turn her into?" I asked. The question caused my heart to thud just a bit faster in my chest. I dreaded the answer because deep down, I knew what it would be. Whether I wanted to or not, I was going to taint her. If she really had that goodness in her, it would eventually wither and die.

He shrugged. "It didn't matter either way. I just tried to keep her at bay, but the more she got close to you, the more I was trying to get close to her, to keep her safe, and then I grew attached. And when she decided to stay…" He shook his head. "I loved her too much already to let her suffer along with us."

"She wanted to stay?" *Fuck!* I hated how my voice sounded - almost hopeful.

Archibald cocked his head to the side; he'd picked up on that and it made me even angrier at her.

"Yes, she did. And while she affirmed she wanted to stay only for me, I feared that deep down, she had another reason." He pursed his lips, his eyes hard as he detailed me. And I knew what he was not saying. He had feared she'd stay for me.

How ironic could it be? One man's fear was another man's hope.

"I know she asked me to stay out of it, but I'm getting tired of you making her out to be a cold, conniving, calculating bitch without a soul. She is not *us*, Caleb!"

"Apparently, you're not very good at listening either, are you?"

We both froze at the strained, velvety voice and turned slowly around. Her voice was deeper than usual, probably due to the water she'd inhaled. She was still so pale and she looked frail in her red dressing gown. She was leaning against the doorframe, clearly to help support herself.

She was furiously stubborn and endearingly strong.

"You should be in bed," I snapped. Her lack of concern for her own well-being added some more fuel to my anger. "The doctor should be here any minute."

Archibald turned to her, his face morphing instantly to concern and love. How nice was it to acknowledge how you felt? To not play games… He was admitting his weakness to me, but he couldn't care less… Maybe he'd accepted what I still refused to: that we shared the same weak point.

"You look like shit, sister of mine." He chuckled, but his voice carried his relief.

She gave him a crooked smile. "Always so kind, brother." She took a deep breath turning to me, looking at me seriously. "I didn't try to kill myself, Caleb. You have to believe me."

"I believe you!" Archibald offered as he moved closer to her, taking her arm.

She leaned on him, making me feel like a sick man for being jealous of the closeness she shared with her own brother.

"Esmeralda," I sighed. I didn't even feel like fighting her anymore. "Just don't."

"No." She stood straighter with her brother's help. "I didn't do that, Caleb. I remember more now and I only had the wine you left me."

"You left her wine?" Archibald asked, judgment clear in his voice.

"No, I didn't."

"Yes you did!" She insisted. "You left a bottle of a weird-named white wine. Check in the kitchen."

"There is no wine in the kitchen, Esmeralda. Just admit the truth now. Blood tests don't lie."

"Don't they?" Archibald asked.

We both knew how easy it was to alter medical records. We'd done it before when the situation had needed it, but Dr. Willis had no reason to lie. He had much more to lose here than to gain. I shook my head. Archibald clearly still believed she was innocent. And I, despite everything, could only think about now was that she'd wanted to stay.

"Esmeralda…" I began, but I was interrupted by Benjamin standing behind Esmeralda.

"Excuse me for interrupting, Sirs, Madam, but Dr. Willis is here," he announced, bowing his head.

"Send him to Miss Forbes's room. She will be right up."

Esmeralda glared at me. I was quite pleased by that. She hadn't lost her spunk.

I took a step toward her, but she shook her head.

"No." She raised her hand. "You don't believe me." She turned toward Archibald. "Help me, please?"

He wrapped an arm around her and kissed the top of her head. "Always," he said before giving me a hard look.

I watched them walk away and close the door behind them. I snorted at the irony of the moment and grabbed a bottle of whiskey. I was clearly not wanted nor needed here; I might just have to go to see the only person to whom I ever mattered.

Chapter 9 - Esme

"You know you'll have to tell me everything right?" Archie whispered as he helped me back into my room on shaky legs. "I know - I know you didn't try to kill yourself, don't get me wrong, but…"

I nodded. "I know, but the thing is –" I threw him a sideways glance. He looked down at me, expectantly. "You're going to get angry with me."

"I see..." He said with a twitch of his jaw. "Well, let's see the doctor first and make sure you have no permanent damage before I start shouting at you. You don't mind if I stay, right?"

I could only see concern on his face and there was no way I'd deny him the reassurance that I was okay, especially since I suspected it was my actions which had caused the incident to start with.

The doctor was already waiting for me in the room when we walked in. Archie squeezed my arm before letting me go.

"Good morning, Ms. Forbes. I'm happy to see you up."

"Thank you, Dr. Willis."

"Why don't you come sit here and let me give you a checkup." He looked up at Archie. "Maybe you could go get her some food? She needs some replenishment."

Archie crossed his arms on his chest, his face set in the stubborn scowl I'd come to know very well. "I'm not going anywhere. I'll ring for food."

The doctor turned toward me and I nodded my approval. I didn't think they could have removed him anyway, even if I'd wanted them to.

"Very well then. Let's begin." He listened to my heart, checked my stats and reflexes, shone the brightest light possible in my eyes, and asked me a series of random questions ranging from what year it was to the name of my brother, before determining that I had been extremely lucky as I'd suffered no permanent damage from the accident.

"Talking about accidents," he said, pushing his round glasses up his nose. "I have a duty to determine if you might be a danger to yourself…" He trailed off, looking at my brother's back as he was setting the platter of food that had just been delivered, onto my vanity.

"I didn't try to kill myself, Dr. Willis."

He sighed. "Miss Forbes, I ran the tests twice and the results are–"

"Correct," I nodded. I needed to change my strategy with the man. He was obviously as suspicious as Caleb so a lie would be better than the truth here.

"This is what my brother and I were just discussing," I said. "It makes no sense, but it seems that my future mother-in-law is using decoy pill bottles to hide her medications. I had a bad headache last night and took some of her paracetamol and some of her ibuprofen a little later, but it seems that neither was what I thought it was. We just checked the bottles now." It was not too much of a stretch. Caleb told me what his mother had in her medicine cabinet and I was sure that their doctor knew she was a pill-popping housewife.

The doctor's face eased with obvious relief. Was it for my health or the tedious task it would have been to put me on suicide-watch? But whatever the reason, he'd bought it and that was all that mattered.

"Ah," he nodded. "I understand. Say no more. Just take it easy for the next few days. You might also develop a cough due to the drowning if bacteria develops in your lungs." He rested a card on my night table. "This is my direct number. Should you feel any discomfort, call me day or night."

I looked down at the card. Being rich was a perk I still hadn't gotten used to. I thought back on the times Luke and I had had to wait hours in overcrowded, understaffed free clinics whenever I'd been sick.

"Money really buys it all, doesn't it?" I asked no one in particular, my voice full of weariness.

Dr. Willis's eyes softened. "You take care." He patted my arm before nodding toward Archie and exiting the room.

Archie gestured me toward the vanity and the platter filled with cereal, fresh fruits, toast…

"I'm only one person, you know," I joked, sitting down and reaching for a slice of buttered toast.

"I know. I'll share." He gave me a boyish grin that reminded me of Luke and sat on the bed with a piece of toast too. I didn't think he would like to know that there was some Luke in him - or maybe he would. He was the spitting image of our uncle. I'd thought he'd looked a bit like him when we'd first met, but I could see more in him now. Maybe it was because I also knew his soul was not as dark as I had anticipated. Perhaps it was because I loved him.

"You just lied to that doctor; it came out so smoothly." He sighed. "I didn't expect that."

"Impressed?" I asked, my mouth still full of food.

"I'm not sure," he replied, meeting my eyes in the mirror. Sorrow was set deep inside them.

I sighed. "I'm still the same girl, Archie."

He shook his head. "No, you're not, and that's okay. Just don't let this life stain you. Don't let me or him stain you."

I opened my mouth to tell him he was mistaken, but he wasn't. I knew it. I had become more calculating, warier. "I promise the essence of me is still here, Archie. I need to adapt for now, but I'm still me."

"Yeah," he said with a nod, but I could see the doubt on his face – doubts I couldn't ease because I had them too.

"So, tell me everything now. Because, not to side with Caleb, but why would anyone leave you a bottle of wine to kill you?"

"Ah yes, that." I took a sip of coffee. I twirled around on my seat to look at him for when I told him the beautiful way I'd fucked up. But as I finally concentrated on him again, I noticed little details that worried me. While he was still impeccably dressed, his blue dress shirt was creased and untucked from his black dress pants. The dark hair he usually styled to perfection was a mess on top of his head. His eyes were shadowed with dark circles. His face carried a stubble I'd never seen before.

"Are *you* okay?" I leaned toward him.

He looked away and ran his hand through his hair. "What do you want me to say, Esme? Because I felt it." He tapped the center of his chest. "I woke up with the irrational fear that something was wrong without knowing what. Then we got the call about your accident... I felt like I'd died, Esme. My heart stopped, but I had to keep my face smooth even though all I'd wanted to do was vomit. So yeah, I was scared."

"Archie..." I sat beside him on the bed, resting my head on his shoulder. "I didn't mean for anything like that to happen...ever."

He sighed and kissed the crown of my head. "Now tell me what you did so I can get mad instead of sad."

I chuckled at that, grateful for my brother's playfulness. I stood up and began to pace the room.

"Okay, so you've read mom's journal and you noticed pages were missing, right?"

He nodded. "Yes, the pages you left for me in my safe place."

I grimaced, cocking my head to the side. "Well... Yeah, but I also took a few extra pages, five to be exact, and sent them to someone else."

I threw him a quick look. His face was now set in a scowl.

"Do I dare to guess who you sent the pages to?"

I winced. "I just couldn't bear the idea of him hating me, Archie!" I threw my hands up in exasperation. "I thought if I showed him our mother was not the homewrecker he thought she was, maybe –"

"Maybe what?" he asked, standing up too now, visibly agitated by my revelation, and I couldn't blame him; it had been a mistake.

I thought that maybe he would forgive me for my betrayal. I shook my head. "It doesn't matter what I thought because he never received the pages. Somebody intercepted the mail."

He nodded, burying his hands in his pants' pockets, his back straight, jaw flexing. He was clearly beyond furious, but was trying his best to restrain himself from exploding into a rage. "If I'm clear, then somebody, other than you, me, and the mystery postman, knows about that journal. So basically, not only have we lost our element of surprise, but the investigation is turning dangerous a lot sooner than we'd anticipated."

I stopped pacing, my legs still weaker than I'd thought. "I'm sorry," I said contritely as I sat back on the bed in defeat, trailing my fingers over the soft blanket. "I didn't think it would be such a big deal, but on the plus side, we know that the journal is important now."

"Because somebody tried to kill you for it?" he asked, his face now red with anger. I knew I had made a huge mistake.

"No, I mean yes... Maybe?" I gave him a sheepish smile. "What's done is done now, isn't it?"

He shook his head. "You're living in a house without protection, and someone has decided to hurt you." He nodded. "Yeah, things are great!"

"The sarcasm is strong with this one," I said in an attempt at humor.

"You think?" I didn't think his scowl could darken any more; I was wrong because boy, did it.

He resumed his pacing, cocking his head to the side every so often as if he was having an internal debate.

I stood up. "Well, while you discuss with yourself, I'll take a shower."

"Uh-huh.," He raised his hand.

I took a quick shower, the hot water doing wonders for my bone-weary body and helping me unlock my sore muscles. I was not feeling totally like myself, but I was getting there.

When I came out, Archie was standing with his back to me, looking out of the window.

"Maybe you should tell him," he breathed.

"Tell what? To whom?" I sat down on the armchair to put my sneakers on.

"Caleb. Tell him what's happening."

"Are you high? Since when do you trust Caleb Astor?"

"I know, but…" He looked heavenward before concentrating on me again. "It hurts me to admit it, but he really cares about you. I didn't think he did, but he's coming undone over you. Maybe if he knew, he could keep you safe here."

"He is mad, not upset," I corrected him.

"With Caleb? It's one and the same. He is the boy with no feelings – or at least so few that he can't really express them, but I know what I see."

I sighed, both at the warmth that filled my chest with this revelation and the Pandora's Box that could open. "Even if he cares, can you be sure his loyalty lies with us? You know there is still a strong possibility that his father is involved in all this."

"I know that, Esme."

I nodded. "Okay, so what then? If we find out his father's involved, can you honestly say he would choose to side with me?" I shook my head. "He hates that he feels something for me, whatever it is. Are you willing to take the risk? Are you certain he won't betray us when it matters?" It hurt me to say that, to admit that we couldn't trust him, but I was done working on blind faith.

He shook his head, crossing his arms on his chest. "No, I can't."

I stood up. "You see?" I grabbed my jacket.

"Where do you think you're going?"

"I almost died last night, Archie." I pointed to the door. "I want to have a quick word with Caleb because I don't want him thinking I tried to kill myself. I don't know why. I just...don't."

His eyes softened and he took a step toward me, resting his hand on my shoulder. "I think I know why, but how are you going to do that without telling him at least part of the truth?"

I chewed on my lip, looking at my closed bedroom door as if Caleb was on the other side. "I haven't figured out the specifics yet." I hadn't figured out anything about anything to be fair. "And then I want to go see Tay and go for a coffee and a muffin, anything really. I just need to get out."

"I'll drive you."

I wanted to argue that I could do it, but to be honest, I was not completely certain I could, and I knew my brother would jump at any chance to see Taylor. I stopped by the door and looked at him. Would telling him the truth about Antoine and Taylor really be a betrayal? My brother had put me first on so many occasions and I felt like I was betraying him by not easing his mind about them. If only I knew what had caused all of this.

"Maybe you coming with me is not the best idea."

"Maybe," he conceded. "But I need to."

"What do you need to do? Take me there or see her?"

He looked at me, a forbidden look on his face.

"What did you do, Archie? Honestly, what did you do to her?"

He looked down, his cheeks tainted with shame as he balled his hands into fists. "Nothing I can justify or be proud of. I was a different person then, a stupid boy full of pain and anger." He looked up at me, his grey eyes reflecting a raw anguish that hurt my soul. "Something I pray every day you won't find out about until you really know me, until I know for sure you won't stop loving me."

"I won't. Of course I won't!" I scoffed. He was my brother, my twin. Even if we'd spent seventeen years apart, I felt connected with him in ways I'd never thought possible.

"You might and I wouldn't blame you, but…" He brought his hand to my cheek and brushed his lips against my forehead. "Just the thought of you looking at me the way I know you would if you knew, kills me, Esme. I can't, not yet."

And I knew the unspoken words - *not ever.*

"I won't stop loving you Archie, but okay." I nodded. Reaching for his arm, I interlinked his with mine. "When you're ready."

I found Benjamin downstairs. I saw his face morph with relief when he saw me standing.

"I'm glad to see you well, Ms. Forbes."

"Thank you, Benjamin. I'm sorry for scaring you. I need to speak with Caleb; is he in his office?"

"No, miss. I–" He faltered; he never faltered. "Mr. Forbes left quite upset with a bottle of scotch. I'm unsure where he went," he added, his face filling with worry once more. It didn't matter how Caleb talked to him; the old man obviously cared for him.

"I'll find him. It's okay." I rested my hand on his forearm.

Benjamin looked down at my hand as if this gesture was so unnatural, so uncommon, and it probably was. Nobody in this house knew how to care, to nurture, to simply love, and all of this made me hurt for the little boy Caleb had once been.

"I will take care of him, Benjamin. I'll bring him back."

I got the keys out of my pocket, but Archie caught my hand. "What do you think you're doing?" he asked, an eyebrow arched as if I was crazy.

"Change of plan. I need to look for Caleb."

"Okay..." He gently took the keys out of my hand and put them in his pants pocket. "And I'm not saying you can't or shouldn't – I'm just going to keep an eye on you and drive you wherever you need to go. You almost died yesterday, Esme. Please be reasonable."

I looked up at him. If it had been anything other than genuine concern on his face, I would have told him to butt out. But he was not trying to control me or tell me what to do; he was only trying to keep me safe. How could I deny him?

"Okay, fine."

"Oh, and Ms. Forbes," Benjamin called just as we were about to exit the house.

I turned around and met his eyes. "Yes?"

"I thought you'd like to know that Mr. and Mrs. Astor will be back today. Maybe it would be best if young Mr. Astor was back in before them and in full form."

"I understand, Benjamin. I'll do my best."

"So, where to?" Archie asked as we settled into the car.

"The cemetery."

"The–" Archie arched an eyebrow at me. "Seriously?"

I nodded. "Yes, it's just a hunch."

"Okay, as you wish."

We drove to the cemetery in companionable silence. Once there, I let out a sigh of relief when I saw the Aston Martin parked across the street.

"How did you know?" Archie asked, clearly impressed.

I shrugged. "Caleb thinks only his brother cared for him unconditionally."

"Based on the way you're looking out for him now, I would say he is wrong to think that. Isn't he, sister?"

"Maybe," I admitted, keeping my eyes on the wrought-iron gate of the entrance. "You can go now." I turned toward him. "Please, I needed to do this alone. I'll have to drive him home anyway."

"Esme, I don't think you should yet."

"Archie, trust me. I know what I'm doing. I wouldn't put his life or mine in danger, but if you come with me, he will close up."

Archie sighed, looking behind me, his mouth twisted with indecision.

"I need to do this, Archie," I insisted. "He saved my life."

He nodded. "Fine, but call me if you need anything at any time."

"Yes, thank you."

"Don't make me regret this, Esme."

I smiled at him, leaning down on the seat to kiss his cheek. "I won't, brother of mine."

He hesitated one more second, detailing my face as if he was looking for something before agreeing. He finally turned in his seat again, and I knew that I had won.

"Just call me when you get home?"

"Promise." I leaned over and kissed his cheek soundly. No matter how bad things were, or how my life changed, I would do it all over again for the love of my brother. This was such a nice feeling, this powerful sibling bond that hadn't even existed a few months ago. Now I could hardly imagine a life without Archie in it.

I entered the cemetery by the small side door. An unforgiving gush of frigid wind reminded me that we were still very much in the heart of winter.

I tightened my red cashmere coat around me and looked up at the heavy grey sky. Snow was definitely on the way.

I sighed, making my way to the hill where Theo's grave lay. It was a secluded, quiet area close to a weeping willow. How fitting.

The cemetery was quite deserted except for an old man holding a single red rose in his hand, hunching against a grave, his pain so profound. I couldn't help but glance at the date of death when I passed the grave. Four years. Yet his pain looked so raw, so new. Was that what it was like to lose the love of your life?

Without invitation Caleb's face flashed in my mind. I faltered. Caleb was not the love of my life. He was an angry young man hell-bent on torturing me.

Please Esme, don't make that mistake. Don't get in any deeper with that broken man. My train of thought was interrupted when I finally spotted Caleb. I stopped a few feet from the grave, remaining unseen.

He was sitting beside the grave, his back leaning against the tombstone, head back, eyes closed. One leg was stretched out, the other folded at the knee. His arm rested on it as he precariously held the half-empty bottle of whiskey. He was only wearing a thin jacket; he had to be freezing. I looked more closely at his face. Even with his eyes closed, he looked tense. His face was so much paler than usual, his pursed lips taking on a little taint of blue.

"What do you want, Esmeralda?" He asked with a sigh, his eyes still closed.

I frowned. "How?" I asked out loud, walking closer to him now. The paleness of his skin was even more striking. I was no specialist, but hypothermia couldn't be far off.

"The wind… I could smell you."

He opened his blue eyes. They looked paler somehow, with the slight haze of intoxication, a haze I knew very well after seeing it so many times in Luke's eyes.

"What are you doing here, Caleb?"

He gave me a small smile, but it lacked its usual bitterness; it was just sad… So weary it made me miss the bitter ones. "It's a good place to be haunted."

"Why are you haunted?"

He shook his head. "Because of what is, what was, what could have been, by maybes and empty promises. I don't expect you to understand."

He rested his hand on the ground, laboriously trying to help himself up.

I reached down to help him.

"No, don't. I can do it."

I sighed and looked at him struggling to stand. He grabbed the headstone, resting his hand on it for help.

"You know you didn't have to go to such extreme measures," he commented after steadying himself.

"Caleb, I didn't try to kill myself."

He looked at me with uncertainty. "But you're unhappy."

Was he joking? He had spent every waking moment since my return torturing me. "Why? Are you trying to make me happy?"

He shook his head, looking down at the headstone as he ran his hand back and forth on the smooth marble.

"You won," he said barely louder than a whisper before taking a swig of his bottle.

"I don't understand." I rested my hand on his shoulder. He froze, looking back at me with some realization and fear.

"I'm letting you go."

It was my turn to freeze as dread filled me. If he let me go, it would ruin my whole investigation, but I knew deep down there was more to it than that, and it terrified me even more. I wasn't sure I wanted him to give up on me.

"Caleb, no. There is more at stake than what you think."

He kept shaking his head, stubbornly gripping the stone even more. "No, I won't have someone's death on my conscience. I've already got enough on it. Just give me a few days. I'll find a way. I'll figure out a solution that will work for everybody. You'll be free."

He was delusional if he thought that would happen. Though what if it could? I wasn't even sure what freedom meant anymore, but I couldn't leave, not while I had a murder to solve.

I looked around the cemetery at the dying flowers on the graves. "Do you know why the dead receive more flowers than the living?"

He finally looked at me again, obviously surprised by the change of subject. "No, tell me."

"Because regrets are so much more powerful than anything else. More powerful than gratitude. Don't let them swallow you whole and take you under. You're so much more than this."

I took the bottle from his hand. He didn't fight me. "Don't do anything rash or irremediable while you're under a misconception." I extended my hand toward him. "Let me drive us home. Give me your keys."

He got his keys out of his pocket, but kept them in his hand. "I said I'd never let you drive my car."

"And if you don't let me drive and you drive us in this state, you really *will* have my death on your conscience." He winced as I nudged my hand toward him. It was a cheap shot, but his lips were truly blue now. I couldn't have his death on my conscience either.

"Fine!" he snapped, slapping the keys into my hand. I forced him to take my arm after seeing his lack of coordination as he tried to walk. It was eerily like a toddler taking his first steps.

"If you tell anyone…" he started after I helped him to the car and took the driver's seat. He tried to threaten me, but his voice was heavy, his speech slower, the alcohol finally taking him down.

I blasted the heating to the maximum to warm him up as I rolled my eyes. "What happens between us stays between us, Caleb. You've got to start trusting me."

He snorted, resting his head against the window. "Been there, done that, got the tee-shirt. Wouldn't recommend it," he mumbled.

"What?" I asked. "What do you mean?" I glanced his way, but he was slouched more heavily in his seat, his eyes still closed.

Was I cursed to take care of drunken men: Luke, then Archie, and now Caleb? That was really a pattern I didn't want to continue.

As we pulled up at the mansion, I was pleased when Benjamin came to meet me by the car to help me carry the dead weight that was Caleb back to his room.

"Can you please tell his parents that he is resting after keeping an eye on me all night?" I huffed as we struggled up the stairs. Caleb was lean but much heavier than I'd thought.

"Of course," Benjamin replied. "Thank you."

"You really care for him, don't you?" I asked Benjamin as he helped me set Caleb on his bed.

He looked at Caleb and nodded. "Young Mister Astor didn't have an easy upbringing; he is not as unbreakable as he lets on."

It was my turn to look at the comatose Caleb. "I agree. Thank you for your help. I will take it from here."

After Benjamin left us, I removed his oxfords and his jacket before leaving to fetch a blanket. When I came back from my bedroom with the spare blanket I had there, Caleb was lying on his stomach. His shirt had ridden up his back, revealing the bottom of his spine and some blue and red ink. I hadn't been mistaken the other night. Caleb Astor was tattooed.

I walked closer to him. Resting the blanket by his feet, I tried to work out what this tattoo could be. I would have never expected this proper golden son to be tattooed, especially not to the extent the couple of glimpses I got seemed to suggest.

Did his father even know? Again, I could hardly picture James Astor being on board with his son's decision.

I let my hand hover over the hem of his shirt, my fingers almost tingling with the desire to pull it up and see more. As I touched the soft material, he turned his face to the side with a soft moan. It made me move my hand sharply as if it had burned him.

Shame engulfed me. I had no right to touch him without his consent. Just the thought had been shameful.

I shook my head. *Get a grip, Esme. He'll show you if he wants you to see.*

I looked at his sleeping face. Even in his alcohol-induced slumber, he looked tortured, in pain. "What is it, Caleb?" I murmured. "What is hurting you so much?" I reached for his face and ran my fingertips over his cheekbone. "Let me help you, please. While there is some time left, while I'm still here, let me help you."

I stayed there by his bed for a few more minutes just looking at him. It was hard to admit how much I'd come to care for this cruel, broken, elitist idiot. Someone too stubborn to believe me even if I told him so.

Chapter 10 - Esme

I should have known better than to think I had any luck left in my life. It was a big house, gigantic in fact. I had been pretty confident that I could avoid the Astors. It was not like they were going to seek me out.

Caleb's mother hated me on principle, probably associating me with the false image she had of my mother. As for James, he gave me the creeps. I shuddered over what he had done to my mother, what he had wanted to do. He had no reason to look for me. I was nothing to him, good or bad.

When I'd woken up before the sun this morning, I'd taken a run around the icy grounds to unwind the events of the past few days and to make sure the drowning hadn't caused any more damage than it seemed. I'd run for longer than I'd thought, having enjoyed the pure silence only interrupted by the rhythmic sound of my sneakers on the gravel. The cold air had filled my lungs, waking every part of my brain and my body. I had enjoyed the burn of my leg muscles as I'd pushed more, went faster. I had liked feeling my body waking up, showing me I was alive and that everybody who had tried to smother the life in me, had failed. I was just as powerful as I'd always been.

It had taken me an hour of running to feel like myself again. After the last few days and the stress of Caleb's parents being back, I hadn't been sure how to keep pretending.

I should have known better than to expect a break from life, I really should have, and yet I was cursing everything that was holy when I found James lurking around my bedroom door. The sun was barely up. He had no business on this side of the house.

He turned to look at me, his smile turning predatory as he detailed me, his eyes taking on a light that made me so uncomfortable I wanted to crawl out of my skin.

I wanted to slap myself. Why did I have to remove my running jacket as soon as I'd walked in? Why didn't I wait until I was in the comfort of my room to do that? Why? Because I was dressed in an acceptable crop top and leggings, because there was nothing indecent about my outfit, because I shouldn't have to be wary of creepy perverted married middle-age men coming on to me.

He licked his lips as his eyes settled on my chest and I could barely contain my gag.

"Ah, my dear Esmeralda! I was looking for you." The joviality of his tone didn't really match the twisted desire in his brown eyes.

I looked past him in the corridor, but there was no help.

I forced a smile but remained where I stood, not coming any closer to him. "Isn't it a bit early in the day to go looking for your future daughter-in-law?" I joked, a good way to remind him of our relationship status and how deviant he was being right now.

He took a few steps toward me. I didn't realize I'd taken a step back until my sweaty back connected with the cold wall of the corridor.

"Yes, this is why I think we should try to know each other better, don't you think?" He took a deep breath as if he was breathing me in. "I'm so pleased Caleb found you. I tried to find you too, you know. Tell me, Esmeralda, will you try to run again? Do we need to clip your wings?" He was crowding my space now, hovering over me, his sickly-sweet cologne surrounding me. I could just knee him in the balls, but I knew it would be counterproductive.

"That won't be necessary; I learn quickly." I hated how small and trembling my voice sounded.

"You look so much like her, you know," he said a little wistfully, wrapping a strand of hair that had escaped my ponytail around his forefinger.

"So I've been told." I looked away down the corridor, praying for Caleb to open the door, but also dreading it. I knew how little he thought of me and no matter how dejected and uncomfortable I looked, he'd never see anything other than what he wanted to see.

"You know, your mother and I were very close friends."

That caught my attention and I turned my head to meet his eyes. I couldn't believe I had ever found those eyes friendly; now they were downright predatory.

"Oh, were you?" Was he baiting me? Trying to see how much I knew about the real situation? *Did he have the journal pages?*

He nodded, letting go of my strand of hair before trailing his fingers against my collarbone. "Yes, the best of friends." He took another step closer, so close I could smell the coffee on his breath. My stomach dropped. I was going to be sick. *Please God. Someone help me.*

"What about you and I being friends too?" he added, either oblivious to my discomfort, completely uncaring, or worst of all getting off on it. Knowing this family, it was probably the latter. "I could make it worthwhile for both of us."

The bile rose up my throat. I was going to vomit on his expensive polo shirt and I wouldn't even be sorry for it.

"Father." Caleb's voice came as a beacon of hope in the darkness and I couldn't contain the little tearless sob of relief at the sound of his voice.

I turned my head toward him. He looked ready to kill, his hands balled into tight fists at his sides. He had showered and was dressed as impeccably as he always was, but he was paler than usual, clearly still suffering from the epic hangover.

James slowly took a step back and turned his head, keeping his body directed toward me as if he was not doing anything shameful, as if sexually harassing me wasn't a big deal – and it probably wasn't for men like him.

"Ah, son, you're up early."

"Not early enough I see." He threw me a look that seemed to say 'are you okay?' or maybe it was just something I wanted to see. All in all it did feel good.

I nodded just in case.

He concentrated on James again. "There are a few things I need to discuss with you about the business."

James nodded, finally taking a step back and allowing me to breathe better. "Of course, business first as always. Let's go to the office." He smiled at me, throwing me a playful wink. "I'll get to know my sweet daughter-in-law more tonight."

Did he really think I'd enjoyed any part of our interaction?

Caleb frowned, walking toward his father, but stopping beside me. "Why tonight?"

"Family dinner of course!" He said as if this was self-evident, but one didn't have to know them long to know that this was not something these people did.

"But we don't have family dinners," Caleb said, confirming my suspicion.

James's jovial smile slipped, showing a glimpse of the real monster I suspected he was. "We do now. Do you have a problem with this, son?"

I wrapped my pinkie finger around Caleb's and nudged it. Now was not the time to get James angry.

I forced a laugh. "Of course he doesn't. Right, Caleb? I'm more than happy to get to know my future in-laws."

"Marvelous," he said, his smile back in place. "Son?" He gestured toward the corridor. "You wanted to talk, let's talk now."

Caleb nodded, but stayed beside me. "Yes, I'll be right down. I just want to have a word with my sweet fiancée first." He smiled, grabbed my ponytail, and pulled me into a scorching kiss that reminded me of the passion we had shared on our night together. It was bruising and hard, part punishment, part possession, and I knew it was his way of marking his territory. Still, it was a much cleaner way than pissing on my leg.

He finally broke the kiss, leaving me breathless and a little flushed. It unnerved me to still react like this after everything he'd said to me, after everything he'd put me through.

His father chuckled. "I can't blame you. Five minutes, Caleb. I have things to do."

Other than harass your barely legal future daughter-in-law? I thought but remained silent.

"Yeah," Caleb's voice was rougher somehow, his eyes a little glazed. It comforted me to know that he was not completely in control either, that even if he wanted to deny it, there was something there too.

As soon as James disappeared down the corridor, I unlocked my bedroom door and let Caleb in.

"Caleb, I swear I was not trying to entice him or whatever you think I want." I shook my head before locking eyes with his, hoping he'd see the truth in them.

"I know."

"You do?"

He scoffed. "Of course I do."

"But you said–"

He raised his hand. "I know what I said and I didn't mean that."

"Yes you did."

He sighed, running his hand through his hair. "And now I don't anymore."

"Are you saying that you believe me now or you're being decent because you're scared I'll kill myself?"

I ignored my phone vibrating in my armband.

Caleb looked at my phone, his face darkening. "Stay away from him."

"I'm trying."

"Try better."

I growled. He was so frustrating. How was I supposed to try?! It was their house and he'd been waiting in front of my door.

"Just…" Caleb looked heavenward. "He is not safe."

I snorted. "Yeah, I noticed."

"And while you're at it, avoid my mother. She's…"

"Crazy?"

He threw me a dark look. "Confused."

Yeah... That was one way of putting it.

"You have a phone now," he said, pointing at my armband. "If you need to go around or if you get uncomfortable again, just text me."

That sort of thwarted my plans of searching the house for any kind of evidence. "You know if you're not careful, I'll start to think you care about me."

It was his turn to snort. "I merely want to avoid any more drama in this house."

"Okay..." I turned around to hide my smile. It was so obviously a lie, but he wasn't going to admit it.

"I'll come pick you up for dinner, okay? Don't go without me."

I turned around at the concern in his voice. He was now standing by the door, his hand on the doorknob.

The concern was genuine and reflected in his face. He wanted to keep me safe even against his own instincts.

"I promise."

He nodded once and left without another word.

I took a quick shower, trying to get rid of both the sweat and James's sweet scent which seemed to be ingrained in my skin.

After three full body scrubs, I was finally satisfied that James's aura was completely expelled. Then I went back to my room where I decided to spend the day and maybe catch up on my homework.

I was far from stupid, but the classes at Brentwood were challenging compared to my old school, and being a rich heiress investigating a murder was not a reason to slack off.

I'd just settled at my desk when I noticed the little blue light of my phone, reminding me of the text I had received when I was chatting with Caleb.

It was from Ben. *I'm excited. I'll get my bike next weekend.*

I frowned. *Already?* I typed, but deleted it. I didn't want him to think I was having second thoughts even though I was – not because I was not ready to go to extreme lengths to avenge my mother's death, but because I didn't want to put Ben, or anyone else, in any kind of danger to resolve this.

This was where my brother and I were still very different. He didn't have any consideration for anyone other than the people he loved and those people could be counted on one hand. Whereas I still had a fully functioning conscience. Putting anyone at risk, no matter how I felt about them, still didn't feel right.

Okay, great! I'll see it soon. I replied and toyed with my phone. I needed to set things in motion now.

I texted our group 'study session' which was composed of Antoine, Archie, and Taylor. Part of me really disliked doing everything behind Caleb's back, but he resented Archie and I too much for me to involve him. I wasn't sure he wouldn't reveal everything just to watch us bleed. It hurt me not being able to trust him; it really did.

Me*:* *Need to meet tomorrow before class.*

Antoine: *Told you we can't have sex. I'm in a committed relationship with your best friend.*

Leave it to Antoine to stir shit any chance he got.

Archie: *Don't worry, sis. You ain't missing much.*

Antoine: *Fuck you, Forbes. My dick is decent. Let's ask Taylor. Taylor, babe, tell Astor I have an epic dick.*

Archie: *I didn't think your ego was so fragile, Antoine. If you need it stroking maybe Taylor should reconsider her choices in men. Your cock is 'decent' – wow every girl's dream.*

My brother really enjoyed playing with fire.

Antoine: *I love being stroked, and don't worry, it's dealt with.*

I rolled my eyes as Taylor messaged me privately.

Taylor: *I can't deal with these petulant children; I might kill one of them. Tomorrow science lab 7:30?*

Me: *Yes, see you then. I'll deal with them.*

Me: *Guys, nobody cares. Tomorrow 7:30 science lab.* I texted, ready to move on.

It was Archie's turn to text me off the group chat. Why did we even bother?

Archie: *Do you want me to pop over? We can discuss now.*

I sighed. It was still difficult for me to get used to the overprotective brother, but I knew he was not going to take no for an answer.

Me: *Can't, have a family dinner with the in-laws.*

Archie: *Fuck, I'm sorry. That's gonna suck.*

"You think?" I muttered. *It's fine. It's only dinner.*

Archie: *Call me when it's done?*

Me: *Sure. Love you.*

It took him a few moments to answer. I knew that these words were still unsettling to him, but I was going to tell him over and over again until it was natural for him.

Archie: *I love you too, sister.*

I stayed in my room the whole day, ringing for lunch to be sent up in between studying and trying to catch up on my month away.

When evening came, I almost gave myself a brain aneurysm trying to figure out what to wear for dinner. After what had happened this morning, I didn't want to show any skin. I would even wear a ski suit if I could.

I settled for a knee-length black dress with a neck-high collar and flats. I tightened my hair into a straight bun and kept my face devoid of make-up. I looked so small, young, and austere all at the same time. The dress was also on the larger side, hiding all my curves. How sad was it that I had to do that?

That's what happens when you live with a sexual predator, I reminded myself, smoothing my dress with my hands.

It was strange to trust Caleb to keep me safe, to shield me from both the verbal bullets coming from his mother and the barely veiled sexual attention coming from his father.

Caleb was the most conflicted person I'd ever met. He was also the person causing me the most conflicting feelings. I'd never been indecisive, but with him I never knew what to expect. Part of me would even prefer him to be hateful all the time. At least I would know where to stand. But no, despite all of his darkness, there was some light shining through the cracks every so often, a light so bright that I couldn't stop the restoration of hope or the acceleration of my heart whenever he touched me, whenever he looked at me.

I hadn't recalled much about the swimming pool incident, but I remembered him begging me to stay. I had heard his voice in the void swallowing me and somehow I had fought to come back for him. This realization had shaken me, making me unsure if I could ever completely move on from him.

Don't lie to yourself. You know you won't.

The light knock on the door brought me back to reality. I looked at it, unsure of what to say or do. Was it really Caleb? If it wasn't and I answered, it wouldn't be possible for me to close the door again.

"Esmeralda, it's me." His deep voice made me sigh with relief.

I opened the door and he detailed me from head to toe before nodding his approval. "Wise choice," he said as he extended his hand to me.

I took a second to do the same. He was dressed casually - well casually for Caleb which meant black dress pants and a pale blue shirt that matched his eyes. He'd rolled up the sleeves to his elbows, showing his powerful forearms. His strong pale smooth hand extended toward me.

"We have to be the image of the happy couple, Esmeralda. Hopefully it will help with both of my parents. I know you don't want to touch me, but I think now is the time to use your acting skills again."

I looked at him. Despite the perpetual scowl on his face, I saw genuine dismay. I understood that he took my delay in taking his hand as rejection.

I shook my head. "Caleb, it's not that I–"

He nudged his hand toward me. "It doesn't matter." That was a lie and we both knew it. "Just take my hand and let's go. My father doesn't forgo tardiness."

We found his parents already waiting in the dining room. His father was standing by the fireplace in a position eerily similar to the one Caleb had adopted the night he had given me the car.

Like father, like son. I hoped as hell that saying was wrong.

James turned toward us, the light in his eyes turning lustful. Caleb squeezed my hand almost to the point of pain. I didn't think he'd realized it, and somehow that made me feel better. He was protective of me even if he didn't want to be.

"Ah, the lovebirds!" James beamed. He came over to us and kissed my cheeks, trailing his lips on my cheekbones and making me want to gag.

I forced a smile as Caleb squeezed my hand, though in warning or comfort I wasn't sure.

"Don't hold her hand so tight, dear. She is not going to run away, is she? Oh wait…" Jacklyn cackled, her voice taunting and dripping with venom.

I turned toward the seating area where she was sitting in an armchair. She wore a stunning purple dress and was holding a glass of white wine. She met my eyes, raising her glass toward me in a greeting gesture.

"Jacklyn," James sighed. "Just drink your wine."

Oh yeah, because getting her drunk was definitely the solution. I thought.

"Mrs. Astor," I bowed my head at her. I was not going to take the bait. "You look stunning," I added, and it was not a lie. She was a beautiful woman despite the alcohol, pill cocktails, and God knows what else. *An amazing surgeon,* Taylor would have added. I chuckled under my breath at that, getting a questioning glance from Caleb.

"I really wish I could say the same, dear. Did you misunderstand dinner for a funeral?"

The funeral of my peace of mind, certainly. I smiled wider. "I'm truly sorry my choice of garment doesn't meet your approval."

She stood up, helping herself by using the back of her seat. How much had she had to drink already? Or was it the pills playing their part? She didn't look high, but…. "Maybe it's a funeral after all. Freedom is a hard thing to give up, isn't it Esmeralda Forbes?" Her words felt like a whip.

Caleb's hand was now squeezing mine to the point of pain again. I would almost have said he was scared, but that was a ludicrous idea. The woman was just a pill-popping alcoholic barely taller than me and so thin I couldn't see her sideways. She was not a real threat.

James sighed, rolling his eyes at me conspiratorially as if we were best friends before turning back to his wife. "Just one evening, Jacklyn. Why don't we top up your glass of wine?" he added, gesturing the serving staff closer.

She nodded, extending her glass toward him. She looked resigned, which wasn't really a look I expected.

"Sorry," Caleb whispered so softly that I wasn't sure I'd heard him right.

I looked up at him, but he was looking straight ahead. "Let's sit down," he added, letting go of my hand to rest his on the small of my back, directing me to a chair.

"Why don't you let your beautiful fiancée sit beside me?" James beamed, already pulling out the chair closest to him.

Caleb tensed, his fingers digging in my back. "No, I think it's better for me to sit beside you so we can discuss a few business points. I'm not sure Esmeralda would like to be caught in the middle of a business talk." He pushed me toward the chair he'd pointed at and sat on the chair his father had pulled out, creating a buffer between me and his father. Based on James's pursed lips though, Caleb would have to pay for this.

The evening was just as painful as I knew it would be with James's eyes always drifting over me with the glint I hated. With every look Caleb tensed and his mother drank. I couldn't believe the woman had any liver left, she was drinking so much.

Finally, after dessert I couldn't do it anymore and faked a yawn. "I'm sorry, but it has been a busy day of studying. I had quite a lot to make up for."

"Of course," Caleb stood up, extending his hand to me. "Let me walk you back."

"That's what happens when we run away like a petulant child," Jacklyn snorted into her glass.

"That's enough!" James bellowed. Slamming his fist on the table, he caused his crystal wine glass to fall on the floor and shatter into a hundred pieces.

"What?" She threw him a matching glare, her own glass still secured in her hand. "Are we going to pretend it didn't happen? That she belongs?" She looked me in the eyes. "This girl doesn't belong in this house, in our lives, in Stonewood."

"She belongs more than you do, Jacklyn. Remember where *you* came from. She has founder blood in her; you don't. Just…just be careful."

I hated that he was threatening her because of me. I didn't want to be the reason for any fight between them.

"Please don't. It's okay. She is right to be upset. I did break the trust when I left. There is nothing she can say that I don't deserve." Actually, I didn't deserve any of it, but it didn't bother me. I really didn't care what the senior Astors thought of me.

"You never broke my trust; you didn't have it in the first place," she cackled before taking a long swig of her drink. "I'm not an idiot driven by the Astor hormones for whom your genes seem to be kryptonite."

"Mother–" Caleb sighed with weariness before turning toward me. "Let me walk you back."

"Oh, and Caleb," James interjected, "please make sure to come back right after. I will be waiting for you in my office. I need to talk to you."

I winced at the barely veiled threat of his tone and couldn't help but worry about Caleb, unsure what his father was going to do to him.

"Thank you for the meal," I said to James with a small smile, hoping to pacify his anger toward Caleb.

He smiled at me, the threat in his eyes dimming slightly. "It was a true pleasure, Esmeralda dear. I'll see you real soon."

I nodded, hating the sound of that promise.

"I'm sorry," I told Caleb as soon as we were out of earshot.

His steps faltered with surprise. "What are you apologizing for?"

For the parents you have, for the love you never got, for walking away and betraying you when I didn't think you'd care, for crushing the little trust you managed to give me, for not showing you that you were worth fighting for… Take your pick I thought. But all I could do was shrug and say, "I don't know."

His face softened as if he could read all of this on mine. His grip on my hand relaxed as his thumb started to gently rub the side of my hand up and down without him realizing it.

"Don't apologize. She was using you as an excuse to start a war. We never have family dinners. They always turn ugly. This is not on you."

"And it shouldn't be on you either," I replied as we stopped in front of my room.

He gave me a sad smile. "Yeah, well, you understand better than anyone that sometimes life deals you a hand that is not what you would have picked for yourself."

Without even thinking, I raised my free hand and cupped his cheek. I wasn't sure why I attempted to show him this tenderness, this comfort. He hadn't done anything to warrant it. Yet, I needed to comfort him more than I needed my next breath. And he accepted it, even if for just a few seconds. He leaned into my touch and closed his eyes. It barely lasted though. He caught himself almost immediately, then straightened up and let go of my hand as if I'd hurt him.

"Don't, Esmeralda. Don't…ever. Not again." He turned around and walked away without another word.

I stood in the corridor for quite some time after his departure. I was surprised by both my need to protect and heal him, as well as the deep response to my comfort, dare I even say the plenitude, that had settled on his face under my touch.

"There might be hope for you yet, Caleb Astor. There might be hope for you after all," I whispered before stepping into my room and locking the door behind me.

Chapter 11 - Caleb

"So, I think that today we need to discuss the subject of the Prom," Archibald said as he opened the council book.

I rested my forehead on the table. "No."

"No? What do you mean, no?"

I looked up. "I just don't care at all, not even a little." And especially not after what my father had said to me the other night after dinner. How he intended for us to share my bride, whether I wanted us to or not. But I would kill him before I let him touch her.

Hell, I'd kill anyone who thought they had rights to her. I might have promised her I'd let her go, but it was still very hard for me not to think of her as mine. I couldn't do that until I knew what they hid from me, until I knew what they were facing together. I hadn't really cared about the pathetic little secret club until what had happened in the swimming pool because if Esmeralda had spoken the truth, which I still wasn't sure she had, then somebody had tried to kill her, and that was not something I wanted to be kept away from. I wanted to find the culprit and burn him to the ground.

Archibald sighed, resting his hand on the book. "Why do you always have to make things so difficult, Astor? This is trivial and yet essential in school life. You wanted the chair at the council. You have it–"

"There are matters which are much more important." I was done playing the idiot.

"Yeah?" Archibald arched an eyebrow mockingly.

I tightened my hands into fists, pushing down my strong desire to smash his face into the table.

"Yeah, like maybe what is happening with Esmeralda and why you're all meeting like little spies behind my back."

I looked at Antoine who had the decency to look down in shame. I'd always considered him as being my friend - my only friend, even if the word didn't really mean much in this world.

As for Archibald and I… Ah, Archibald and I, there was way too much bad blood between us. Too many things had happened while fighting for a crown I was not sure was worth anything anymore.

As for the incident with Taylor, well, I wasn't sure I was really to blame in that. He had made his choice, burning any feelings that might have existed. I'd barely handed him the matches. The consequences were all his.

I cocked my head to the side, thinking for the first time about what I would have done if it had been Esmeralda and I.

Archibald closed the book. "I don't know what you're talking about."

I let out a humorless laugh. "Do you really think you can fool me? I'm the puppet master, remember?"

He shook his head.

"Please," I snorted. "You can deny it all you like. You think you're an evil mastermind, but your little gang is far from being smooth."

I pointed to Antoine who was still avoiding my eyes. "You could at least pretend to teach her some French. Either you're the worst tutor in history or you are not teaching her shit because fuck, she blows at French."

"I– It's…" He opened and closed his mouth like a fish out of water.

I raised my hand. "Don't embarrass yourself and insult me by trying to lie, just keep it closed. And if you don't tell me, I swear I'll burn the fucking world until I find out the secrets you're keeping."

"You should be careful, Caleb." Archibald crossed his arms on his chest. "If you burn the world, you might burn with it."

"And I care because…" I trailed off. I didn't think Archibald really understood the depth of my detachment. Nobody was more dangerous than someone who had nothing left to lose.

"Little lesson, Archibald – to destroy your enemy, you need to be ready to be destroyed." And I was born ready. I even thought that part of me had been chipping away since the day I was born.

Archibald turned to Antoine who shook his head ever so slightly.

Archibald sighed. "To be fair, Caleb, whatever is happening, *if* anything is happening, it has nothing to do with you." He shook his head. "And if you want to know, you'll need to speak with your fiancée."

"Ah yes," I snorted. "My fiancée, your sister…" I turned to Antoine. "Your little secret-keeper."

Antoine paled, realizing I knew more than he wanted me to.

"As you know, your sister has not been forthcoming. She'd rather drown than be with me, so I think that–"

"SHE DIDN'T TRY TO KILL HERSELF!" Archibald snapped, his face reflecting the frustration I felt.

This was a waste of time. They would not come clean. I needed to find out what they were hiding using other methods. Even though it was four against one, they wouldn't stand a chance against me.

I stood up, grabbing my bag. "I'm done with this shit. Meeting adjourned. I'll see you when you decide to stop being backstabbing whores and return to being the powerful kings you used to be."

I smirked. "Now I'll go find Aleksandra and ease my frustration. I'll see you for lunch. It might very well take all of the morning classes."

Archibald's face darkened with anger at the idea of me cheating on his sister. If only he knew the truth and the curse that had affected my dick since I'd taken Esmeralda's virginity.

I also knew that it was my only possible excuse as the bitch was not going to be in school for a few days. She had been texting me nonstop since I'd left her place the night Esmeralda had nearly drowned. She was now on her way to an upscale clinic to get some work done as if she thought it would entice me. Even with or without the Esmeralda curse, she had another thing coming. Had I ever wanted to fuck plastic, I would have ordered a doll. At least then I wouldn't have to pretend to listen to all her crap as I pumped into her.

After exiting the room, I waited behind the lockers for the meeting to be over. Archibald and Antoine didn't have any reason to feel suspicious. But no matter what I felt beyond pathetic following Archibald Forbes like a fucking groupie in heat. How could the tables have turned? I used to be the king, on top, untouchable, and enjoying how it felt above it all. Now I was left behind playing I-Spy to get some scrap of information. Oh, if my father could see me…

Archibald exited and walked into another empty classroom where he took out his phone.

I leaned beside the door, opening it slightly to listen. We still had the minutes before the changing of classes.

"Hey, don't worry. Everything is okay. Yes, Caleb is fine too. Why do you even care?" Archibald snapped and I couldn't help but smile a little. Esmeralda's concern over me was not completely fake and that made me feel better.

"Oh, come on. It's only homeroom… So what?" He sighed. "You're Forbes. Nobody cares if you miss the end of class. Esme. Esme...ESME! Fuck, just listen."

Now I chuckled out loud. I'd found Archibald's master - his sister. *Pot, meet kettle,* a little vicious taunting voice resonated in the back of my mind, sobering me fast.

"You need to talk to him. Tell him. No, I have not lost my mind, but Esme, I think you can trust him. Tell him something, anything. Ease his mind. Make him understand you didn't try to kill yourself. Please, for me."

I was frozen on the spot, my head against the door, not even pretending to be just standing there. Archibald Forbes was pleading my case. Of all the people in the world, he would never have been my pick.

"No, not only for that. I would feel better if he knew something. You would be safer at his place. He cares, Esme. No matter how much he denies it to you, to me, to himself. He cares...deeply."

I cursed under my breath and walked away, deciding to spy another day. How was it that he saw so clearly into me when I always thought I was a mystery?

I did care, and I hated it. I hated it even more now that I knew the world had figured it out. Did my father know? The thought chilled me to the bone. If he did, it would be the end of everything. He would have leverage again, a leverage he'd lost when Theo had died.

I didn't even pretend to be out with Aleks, choosing instead to walk to my next class when the bell rang.

"So what about Aleks?" Archibald asked as we walked in.

"Not here today," I admitted. Just as I sat at my desk, my phone vibrated in my pocket.

Can you meet me by your car at lunch? I need to talk to you.

I looked at Esmeralda's text, cursing myself as my heartrate picked up just at the reception of a message. It was the first one she had ever sent me. I felt like a child as both apprehension and a certain feeling of treacherous hope settled its painful claws into my heart.

Don't betray me again, Esmeralda, I thought.

OK, but don't waste my time, I replied. Just as the class was called to order, I saw the three little dots of Esme's pending reply. Well, our teacher had another thing coming if she thought I would let go of my phone before seeing the answer.

Promise, she simply replied.

As lunch approached, I couldn't help the apprehension that settled in me. It was a new feeling. Ever since Esmeralda had entered my life, I'd started to sometimes feel like a child. It was unnerving. Before, I'd been all contempt and anger. Now... I wasn't sure anymore.

I met her by my car and leaned down bracing my arm on the car beside her face.

People began staring at us with various levels of indiscretion. We were the star couple of Brentwood, but rarely showed any familiarity. People assumed it was simply for decorum, that PDA was against our elitist customs, and not due to the disgust my touch elicited in my fiancée. How ironic.

"Do you mind if we speak in the car? I'm not a fan of an audience," she said. I followed her eyes to the group of vipers who usually trailed behind Aleksandra.

"Ah, yes, but first let's give them something to write home about." I gave her a small smile. The little conspiratorial one she gave me back made me feel lighter. I leaned down, giving her a sweet kiss. I didn't have to do this, but I wanted to, like I always did when she was near.

I usually had a primal need, a desire to conquer her, but also, more often now, I felt a wave of tenderness I didn't really understand. It was not something I ever received or gave and yet...it was there, growing.

I lifted my head. She let out a little sigh, her gray eyes looking stormier and steelier after this kiss. This was one of those moments that recomforted me in my weakness, because I knew that, even if it was on a much lesser level, I affected her too.

I opened the passenger door and gestured her in.

She cleared her throat, shaking her head a little. "Yes, sure, okay, thanks."

I closed the door behind her and couldn't help but grin like an idiot. Maybe I affected her a bit more than I thought.

"So, what did you want to talk about?"

She nodded. Opening her bag, she got out a leather-bound notebook. It wasn't really something I'd expected. She proffered it to me, her face full of apprehension as if she was giving me her most precious belonging.

"Okay…" I trailed off. Taking it from her, I rested it on my lap.

"This is my mother's journal."

"Oh." I looked down at the notebook on my lap with renewed interest. "Did Archibald give it to you?"

She shook her head. "No, I don't know who gave it to me. It was just waiting for me in a brown envelope. This -" she pointed at the notebook on my lap - "should be proof enough that I didn't try to kill myself. This is also why I know my mom is not the homewrecker you seem to think she was."

That was a lot of information to have at once. The journal could contain lies, I thought, but then what would be the point of lying in one's own journal?

"Does it talk about my parents?"

"It does a bit." She grimaced, cocking her head to the side. "It did more."

"What do you mean?"

She looked at me with uncertainty. She wasn't sure how much she wanted to reveal. I wish I could blame her, but I would feel the same if I was in her shoes. Giving me information would give me ammunition. Before that she needed to decide how much she trusted me, which considering our history couldn't be much.

"I…" She sighed as she turned to look ahead, breaking eye contact. "I'd ripped out some pages concerning your family, I'd posted them to you the day I'd left."

"You– I never got them."

"I know that now."

"Why did you?" My mind was reeling. This girl never did anything I expected. Why couldn't she be predictable? It would avoid me being conflicted all the damned time.

She looked down at her hands, fidgeting her fingers.

I rested my hand on top of hers to stop her without thinking of the effect her soft skin always had on me. How a mere touch caused my chest to tighten so much it made it hard to breathe.

"Esmeralda, why did you send those pages to me?" I asked again.

She rested her head against the headrest, then turned toward me. "Because I was conflicted about leaving, because I thought it might make you hate me less." She let out a humorless laugh that broke the little bit of the heart I had left. "What an epic failure, right?"

I opened my mouth to tell her that I didn't hate her, not even a little, not even when I had tried so hard to. I was feeling angry, hurt, betrayed…all of this in one, but no hate, which was quite ironic as, before her, hate had been my most constant feeling. Against my parents, myself, the world… but not her. Never her.

"I don't hate you."

She arched an eyebrow, looking at me with incredulity.

"I don't, but that might be a conversation for another time. So, what about your mother's journal?"

"I want to find out who gave it to me because it means it was someone she trusted, and I need to talk to him or her."

"What are you looking for Esmeralda? Why is this person important?" She was not telling me everything. She was too nervous. There was something more.

"Truthfully, I'm not sure."

I looked at her for a second. She bit her bottom lip, a clear tale of her nervousness, but I wouldn't push her. Maybe it would be progressive. Maybe she'd end up trusting me more.

"Where did you get it?"

"In the library. It was on my desk."

"Okay, who was there?"

"I think – I think it might be the librarian."

I nodded. "Okay, let's go ask her."

She let out a snort, looking at me clearly thinking it was a joke.

"I'm not joking," I added, opening my door and getting out of the car.

"But."" She rushed out of the car and stood in front of me. "It can't be so easy!"

I shrugged. "Why not?"

"Because if she wanted me to know, she would've told me."

I smiled at her. If only she knew how words didn't mean much, not to me. That woman would probably be saying so much more without speaking.

I extended my hand to her. "Do you trust me?"

"To some extent." She took my hand tentatively. "In theory."

I liked the honesty behind her words. I nodded, intertwining our fingers together. "Just follow my lead." I pulled her toward the library as the bell rang to announce the end of lunch.

"Caleb, we're going to be late."

"So? Don't be scared. I won't mess this up. I'm a master manipulator. Don't forget that."

"How could I? This is why I have such a hard time trusting you. This is also one of the reasons why I left. I wasn't sure what to trust."

I froze. How could she reveal something that was so crucial in the middle of a corridor full of students? We didn't have the time to address that now, but it would have to be addressed again because this was a revelation much more critical than she realized.

"Oh, Miss Forbes!" The librarian smiled at her. Her smile slipped a little when she saw me. She wasn't a fan, but not a lot of people were. "Mr. Astor."

I frowned. She looked familiar. "Librarian."

Esmeralda rolled her eyes. She tried to let go of my hand, but I tightened my grip. I was not letting go yet. "It's Ms. White!" She pulled me to the counter.

The librarian pushed her glasses up her nose and leaned on the counter, concentrating on Esmeralda alone.

"How have you been doing? I haven't seen you for a while. I miss seeing you here."

Esmeralda blushed a little with guilt. Why should she feel guilty? This woman was school staff. Esmeralda didn't owe her a thing.

"I was busy with school and family. You know."

"Oh, yes, your trip to Paris and everything!" The woman clapped her hand with glee, but her lips were turned down on one side. She was faking it. "Alors comment était Paris ?"

"Oui," Esmeralda replied with a nod.

Oh, for the love of God! Antoine should have at least *tried* to teach her something during the pretend tutorial sessions. They were not even attempting to make their story stick; it was insulting to me. I laughed, tucking Esmeralda into my side and kissing the side of her face.

"You've got to stop doing that to people. They will think you don't understand." I shook my head while looking at the librarian. "Sorry, she is still very uncomfortable speaking French with anyone other than Antoine St-Vincent. She doesn't even try with me, so she pretends she doesn't understand."

"Esmeralda, please." I squeezed her hand. "If you're uncomfortable, reply in English. I'm sure Ms…"

"White," the librarian offered.

"Yes, I'm sure Ms. White wants to know how Paris was."

"Okay," she sighed, looking at me gratefully before turning toward the librarian. "He told you my secret. I don't like speaking French, but Paris was amazing. The Eiffel towers, the baguettes, the French people with the berets..."

I groaned internally. How did I ever think this girl was a mastermind? She was the worst liar in history. She was a second away from mentioning the garlic-wearing cyclists and Pepe Le Pew.

"She followed her mother's journal; it was quite emotional."

"Her journal?" Ms. White's voice faltered. She didn't know that journal existed, but she didn't like that it did. "That's exciting." No, she was not excited.

She was scared.

I frowned. The signs were few, but undeniable. Her eyes were a bit wide. Her brows were raised and drawn together in a flat line. Her mouth was open, lips slightly tensed. Why did the journal scare her?

"Did you know Esmeralda's mom?"

"Her mom?" She blinked in rapid succession. "No? Why would I know your mom? Has she come to the school in the past five years?" she asked, rubbing her chin. Damn, she was a textbook liar. No, something was wrong with her and I hated that.

"Caleb."" Esmeralda shook her head. "Sorry Ms. White. You see I'm asking because–"

"Because she wanted to know if you have any photos of our parents here somewhere so she can get more photos of her mom."

"Oh." She shook her head sadly. "No, I'm sorry, Esmeralda. I have nothing. I can only imagine how much you miss her. I'm very sorry I couldn't help."

She didn't look sorry; she looked relieved.

I shrugged. "It was worth asking." I looked at my watch. "We better go, babe. We don't want to be too late."

She looked up at me, an eyebrow raised and mouthing the word 'babe'.

The librarian looked at me, trying to hide her contempt. *The dislike is mutual, woman, don't worry.* When she turned to Esmeralda, her smile was once more genuine and her eyes had some warmth. It was the only reason why I didn't try to expose her straight away. "Come see me again soon, okay? I would love to discuss your trip with you."

"Sure, I promise," Esmeralda called as I pulled her out of the library.

"Babe?" she tried.

"Not a fan?"

She grimaced. "No, not really." She pointed at the library as I kept on pulling her down the corridor, not sure where I was taking her. "What was that all about?"

"I'm not sure," I admitted, "but that woman lied. She doesn't know about the journal, but she knows your mom or of her."

"How do you–"

I waved my hand dismissively. We didn't have the time to get into the details. "Just trust me on this. She doesn't like me, but again, who does? She is defensive, even a little scared, and she looked familiar."

"Yes. She is your school librarian."

"No.," I shook my head. "It's something else. Do you think I acknowledge the help?"

She pursed her lips and crossed her arms on her chest. "Why are you like that?"

I rolled my eyes. "We're the elite. You think your brother is better? Think again. But no, there is something about her."

"Antoine said she didn't have any online presence at all." She twisted her mouth, chewing on her bottom lip. "He says she is not good enough to be in Brentwood."

I couldn't help but grin at her. Antoine's findings were confirming my suspicions. I was just that fucking good.

"Here we go," she said. "An ego boost you didn't need."

"We'll find out who gave it to you, I promise."

She raised up on her tiptoes and kissed my cheek. Then walked away to her classroom, leaving me frozen in the corridor like a first-class idiot.

We were making one hell of a team, her and I. Too bad it couldn't last.

Chapter 12 - Esme

"Do we really have to take them?" Archie asked with a childish pout as Antoine and Taylor settled in the back seat.

"He's the specialist, Archie. Who will explain to Ben how to use everything? What if he has questions?"

Archie grumbled, but dropped the subject. I kind of felt bad for breaking up the little boys' group they'd had before I'd arrived. They'd seemed united. Well, by hate and deception, but at least they'd had each other.

"What did you tell Caleb?" Taylor asked as if she was mirroring my thoughts.

"Nothing really. He doesn't seem to care that much." Maybe he was faking it; I wasn't sure. Whilst he was not throwing me death glares anymore, which I considered progress, he still kept his distance. The only exception was at home where he'd been making good on his word to take me everywhere I wanted to go whenever his father was around. I hoped that wouldn't last forever though, as I still had to investigate their house.

"I told him I was going with Archie to Port Harbor for some shopping. He gave me this." I retrieved the black and platinum credit card with my name on it from my phone pocket and waved it over my head to Taylor.

She whistled. "Damn, the boy gave you an Octave."

"Okay?" I looked at the card. It looked just like any piece of plastic to me.

Archie sighed. "It's a very exclusive credit card, Esme. It has no limit and you can only get it if you have ten million or more in your account."

"Oh." I looked down at the card as if it was a treasure and in many ways it was.

Caleb had walked me downstairs just before Archie had come to pick me up. He'd handed me this card as if it was not a big deal and maybe it wasn't. He'd looked as stoic as he always did, but his voice had been a little bit deeper, warmer, when he'd asked me to be good. I'd wanted to remind him that

I was neither a child nor his belonging, and what would be considered 'good' for either of us would be diametrically different, but his eyes had reflected real concern, even a little fear, and so I'd backed down.

When I'd promised him I'd behave, he'd chuckled. "Your brother's going to watch you like a hawk. I'm not too worried, but you know." He pointed at the card. "Just use it if you want a corduroy dress, a hot chocolate or some angel wings," he added, keeping his eyes on my bare neck. I had not worn his necklace since I'd been back. I wasn't sure why because God knew how much I loved it, but it felt like showing him how much I cared and I didn't want to be more obvious to him than I already was.

I sighed, wishing the memory away.

"I won't use it," I said, my voice a little wistful at the memory of my day with Caleb. That was the day my heart had cracked open for a version of Caleb I'd rarely seen since.

Archie threw me a side glance. "I know you won't. If you need anything, just tell me. I'm happy to buy it for you."

"Or me," Taylor piped in.

"Oh, I see we're all doing it? Fine, or me." Antoine added, making me chuckle. I turned around on my seat to give him a grateful look.

"So you told Astor you were going with Archie. What if he finds out Antoine and I joined you?"

"So what? It looks like it is a double date." Antoine shrugged dismissively.

"Sure…" I scrunched up my nose. "A date with my twin brother. Please just park here until I vomit."

"We could always switch," Archie offered with a noncommittal shrug, but I could see how much he wanted to as he glanced at Taylor in the rear-view mirror. She continued looking out of the window as if nothing had been said.

"Switching is a great idea," Antoine beamed. I turned around again, this time looking at him with confusion.

Taylor turned her head and glared at him. If looks could kill, I'd be going to his funeral.

"Is it?" she asked through gritted teeth. "Maybe it will happen over my dead body...or yours."

"Come on! You and Esme, me and Archie. Embracing the pride colors."

Archie chuckled. "You're basically a vagina and my sister has more balls than you, so yeah, it's not much of a stretch."

I knew Antoine had meant it as a joke, but Archie was still not aware of Antoine's sexuality, not that I thought he would care. I just didn't feel like joking about how real it was given how he was compelled to hide it. For Antoine it was surely auto-derision, but I was not used to being in a world where sexuality was a crime. I might have been poor in my old life, but there gays didn't have to hide.

"I don't think you coming along would be an issue. Tay is my best friend and you're friends with Archie. Joining us for a day in Port Harbor is not that much of a stretch."

"Yeah, because everybody knows how close Taylor and Archie are, right?" Antoine always had to point out the elephant in the room.

"You really are a shit-stirrer, aren't you? Is that a French thing?"

Archie snorted. "Nope, whilst they are quite blunt, this is not a French thing; it's an Antoine thing."

Antoine shrugged before grabbing Taylor's hand and looking out of the window. I let my eyes wander to their hands and watched him gently brushed her knuckles with his thumb. They might not be in love in the common sense of the word, but they did love each other. It was cute.

The rest of the drive was much calmer with Archie questioning me about Ben and Antoine telling us about all the material he had gotten from his father's stash.

"Where are we meeting again?" Archie asked as he parked the car at the waterfront.

"Oceanview," I whispered.

Being here again brought a wave of feelings I hadn't really expected. I looked toward the Ferris wheel and couldn't stop my heart tightening in my chest at the memory of Caleb and I up there. I took a couple of steps and stopped again. I looked around at the closed drink cart and the iron trash can. This was the exact spot where he'd kissed me sweetly, tasting the hot chocolate on my lips.

"Are you okay?" Taylor asked, taking my hand.

I turned toward her, blinking away the memories. "I - Yes, sure." I forced a smile, but I could see she didn't buy it.

I looked over her shoulder. Archie was eyeing us both with concern. I smiled at him and he sighed with a small shake of his head. He hated seeing me troubled just as much as I hated it when it was him.

"We still have some time, don't we?" Taylor asked looking around.

I looked at my watch. We were an hour early. Most shops were still closed, including Oceanview.

She pointed to a few shops, including a coffee shop that was open on the other side. "Why don't we go browse for a while? Just to see what's out there."

I nodded, grateful that the coffee kiosk and the jewelry store were closed.

She followed my eyes to the locked storefront. "Want some bling?" She nudged me playfully. "Don't bother with this here. This is my family business. Let me hook you up, dawg."

I laughed, turning toward her, the weight of the memory on my chest finally easing up. "Did you just call me dawg?"

She grinned. "Maybe?"

I pulled her into a hug. "I love you, Taylor Oppenheimer. I really do."

Archie looked at us with a small smile, longing in his eyes. He could not hide in this moment how heartbroken and mournful he was. My eyes slid to Antoine who was also looking at my brother, his eyes reflecting some of the pain. No matter what he said, no matter how much he cared for Taylor, he didn't like to see Archie hurting either.

"We're going to check the stores," Taylor said, turning to both Archie and Antoine. "Do you guys want to join us?"

Archie and Antoine looked at each other. "Hard pass."

I chuckled. "Yeah, thought so. Let's just meet in front of Oceanview in forty minutes. Deal?" I pointed at the store where Alice worked.

"Okay, but here," Archie came closer and extended me $300. "Just use this okay? Don't use his card."

I looked down at the money in my hands. I knew we were rich, but he'd just handed over $300 like Luke would have handed me a fiver.

I nodded. "Okay, thank you."

"You know you'll have to tell the truth eventually," I told Taylor as we entered the antique and second-hand shop.

She shrugged, looking at some old coins in a case as if they were the most fascinating thing she'd ever seen. "I have a plan. It won't be forever, only until graduation."

"Why?"

She shrugged again. "I'm going away to college."

"Uh huh…" I trailed off, knowing there was something more. "One way or another you'll have to 'break-up'."

"Yeah, we've not yet figured out that part. Why is it so important?"

It was my turn to shrug and walk around the small, stuffy store. It smelled like mothballs, making my nose itch. "I know I'm a source of trouble for their group, but this relationship is tearing them apart and it's hurting my brother. I know you probably have every reason to do that and frankly, based on how he treated me when I first got here, I know he's no saint, but I'm just very conflicted at being in the middle, knowing that one word from me could make it hurt less for him."

She stopped walking and turned toward me. "I understand that and it makes me feel guilty. Believe it or not, I don't enjoy seeing him suffer, not at all. I just need him to stay away, but I am not as strong as I thought I was. I sunk back while you were away and he was trying to get back into my life and, just for a minute, I was that girl again, standing on the edge of a bridge looking down at the dark water, contemplating…" She shook her head as she picked up a creepy-looking doll from the counter.

"Tay, did you try to–" I couldn't imagine my friend in such a state of despair that she would contemplate ending her life.

"I really don't want to talk about it, any of it. Not now and probably not ever. I'm sorry it leaves you in the dark for a part of my life and maybe Archie will grow balls and tell you himself, but I won't."

I nodded. "Okay." Her voice had been even, but her mouth was tight and her back straight. She was poised, trying to avoid making a scene.

I pulled her into a side hug and kissed the side of her face. "It's okay. Do what you need to do to protect yourself. I understand." And boy did I understand. Every day I was fighting my growing feelings for the wannabe sociopath sharing my life.

"What do you think of those wigs?" I pointed to the horrendous synthetic pieces on the plastic mannequin's head. "Do you think we need these for our disguises?"

She snorted. "I'll be caught dead before trying these flea-infested head rugs. No offence," she added when she met the eyes of the glaring clerk.

I gave the woman a sheepish smile. Parting from Taylor, I looked more closely around the store for something to buy. I felt guilty now for insulting her store so I was going to find something, anything really, to restore some karma points.

I picked up a couple of random items before stopping dead in front of a small velvety box that was holding a pair of angel-wings cufflinks. They seemed to be silver and vintage. They were small enough to not look too ostentatious. What shook me was that I didn't want to buy them for my brother, but the icy young man I was engaged to.

I turned to look for Taylor and found her going through vinyl records, too engrossed to notice my stupid weakness.

"Excuse me. How much for those?" I pointed at the cufflinks through the glass casing.

The woman walked toward me, her scowl still quite present on her face. I couldn't really blame her. We had just insulted her store.

"These are 1920s vintage sterling silver gothic wing cufflinks."

"Yes." I leaned down. The details were perfect. The wings were open in flight, giving them a steampunk vibe. "I love them. How much?"

The woman looked at me, trying to figure how much she could milk from me. "$100."

I sighed, looking at the cufflinks again before turning to Taylor. She had four vinyls under her arm and was going through the last rack. I had minutes before she came to join me and question the very masculine gift which was not destined for my brother.

"Fine," I told the woman, resting the few other items on the display case. "I'll take them and these too."

I was just getting my $22.95 change from the $200 I gave the woman, when Taylor appeared with her pile of vinyls.

"I didn't know you were into classics," I admitted, looking at the woman ringing each one. "Queen, Abba, Lionel Richie... Quite eclectic."

She smiled, running her hand over the cover of Queen's 'News Of The World' album. "They're not for me; they're for my dad. It's our thing. I know I'm quite into modern stuff, but dad is a crazy music buff and he passed it on to me. We went through his vinyl collection together. He had more than eight hundred, you know? All in the basement music room. I'll show it to you sometime. So now when I go out, I look to get some more. We will probably listen to them tonight together in the music room."

All the sorrow from before had escaped her when she talked about her father. The genuinely bright smile she usually sported was back in place. I'd known she loved her father. It was obvious, but I hadn't known it ran that deep. He was her hero and that tightened my heart because I'd never had that, not even with Luke who I loved very deeply. I'd never really managed to lean on him, not with his alcohol problems and sorrow from losing my mother. I was the one who had stepped up much younger than I should have. Maybe it was why I was the way I was. Maybe not being able to rely on anyone made me too pragmatic.

I shook my head. "That's lovely."

She nodded, paying for her purchases, oblivious to my internal debate which I was grateful for.

We stopped at a clothes store where I indulged in a new oversized hoodie, much to her despair, before getting some coffees to go and meeting the guys in front of Oceanview.

"How was the shopping spree?" Archie asked, extending his hand to take my bags.

I shrugged. "It was okay." I gave him my bags before looking into my handbag. "I've got some change for you–"

"Don't insult me, Esme. Keep it." He pointed at the store window. "I believe this is the cousin you mentioned?"

I looked up to see a glaring Alice. She was obviously not thrilled to have us here and I couldn't blame her. Secret meetings in the back of her store were not something that the girl probably wanted. *And you do?*

I gave her a tentative smile. Her scowl softened a little, but her stance was still quite unwelcoming.

"Maybe we should have met somewhere else," Antoine commented.

I shrugged. "It was the safest place. Let's get this over with."

I decided to play the friendly card as soon as we walked in to prevent my haughty brother from making even more of a mess of things.

"Hi, Alice. It's very nice of you to let us use your–"

"He is waiting in the kitchenette in the back," Alice interjected, cutting me off.

"Okay then…" Antoine muttered as we walked in a perfect line to the kitchen.

"Right on time." I heard Ben's voice, but Archie's back was blocking my view. *Stupid giant!*

Antoine chuckled as we fanned out. "I feel like we're in a James Bond movie. It's so cool." He grinned, cocking an eyebrow. "I'm quite dashing enough to be James Bond."

Archie snorted, pointing at the bag Antoine was holding. "Not even in your dreams, French boy. You're literally the goodies' guy. You're Q at best."

"Q?" Antoine rested his hand on his heart. "How dare you? I dress way better and who would you be, Forbes? Bond himself?"

Archie looked smug, crossing his arms on his chest. "I'm tall, handsome, athletic, and with class. Obviously, I'm Bond!"

I rolled my eyes and dodged my brother when they started to argue about the European charm that Antoine had, but Archie was lacking.

I finally met Ben's dark orbs and his frown immediately changed into a beautiful smile.

"Hi, beautiful!" He opened his arms invitingly.

I stepped into his bone-crushing hug as he wrapped himself around me. I realized how much I'd changed. My heart still ached with longing, missing my friend and the life I had, but it was not the same. The crush… It wasn't there anymore.

"Are they always like that?" Ben asked once he let me go.

"So you're the secondary love interest?" Archie asked.

Taylor chuckled at that. Archie beamed at her and she sobered straight away, pretending to look at the crochet blankets on the shelves.

"Yeah, and you're the miserable SOB of a brother who used to make Esme suffer?"

Archie's face paled before reddening with anger. "You listen–"

"And I'm the comic relief!" Antoine blurted, stepping in front of Archie.

"You don't say…" Ben trailed off, eyeing Antoine up and down.

I never thought of Ben as judgmental, but right now I was not particularly keen on how he was looking at my new friend.

"Listen, Ben," I said. "If you don't want to, it's okay. I understand, really. I'm not comfortable either with letting you do this."

"No, Esme, that's not it. Really." He let out a sigh. "It's fine. I'm going to New York anyway."

"Okay." I was still not convinced.

He smiled at me. "I have a present for you in the storeroom though. Come. I'll show you."

"Is it your penis?" Antoine asked seriously. "Because I've tried that tactic before and the success rate is pretty low."

Archie snorted and looked at Antoine, sharing a smile of connivance with him. Ah, the friendship was still there. It just needed a common enemy to bring it back. Too bad that had to be sweet Ben Deluca.

I rolled my eyes at them. "Whatever it is, Ben, you can show them. They are my friends."

He stood up. "One thing for sure, is that I'm pleased you came back to your senses and didn't bring the sociopath."

Archie nodded. "Ah, he does know your fiancé pretty well. It's impressive."

"Shut up, Archibald," I snapped.

He raised a questioning eyebrow at me. Didn't he know I cared for Caleb? He must do.

"We're not here to talk about Caleb. We're here to solve a murder. I think it's time to keep our priorities straight!"

The room turned silent as everyone looked toward me as if I'd grown an extra head. It was the first time I'd really lost my temper, so everyone was giving me varying degrees of wariness. Well, except for Antoine who had a little side smile, seemingly saying, 'I can see right through you'.

Archie nodded. "You're right. I'm sorry."

Ben sighed. "Sure." He pointed to the storage door again. "Why don't you go see your surprise while these guys show me the things I need."

"Okay…" I trailed off.

"I'm coming with you," Archie stated in a tone which left no place for argument.

Antoine stepped forward with a cheeky grin promising pain. "I'll take care of your little boy toy. Go see your surprise."

My worries vanished as soon as I saw Luke sitting on a stool.

"Esme!" He stood up.

"Dad!" I gasped, running into his arms and holding him tight.

He kissed the top of my head. "Oh, I missed you."

"I missed you too," I mumbled, my face still buried in his chest. It was just so good to see him after eight months.

I stayed in his arms a few more minutes just reeling in his warmth, his smell of cheap soap and cologne that even now, after everything, still gave me a sense of security like it had when I was a little girl.

When I finally stepped out of his arms, he turned to Archie with a small smile.

"Archibald, I'm so happy to meet you." Luke took a step toward him, but Archie took a step back throwing him a chilly look.

"I'd like to say likewise, but…"

"Archie!"

Luke raised his hand. "No, it's alright, Esme. I understand."

"Do you?" Archie asked, crossing his arms on his chest. "You lost your sister. Did you even imagine the agony I was in for not having mine?"

"It was much more complicated than that and I know you know that now." Luke pointed at my engagement ring. "We both know there was a fate we wanted her to avoid. You tried to help her leave. I can imagine quite well how making this choice ripped you apart."

Archie stood closer to me and wrapped an arm around my waist. "It was a painful and yet easy choice to make."

I leaned against him, resting my head on his chest. "I love you, brother."

Luke took the scene in with a small smile on his face. "But I'm happy she has you. I really am. At least I know that even in the midst of all of this, she has someone who loves her unconditionally and who will sacrifice everything for her. It helps me stay away knowing that I have you to protect her even in her crazy plan to find out who killed Victoria."

Archie stood straighter. "I'll do everything I have to do to keep her safe. There is no stopping her when she wants something." He looked down at me with a fondness that made my heart ache. "I rather be by her side every step of the way than to have her do stupid things behind my back."

Luke laughed at that. "Yes, our Esme always had a mind of her own."

I looked at Luke. He looked much better now – even better than before I'd left. "You look good."

He nodded. "Thank you, yes. I took this detox as a fresh start. I have a new steady job, you know. It's turned my life around. The lawyer your friend Taylor sent said that in another six months William will not be able to bring any action against me. You'll be able to come home then."

Archie's hand tightened almost painfully on my back, tension radiating from him.

"I see." I nodded. It was something that I was sure William knew himself. This was probably why he set the wedding just after graduation, still within the six months where he still had a pressure point. "But it doesn't really matter," I said. "I'm not leaving Archie."

Luke took a step back, rejection flashing on his face.

"I'm sorry. You know I love you, and no matter what DNA says, you are and always will be my father. I hope that if one day I truly marry I will have you walking me down the aisle, but Archie is my brother and I won't leave him behind no matter what – even if he begs me to."

"What are you saying?"

I shrugged. "I'm saying that, well, we haven't discussed it yet, so it's a little awkward, but I'm planning to move with him to Providence and do my thing. Study there."

Archie's face lightened so much I knew it was the right choice. "Of course, you'll move in with me! And I have enough pull. I'll get you in Brown too."

Luke's look was full of sorrow and I was sad, but I knew he understood. He had loved Victoria deeply. He'd chosen her too when he'd taken me in, breaking the law.

He nodded. "I'm reassured you're okay, but if you need anything...both of you...I'm only a call away."

Archie nodded. "Thank you," he offered and I knew it was a genuine gesture from him. I knew him enough to know his answer would normally have been 'we don't need anyone'.

"Are you leaving already?"

"Yes. Coming here was already quite risky, but when Ben told me he was meeting with you I wanted to check on you in person just to make sure that what you said on the phone was correct. That you were well. You're my baby girl. The fact that you're eighteen and obviously well protected -" he pointed to Archie - "still won't stop me from worrying."

I nodded, thanking God that I didn't tell him I'd moved in with Caleb and that we strongly suspected someone had tried to kill me.

"Everything's fine, Dad."

He nodded again, taking off his cap. He ran his hand through his hair before putting it back on. It was something he did when he was nervous.

"What is it?"

"You know what you're doing with Ben for your mom?"

"Ben's not in danger,"

He sighed. "No, I know that, but I hope you both know how dangerous the path you're taking is."

I felt Archie turn to stone beside me and I knew he was about to lash out.

"No offense, sir, but I think I know this life a little bit more than you do. I'm not saying it is without danger, but I'll protect Esmeralda with my own life if I need to. You, on the other hand, were not even able to protect her from your own weaknesses."

Luke looked down in shame as I elbowed Archie as hard as I could in the stomach.

"What was that for?" he asked breathlessly, rubbing the spot.

"Because you're being an ass and I don't like this version of you." I stepped away from his embrace and went to stand in front of Luke, taking his hand in mine.

"You did a great job with me, Dad. Look what I turned out to be." I smiled at him as he still avoided my eyes. "William has tried everything to break me, but he failed. I'm strong and smart and all that is because of you. Don't listen to Archie. He is angry. You did a great job and I love you so very much."

Luke finally looked at me, his eyes shining with tears. "I'm so proud of you, my girl. I'll see you soon, okay?"

"Of course."

He nodded toward Archie. "Archibald, take good care of our girl."

Archie nodded back. "Always."

Luke gave me another quick kiss on the top of my head before leaving.

Once the door closed quietly behind Luke, I turned around ready to give Archie an earful for his rudeness, but the sad look on his face stopped me in my tracks.

"He has mom's eyes," he whispered, his eyes on the door.

I nodded. "Yes, he does."

He finally looked down at me. "You look just like her, but those eyes…" He shook his head. "I didn't expect to ever see them again."

This drained the last of my frustration away and I gave him a hug. "I know and I'm sorry."

He sighed, wrapping me in his arms and resting his cheek on top of my head. "At least I have you, and knowing you want to come with me to Providence…it's the best news ever."

I nodded in his embrace. "Well, we better go back now."

"Yeah, let's get this over with."

"Is everything okay?" Taylor asked, taking in the look on both of our faces.

I nodded before looking at Ben with a small smile on my face. "Yes, Ben brought Luke. Thank you so much."

Ben put down the little round plastic thing he was holding and gave me a smile. "You're welcome, Esme. I'm pleased I could do that for you."

"How is it going?" Archie asked Antoine, clearly eager to leave.

Okay… He really wanted to get it over with.

Antoine started to pack his bag up. "We're done actually. It's quite straightforward and the boy is smart enough."

I looked at Ben. "You're good."

"Yes, but it's unbelievable, all of this. I feel like I'm in some spy movie. It's crazy." He shook his head.

"Yeah, like you're James Bond and he is Q?" Archie asked with a little teasing smile.

"Yes exactly!" Ben exclaimed. "You're Q."

Antoine glared at Archie. "Vas te faire foutre, Forbes."

Ben gave me a clueless look and I was pleased for once that I was not the only one who didn't speak French.

"He said 'Fuck you, Forbes'." Taylor piped in, way too happy to assist.

I rolled my eyes. "It's amazing all the tech, right?" I commented, trying to redirect the conversation.

"Yeah, it's like in the films!" He showed me a small round see-through sticker. "Can you believe this is a listening device?! Just stick it on his phone and bang! We hear it all." He looked at it with amazement. "I feel like we're in Gattaca or some shit."

Antoine nodded. "Most of what I've given you today is priceless, created for the highest level of our– your intelligence. These are not toys."

God, was he serious when he talked about his spy stuff.

Ben nodded. "Yeah, got it. It's easy. There won't be a problem."

"Do you have any other questions?" Archie asked, looking at his watch. "We really appreciate everything you're doing for us, but we won't be able to stay much longer."

"No, no questions, and I'm not doing it for you. I'm doing it for Esme," he added, keeping his eyes on me, the heat in them unmissable.

"Uh huh…" Archie's eyes narrowed into slits. "That's nice." His tone was so cold I shivered.

"Okay guys, why don't you wait for me out front? I'll walk Ben back to his bike," I offered before Archie could say something mean yet again. "You don't mind, do you?" I asked Ben.

"No. Actually, I'd like to talk to you alone too."

"Okay." I took a step forward. "Let's go."

Archie caught my wrist. "Esme, maybe I should come with you. It's not like–"

"No, don't, Archie, please. Don't be like Caleb or Father. Don't try to control me. Not you."

He let go of my wrist as if I'd burned him. I knew it hurt him to be compared to them, most of all our father.

"Esme, no, never."

"And yet–" I pointed at Ben who was waiting by the door, the little bag of spying devices secured in his hand. "He is my friend, someone who has always been there for me. I'm just going in the back for a few minutes to have some alone time with my friend. This is not something you should consider as an issue. Archie, don't smother me. I wouldn't survive it."

He looked pained and took a step back. "Never. We'll wait out front. I love you."

I smiled back. I knew how much it cost him to say those words, especially in public. "I love you too."

Ben and I walked outside, remaining silent until we reached his bike.

"Your friends are...interesting."

I laughed. "That's one way of putting it."

He leaned against his bike.

"You know, you don't have to do it if you don't want to," I said. "It can be dangerous and New York's not close."

"What are you saying? Don't you think I can do it?"

"No!" I shook my head. "Of course you can. But I feel guilty, you know? I keep putting people in danger with this."

He raised his hand to stop me. "If your mother was murdered and I didn't help you out, I wouldn't be able to look at myself in the mirror. Plus, as I said, I was going to New York next week anyway."

"You were? Why?"

Ben blushed, rubbing the back of his neck. "I've been contacted by NYU. They are offering a full ride."

"Oh! Oh my God, Ben, this is big!" I threw myself at him to hug him. I was lucky he was so big as I almost took him and the bike down with me.

He chuckled. "Wow, that's an enthusiasm I missed."

I tried to pull away, but I realized my mistake as his arms stayed wrapped around me, his eyes detailing my face before lingering on my lips.

"I truly missed you, Esme. I missed everything we did together and all our missed opportunities," he added before leaning down.

I turned my head at the last second, his lips connecting with my cheek. I wiggled out of his hold.

"I'm sorry!" He straightened up visibly embarrassed. "I just thought–" He shook his head. "The fiancé wasn't with you. I thought–"

"No, Ben, don't apologize. My situation is complicated and I don't want you to think either way. I don't know where I stand right now. I don't want to make any promises I can't keep."

"Please, Esme, don't. You didn't promise me anything. It was just me being…" He sighed. "I don't know what I was thinking."

"I–" I bit my lip. "Your help's not in the view of–"

He growled. "Fuck, I really made a mess of things, didn't I? No, it has nothing to do with my feelings for you. As I said, you're my friend and that's the right thing to do. Your friend Antoine gave me a burner and his number. I'll text him when it's done."

"Thank you, Ben, and thank you for bringing my dad. It meant much more than you think."

He nodded, straddling his bike. "It's alright, Esme. I'm happy to help. Oh, and when things get less complicated, give me a call. I'll be waiting."

I smiled. "Okay," I replied, but all I could think about was Caleb and that didn't predict anything good.

When I walked back into the backroom, only Archie was waiting for me.

"Is everything okay?"

"Yeah, I think so. Where did the crazy kids go?"

Archie rolled his eyes. "Taylor's buying half the store. She wants to thank the girl for loaning the space."

"I can understand that. Let's buy some stuff too."

Eighteen hundred dollars later, we were on our way back to the car, weighed down by bags.

"Did you really need ten crochet blankets?" Antoine asked Taylor as he set the bags in the trunk.

Taylor shrugged. "They're great presents. They were pretty and kitsch and shut up."

The drive back was done in silence, but it was not tense as it'd been on the way to Port Harbor. We were all lost in our thoughts, me mostly thinking of Luke, Ben's attempt at a kiss, and the stupid present I'd bought Caleb.

Thinking of Caleb, I decided to text him that we were on our way back. As usual, his answer was one word – 'fine'. But then he was waiting for me by the main door as Archie pulled up in front of the house.

"Be safe," Archie whispered kissing my forehead, his eyes never wavering from Caleb's.

"Always," I replied exiting the car and meeting Caleb by the stairs.

"How was Port Harbor?"

"Bittersweet," I admitted. It was true for so many reasons, including us and the realization that the girl I had been was gone for good, that I could not long for a life that was not mine anymore. I was not Esme Danvers anymore, but I was not exactly Esmeralda Forbes either. I wasn't sure who I was.

His face softened a bit and he trailed his knuckles ever so slightly against the back of my hand. "I have some good news for you."

"Yeah? What is it?"

"My father has been called away on business. He is leaving tomorrow for a week."

I smiled, relief going through me. "Is your mom going too?"

Caleb chuckled at the hope in my voice. "I said good news, not great news."

"Ah." I shrugged. "I'll take what I can get."

He nodded toward my shopping bags. "You did some shopping."

"I didn't use the card."

"Okay?" He seemed to be taken aback by the statement. "Why not?"

"Archie wanted to buy everything. Even something he didn't realize was a present for you so, you know…" I gave him a little mischievous smile. "That will be something to tease him about."

"A present? For me?" he asked again, still staring at the bags. Did he even get any presents? This man was breaking me.

I nodded. "Come to my room. I'll give it to you."

His eyes darkened a little and I blushed under the implication of my own words. Shaking my head, I started up the stairs with a silent Caleb trailing behind me.

As soon as we walked in, I started rummaging through my bags for the small box. I found it and wrapped my hand around it, suddenly second-guessing my impulse to buy him them; it was ridiculous.

"Don't give yourself a brain aneurysm, Esmeralda, just give me the box." The cool detachment of his voice didn't match the heat of excitement in his eyes as he stared at the box.

"I– umm… yeah." I fidgeted. "Here." I gave him the box.

He looked down at it and opened it carefully like it was precious.

"So, yeah, it's not much and I didn't pay with your card, but I know you love cufflinks. I've seen them in your bedroom. I mean, I know they are not the same quality and all, but–"

"Can you just stop rambling for a minute?" he asked calmly.

"I–" I took a deep breath. "Yeah."

He chuckled. "The rambling when you're nervous is quite endearing, but it makes it difficult to say anything."

Had he said 'endearing'? I cocked my head to the side. Things had gotten better between us since the incident, but we were still a way off niceties, especially when it was only the two of us.

"Do you like them?"

He shook his head. "No."

I couldn't help but feel a little disappointed, even if I should have expected that much. Wings were tacky and they didn't have the same significance for him that they had for me.

"It's okay. I can–"

"I love them"

"You what?"

He gave me a small smile. "I love them, really." He took another couple of steps forward.

"You do?" I asked, arching my eyebrows with surprise.

His smile widened. "Uh huh." He leaned down, slowly, and brushed his lips against mine, making me shiver.

I took a sharp breath. Without thinking, I stood on my tiptoes and pressed my lips a bit more firmly against his.

He wrapped his arm around my waist and gave me a few slow open-mouth kisses.

It was like time had stopped. His lips remained on mine. He pulled me closer to him. The flutter in my chest intensified. My heart pounded in my chest and my knees got weaker. Everything disappeared except the heat of his skin on mine, the smell of his cologne as it addictively invaded my senses.

When he broke the kiss, he kept me in his arms. I looked at him, my body tingling, my lips parted. His blue eyes were so full of turmoil, looking right into me and filling me with a wave of warmth that engulfed me completely. It curled my toes, unfurled all of my senses, as his closeness managed to silence all my thoughts.

He pulled me in again, claiming my mouth, hungrily and intensely until my knees gave in and only his arms kept me up.

He broke the kiss, leaving both of us breathless, but he kept his arms around me until I could feel my legs once more. Again, I was grateful.

He finally let me go, walking backward to the door. "Goodnight, Esmeralda." His voice was a bit deeper than usual.

"Goodnight," I squeaked as he left the room

Yeah, right, like I'll be able to sleep after that.

Chapter 13 – Esme

When I pulled into the school parking lot this morning, I was feeling lighter than I had since I'd come back from California. Maybe it was because we were finally making some progress on solving my mother's murder or maybe it was because my relationship with Caleb had shifted some more. The hate and anger had been replaced by some connivance and a light, dare I say 'friendship'. With his father gone and his mother holed up in her quarters, the house had become ours again. We dined together, even read last night in the library in a companionable silence. I even started to hope that–

A knock on my car window made me jump. I was about to bitch at whoever had scared me when I noticed the grim look on my brother's face.

"What's happened?" I asked, opening the door. Couldn't I just catch a break?!

"Father's summoning you and Caleb for dinner tomorrow night."

I frowned. There was no lost love between my evil father and myself. I hadn't heard from him since I came back and I'd only shared a couple of calls with poor Sophia.

"Why? The man has not talked to me in weeks."

"I don't know."

I sighed. "Did you tell Caleb?"

He nodded. "Yes, but Father had already called him to inform him of the request."

"And what did he say?"

Archie shrugged. "He said he'll do what you want to do."

I smiled at that. Yes, Caleb had changed since I'd given him the cufflinks. Who would have thought they would make such a difference?

"You two…" Archie trailed off.

"Yes?

"Are you…*a thing*?" He asked with a grimace.

"Don't look so disgusted. It's offensive, and no, we're not a 'thing'."

Our phones beeped at the same time. I looked up and saw Caleb and Antoine reach for theirs too – that didn't bode anything good.

Meet me in the council room. I've got news. T

"Oppenheimer texting me willingly? It has to be life-altering," Archie joked, but I could see he meant it.

"What do you think she wants?" Antoine asked as we met by the council room door.

Archie unlocked it and gestured us in. "I don't know, man. She's your girlfriend. You tell me."

Caleb looked at me and rolled his eyes. We exchanged a grin; this still-fragile friendship felt nice.

"So did Archie tell you about dinner with your father?" he whispered, coming to stand closer to me than necessary, but I was not going to complain. I shamefully had to admit I was somehow addicted to the earthy smell of his cologne.

"He just did, before Taylor's summons."

"How are you feeling about it?"

I looked at his face. The concern was genuine, opening the breach in my heart a bit more, letting more of him slip in. "I want to know what he wants, and I'll have you and Archie at my back."

He smiled and it was one of those smiles he used to give me after Port Harbor, but before I'd left him. It was a smile I had missed more than I thought I would and it made my heart jump in my chest.

Taylor chose this moment to walk in, holding a moss green leather-bound book in her arms.

"You called?" Archie sniggered.

She turned to me. "Best friend." She then looked to Antoine, Caleb, and Archie, calling them respectively, "Daphne, Velma, Shaggy. Sorry to interrupt the investigations of Mystery Incorporated but I have news."

Archie pointed at himself. "I'm Shaggy?!" he asked offended.

Taylor raised her eyebrow in silent confirmation.

"Oh, come on! I'm at least a Fred!" He turned to Caleb and Antoine. "Go on, tell her you're not Daphne or Velma."

Caleb shrugged. "Velma's the brains. I'll take it."

Antoine winked at Taylor. "And Daphne is the pretty one. I'm good too."

"Anyway," I started, trying to bring back the conversation on a safer ground. "What did you want to say?"

"Ah, yes." Taylor shook her head. "While you were all busy using your spying systems, super-computer, and your spy networks," she snorted, "you forgot to look at the basics."

"Care to explain?" Caleb asked, gesturing toward the table.

"You were so busy trying to find what was there instead of noticing what wasn't." She slammed the book on the table. "Your answers are here."

"Okay…" Antoine trailed off, coming to stand beside her. "No offense, babe, but how can a yearbook from over twenty years ago provide us with an answer?"

She rolled her eyes. "I went to the library and looked for our Father's yearbook, thinking that maybe there was something there. And you know what's strange? Their final year at Brentwood and the three years after that were missing."

I frowned, looking at Archie. "Okay, that's strange."

She snorted. "You think? Especially since you can't check out yearbooks. So I went to my dad and asked him to see the yearbook of his last year at Brentwood as a memento for my last year here too." She shrugged. "He gave it to me and here we go."

She opened the book to where she'd stuck a red tag and turned it toward me.

It was my father holding a debate trophy. It was scary how much he and Archie looked alike, but he had this wickedness in his eyes that my brother was missing.

I cringed at that photo, at all of the surroundings and the people almost bowing to him as though he was a king.

Archie glowered, probably hating the reminder of how similar he was to our father. "I don't–"

Taylor tapped her perfectly manicured fingernail to the left corner of the photo. "Look closer."

We all leaned down at the same time. I gasped when I saw it, jerking straight. She was a child there, with crazy hair and braces, but it was unmistakable. Ms. White was looking up at my father adoringly.

I looked at Caleb and I was sure that I had the same look on my face as he did. I was impressed by my friend. She'd been the quiet one in the background. Yet, she was providing us with gold while Antoine and his thousands of dollars, hadn't even gotten us anywhere close to a breakthrough.

"Who is she?" Antoine asked, turning the yearbook toward him to have a better look.

"It's our librarian, Ms. White."

He nodded. "Ah, the fishy one. The woman without a past."

"Turn to the blue tab."

She tapped on the yearbook photo. "Anna-Maria Valkoinen has a past. I'm sure you'll find plenty."

"Valkoinen. It means 'white' in Finnish." He cocked his head to the side. "Minus seven for lack of originality."

"How would you even know that, Sherlock?" my brother asked, trying not to show how impressed he was.

"Because I'm European and we're cultured, contrary to you lot."

"Smug asshole," Caleb grumbled.

"I second that," Archie confirmed, grinning at Caleb.

Antoine snorted. "You're just jealous."

"You were right," I said to Caleb. "She lied to me."

He nodded. "Yes, it was obvious."

"Takes a liar to know a liar." Archie went straight for the guts.

Caleb's face closed in the cool impassive mask of indifference that I knew now was an evidence of hurt. "Yeah, so?"

"I need to talk with her."

Caleb grabbed my arm before I could exit the room. It was a possessive, firm grip, but somehow still soft enough not to hurt me. It was Caleb's contradiction in a nutshell. "You're not going by yourself."

"Oh, come on Caleb. She's a middle-aged librarian, not the boss of a Mexican cartel."

Caleb sighed. I knew he was about to start a tirade, but Archie interrupted. "I think Astor is right."

Everybody froze and turned to Archie, looking at him as if he'd just grown a second head.

"What?"

"You're agreeing? With me?"

Archie shrugged. "There's a first for everything, but Caleb's right. Going by yourself is not the way to go. Besides, she will be busy now. Let's go together at the end of the day, okay?"

Caleb frowned. "I'm the expert, remember? I can see right through her."

"Maybe, but it's not your mother; it's ours." Archie stood beside me. "No offence."

Caleb rolled his eyes. "I don't think–"

I rested my hand on Caleb's arm. "I'll go with Archie, but I'll tell you what she says."

Caleb detailed me in a way that made me rethink all of my life choices. He sighed in rendition. "Fine. It's your mystery to solve."

I could hardly believe he'd given in so easily. Based on Archie's incredulous look he couldn't either.

"Okay?"

He nodded. "Fine." He turned to Antoine. "Look her up with her true name."

Antoine waved his iPad. "Already on it."

"Thank you, Tay. Really."

She winked at me. "Anything for you, bestie."

The day seemed to last an eternity. When the bell of the final class rang, I almost skipped on my way to the library. I found Archie already waiting in front of it.

"Ready?" he asked, hooking his arm with mine.

"As ready as I'll ever be. Let's go."

"You lied to her," Archie announced just as we walked into the library.

Okay, then. I rolled my eyes, instantly regretting not taking Caleb with me. At least he had a modicum of restraint and patience.

Anne White frowned. She looked around the library, but it was deserted as usual.

"Ms. White–"

"–or should we say Ms. Valkoinen?" Archie interrupted me.

I glared at him. This was not the way to deal with things. "Archie could you just, just...not."

He grumbled under his breath, but stopped talking.

"I… Just a minute." She rushed to the door and locked it before coming back and gesturing us to the closest table.

"How did you find out?" she asked, resting her elbows on the surface.

"I don't think that's really relevant now, is it?" I asked, sounding sterner than usual.

"No, I suppose not."

"I asked you if you knew my mother. You said you didn't."

She sighed. "Listen, Esmeralda. It took me years to get out of that life."

"You seemed to have been in love with my father." Antoine had already found a few things for us during lunch. "It was even said you were to get married."

She nodded. "Yes, but your mother saved me from that fate." She shook her head with a weary sigh. "She took my curse and I was too chickened to help her. As you probably know, my family promised me to William when I was only fourteen. He was eighteen, but was already powerful and charismatic. I was the shy freshman. He was the all-powerful senior." She pointed to Archie. "Actually, he was a lot like you are now."

Archie scowled at her, his jaw twitching. He hated being reminded how similar he was to our father.

I rested my hand on top of his in an attempt to soothe him.

"So you were in love with our father."

"For a while," she continued. "Or at least I thought I was until I saw he was not for me, until I fell in love with someone else." She sighed. "Until I realized it was not a world I wanted to be stuck in. But I couldn't really do anything. My father's business was dependent on this union. Then your father left for university while I stayed here and studied. At least there was that. But you know, even though I was not yet officially engaged to your father, I'd already been claimed. Therefore every boy around this town stayed away from me."

I winced. I know she'd lied, but I could only imagine how she'd felt. Her realization at being stuck in something so much bigger than she was, something my mother had experienced first-hand too.

"What I wanted didn't seem to matter anymore, you know? And instead of going to university to study literature as I'd always wanted, I ended up being sent to Grindelwald in the Swiss Alps – a school for reformed girls." Her mouth tipped down in obvious disgust. "It was basically three years of learning how to be a proper lady. With the Guide of a Good Socialite Woman its Bible, all you really learned was how to be a perfect wife, perfect hostess. How to be smart enough to make your husband shine and make yourself valuable, but without being smart or independent enough to ever outshine your man."

This couldn't be real. Such a place couldn't exist.

I turned toward Archie for confirmation, but he nodded with a grimace.

"Was I to be sent there?"

"You still might," Ms. White warned me. "If you keep going down this path, you will."

"I'd never allow it."

"You're just a boy, Archibald Forbes. You've got much less power than you seem to think."

Archie leaned toward her, molten anger vibrating off of him. "And I think you're underestimating me greatly," he replied darkly.

She scoffed. "I hope you're right, but I think you're both overestimating your odds here. This will be your downfall. You are biting off far more than you can chew. Mark my words. The best thing you can do is make yourself inconsequential like I did."

"That is not in my nature." He grabbed my hand. "Not in *our* nature."

She shrugged. "I hope for Esmeralda's sake that you're right."

"So what happened next?" I asked her. We didn't have all day and I didn't think that Archie asserting his power on the librarian would be productive in any way.

"I went to school. I was in the middle of my second year when I was called back. I thought it was to make the engagement official, but that wasn't the case. Your father had a huge party where he announced his engagement to your mother."

"And you felt betrayed and cheated," Archie offered.

I gave him a side look. God, he was so obvious. I really regretted not bringing Caleb. He was much more calculating.

She started to laugh. "Cheated? Lord no! I was so happy, I could've cried! I mean, I felt bad for your mother. I really did. She didn't know what she was stepping into and I didn't warn her." She looked down at her hands resting flat on the table. "You see, I was just too happy to be free. I would have never been allowed to step away. As backward as it seemed, he was the only one able to grant me my freedom."

Her words took me back to the cemetery when Caleb, as drunk as he'd been, had told me he was giving me my freedom back. Was that what he had meant?

"My father wanted me to go after your father and ask for compensation or force him into marriage, especially since…" She blushed, looking away. I knew what she didn't say though. My father had taken her innocence. "But I refused and my father disowned me." She took a deep breath. "I took this chance and went away, changed my name, and started afresh."

"If you wanted to start afresh, why did you come back?" Archie asked, crossing his arms on his chest. That was a fair question.

She nodded. "I know it's strange, but it's my home. Once my father moved, I wanted to come back. As you both know, Brentwood pays extremely well. I'm making more here in a quarter than I'd make in a full school year anywhere else." She shrugged. "I didn't care about William and his wife. He owed me and I wanted the job."

"What about my mom?"

She turned to me, her face softening. "I was not lying when I said I didn't know your mom. I moved here only a few months before her accident."

I threw a quick side glance at Archie. *Accident? Right.*

"She came to see me once here. She had told me she was aware about the engagement and that she was sorry. She'd looked so tired and weary. I told her I was sorry about not warning her. She was so nice, saying it didn't matter, that everything would be okay very soon."

"Why not tell me that last time?"

She shook her head. "Because it's a part of my life that I'd rather forget and because it has nothing to do with you. It was a long time before you, Esmeralda. Why bring back a past that has no reason for being?"

I was about to comment that it was a question of trust, when the main door opened to reveal the janitor.

"Oh, I'm sorry!" He looked at the three of us. "Is everything okay in here? The school closed over thirty minutes ago."

I looked at my watch, surprised by how quickly time had gone and shocked that Caleb hadn't tried to come in all guns blazing.

"It's okay, Javier. We're done anyway." Ms. White smiled at him before turning to me. "Are we good?"

"For now." Archie stood up and walked out without a look back.

I wasn't sure why he was so upset. It was not like he didn't know what a prick our father really was. I didn't expect it to come as a shock.

I was about to leave when Ms. White caught my wrist. "I don't know what you are looking for, but stop now. Give up." The urgency of her tone made my heart race.

"Why?"

"Because you don't know what or who you're messing with. I would be sad to see something happen to you and it will… If you continue down this path, it will."

My heart started to hammer in my chest. Something was already happening to me. The failed attempt on my life last month was proof enough.

"Esme?" I turned to see Archie back at the door, frowning at Ms. White's hand around my wrist. "It's getting late. Let's go."

"Just let it go," Ms. White whispered again before dropping my wrist.

"What was that all about?" Archie asked as we exited the darkened school. It definitely had a weird vibe, being here when it was empty.

"I'm not sure. She was telling me to be careful I guess."

"Uh-huh… I still don't like her."

I chuckled. "You don't like anyone."

"That's not true. I like you."

"No you don't; you love me."

He sighed, burying his hands in his pockets. "That I do. So, what do you think of her sob story?" He asked as we stopped by my car.

I leaned against the driver's door. "I believe it. I'm sure Antoine will be able to check her story now, to see if it's true."

"Yeah. I'm still not a fan."

"Yeah, Caleb's not either. I mean, he knew she was lying about mom from the moment he saw her."

He cocked his head to the side. "You sound impressed."

"I am."

"Talking about Caleb, I noticed that you guys seem to be…friendlier with each other. How did that happen?"

Ah, this morning's interrupted chat had not been forgotten.

I did my best to contain my grin. Archie was pretending it was not a big deal, but I could see how much he wanted to know.

"Does it matter?"

He shrugged, but I didn't miss the frustration flash across his face.

I sighed. "I'm not sure. I think he is forgiving me for walking away. I think he is starting to see I'm not the conniving bitch he thought I was. At least...I hope so."

Archie snorted. "Took him long enough. For an evil genius, he can be so dim sometimes." He detailed my face. "You care for him, don't you?"

I nodded. "Of course I do. I know he won't believe it. I even know it doesn't make much sense, but…" I shook my head. "I think you were right. I'm going to tell him everything. I don't think he'll betray us. He didn't with White and he's kept me shielded at his house even though he could have just thrown me to the wolves for the entertainment factor."

"Maybe just wait until after dinner with father. He has something up his sleeve. I know that. I just–" He growled in frustration. "He's not telling me much these days for some reason."

"Do you think he knows?" I paled, panicking at the thought of Archie being made responsible. The price he would have to pay for betraying our father would be of biblical proportions.

"About us?" He shrugged. "Maybe, but you know what? I don't care. If he does, we'll figure something out."

"Yeah." But my voice didn't convince him nor me. "I'll still tell Caleb about what White said though."

"Of course." He leaned down to kiss my forehead. "Okay, well, I'll see you tomorrow."

"Yep, I'll text you when I get home."

"Okay, and hey, don't worry too much. We've got each other's back. We'll be fine. Nothing's going to happen to you. I would not allow it."

"I know Archie. It's just getting all too real."

"I get that." He looked at his car. "There's no turning back now."

No there wasn't. Though truth be told, I didn't think there had ever been a way to turn back. Everything had been set in motion as soon as I'd opened our mother's journal. There was nothing that could have changed that.

Chapter 14 - Caleb

I was not looking forward to dinner at the Forbes Mansion. How could I? I'd always disliked William and his stupid trophy wife. Archibald and I had been friends once upon a time. It was before I'd realized that he was not as broken as I was, that he was the shiny one. Then I'd wanted him broken just like I had been. Why didn't he wear scars too? So, I'd helped him lose the only thing he'd wanted, the only thing that had mattered to him - Taylor Oppenheimer.

I sighed, adjusting the cufflinks Esmeralda had bought me. They were not really my style. I was more into clean lines and abstract concepts, but they'd come from her. I knew what the wings meant. The fact that she'd given them to me meant a lot. I wanted her to know that.

A soft knock at my door brought me back to reality. I knew who it was before opening it. Everything about her was gentle, even her knocking.

I was as awestruck as I usually was whenever I looked at her. She was dressed simply in a knee-length, purple dress. There was just enough cleavage to entice me and show the wings necklace I'd given her in Port Harbor. Her hair was up, revealing her slender, delicate neck. I wanted to kiss, bite, lick…own it. I let my eyes trail down her shapely legs to her stiletto-clad feet.

"You look absolutely stunning, Esmeralda." If only she knew the effect she had on me. Controlling my cock was almost an impossible job, although maybe it was better she didn't know. She already had so much power over me. I should just be grateful she didn't know the extent.

She blushed and *fuck me!* When I didn't think she could get more enticing, she went and did that.

"You scrub up well, too." She took a step closer and rearranged my tie knot before patting me gently on the chest.

"How domestic of you." I jested before raising my arm to take hers.

She took my arm. Noticing the cufflinks, her smile turned so vibrant, wearing them suddenly became worth it. Fuck, I was a sucker for this girl.

"You really like them?"

"Of course I do." I walked her down and helped her to the car, acting as if it was a date and not a dinner in Doomland that was waiting at the end of the road.

"You know we can always pretend I'm sick if you don't want to go," I offered as she chewed on her bottom lip in an obvious sign of anxiety.

She shook her head. "No. Well–" She cocked her head to the side. "I can't say I'm thrilled to spend time with my father, but I haven't seen Sophia for so long. She was always nice to me and–" She shrugged.

"You know you could have spent time with her whenever you wanted. You are not a prisoner."

"No, I know, but I don't think my father would have seen that too kindly."

"Ah."" I nodded. She was worried and protective of Sophia. Was Sophia's life how she imagined how her life with me would be? "No matter what, that would never have been you."

"What?"

"Sophia. If you marry me or anyone else, you would never become her."

"And how do you know that?"

I chuckled. "You're so much stronger than anyone I've met, my little hellfire. You can be bent, but not broken."

"I came close to being broken. Too close," she whispered.

I glanced her way, but she was looking out of the window.

"Is that why you left?"

She sighed. "You know why I left."

"Not all, not everything."

"No, that's true," she admitted. I was surprised by such an easy acknowledgement. "But you will. I'll tell you everything".

"When?"

She sighed again. "I'm not sure."

This evasive answer angered me, but I took a deep breath, trying to rein it in. Now was not the time nor place for a discussion that was bound to end in our usual fight.

As soon as we parked in the driveway, the door opened. Sophia Forbes stood by the door, beaming at Esmeralda.

It was quite a lack of decorum she was showing. I was sure she would be told off for it by her husband, but I didn't think she really cared. There was much more life in her face than I'd ever seen before.

I couldn't help but look at Esmeralda with fondness as she looked at her stepmother with a kind smile of her own. She really was impossible not to care for.

Esmeralda exited the car before I even had the chance to round the car and let her out. Then she ran up the stairs to meet and hug the other woman. They whispered things to each other, but they stopped as soon as I reached Esmeralda's side.

Sophia looked at me. She'd always regarded me with her robotic emotionless smile and dead eyes; this time was different. It seemed Esmeralda had brought some life into her as she had in me.

"Please come. Archibald and William are already waiting in the dining room."

As she walked a couple of steps ahead of us, I reached for Esmeralda's hand as if it was second nature. I could lie to myself and say it was all for show, but it wasn't. Touching her was becoming something of a reflex. And the way she immediately intertwined our fingers, squeezing my hand... I dared to hope it was the same for her.

"What did she tell you?" I whispered, leaning toward her.

"She said I looked happy and that she'd been right - you weren't a terrible match after all."

"Oh, did she, now? And what did you reply?"

She shrugged, but I could see the little teasing smile tucked at the side of her face. "I said you were not bad and hot enough to forgo your shortcomings."

I chuckled. "Good to know that my hotness is giving me–"

"Isn't that adorable?!" William exclaimed as we entered the room. Any joy Esmeralda might have felt, drained in a second. Her face turned paler, guarded, and wary. I didn't like this look on her face, not when I couldn't control it at least.

She was just frozen, her hand gripping mine as if I was a lifeline.

"William, thank you for inviting us," I offered when I realized she was not going to talk.

Archibald, who was standing behind William, threw Esmeralda a small smile before sending me a worried look. *You and I both, brother.*

I nudged her. "Isn't that what you said before, sweetheart?" I leaned down and kissed the side of her face.

She looked at me, the worry fading a little. "Ah, yes, very nice."

William looked at our hands. "Ah, are you worried she'll escape again?" He laughed, but it was not humorous. It was cold and calculating as if he was trying to make me angry.

I chuckled. "She is free to go wherever she wants. She is my fiancée, not my prisoner. Although I presume that is a concept still mixed together for some people."

William's nostrils flared. Archie turned his head to hide his grin. One for Caleb. Zero for William.

"Very well." He gestured to the table. "Let's take our seats."

The starters were eaten in a very uncomfortable silence. The more it went on, the more Esmeralda tensed.

"So, Esmeralda, how is life in Brentwood?" Sophia started.

I felt grateful for her attempt to ease the atmosphere. It was not something I could do. I couldn't show that the tension bothered me and most of all, not on Esmeralda's behalf. If I showed I cared more than what I was supposed to, William, and consequently my father, would have a new pressure point against me.

Esmeralda sighed with relief. "It's okay. I like this school. The classes are really challenging."

William snorted. "Anything would be better than the popper school you used to attend. It was a simulacrum of education, set to create failures. Why don't you two speak about dresses and make-up. It's what you're experts on, aren't you?"

"Actually, Esmeralda is doing very well. She is in the top percentile of the class," Archie intervened. It was his first mistake of the night, although I suspected not his last.

"Oh, is she?" William concentrated all his attention on his son. "And why would you care what her grades are? She is a woman, a wife-to-be. How does it matter?"

I cringed internally, only imagining what Esmeralda could think right now. A glance at her face told me everything I needed to know. The way she glowered at the chicken on her plate, she looked as if it had personally offended her.

"I don't care. I just want to make sure that she is still far enough away from me that people know who the smart one is."

Don't pull at your ear! Don't pull at your ear! I winced as Archie reached up and pulled his earlobe, a gesture that William didn't miss either.

I should tell him about his tell. I really should, but I'd never claimed to be a good man and keeping this edge on him had seemed more important than coming clean.

"Uh-huh..." William kept his eyes on his son for a few seconds more before turning toward me. "So." He wiped his mouth and rested his napkin on the side of his plate, eyeing me silently. I hated the calculation there. It was something I knew very well. Dinner had been a set-up and we'd fallen for it.

He smiled. "I've got news for you."

"For me?" I asked, pointing at myself.

"Both of you." He gestured toward Esmeralda and I. "I had a discussion with James and it seems you two are happy together."

I felt Esmeralda's eyes on me. I looked down at her to see wariness and even a little fear. She was looking at me like I was her hero, like I could ease her worries, but I couldn't. Not with William, not yet anyway.

I rested my hand on her leg and squeezed. It was a feeble attempt at comfort, but the only one I could really give her.

"What is it?" I asked. I was better than her at pretending, at faking. It would be for the best if I took the lead and avoided falling into William's trap.

"James and I talked and we believe it would be for the best if we moved your wedding to the Cherry Blossoms festival. The Country Club has an opening and it will be a stunning occasion for a wedding."

I froze, my hand tightening around Esmeralda's knee.

"The Cherry Blossoms Festival is in five weeks," I reminded him.

Esmeralda tensed beside me. Even if I knew better, it stung to notice once more how strongly she rejected the idea of a marriage with me.

"So?" William shrugged. "It's plenty of time."

"But." I shook my head.

"Father, you can't be serious. Nobody can throw a wedding in five weeks, I–"

"I don't remember asking for your opinion, Archibald. Remember your place," William snapped.

I frowned at this. William rarely mocked Archibald in public. Based on Archibald's shocked face, he hadn't expected that either.

"But William, we haven't even looked for a dress!" Sophia gasped with a good humor I suspected was as fake as her cleavage.

"Really, Sophia?" He glared at her. When she recoiled as if his eyes could physically hurt her, I suspected she would pay for this tonight.

I turned to Esmeralda who was paler than usual. Tiny beads of sweat pearled her forehead. She was having a full-blown panic attack. Did she think a marriage with me would be like Sophia's marriage to her father? Was that why she was so reluctant to the idea?

I knew she cared for me on some level. I knew she was attracted to me. I saw that whenever she looked at me. Her body reacted to mine when I touched her, kissed her. That was not something one could easily fake, especially not someone as inexperienced as she. Maybe if she knew that marrying me was not marrying her father, or God forbid, mine, then maybe we wouldn't end up miserable.

"Sir, you know how much I value your input, but this wedding is mine and incidentally, Esmeralda's. After graduation, was ideal for me. I could then take her to Italy and spend all day, every day trying to make you a grandfather. That is not something that can easily be done in my parents' house."

Esmeralda blushed furiously as Archibald growled… *So much for the poker face, asshole!*

I laughed along with William. Wrapping my arm around Esmeralda, I pulled her against me in a possessive gesture.

William nodded. "I understand that, son, but everybody knows that ship has already sailed."

He raised his hand to stop me from talking. "But–" He sighed, shaking his head. "Ah, I'm going to ruin the surprise. James is going to kill me. We decided, as a wedding present, to buy you the Wagner's mansion."

"You– what?" The Wagner's mansion was probably the smallest mansion on Mount Hill. All things considered, it still had twelve bedrooms, two tennis courts, and a heated swimming pool, but it was way too close to both our parents' places and much too real.

"Surprise!" William beamed, but the fakeness of his tone didn't manage to convince me.

"Sir -"

William stood. "Caleb, I would like to talk to you in my office now."

"I– Sure."

Esmeralda threw me a look full of alarm as I stood, but I gave her a small smile, hoping to convey some reassurance. I was going to make it all okay. I wasn't sure how, but I would.

"Where are you going?" William asked Archibald as he stood up to come with us.

"I was thinking I'd come with you for a bourbon and let the women discuss wedding dresses."

William's smile turned predatory. "No, you're not welcome in this instance. Stay with your dear sister. We both know how devoted to her you are," he added before swirling on his heel and leaving the room with commanding steps.

Esmeralda and Archibald looked at each other, both sickening pale as they realized that they'd been played.

I could have told them. William and James were still the masters. They should have been more careful, more refined. This was also the reason why I was always a step closer to the crown than Archibald was. I never made the grave mistake he'd clearly made – to underestimate our fathers.

I sighed and followed William to his office. Maybe I could fix whatever had caused this.

As soon as we walked in, William strode over to his bar. After helping himself to some bourbon, he looked at me with the crystal decanter still in his hand.

"Please." I nodded.

"Your father informed me you wished to delay the wedding. I can't help but wonder why?" he started. Extending me the glass, he gestured me toward the chair across from his desk.

I shook my head. "No, this is not an issue. I want as grand a wedding as I can get. St-Vincent told me about Château de Vaux-le-Vicomte in France and I believe it will be a perfect venue. It'll give our union the grandeur it deserves."

It was also the only venue which was famous enough not to be bullied by our families and didn't have an opening for the next eighteen months. I had promised Esmeralda, against my better judgement, to set her free. I needed time to secure this.

William leaned back in his seat. "Don't you want to marry Esmeralda? I knew it took some convincing at first."

I wanted to laugh, but kept my face blank. That was an understatement. Threats, that's what it had taken to make me come to heel. My father was a piece of shit and he'd known Theo had always been my weakness. He'd spent most of his time threatening to send him to horrible centers far away if I didn't keep in line and I'd known the man was cruel enough to act on it.

"No offense, sir, but you were not that thrilled at the idea of a match between your daughter and myself."

"A Forbes-Astor union is as powerful as it can get. There's no reason for me not to be happy about it."

I cocked my head to the side. My father admitted he had exchanged this union against a favor, but William Forbes would rather die than admit having been bested. This much I knew.

"So, Esmeralda?"

"What I want is not relevant. To be honest with you though, I believe your daughter is actually a wise choice." I gave him a suggestive smile.

It was not a lie. Physically she was perfect for me. The sex with her had been mind-blowing in ways I'd never thought possible. She was also funny and sweet and unbelievably kind. So unlike anybody I knew. Maybe that was why I was reluctant to marry her – to condemn her and myself to a loveless, miserable life.

I would not be my parents. I used not to care. A wife was only a body to produce an heir and look good. To be honest I'd never thought I had it in me to care for anyone other than Theo, but I'd been wrong.

"We've done you a favor, Caleb. Esmeralda and her brother, they are betraying us."

I kept my face blank. "They wouldn't dare."

He chuckled. "Or so I thought, at least about Archibald. But don't worry, he will be sent to rehabilitation camp this summer. He needs to reassess his priorities in life."

I nodded with a smile. "If he is against us? Yes, absolutely." I frowned. "I can't believe he would dare come against you. He should know better."

I needed to thank my family for breaking me and making me an emotionless robot most of the time, making me into someone who could ignore what he felt so well that he became a master manipulator.

William sighed. "I know. I'm disappointed by his lack of judgement and frankly, his stupidity."

I gave him a half-smile. "Archibald has always been easy to toy with."

William's own smile widened. He was just as sick as my father, enjoying the hurt and downfall of his own child. "And you've always been so good at it."

I tilted my glass to him.

"And this is why I want to help you," he said, sliding a folder toward me.

"These were taken last week." He raised his hand. "I know you've told me you'd handle Esmeralda, but she is still carrying my name and this -" he leaned over the desk, tapping his forefinger on the file - "can cause damage to both of us."

I opened the file. The photo was of Archie, Esmeralda, Antoine, and Taylor in front of a store in Port Harbor.

I looked up at William. "Yes, they were in Port Harbor last week. I'm aware."

He jerked his head toward the folder. "Keep going."

I looked at the second photo. The pain and betrayal I felt were so overwhelming I was not certain that my mask of indifference was still in place.

Esmeralda was exiting the store by the back door with Ben Deluca. In the next photo, he was leaning against his bike and she was standing too close to him for my comfort. In the next one she was hugging him and in the last, he had his arms around her and looking at her lips as if he wanted to eat her alive. I didn't need to be familiar with the man to recognize that look. It was the one I always had when Esmeralda was close to me.

"I'm sorry."

"No, you're not." I was done playing games for tonight. I stood up, adjusting my jacket. "I'll deal with this." I pointed down at the photos. "May I?"

William nodded. "Please. They are yours."

I picked up the photos and slid them back into the folder. "We'll be calling it a night."

"Yes, I understand. Oh, and Caleb?" He called just as I reached the door.

I kept my back to him, but turned my head to the side. "Yes?"

"So, I guess you agree with the Cherry Blossoms festival as your wedding date?"

"Yes," I replied before exiting the room.

I walked stiffly back to the salon where Esme was sitting on the loveseat with Archibald and talking with Sophia.

The coal of betrayal was burning deep in my chest. I'd thought we'd turned a page. She'd bought me this heartfelt gift and I'd felt like a fool again. But not anymore. This time I was really done.

Esmeralda smiled at me. Lines of worry marked her face when I didn't return the gesture. Was she worried about me or about herself? I snorted internally. Why would she worry about me? I meant nothing to her.

I gave her a sharp nod. "Are you ready to leave now?" I asked, my voice leaving no room for argument.

"I– Yes, sure." She stood up, detailing me with confusion.

I turned from her and met Archibald's glare. He didn't even know how damaging he was to his own sister. Maybe his desire to punish me clouded his judgement. He couldn't be that stupid.

"Perfect. Mrs. Forbes." I nodded to Sophia before gesturing Esmeralda toward the door.

"Is everything okay?" she whispered as we sat in the car.

"You tell me, Esmeralda."

She remained quiet as I drove, my dark mood swallowing me more and more to the point of choking.

I parked on the side of the road and kept the door locked. At least she'd have to listen here.

I removed the cufflinks and handed them back to her. "Here. I don't want them. They are much too tacky and frankly, childish."

She looked down at her hands. "But I bought them for you," she whispered, the look of pain and rejection so plain in her face. "You said you liked them."

"We all lie, Esmeralda. You and I both know that." I shook my head with weariness. "I don't know what game you're playing. Hell, I don't even think *you* know what game you're playing, but you have to be careful as some players might not have some of the moral consideration - " *or stupid feelings* - "as I have."

I threw the folder onto her lap. "Don't rely too much on Archibald; he is not foolproof."

She looked at the photos and took a sharp intake of breath. "No. Caleb, I swear, this is not what you think," she claimed waving the last photo at me.

"No?" I turned in my seat to face her, crossing my arms on my chest. "It is not a secret meeting with your former boyfriend in Port Harbor? A secret love tryst sanctioned by brother dear?"

"No." Her silvery bewitching eyes stayed locked with mine, her voice strong and unwavering.

"What was it then?" I asked challengingly as a treacherous, poisonous hope filled me. *Lie to me if you have to. Just make it stop hurting.*

"I – I can't tell you," she whispered, breaking eye contact and looking down in shame.

I felt it right through my chest. The last fragments of trust. It was so painful that I had to show her who she was putting her trust into.

She couldn't treat me as both her savior and her enemy. I could not be both. I *wouldn't* be both.

"Fine." I started the car and turned left.

"This is not the way home." Her voice carried a fear that angered me even more. She was scared? Of *me*?

I growled. "You've got nothing to fear from me Esmeralda. Not anymore."

"Anymore?" Her voice was small, but I refused to look at her, to let her make me feel guilty.

"I'm done with all of this, but you need to see something."

I drove past the 'private property' sign attached to the faded sign that had once said Fairmont Park and stopped the car. My lights illuminated the reminiscence of the burned gazebo that used to be in the middle of the park.

"This is your brother's doing, Esmeralda!" I pointed to the gazebo. "This is what he does and this is what he'll do to your life too!"

"He burned that gazebo?" She asked with puzzlement.

"No, the gazebo is a reminder of what your brother did. This abandoned park is a screaming truth of his nature."

"I don't–"

"This is what his actions toward Taylor Oppenheimer caused! I have half a mind to tell you everything and let you see your brother for the spineless monster he really is." But the story depicted me as a monster too, a vile manipulator with no morals. "But it would sound petty and unbelievable. Just– Get out."

She frowned. "What?"

"I've had enough of you for now. Get out. I need to unwind and you won't like how."

She opened the door, but remained seated. "You can't just let me out here! It's night and my phone's at home."

I shrugged. "Don't care." I pointed to the left. "You better start walking."

She didn't know it, but the property was just behind the high trees. She would be back inside in less than ten minutes, but I needed to be away from her now…or I feared I would break down and show her the extent of my scars, the extent of my broken mind…the extent of the weaknesses she caused in me.

"Out."

She sniffled and I knew she was crying even if it was too dark to see.

She stepped out, but kept the door open. "Stay. Let's talk. Don't walk away. You do it all the time. Please, Caleb, don't go to her. Please, I beg you…" Her voice broke. She was not trying to hide her tears and it tore me apart.

Was it always about Aleksandra? Was there no other reason for her outcry?

"Don't worry, Esmeralda, there will be no Aleksandra. She is not discreet enough. From now on my indiscretion will be more socially acceptable for you," I added and drove off before she could see how much of a lie that really was.

Chapter 15 - Caleb

When I made it to the Stonewood Club, I walked directly to the bar and ordered a bottle of bourbon. I sat down by the fire and checked the security feed on my phone just to make sure that Esmeralda had made it home safe. I was furious and betrayed, but couldn't stop caring even if I wanted to.

I ran my hand over my face, trying to wash away the weariness that only physical exertion could really get rid of.

I gestured for the Majordomo to come forward.

He bowed slightly. "How may I help you, sir?"

"Is there anyone available for fencing or squash?"

"Mr. Stuart McAllister just requested a fencing partner. Would you like me to inform him of your wish to fence?"

I nodded. "Yes, I'll be in the fencing room in a few minutes. I'm going to change in my family quarters." The quarters were actually only a room and a small bathroom, but were still a luxury that only very few members could afford in this club. Being the blood of a founding member ensured I was one of them.

Stuart was already in the room when I arrived, tightening the laces on his fencing shoes. He threw me a look and I knew he could see my anger and sourness. It would be hidden under my mask in a few minutes, then I'd start inflicting as much pain as I could, imagining that instead of Stuart, it was a myriad of people who had offended me and caused me pain. Strangely enough, I never pictured Esmeralda even though she was the source of most of my issues these days.

But instead of asking any questions, Stuart nodded a hello before concentrating on his shoes again. I stood beside him, finishing my set-up in silence.

This was something I liked about the older McAllister brother. He didn't pry, probably because he didn't care. He was at university studying medicine. His father was a renowned plastic surgeon. His mother was the heiress of a global restaurant chain. They were old blood too, rich – maybe not as rich as me, but then who really was?

We fenced for thirty minutes straight. The anger had only started to fade when Stuart raised his hand for a break.

"No, not now," I growled.

Stuart removed his helmet, forcing me to stand down. His face was soaked with perspiration, his breathing short. Dark curls stuck to his forehead.

"Man, you're killing me," he huffed. "I expected a gentle match, not this. I need water." He limped to the bench and sat down heavily.

I stayed on the piste, staring at him, my mask still on.

He took a big gulp of water from his bottle. "You won eight bouts out of ten. I clearly can't catch up." He was still breathing heavily. "I concede defeat. I've got to go home and study."

That was something weird with him; he didn't mind losing. There was something wired wrong in his brain. That had me thinking about the rest of his family, his sister, Anne.

I removed my helmet and walked closer to him.

"Your sister has been shunned, hasn't she?"

He looked at me, his jaw set. "If you've decided to talk shit, you better just walk away. It won't make me want to fight you, but it will make me reconsider any future bouts and you know you won't find a better opponent here."

"I'm not asking to mock. I just want to understand. You didn't fight it. She didn't either."

Stuart sighed. "Why? Are you planning to shun your fiancée?"

I looked down, removing my shoes. That was the million-dollar question.

He sighed after a while when he realized he would not get any more information from me. I knew I wasn't being fair, but it was the way it worked.

"I didn't fight it because it was what she wanted. Her fiancé had a little conscience and didn't want an unwilling wife. Anne was, is, in love with a good man. He's a working man and she slept with him long before she was forced into that stupid betrothal. They came to an agreement. He shunned her through a contract. She was on her own. My family had no more rights over her." He shrugged. "She is married to the man she loves. She has a nice little house in Boston, which is probably no bigger than your pool house, but she is pregnant and so blissfully happy. She's been gone three years and she doesn't miss the money, not even a little."

"I see."

He laughed. "No, I don't think you do. I don't think most of us do," he added quickly when he noticed I was about to argue. "We've got it all, you even more than me. I don't think I've ever been as happy as she is now. She's free whereas we're not, not really. We can fool each other as much as we want, but we wear those chains too."

"Thanks for the game. Until next time." I nodded at him and exited the room, leaving him behind. I didn't even know if he'd added something. I was just too busy thinking about how I could actually pull this off without completely destroying things with my father...and how I could do it without missing her too much.

Once more, I drank myself into oblivion. Since Esmeralda had entered my life, I'd really started to become a clinical alcoholic. Was this what feelings turned people into?

****

I woke up with a banging headache way later than I should have. I reached for my phone, but it was off, so I looked at my watch, squinting.

Ten. I growled, forcing myself up. I wasn't sure any amount of coffee would save me.

But contrary to all odds, thirty minutes after a hot shower, my bodyweight in coffee, and two Tylenol, I felt human again. A beat-up one, but still.

I couldn't stop thinking about what McAllister had said last night. That was the only solution. As much as part of me hated there was an actual way out, I could not spend a life with someone who didn't want me the way I wanted her.

Going to school was out of the question today. I felt functioning, but not enough to sit for hours during boring lectures. I had things to do, relationships to break, and I had to do all that before I changed my mind like the fickle man I was becoming. I had to do it before Esmeralda did something that would allow that insidious, poisonous hope to take hold of my heart once more.

I went home and was not surprised that Esmeralda's car wasn't in the driveway. She was at school, like the good little angel she was.

Now I just needed to go into my father's office and find the contact details of the lawyer who could help me draft a stupid contract that would help her escape me. Something strong enough to protect her from me when I'd inevitably change my mind and chase her down. Something that will actually stop me from going to her when I was at my weakest.

I looked up the stairs wistfully. I should go to the office and get what I needed. Yet I hated that I'd returned the cufflinks. I never should have given them back. They were a memory of her, a present I wanted returned.

I rolled my eyes and went upstairs. Just a few minutes wouldn't hurt the schedule. I wanted those stupid things back and they belonged to me anyway.

I had my hand on the doorknob when I was interrupted. "She's gone."

I tensed, turning around slowly to look at my mother standing in front of me in her silk dressing gown. A glass of white wine was in her hand. She looked like a leading lady from the stupid 70s shows that reran late at night.

I pointed to the glass in her hand. "It's not even eleven, mother. Really?"

She shrugged, taking a long sip. "It's five o'clock somewhere."

I sighed. "And I know she's gone. She's at school."

My mother shook her head, a small smile on her face. "Where you should also be, shouldn't you?"

I snorted. "Are you trying your hand at parenting?" I raised an eyebrow with incredulity. A Greek tragedy showed more mercy than this woman had ever shown me.

She looked away, pursing her lips. "And it's not what I mean. She left this morning with a suitcase." She took a deep breath and nodded. "It's best this way."

"For whom?" I asked mockingly.

"Everyone."

"We both know how much you loved her. I'm sure you're heartbroken," I taunted.

"About not having a teenage hussy roaming our corridors under your father's wanting eyes?" She snorted. "Hardly."

I recoiled in surprise; did she know about father's tendency to like young women?

She spotted my reaction and sighed. "I'm slightly impaired, son, not stupid."

"Esmeralda's not a hussy." I didn't know why I felt the need to defend her, least of all to my mother. That woman's opinion didn't matter and had stopped mattering so long ago.

She shrugged one shoulder. "She gave you her virginity awfully fast."

I tightened my hands into fists. "We are engaged."

"On paper maybe, but we both know this is all pretend. Please don't try to make me believe you ever thought it was true."

I did, sometimes I did, and before last night I'd dared to hope. I shook my head. "No, of course not."

My mother eyed me critically as if she wanted to see the truth behind my words. Ah, it was a good thing we were basically strangers.

She shook her head, taking another sip of her wine. "It's better this way, Caleb. You should have disowned her when you had the chance. Let her go back where she came from. She doesn't belong here. She never did."

"She is a Forbes!"

"Not by choice. She doesn't want to be here and I don't want her here." She waved her finger in a dismissive gesture.

"Let her run back to the miserable insignificant life she wants so much."

I sneered. "If I didn't know better, mother, it would almost look like you want to protect her from me."

"But you know better, don't you, son?" She finished her glass. "Anyway, I need to go and get a refill," she announced, waving the glass in my face.

"Ah, yes. Please go ahead. We wouldn't want to be lucid for too long, would we, mother?"

"Lord no!" she scoffed.

"Why?" I asked when she turned her back to me. "Is the past haunting you then?"

Her stride faltered and she stopped, keeping her back to me. "Past, present, and even future," she replied barely louder than a whisper before resuming her walk down the corridor.

I'd never noticed until now how frail she'd become since Theo's death. *The only son she'd ever loved.* I was not bitter about that. Theo was the light to my darkness, the kindness to my cruelty. It was an easy choice to make, even if the irony of all that was, it had been her who made me the way I was.

I shook my head. Now was not the time to dwell on the past. I looked at Esmeralda's door once more, but gave up on my quest for now. If my mother spoke the truth, I could find the cufflinks later. First, I needed to speak to Esmeralda. I wasn't sure where she was going to move in with, so I would need to get to her before school was out.

My father always locked his office when he was away, but he'd given me a key a while ago. I was not naive enough to believe he fully trusted me. I was sure that all of the things he didn't want me to see were locked in places I had no access to, but it still felt like a gesture from the man who enjoyed torturing me in every way he could. A man who'd made it his life's mission to transform me into him. A mission I'd genuinely thought was complete until Esmeralda had appeared in my life, waking up a myriad of feelings I'd believed were long dead.

I sat on his chair and soaked in the ominous feeling of the office for a minute. It was the throne room of a king, a king I would one day replace.

I trailed my hand on the smooth surface of his desk. He was going to be furious. He wanted Esmeralda and I was taking her away from him. But I also knew that he needed me more than I needed him. He needed an heir and I was it. He could maybe try to have another one, I supposed, but that child would always be the bastard son. He would never have my legitimacy.

He'd forgive me in time. Even if he punished me though, it wouldn't hurt. Not when compared to the pain of seeing Esmeralda choose an insignificant man and an insignificant life over me and all the treasures I could have given her.

Why did you think she would pick you? You've never been picked first, not even once in your life, Caleb Astor. You always were and always would be a second choice, a voice taunted in the back of my head. A voice that sounded just like my mother's.

I looked through my father's address book on the computer. He had seven law firms on retainers, so it took me over an hour to find the appropriate lawyer, then another fifteen minutes to secure an appointment for later today.

I kept on looking through the files, frowning when I saw one titled 'ED' in the annual accounts.

Opening it, I found emails sent by Luke, Esmeralda's adoptive father, thanking my father for his help with Esmeralda's future tuition. I snorted. The man was so delusional, but now I knew how William Forbes had managed to know about Esmeralda's existence.

There were photos of her before her world had been turned upside down. Some were of her at school, wearing her football team's colors, cheering with a big smile on her face. She was looking at a jersey that read, '12 Deluca'.

My heart squeezed with envy and jealousy as I kept looking through the files. There were photos of her working as a lifeguard, shopping at the mall with a blonde girl, standing with Luke at a barbecue, and hanging out with Ben Deluca at school...always Ben Deluca.

I reached for my phone. Grinding my teeth, I dialed the number I had saved under 'insignificant'.

"Do you love her?" I asked as soon as he'd answered the phone.

"Excuse me?"

I sighed, keeping my eyes on the photo where he was giving her a piggyback ride. "Esmeralda. Do you love her?"

"Sociopath? Is that you?"

I growled. His lack of respect was infuriating. He was a bug. He knew that I could easily destroy him, yet he stood up to me. It was good though; Esmeralda might need to lean on him in the future.

"Answer the question."

"What's not to love?" he replied. Whilst he didn't say the words, I knew exactly what he'd meant.

"You need to be strong for her. You need to remember that what Esmeralda wants and what is good for her might sometimes be two diametrically opposed concepts."

"Why are you telling me all this?"

"Because I know what you did in Port Harbor."

"Oh…"

I leaned back in the chair and closed my eyes.

"Did she tell you?"

"Does it matter who told me?"

He laughed. "Yes, it does. Because if she had, you wouldn't be calling me conceding defeat."

I opened my eyes, looking at the door. "I'm not conceding anything. She isn't mine to keep."

He sighed. "Listen, man. It's no secret I care about her a lot. I kick myself every day for letting her go without telling her, but it's done now and there is no turning back."

"What do you mean?"

"I mean that I tried to kiss her in Port Harbor and she pushed me back. She never said it was for you, but–"

"It wasn't for me." I'd made up my mind; we were bad for each other. I was dimming her light and she was driving me to the borders of insanity.

"If you say so. But I promise, I'll keep her safe."

"Your statement lacks conviction."

"Because she's not coming back. I'd like her to. I really would, but she won't."

I shook my head. "Okay, whatever, just... Just be good to her." I hung up before I could hear his irritating voice anymore.

I needed to go to school now, speak with Esmeralda and Archibald. We needed to decide on a plan of action before Esmeralda and I went to the lawyers. I knew Luke had contacted my father to help him pay for college. It was something that Archibald and I could easily do.

I was halfway down Mount Hill when I was stopped by a barricade of police cars.

I hit the horn with frustration. Fucking stupid kid had probably raced down the hill with his new sports car without any idea of how to control the horsepower. It happened all the time.

A policeman approached me.

"I need to go through," I growled. We owned the police. There was no reason to pretend we didn't.

"I'm sorry, Mr. Astor. I wish I could let you, but there's a casualty on the scene. You have no other choice than to turn around."

I followed his gesture with my eyes to the coroner's truck and I froze. Between the police lines and truck, there was a flash of red. Even from this distance, I could not miss the license plate, the one I had customized to say, 'Ang3l5'. Bile rose up my throat as cold sweat ran down my spine. It couldn't be…

I opened my door, dodged the chubby cop, and ran to the accident scene, all the while ignoring the screaming man behind me.

My knees gave in. I hadn't even realized they had until they met the unforgiving asphalt.

The car was wrapped around a tree. The lifeless body that had gone through the windshield was resting crookedly on what was left of the bonnet. Her long brown hair was caked with blood. Her lifeless mangled arms dangled, dropping blood on the pavement. This was the moment I felt it - my death. I'd thought it was a figure of speech, but it wasn't. Esmeralda was dead and I was dying inside.

My heart stopped. My breathing stopped. Fuck, my *life* stopped as I realized, much too late, that I couldn't do this without her.

My stomach heaved. I rested my hands on the ground as my vision turned blurry.

Fuck, I loved her! I loved her with every part of my broken heart, dark conscience, and tainted soul. I shook my head as tears spilled from my eyes, tears that I, for once, wasn't trying to hide.

I shook my head. I wouldn't survive her. I couldn't.

I didn't want to.

Her leaving me, I could have accepted, could have come to terms with as long as she was happy. My heart would have kept on going, beating inside her chest, beside her beautiful heart.

I heard her shout my name and this time, I let out a sob. I was losing my mind. Her voice was calling me over and over again and I didn't want it to stop. I would much rather take this madness than lose her completely.

Suddenly, I felt hands on my cheeks. Hands that forced me to look up. Despite the blurriness of tears, I saw her.

"Esmeralda?" I tried.

"Yes," she replied breathlessly. I blinked away my tears. She was kneeling in front of me, her eyes reflecting my sadness. "Caleb, it's me."

I turned toward her body lying on top of the car. "Am I dead too?" I smiled at the thought; at least I was with her now.

She shook her head, ran her thumb on my cheekbone. "No. I'm here, Caleb. I'm alive."

"Please, God, don't let it be a dream, don't be that cruel," I let out as a pained prayer with a voice I barely recognized.

I saw her heart break in her eyes as she turned toward the car, her face paling. "That is not me. I–"

I grabbed her face. "I don't care." I pulled her to me, giving her the kiss I should have given her before. The kiss that I hoped conveyed everything I felt for her.

"There is a time and place for this, and now is not it," Archibald warned coldly, interrupting us before I could deepen the kiss.

I pulled Esmeralda into my arms, resting my face in the crook of her neck. She ran her hand in my hair soothingly.

"Take him home. I'll deal with this," he commanded Esmeralda.

I didn't like his tone, but I didn't seem to care right now. I was still having a hard time believing I was holding her. For the first time in my life, it was like my brain and heart couldn't believe they were so lucky, that the warm soft girl I was holding, was really her.

Don't leave me.

"I won't," she replied when I expressed my thoughts aloud. "Come on. Let's go home."

Chapter 16- Esme

It took us over fifteen minutes to get to Caleb's bedroom. The house was not even five minutes away, but driving had been difficult because Caleb had refused to let go of my hand. He kept looking at me like I was a vision; my heart broke all over again.

I had been coming back early because my car had been stolen by some bitch at school – a bitch who was now dead. Despite the guilt I felt at having the death of a human on my conscience because it was my car that had caused this, I had to let it go for now. Caleb was unravelling and he was my priority. I couldn't afford to care about the dead student right now, not after seeing Caleb so broken when he'd thought it'd been me.

When I'd seen him on his knees sobbing, my heart had split in two. I'd realized that no matter how much he'd denied it, he loved me. In his way he loved me. And no matter how much I wanted to deny it, I loved him too. God help me, I loved him too.

He turned toward me as soon as I'd closed the door and ran his hands up and down my arms. "I'm not a sociopath."

I frowned. That had come out of the blue. "I never said you were."

He sighed, finally letting go of me. Some of his tension faded a little.

"Yes, you did. Just like everybody else." He shrugged as he started to unbutton his shirt. "I might have sociopathic tendencies, or it might just be the consequences of the fucked-up childhood I had, but I do feel... Less often maybe, mostly negatively I admit, but when I feel, it is all powerful, all-consuming, and it swallows everything in its wake."

"What are you feeling for me, Caleb Astor?" I asked, my voice carrying the tension I felt. His answer was paramount.

He froze. "Everything," he whispered, as if admitting his feelings could cause him damage.

He turned his back to me and let his shirt fall to the floor, revealing his tattooed back. It was a Japanese bearded dragon, black and grey, its mouth spewing unforgiving blood-red fire. Its fangs pointed aggressively. Its eyes were pulled in a dark angry scowl. A quote was printed at the bottom of Caleb's spine, held between the talons of the mythical beast: *"Pain gave me motivation."*

It truly was as if this was his way to surrender some of his control to me.

I took a couple of steps closer, detailing the tattoo more closely. The more I looked, the more I noticed the slight unevenness of scars on his skin.

I gasped at the number of them. There were at least six. I then understood the purpose of the tattoo; he'd wanted them to disappear.

His head hung low, his shoulders hunched. "This is how the hopeful child was smothered out of me," he confessed, keeping his back to me. "This is helping me realize the world we live in has no place for love, tenderness, nor trust. The darkness became me. There is no turning back."

I took a final step closer. Caleb took a sharp intake of breath when I ran my trembling hands down his back, gently stroking it.

I rested my hands on his shoulder blades, letting the heat of his skin seep into my freezing hands.

"We all have scars. I don't have all the words to say what I would like to, but–" I suddenly felt bold and gave his back a small kiss. "I am feeling what you feel every day and I don't want you to sink deeper into this. We're alone now, you and I…" I kissed his back once more, trying to kiss each scar. "Please let down your guard."

I reluctantly let him go and took a couple of steps back. "Turn around," I begged.

He turned slowly, keeping his eyes trained on the floor. But how could he be ashamed? I wondered. Exposing himself in such a raw manner was the bravest thing he could have ever done.

I looked at the lone tattoo on his chest, just over his heart. I trailed my fingers over it. It was a heart topped by a crown. The bottom of the heart twisted on top of an eternity symbol.

"Please look at me. Caleb, please, trust me." I couldn't help my voice from breaking as my eyes filled with tears over his pain.

He looked up, his face a turmoil of emotion, an exposed nerve. "No, don't cry for me." He raised his hand helplessly, reaching for me. "I asked once before if you would cry for me, but I'm not deserving of your tears."

I shook my head. "You deserve my tears and more. You're a good man, Caleb. Even if you don't want to admit it. Even if you don't believe it. I'm sorry for keeping you at arm's length. You didn't deserve that."

My heart accelerated as I reached for his belt, undoing it.

"Your scars, your pain... They don't make you any less strong. You deserve to be revered and loved and cherished."

I sank to my knees in front of him, grateful for the luxuriously plush carpet, and unbuttoned his pants.

"Esmeralda." He looked down at me. Instead of the dominance that had been there the last time I'd been on my knees in front of him, there was awe. It was as if he couldn't believe this was happening.

"I thought you would never get on your knees for me," he breathed, his voice thick with desire.

"And I thought you would never love me. We were both wrong. Now let me revere you, Caleb Astor," I added, a reminder of his own usage of the word when he'd made love to me our first time.

I pulled his pants and briefs down just enough to free his penis, which was already at half-mast.

I wrapped my hand around it, squeezing gently. It was quite ironic that this strong, imposing, and powerful part of him was also so soft and warm.

I pumped him a couple of times, watching as it grew bigger and harder in my hand. I had no real clue what I was doing, but I'd heard girls talk about it at school. *Like a popsicle,* they had said.

I gave the tip a lick. Caleb hissed. "Do that again."

I smiled and licked the tip once more, longer this time, before putting the tip in my mouth. I then swirled my tongue around it.

"You're killing me Esmeralda," Caleb growled. Thrusting his hips slightly, he threw his head back in surrender.

I let go and looked up, floored at how undone he'd become. I might have been the one on my knees, but I was in charge. Seeing him like this, in pure bliss… It pleased me, knowing I was the one unravelling him. I was enjoying our predicament much more than I'd thought I would.

I repeated the action again, this time taking him a bit deeper in my mouth. The animalistic sounds and unintelligible words coming from Caleb were enough to let me know I was doing something right.

I repeated the motion, taking him deeper still, working my jaw to accommodate more of him while wrapping my fingers around the base of his length.

He slid his hand through my hair. Gently cupping the back of my head, he locked me in place as he started to rock his hips slowly, going deeper with each thrust. I rested one hand on his hip to keep the balance as he increased the pace. I gladly relinquished the control, letting him chase his pleasure. Seeing this powerful man come undone with the ecstasy my mouth gave him, aroused me in a powerful way I had never expected.

"No," he growled, pushing me off his penis. "I'm too close," he added breathlessly.

I frowned. "Is that a bad thing?"

He yanked me up. "Today it is. Today I want to enjoy the moment, enjoy it like it might be the last."

"I'm not leaving you Caleb. I'm–" I couldn't finish as his lips crashed on mine. His teeth nibbled on my bottom lip, demanding entrance to my mouth. Once granted, his tongue possessed me, tasting me as if I was his favorite dessert. The frenzy of the kiss had both of us moaning with pleasure.

He walked me back to his bed, never breaking the kiss. He laid me gently on the mattress before pulling away and detailing me, his eyes hooded with desire.

"I'm enjoying this Catholic schoolgirl look," he grinned, trailing his hands under my skirt. His fingertips left a trail of fire on my skin. Hooking his fingers under my panties, he brought them down slowly.

"The skirt is going to stay," he instructed, crawling over me while unbuttoning my shirt. He kissed my exposed skin between each button. When he reached my navel, he swirled his tongue around it before flicking down into its hollow. "Bra off," he commanded before trailing kisses back up.

I arched my back and hurried to discard the bra before his mouth reached my breasts and already-erect nipples.

He smiled at the sight. "I missed you too, my friends. More than I can say."

I chuckled at the passionate, one-sided discussion Caleb was having with my breasts. It helped me alleviate some of the tension about what was still to come.

He bent down, taking one nipple in his mouth as his hand trailed down to my most intimate place. Suddenly, all coherent thoughts escaped me.

All that mattered was his wicked mouth worshipping my breasts and his fingers between my thighs, brushing against my tender, needing flesh. He gently slid a finger inside of me and then another.

"You're so wet for me, Esmeralda," he breathed huskily, letting go of my nipple. He trailed his nose up the swell of my breast and across the column of my neck, until he reached my ear.

"Always." And it was true. His eyes could light a fire in me like an inferno.

He nipped at my earlobe. "Good to know because I'm always hard for you."

He settled between my legs, parting them wider to accommodate his tapered hips. He entered me slowly, letting my body adjust to his invasion. His eyes locked with mine, showing me all the feelings he couldn't put into words.

Once he was in to the hilt, he stopped and kissed me sweetly. "You feel amazing. Nothing can compare to you."

I squeezed him, making him hiss.

"So tight," he growled, nibbling at my jaw. He thrust shallowly and slowly. It was a sweet, blissful torture that I wasn't sure I could endure much longer.

I trailed my hand up his back. "Faster, harder," I begged, arching my back.

"With pleasure." He pulled out and entered me again in one powerful motion. He started to thrust harder, longer, deeper until the headboard was hitting the wall, until our moans of pleasure turned into animalist screams. His hand came between us. His thumb stroked my clit. I saw stars, experiencing an orgasm so powerful that I finally understood why some people called it *la petite mort.* The little death as Antoine taught me in his attempt to rail me with his hedonist nature. I felt like an exposed nerve, all my senses heightened.

Caleb gave one final thrust and came deep inside of me with a roar of pleasure. I was too happy and satisfied to even care.

Caleb pulled out and rolled over, pulling me against him.

"We need to be careful next time," I sighed, kissing his neck. I'd just finished my period so we were safe, but we couldn't have a baby yet.

"Yeah, I got a little carried away." He kissed the top of my head. "I'm just glad to know you want a next time."

Lord, I hope so! I thought. If sex was always like this, I wondered how people even managed to make it out of bed

He pulled me tighter against him. His eyes were heavy, but I could see he was fighting it.

"Why don't you sleep a bit?" I suggested, tracing his chest tattoo.

"Because last time I did, you disappeared."

My heart squeezed in my chest as a wave of guilt engulfed me once again. "I won't. I promise."

"My mother saw you leave with a suitcase this morning."

"I see. Was she gloating?"

He shrugged one shoulder. "Well, she was morning drinking, which is something she does to celebrate days ending in 'Y'."

"I only took a small suitcase. Things hadn't ended well last night, and I wanted to spend a couple of days at Taylor's just to figure it out."

"Figure what out?" he asked. I could feel his muscles tense with apprehension.

"How to tell you everything."

"I see. Did you figure it out?" he asked, his thumb tracing idle patterns on my bare back.

"My mother was murdered," I let out.

He froze. "Sorry?"

"My mother," I sighed. It felt good to finally come clean. "She was murdered," I repeated. Then I unleashed everything on him, from the moment I'd found the note in the journal, every single detail up to my trip to Port Harbor. I got through the whole story without even a single word from Caleb.

"Are you still alive?" I asked him, trying to lighten the mood.

He nudged me. I reluctantly moved from my spot on his chest. Standing up, he pulled on his pants.

He started to pace up and down at the foot of the bed. "So, you are telling me that you were investigating a murder and that someone tried to kill you, here, in my house?" His tone was calm, but his overall demeanor was angry.

"I told you I didn't try to kill myself."

He threw me an exasperated look. "But you'd left out a crucial element there, Esmeralda. Don't do that."

"I'm sorry."

He shook his head, glancing my way, his eyes darkening again. "And you'd called Ben just so you'd be caught in Carmel, not because of a lover's lament."

I tried my best to stop my smile from spreading. Jealous Caleb did have his appeal. I shook my head. "No, it had nothing to do with love, but he was the only person I thought would be believable."

"And Port Harbor?"

I shook my head again. "I told you. I needed someone to bug David Phang. It was not – how did you call it? A sanctioned lovers' tryst?"

He rolled his eyes and sighed, letting go of his tension. "You should have told me."

"I know."

"I would have protected you."

"I know."

He sat beside me on the bed, gently brushing away the hair on my forehead. "I want in. Please let me be there for you."

I gripped his hand and kissed the back of it. "Of course."

"All in?"

"All in."

He smiled, letting his knuckles trail down my bare chest before circling my nipple. "Maybe we can seal the deal by–"

But he was stopped by my phone blaring out Archie's ringtone. "It's Archie." I pointed at my blazer on the floor.

"Fine, later." He gave me my phone.

"Brother!" I smiled as I answered.

"I'm in front of the gates. I've got news." His voice was cold, preoccupied...and it suddenly burst my loving bubble and sexual satisfaction. Someone had died, someone that should have been me.

"Archie is here."

Caleb sighed with a nod. "Yeah, it was too good to last." He jerked his head toward the door. "I'll keep him occupied. Go take a shower."

I looked down and blushed furiously at the proof of our lovemaking on my skin. I jumped up off the bed and wrapped my shirt around me. "See you in a bit."

"Wait," he called as I reached the door.

I turned around with a questioning look. He walked to me like a man on a mission, caught my face between his hands, and kissed me passionately.

"Don't be too long," he growled against my lips after breaking the kiss.

I staggered on my feet. "I'll do my best," I replied breathlessly, unsure if I could even walk back to my room after everything we'd shared. The wicked smile forming on his face clearly showed that he knew it too.

Chapter 17 - Caleb

I still couldn't believe that everything could change so much just in the space of a few hours. I'd been so determined to let her go for her own good, but then when I'd thought I'd lost her, I'd felt a pain so intense, so raw, that I knew I couldn't. I shivered at the reminder. Some residual pain still echoed in my chest as I retrieved my discarded shirt from the floor.

But the impossible had happened. She had shown me that she cared, truly – although maybe not in the obsessive way than I did. She had also shown me that she hadn't betrayed me. That was worth all the pain I'd experienced

"Where's my sister?" Archibald asked as soon as I met him in the small library.

"Taking a shower. She'll join us in a moment." I gestured him toward one of the maroon leather chairs surrounding the rectangular coffee table.

Archibald detailed me. His mouth turned down in a disgusted pout. "I don't think I'll ever be okay with you defiling my sister."

I sighed. I was going to be the mature one and not say that if it was my decision, I would 'defile' her in every room of this house.

"And I can't say I like the light in your eyes at whatever you're thinking, but–"

"But?"

He shook his head, sitting on the chair I'd pointed him toward. "But I'm glad she has you. With what's to come, she'll need all the help she can get and I saw it today. You love her."

There was no point denying it, but I wouldn't confirm it either. She deserved to be the first to hear it. "What happened?"

"Let's wait for Esme."

I rang for tea and coffee just as Esmeralda walked in. How was it that she looked breath-taking with her face bare of makeup and her body clothed in a simple pair of jeans and sweatshirt?

"You look grim, brother," she said, giving him a hug before coming to stand beside me. It felt so good to have her stay by my side.

I wrapped my arm around her waist and kissed her cheek.

Archibald looked at both of us and sighed. "Your car was tampered with Esme. Your brake line was severed."

I froze as she tensed beside me.

"What did you say?" I asked slowly. *Please tell me I'd heard wrong.*

"Somebody's really trying to kill her." Archibald's eyes reflected the dread I was feeling inside.

I pulled her closer as if I could shield her by making her a part of me.

"Oh..." She paled. I feared she was going to pass out.

I pulled her to the loveseat and sat as close as I could beside her.

"Esmeralda, it's okay. I'll keep you safe." I looked at Archibald sitting across from me and added, "*We'll* keep you safe."

"Do you think that's what happened to mom?" she asked.

Archibald sighed. "Maybe. I…" He stopped talking when Benjamin entered with the cart containing coffee and tea.

"Thank you, Benjamin. You may go now." I looked at the cart before standing up. "I think this discussion calls for something stronger." I walked to the well-stocked bar. It was one of the perks of living with high-functioning alcoholics. "Name your poison."

Archibald rubbed his hand over his face. "Bourbon, double, neat."

Ah, it would be that kind of conversation. I turned to Esmeralda. I wasn't keen on her drinking alcohol, so I was relieved when she shook her head.

"No thanks. I'll stick to tea."

I copied Archibald's choice before taking my seat beside Esmeralda again. "So?"

Archibald took a long sip. "So, yeah, I went to the station and asked for the car to be looked at as a priority. After less than thirty minutes, the expert told me the brakes had been tampered with."

"Couldn't it have been just a fault?" Esmeralda tried, much paler than usual. I couldn't blame her. The thought of having someone out there wanting to end her life was terrifying for all of us.

Archibald shook his head, finally showing the extent of his weariness and worry. I felt sorry for him. "No, I asked the same question. The man showed me a photo. The cut was too even, but it seemed to be amateurishly done."

"Amateur?" I asked. That didn't sound like something belonging to our lives. Nothing was done by amateurs.

"Why does it matter?" Esmeralda asked, still paler than a ghost.

I squeezed her knee. "I'm not sure yet, but it just…"

"Doesn't fit?" Archibald offered.

I rubbed my jaw. "Yeah…".

Archibald shrugged. "Unless it was not planned – something done in the spur of the moment."

"Do you think they know about David Phang?" Esmeralda asked.

Archibald cocked his head to the side, twisting his mouth with uncertainty. "I doubt it, but it might just be a sloppy professional job too."

"Who? Oh God," Esmeralda rested her hand on her mouth as if she'd finally caught-on to something. "Who was driving?"

I knew the answer before Archibald uttered a word. She looked enough like Esmeralda for me to believe that she had died. She had also been the reason why I'd picked her as my preferred sextoy for my sexual needs after meeting Esmeralda– so I could pretend she had been the woman sitting before me.

"Aleksandra Dermot."

"It's horrible. If she hadn't–"

"Don't." I took Esme's hand, intertwining our fingers together. "Don't do this. Don't feel guilty. She did what she did because it was the person she was. I can't feel sad. The only thing I can feel is relief because you're sitting beside me. I know it sounds cold and uncaring, but I couldn't care less about who was in that car as long as it wasn't you."

"She was a daughter, Caleb. A sister. What she did to me was petty, but it was harmless and –"

"Her parents wanted to sue you for the car tonight, Esme," Archibald interrupted.

She looked at him, blinking back the tears, guilt morphing into confusion. "What?"

"When those people should have been at home mourning the loss of their daughter, they were at the police station with their lawyers wanting to know who the car belonged to. When they heard the name Forbes, I swear their faces morphed and dollar signs appeared in their eyes."

"How do you know?"

"I know because I was there trying to figure out what had happened to your car, because I've seen enough gold-digging assholes in my life to recognize one even with my eyes closed, and because Aleskandra didn't become who she was by accident. Her parents always wanted more money. Their money was drying up and they were desperate."

"What did you do then? Offer them some?"

Archibald snorted. "Hardly! Those people won't get a penny from me! No, I walked up beside them and told the police officer I wanted to press charges against their dead daughter for theft."

Esmeralda looked a bit disappointed in him. "You said that after they'd just lost their daughter?"

"Did you miss the part where I said they wanted to sue us?"

She shrugged. "It doesn't matter. A life was lost, Archie. You can't be so dismissive."

But he could be, just like I could be. She was too good. She was untainted. This, I knew, was something that Archibald and I agreed on. We would do anything in the universe to keep her that way.

"Archibald did what he was supposed to, Esmeralda." I couldn't believe I was defending him and yet – "I would have done the same."

"But, it's not right! I–"

"Later, okay?" I tried. I would do what needed to be done to pacify her, even if that meant giving those fucking leeches some money. I loved her enough to do just that. I wanted to give her some peace, some closure.

"Yeah, sure." She thought I was humoring her, but she'd learn to trust me. With time, she would.

"So, I guess you had weeks to investigate. Who's on the list of suspects?" I asked, turning the discussion back to what really mattered to me - Esmeralda's safety.

Archibald flushed slightly and I knew I would not like the answer. "Mainly?"

"Uh huh."

"Our father and…your parents."

I was startled by the admission, not that it should have come as a shock, but still. I knew my parents were not good people, but to the claim that they would try to kill a mother and daughter...

"It wasn't my father who tried to hurt Esmeralda. It's not possible."

Archibald looked at Esmeralda with uncertainty. Did he take my statement for a stupid attachment to my genitor?

"I'm not saying he is not capable of doing that. He very much would and it would not stop him from sleeping. But he is fascinated by Esmeralda – fascinated in a way that I'm anything but comfortable with. No, he would not do that." *My mother, on the other hand...*

Esmeralda looked at me and I could see she understood where my thoughts were going. She squeezed my hand.

"What about your mom?" she asked, mirroring my thoughts.

"Ah, that's the question, isn't it? I'd like to say she has nothing to do with this, but there are things about my mother you don't know." I looked down, somehow ashamed even if I had no logical reason to be. "So no, Esmeralda, I can't say my mother has not tried to kill you or taken part in your mother's death." I shook my head. I hated the idea.

Esmeralda pulled my hand to rest it on her lap. "Caleb, I'm sure she has nothing to do with this. Why would she try to kill me anyway?"

"Yeah..." I was so uncomfortable. I hated saying all of this in front of Archibald even if he knew some of it and suspected the rest. Saying things aloud were much more difficult. "My mother is not… She is quite unstable."

"Okay…" Esmeralda trailed off.

I looked heavenward. Pulling Esmeralda's hand to my lips, I kissed the back of it before resting it on my lap. "For you to understand, I need to start from the beginning."

"We can discuss it later if you want, when it's only the two of us."

I threw my hands up. "Oh, what the hell. It might be best if I get it all out now. We're family now aren't we, Archibald?"

He smirked. "Whoever takes care of my sister is my family, Astor. You do care for her, don't you?"

"I would die for her," I replied, my voice neutral, but somehow hurt and vexed that he felt the need to ask. "I felt her loss twice. I never want to experience that again."

Archibald nodded, taking a sip of his drink. "Then we're good. Well at least as far as Esme is concerned."

I snorted. Like I needed a reminder that nothing could ever save our former friendship.

"You've both seen the scars, but–" I leaned back in my seat. "What you don't know is that my mother was the one who gave them to me."

Esmeralda gasped and scooted closer to me on the loveseat. As unlikely as it seemed, having her closer helped me so much more than I cared to admit.

Archibald looked away and I was grateful. He didn't want to show me whatever it made him feel and I approved. I didn't think I could have handled seeing the pity in his eyes.

"She had a psychotic episode. I was five when I woke up to my mother standing above me with a knife in her hand. She'd stabbed me six times as I tried to crawl away before Benjamin came in and stopped her."

"Ah." Archibald looked down at his hands clasped together. "Is that why she left for a trip to Switzerland?"

I laughed. "Yes, to one of the best loony bins in the world." I shrugged, but held Esmeralda's hand as if it was a lifeline. In many ways it was. "She wanted to kill my father's heir as she was certain your mother had had an affair with my dad."

Archibald looked up sharply. "She didn't."

"He knows that now. Caleb, don't you?" Esmeralda said.

I looked into her eyes and I couldn't deny her. She believed that and her mother's diary. No matter my doubts, I couldn't foist them upon her.

I leaned over and kissed her forehead. "Of course I do. But what I believe or not doesn't matter. My mother believes that and my father's attention toward you could be a trigger." I shook my head. "That and the white wine."

"The Jägermeister?" She asked.

I chuckled, only she could make me laugh in such a moment. "The Gewurztraminer, yes. It's my mother's favorite wine."

Esmeralda looked at her brother again just as Benjamin appeared to let us know that Antoine and Taylor had arrived.

I nodded. I felt raw. It had been thirteen years and I could still see her crazed eyes as she'd stood over my bed that night. I could still feel the blade entering my back.

I let go of Esmeralda's hand and jerked up from my seat. "Let them in." I looked at Esmeralda. "I'm just going to get some fresh air for a few minutes. Just catch them up, okay?"

I walked out onto the library balcony, closing the French doors behind me. I took a deep breath before leaning against the balcony rail and looking out at the dark garden.

The door clicked open and I breathed a little easier. I had hoped she would come to me, join me in my pain.

She stood beside me, her hands on the rail looking straight ahead. "I hope you don't mind. I wanted to be here with you."

"No, I don't mind." I moved my hand to rest it on top of hers. We stayed there for a few minutes in silence. It was nice, peaceful, but I needed to tell her the rest - things I hadn't wanted to admit in front of Archibald.

"You know my mother adored Theo. I mean, what was not to like? He was precious."

"He was," she replied carefully. "I cared for him deeply and miss our games, but Theo being precious doesn't make *you* any less precious."

Straight to the heart! How did she do it?! Read between my words? Know exactly what she should say? How did I even think I stood a chance against her?

"I suspect my conception was not completely–" I looked down at the dark pit the world was and knew my next words would have consequences. They would be words I would never be able to take back. "I suspect my conception was not really consensual." I let out in a breath. The only sign that Esmeralda had heard me was her hand tensing beneath mine. "I can't be sure of course, but I've caught some arguments over the years. In times when my mom was not high on alcohol or pills. She only wanted Theo. My father considered him a flaw and he wanted an heir that was functional. After I was born and considered normal, he sent Theo away. Maybe to punish her because of the sick man he was or maybe because Theo didn't fit the picture of the perfect family he wanted so hard to present."

Esmeralda scooted closer to me, resting her head on my shoulder. A simple gesture that spoke volumes. A silent support that meant everything.

"She hated me from the moment I was conceived and–" I sighed. "There it is."

"Look at the sky," she whispered, her warm breath caressing my neck.

I looked up at the darkness, confused. "I don't–"

"Look closely. The more you look, the more you see the stars. At first, all you see is darkness, but then your vision adapts and you start seeing more and more stars."

"Okay…" I replied, keeping my head up. And it was true, the sky was now lit with hundreds of stars that I hadn't seen before.

She moved from her space on my neck and I regretted it, but I kept on looking up. I could feel her eyes on me, detailing my face.

"It means that it takes the darkest night to see the most beautiful stars, Caleb. Not everything is bad. Even in darkness there can be light. Even in the most twisted, fucked-up life, there's hope."

I turned toward her. She was looking at me earnestly with so much hope. "What are you trying to say? That you'll be my light? My hope?"

She shrugged. "If you want me to be."

I snorted, but it sounded more painful than snide even to myself. "You left me." I reminded her, as well as myself. I couldn't allow myself to lean on her too much. She didn't deserve the responsibility and I couldn't afford the risk.

"I came back."

I shook my head. "Not for me."

"I missed you. From the moment I left, I missed you," she admitted, but I didn't miss the fact that she didn't deny my statement. "I wanted to stay for Archie, but also for you and it was terrifying."

I turned toward her. "I understand that fear," I admitted, "better than you think because I'm so in love with you, Esmeralda."

She took a sharp intake of breath at the surprise. That made two of us. I'd never expected to be saying it now, not like this, not yet, but somehow it was perfect.

"Caleb, I–"

I leaned down, stopping her words with a soft kiss. "Don't–"

She frowned, cocking her head. "I don't understand."

"Either you're about to tell me that you need time or something along these lines, and I'm not really in a good emotional place to hear it, or you're about to reciprocate, and I wouldn't believe it."

"Why?"

She really had to strip me of any defenses I had. "Because I want you to say anything you have to say when there's no pressure, no incentive, no remaining fear. Let's solve your mother's murder and find out who is trying to hurt you. After that, we can discuss this, okay?"

"But what if I want to say things now?" She trailed her hands up my arms before wrapping them around my neck.

I wrapped my arms around her waist and pulled her to me. She was where she belonged - in my arms, nowhere else. Now I just needed her to figure it out too without pressure or anything at stake.

"Please don't, for me?" I kissed her forehead once more. "You haven't seen the extent of the monster lurking inside me." She didn't know all the lives I'd had the pleasure trying to destroy, starting with her best friend and her brother.

I leaned toward her slowly, giving her time to turn her head, but she didn't. She closed the distance and meet my lips, kissing me hesitantly. She was obviously not used to taking the lead. I let my hand trail up her back, to her neck, deepening the kiss and kissing her until my lips were numb.

I finally broke our kiss and couldn't help the male egotistical grin that settled on my face at her glazed eyes, satisfied look, and swollen lip.

"I'll accept it, you know," she whispered after a while, once her breathing was back to normal.

"Accept what?" I asked, resting my cheek on top of her head.

"Your monster."

I looked up at the night sky, not sure what I could even say. She might think so, but she didn't know the extent of it and I was too scared to test her theory.

I knew everything was fucked up, but these few minutes with her on this balcony, away from the impeding drama, were priceless.

A fleeting moment when I didn't have to fake, to protect myself from snakes looking for a weakness they could use to their advantage. It was freeing. This was what this woman was for me - freedom. And that was the irony of it all.

She was freeing me whilst I was locking her in. How could it not be doomed?

I sighed, kissing the crown of her head. "Let's go back in. We wouldn't want your brother and St-Vincent to start a war."

She looked into my eyes for a few seconds before sighing. "You're right. Let's go in."

We had only just passed through the door when Taylor threw herself at Esmeralda. "You really have to stop trying to die on us," she sniffed, holding Esmeralda in a bear hug.

Esmeralda returned the hug with a small smile. "I'm not going anywhere. I promise."

Taylor let her go, but kept her hands on her shoulders. "It's sad that Aleksandra had to die though."

Esmeralda threw me a look that seemed to say, 'See, that's how people *SHOULD* react.'

"Well... Better her than you so..." Taylor continued and it was my turn to smirk at Esmeralda. Oppenheimer might have been an imported piece, but she was still one of us no matter what she said.

"How come you're here anyway?" Esmeralda asked, looking at Taylor and then St-Vincent.

"Archibald called us to say he had news. I had news too, so I thought it would be best if we tackled everything now," Antoine started, taking a drink from his teacup.

"What's your news?" I asked. Esmeralda threw me a grateful look, clearly pleased to have the spotlight directed somewhere else.

"The background on White checks out. What she told you seems to be the truth. I even found her father's petition to sue yours and the document she'd actually signed refusing any pursuit."

"I guess your father helped her get the job as an 'IOU' for something or a guilty conscience for what he had caused her."

Archibald snorted. "I'll buy the IOU, but not the other explanation. Our father doesn't have one."

"A guilty conscience?" Esmeralda ventured.

Archibald gave her a sad smile. "A conscience at all."

She grimaced, but didn't reply.

"Yes, anyway, she seems legit."

"I still don't like her," I mumbled stubbornly as I sat beside Esmeralda.

"Yeah, well, who *do* you like?" Taylor asked. I knew it was a rhetorical question, but my eyes met Esmeralda's straight away.

Her. I like her. I love her... Just her, only her.

She gave me a gentle smile, reaching for my hand again. She didn't need the words; she understood.

"Also, your boy-toy pulled through and the monitoring devices are up and running at Phang's restaurant."

I couldn't help but tense as jealousy reared its ugly head at the mention of Deluca. Deluca who'd come through for Esmeralda when I'd failed her over and over again. Deluca who believed her on principle when she said something, unlike me. Not damaged, not broken… On paper he was so much better for her than I was.

Esmeralda nudged me, bringing me back to reality. "Caleb?"

"Umm?"

"Where were you?" she whispered with concern.

"Nowhere I wanted to be." I turned to the group. "What were you saying?"

"I'd said it's time to set the bait, so I was offering a group trip to New York for a weekend before spring break." He pointed to Esmeralda. "Then she asked you if you wanted to join."

I looked at Esmeralda like she was dim. Did she really need to ask? Wasn't she with me on the balcony before when I'd professed my love to her? Did she know I'd never said those words before? Of course, she did. She must do. "Wherever she goes, I go."

She gave me a tender smile, her cheeks taking on a lovely pink color. My heart squeezed in my chest. Would this ever feel normal? My love for her? Would I ever be able to breathe normally when she was near me?

Archibald clasped his hands. "Okay, it's settled. Now we just need to make sure Esme will be safe at all times."

Taylor nodded. "School is fine, so that's good. We can take turns giving her a ride to school if Astor can't for some reason, and on weekends, we can always figure out things to do."

"What about the nights here, though?" Antoine asked. "If his mother is in on it…"

"We've got the nights covered," Esmeralda said, eyeing me shyly.

Thank God for this! "Yes, nights are okay," I replied as coolly as I could, but a grin formed on my lips, mirroring hers.

Archibald gagged.

"But how–" Taylor stopped, looking from me to Esmeralda. Her eyes finally widened with realization. "Oh… I see."

Esmeralda blushed furiously and looked down at her nails.

Taylor turned to St-Vincent, extending her hand. "Pay up."

"I don't have cash on me."

She snorted. "Yes, you do. You always do. Pay up."

"Fine," he grumbled, reaching for his wallet and extending five hundred dollars to her.

"What's that all about?" Esmeralda asked, looking at the money changing hands.

"I bet you two would give in to the sexual tension before spring was out."

Antoine shook his head in defeat. "I expected you to wait until graduation."

"You're betting on my love life?" Esmeralda asked, not as angry as she should be. She was merely aggravated.

Taylor shrugged. "Sure, why not?"

Esmeralda rolled her eyes. "I'll be careful. I'll go nowhere by myself. It will be fine; I promise."

I tightened my hold on her hand. Now that I was in on the secret, I would keep her safe. She was going to be fine because life had already been shitty enough with me. It couldn't take the last precious thing I had. I would not allow it.

Chapter 18 - Esme

I knew we were going to New York to solve my mother's murder. Yet, I couldn't help but feel giddy at the idea of going to such a big city. I'd always dreamed of going to New York, visiting Central Park, going to a Broadway show – anything. Just being part of the atmosphere would be enough.

"All ready!" I chimed, getting into the passenger side of the car as the butler set my suitcase in the trunk.

"Only one case?"

"It's only two days."

He chuckled. "I bet Oppenheimer will have at least three."

I wiggled against the leather seat. "It's so comfy."

He chuckled again and I loved the levity in him. Since the day of the accident, his mood was getting lighter and we were getting closer every day. I was so glad we'd decided to tell him everything.

"It better be for the price that Mercedes-AMG charges for a GLS 63."

I nodded as if that meant something, but all I knew was that it was big and super-luxurious.

"Are you going to pick up the others now?"

"Why, don't you want to be alone with me?"

I rolled my eyes. I'd spent every night in Caleb's room since that day. My bed was comfortable, but his was heaven. However, I was not certain if that was due to the custom-made mattress or the man that held me tightly in his arms.

"I've booked us a suite at the hotel with a private jacuzzi and a view of the city. I hope you don't mind."

I blushed at the thoughts this suite brought to my mind. Caleb and I had had sex a few more times since I'd shared his bed. I'd been enjoying it more and more, getting bolder. I couldn't help but wonder what it would be like in a jacuzzi... Practice makes perfect, they say. And I enjoyed practicing with him.

"I'm not sure what's going on in that head of yours, but that blush says I'll be down with the plan."

I grunted, looked out the window. I was not going there now.

"What do you want to do in New York?" he asked as he finally started the car.

"Can we do anything?" I asked, getting even more excited.

"Of course! We have dinner at Phang's restaurant and I have another thing, but the rest of the time belongs to you."

"Oh!" There were so many things I wanted to do. Too many, in fact, to cram into a weekend.

"Hey, don't stress out." He reached over and gently stroked my cheek. "Whatever we can't do now, we can do another time, just the two of us. We can hop in my car and be there in under two hours."

I leaned into his touch. "Okay... But -" I frowned - "what's your secret appointment in New York?"

"It's no secret. There is a famous tattoo artist I've booked an appointment with. I want to add one for Theo."

My heart squeezed in my chest at the thought of Theo. "I miss him," I admitted.

"Me too, so much." All joviality had left Caleb's face.

"Can I come with you?"

He threw me a startled look. "Of course you can. You don't need to ask. You're always welcome wherever I go."

Warmth spread into me and I regretted not telling him everything before. It would have made our relationship so much easier.

However, the conversation had to stop when we picked up Archie in front of the gates.

"Why are you waiting there?" I asked when he set his duffle bag in the trunk.

"Because father would have harassed you both. I don't think he's happy that his attempt to create a divide between all of us failed miserably." He sighed. "At least I don't have to fake it anymore. He knows I'm on your side."

I turned in my seat. "But you're okay, right? He is not making your life too hard, is he? I mean if it's too difficult, you can always move in with us, right Caleb?"

"Sure."

Archie laughed. "Lord no! No offense, sister, but I think both Astor and I would rather get our nails ripped out than share a living space." He leaned back on his seat with a sigh. "And to be fair, there isn't much he can do. He needs his heir."

"Yeah, you might want to rethink that," Caleb started. "You know the rehab camp's an option."

I straightened in my seat. "What's rehab camp?"

Caleb shook his head as he stopped in front of the Oppenheimer House, honking twice. "Nothing good, but it won't happen to Archibald." He looked in the mirror, meeting my brother's eyes. "We will fix it before that."

"Yeah…." I turned to see Taylor and Antoine walking out, her holding one suitcase and him holding two. "See, she only has one."

"You just wait," Caleb chuckled, popping the trunk open." Are we good to go?" he asked when Taylor settled in the backseat.

"No, wait, Antoine needs to get his suitcase and my extra one."

Caleb looked at me with an eyebrow raised and an 'I-told-you-so' half grin. "You don't say."

"You know we're only going for two days, right?" I asked her. "Why four suitcases?"

"Oh, there's only two for clothes. One is for shoes, the other for accessories." She shrugged. "It depends what I'm in the mood for."

"Yeah," Antoine huffed. Joining us in the car, he sat between Archie and Taylor. "Not sure why you need to think so hard for campus tours, but you know."

Archie leaned forward on his seat, trying to look at Taylor. "Are you checking universities? Together?" he asked. He'd tried to sound merely curious, but the tension in his voice was hard to miss.

"Here we go," Caleb grumbled just loud enough for me to hear before starting the car.

"Yeah," Antoine replied. "Tonight after dinner at River Queen, we'll have an early night because tomorrow we're going to see Cornell, Columbia, and NYU."

"NYU? Huh… I thought you were going to Ivy Leagues. I guess we can't all do it," Archie started and Taylor hissed.

Caleb put the music on to drown them out.

"Thank you!"

He nodded with a little grin. "Anytime. Talking about college, have you thought about it?"

"I - Yes. Before–" I shook my head. "I just didn't think it was an option anymore."

"But it is. Archie and I, we can get you in seven of the eight Ivy Leagues...and I'm sure Oppenheimer can get you in the eighth."

"Ah, cool. It's just–"

"It's just what?" he encouraged.

I shook my head. "Nothing. It's nothing. I'll think about it." I looked away feeling stupid. What was I supposed to tell him? That I hope we would last the distance? That after we managed to resolve everything, we might have a future? Was he still set on freeing me from this life and in consequence, from him?

I looked at him. His profile was so serious while he drove. What if I didn't want to be free of him?

He glanced at me again as if he could feel my eyes on him. "What? Esmeralda, what is it?"

I looked at the back. For once the three behind us were chatting instead of arguing.

"You promised. No secrets, remember?"

"What does it mean for us?"

He was silent for a long time, so long I thought he was not going to answer. "I don't know." He shook his head. "I often fool myself, pretending I have all the answers, but I don't, Esmeralda. I've been trying not to think about it, at least not yet. Let's deal with the case at hand first, okay?"

"Yes, of course." I nodded. He was right. One problem at a time was the way to go, but I couldn't stop thinking about the uncertainty of the future.

Once we entered the city, all my worries vanished, at least for now. I couldn't help but gape in awe at the tall buildings, the busy streets, the yellow cabs. It was just like in the movies.

When we stopped at a red light, I turned toward Caleb, then blushed as I saw he was detailing me with a small smile on my face.

"What?" I asked self-consciously.

"Nothing, it's just… It's quite lovely to discover the city for the first time through your eyes. What about going for a walk after check-in?"

"What about me?" Archie piped in, leaning in between the seats.

"What *about* you?" Caleb asked, tensing up as he resumed his drive.

"I know I'm the third...or fifth wheel on this trip, but still, she's my sister."

"Don't you have some meeting with the douches of St. Esperance?"

I looked at my brother for an explanation.

"St. Esperance is an elite private school here in Manhattan. They are our debate team's rivals and we crushed them. When father was quite reluctant to let me come on this trip, I arranged a meeting with the team he couldn't refuse." He turned back to Caleb and added, "And it's tomorrow, but thank you for the concern." His voice was laden with sarcasm.

I reached over and patted his cheek. "Don't worry, Archibald Forbes, you are totally welcome to come with us. You all are," I added, meeting Taylor's eyes in the mirror.

"Sorry, best friend, but it's Fifth Avenue shopping for me. You're welcome to join, but–"

"I'll pass. I can go shopping anywhere. I want to visit!

Taylor sighed. "Oh, Esme, no you can't. Fifth Avenue shopping is a bit like Rodeo Drive shopping – you can't really do that everywhere."

I nodded. "Maybe next time."

"Maybe never," Archie whispered, making us both chuckle.

"I heard that!" Taylor shouted as my brother grunted. I was sure she'd punched him.

"Finally," Caleb sighed as he stopped in front of an old-looking building. A man dressed in a red jacket with big brass buttons opened the car door and gestured for me to come out. "Madam, welcome to the Ritz-Carlton."

I got out, quickly followed by the others as a similarly dressed man opened the trunk of the car to get our luggage.

Caleb gave him the keys of the car along with a fifty-dollar bill.

Who the hell tipped a Grant just to park a car? Forbeses, Astors, and Oppenheimers, that was who.

Caleb took the lead to reception. He had always been the leader of the pack. Even when we'd been enemies, where it was him and the other kings as one, it had been obvious. Not that Archie couldn't take the crown if he wanted to, I was sure. At the very least, he could have threatened Caleb, but I believed that deep down, Archie hadn't wanted it.

"Astor, Forbes, St-Vincent, and Oppenheimer," Caleb announced as he reached the desk.

"Oh, of course," the woman at the VIP front desk fluttered. I wasn't sure if it was due to Caleb's cold command, his striking good looks, or the powers that all of those names put together entailed, but the little jealous voice in me made me stand beside him and reach for his arm.

He looked down at me, his eyes shining with humor. He was not fooled for a second by my reaction, but clearly he was pleased by it.

"Oh, Mr. Astor, sorry, but I have nothing for Oppenheimer. I can–"

"There is no need," Antoine stated, wrapping his arm around Taylor's shoulders. "St. Vincent room for two," he announced, winking down to Taylor.

Archie scowled, his nostrils flaring, but he looked away.

"Ah," she nodded. "Perfect. Mr. St-Vincent and Mr. Forbes, your rooms are on the eighteenth floor with a view over the park. Mr. Astor, your suite is ready; it's on the twenty-second floor." She extended a gold card toward him. "This card will take you to your floor." She pointed to the elevators. "Your luggage will follow in the next few minutes."

"Thank you."

"You went for the suite?" I asked Caleb as we walked toward the elevator. "Don't you think it's a bit much for just one night?"

He glanced behind us at the three bickering about something new. "To get away from them and be sure not to be interrupted for what I have planned for you tonight?" He grinned. "Absolutely not."

I blushed and nudged him playfully. "Wait until you see what I packed."

His pace faltered as he glanced at me, his eyebrows raised with surprise. It was true that I was not playful with him, but I liked how it felt. Now I almost wanted to stay locked in the room all afternoon.

Archie gagged behind us, killing the mood. "Please keep the sexual banter for your suite, guys."

Antoine rolled his eyes. "Stop being a sourpuss because of your blue balls, bro. Call the club; they'll send you a lovely lady. I mean, don't pretend like you don't know. You two used to be VIP members."

"Like a prostitute?" I glanced up at Caleb, who was throwing daggers at Antoine, his lips pursed. I could see he was contemplating murder.

"What?" Antoine scoffed. "It's not like she thought you were virgins or anything. I–"

Taylor put a hand on his mouth. "I really suggest you shut up because I think Astor is about one second away from murdering you in this elevator and blood will be very hard to remove from my dress."

"Wise advice, Oppenheimer," Caleb growled, but I couldn't help but tense at the thought.

I'd known about Aleksandra. Once more, the thought of my nemesis's death brought back a fresh wave of guilt which I pushed back down. Now was not the moment. Caleb had paid for the funeral. He had sent money to her parents. He'd done everything I'd asked. I looked up at him again. He was looking straight ahead, his murderous glare still on.

The elevator opened on the eighteenth floor, letting the three others out before the doors closed again, leaving us alone.

"Whatever you want to ask, just do," he said, his voice weary. "But know it was before I met you. Don't let his stupid mouth ruin it for us."

"No, it's just… How many?"

He sighed when the elevator opened onto our floor. He reached for my hand and pulled me out of the elevator and into the plush cream-carpeted corridor which only had two doors. "Does it really matter?"

I twisted my mouth, pondering the thought. "I suppose not really, but I'd only had you and–"

He opened the suite and pulled me in, fusing his lips with mine in a passionate kiss. "And you are the only one that matters, Esmeralda," he whispered against my lips as we broke the kiss. "Is that not enough?"

"Yes, it is, I– holy shit! Where are we?!" I gasped, stepping out of his embrace and into the room. It had a living room with a giant TV on the wall, a bedroom with a king-size bed, and another giant TV followed by a marble bathroom that I was sure was bigger than my old house. It had an enormous shower, two sinks, and a jacuzzi bathtub facing the gigantic bay window, which gave a full view of Central Park just as it did in the other rooms. "This is…"

"Nice?" Caleb asked, coming behind me and wrapping his arms around me. "I can't wait to try the bathtub tonight... Bathing suit optional."

"It's more than nice. Caleb I feel like a princess."

"As you should." He kissed the side of my neck, making me shiver. "Ready to go roam the streets?"

I nodded. "Yes. Text Archie, please. I don't want him to be miserable."

Caleb sighed. "Fine, let's take him."

For the next couple of hours, we went around Manhattan. It felt nice. I loved the truce between Caleb and Archie. Even if I was not certain it was permanent, I enjoyed it. It was like a family.

I was still in quite high spirits when we all met downstairs for the limousine to take us to Chinatown.

"So how was the shopping?" I asked Taylor as we met in the lobby.

Antoine chuckled.

Taylor threw him a glare. "I got a little carried away."

"Uh huh. What do you mean?" I teased.

"So how are we dealing with Phang today? How do we make sure he takes the bait?" she asked, clearly done with the shopping subject.

"Well, I can take the lead," Caleb offered.

I shook my head. "No, I think Archie should deal with him."

Archie beamed as Caleb frowned. "Esmeralda, I'm sorry, but I think I'm quite a fantastic strategist."

I nodded. "Yes, I know that, but you're too subtle. You should have seen Archie when we spoke with White. It was an absolute bloodbath and we need Phang in a panic. Archie is who we need."

Their expressions switched. Caleb was now smirking, his eyes full of victory, while Archie scowled. It was going to be a long night.

The River Queen was almost full when we got there. I felt like a genius because I'd taken the time to book a table.

"Table for Danvers, please." It felt weird to use this name. I was not Danvers anymore. I never was.

"Excuse me," Caleb asked coldly after we'd ordered.

The waitress approached the table warily. She didn't need to know who we were to be careful. We all breathed money with Rolexes, Prada bags, and huge diamond engagement rings we hated. Caleb's authoritative presence clearly didn't help either.

"I'd like to speak with the owner right now."

"Sir–"

"I said right now!"

I looked down. I knew it was all an act, but I also felt ashamed because she didn't know that, and somehow I was not sure it was an act for Caleb. I was sure it was who he was most of the time.I tt was something still hard for me to swallow.

"Of course." She rushed behind the counter before reappearing with a man I recognized as David Phang, although he was older than the image we'd seen.

"How may I help you?" he asked as he reached our table.

"We ordered fifteen minutes ago and we're still waiting. Do you know who we are?" Caleb asked.

"You're David Phang, aren't you?" Archie asked.

The man looked at Archie and his eyes widened in recognition. No matter how much he hated it, Archie was his father's son.

Archie looked around. "This is quite a restaurant you have. I didn't know being a deputy paid that much. You left the force a few months after my mother's death to open this place. Just what? A few years in the force and you could afford to buy this in the heart of Chinatown?"

Caleb and Taylor looked at me with incredulity. Oh yeah, that man was as subtle as an elephant in a crystal store.

"I... Yes, indeed." He chuckled nervously. "I'm sorry for the delay in the order. The meal will be complementary. I– Yes. I will check the kitchen now."

He left as if his ass was on fire. I was pretty sure we would not see him for the rest of the evening.

As we ate, we talked about our mutual plan for the next day, all silently hoping that our plan had worked. If David didn't take the bait, it wouldn't be good. We would be losing our only real lead. And then what?

"Hey, what's up with you? You've been awfully silent since we met Phang," Caleb said as we exited the limousine, now back at the hotel.

"What if it doesn't work?"

"It will work," Archie scoffed, nudging me. "Did you see the man's face? He almost shit his pants."

"When will we know?" I asked, turning to look at Antoine who was walking a few steps behind us, hand in hand with Taylor.

"A couple of days?" He shrugged. "Maybe a bit more. I'm tracking his calls, not listening to them. It would have raised questions from my father to do that, but don't worry, I'm sure it will work. And I agree with Archibald. He looked terrified. He will act."

I sighed, leaning against Caleb and trying to concentrate on the positives. We had a fantastic room with an amazing view and a killer bathtub. We needed to make the most of it.

"Do you guys want to go grab a drink in the private lounge?" I asked, praying they would say no. But they were taking risks for Archie and I, so I didn't want them to feel dismissed.

Antoine looked at Taylor, who gave me a little cheeky smile. I hadn't fooled her. "Nah, have fun with your lover boy. We need to look at our schedules for tomorrow. It's quite a busy day, but thanks."

I turned to Archie. He glanced at his watch. "I would, but I've got a guest coming soon and I want to freshen up."

I crinkled my nose at the idea of my brother with a prostitute, but it was not my place to comment. "Okay, you guys have fun. See you tomorrow."

"Three o'clock in the lobby. Don't be late!" Caleb called as they exited the lift. "We'll leave without you if you're not back."

"We wouldn't!" I shouted just as the doors closed.

"He is a grown man, you know," Caleb added as we resumed our ride up. "He knows what he is doing."

I shook my head. "I'd rather not think about that. I'd much rather focus on tonight."

"Oh yeah?" A slow smile spread on his face. "Talk to me."

I blushed. I was not usually forward. I was not really used to engaging sex. It felt strange, yet good, to be taking the lead. "Why don't you go get the tub ready and I'll show you what I brought?"

"You don't need to tell me twice." He swatted my butt. "I'll be waiting."

He disappeared into the kitchenette area. I heard the clink of glasses and the fridge open and close as I walked into the bedroom. Then I disappeared into the walk-in closet with what had to be the smallest, most suggestive bikini ever invented.

Smiling, I wrinkled my nose as I held the barely existing pieces of fabric in front of me. It was something to be reckoned with. It was made of very small white crochet triangles held together with pieces of string. I put it on and let my hair down, which flowed nicely to the middle of my back. Then I turned toward the mirror.

My cheeks reddened. It was almost more indecent than being completely naked. I would have considered bailing if I hadn't recalled Caleb's worshipping eyes every time he had looked at me in any state of undress.

I met him in the bathroom and was awed by how quickly he'd been to set the mood. There was some soft music, rose-scented candles, an ice bucket with a bottle of champagne, and two glasses on the side of the tub. Some chocolate-covered strawberries and the man himself was sitting in the bubbling tub. I suspected he was completely naked and ready for me.

"Just let me look at you for a minute…" he growled, his voice full of desire. "You are– Fuck! I feel like I'm going to come like a stupid schoolboy."

"That would be a shame, wouldn't it?" I smiled, taking a step closer, motioning to my bikini-clad self. "I stole it from the swimming cabin. I hope you don't mind."

His eyes raked over my breasts before trailing down slowly and stopping on the triangle covering my core. "God bless my father's taste in women swimsuits."

"Can we not talk about your father? It's bound to make my skin crawl in all the wrong ways."

He shook his head. "That would be a crime. Why don't you come join me?"

I joined him in the tub and straddled his waist. His erection pressed against my core, the fabric of my bikini the only barrier between us.

"Am I close enough?"

He rested his hands on my ass, squeezing and pulling me closer. "You're never close enough, my angel," he whispered in my ear before licking it.

Whimpering, I rocked my hips against him. *Angel.* I loved that nickname. I hoped he would call me that forever.

I wrapped my arms around his neck. "I think I will get a tattoo too tomorrow."

He moved his head, trailing his nose down my jawline. Continuing down the column of my neck, he stopped at my collarbone where he licked the shallow dip.

"And where would this tattoo be?" He asked as he undid the knot between my breasts, instantly freeing them.

He trailed his fingers over my hardened nipples before softly rolling them between his fingers, making me rock against him again.

I took his hand and trailed it down to the hem of the bikini bottom where I slid his fingers in about half an inch.

"Just here, "I whispered as my heart stammered in my chest.

"Ummmm, here?" He ran his fingers back and forth on my skin. "I can't wait to see it. But we'll need to find a woman to do it." He nipped at my bottom lip. "Because there's no way I'll let a man near any part of your body that is for my eyes only."

I shivered at his words. They should annoy me. I was my own person. Yet, his possessiveness made me even hotter for him.

He kept his eyes locked with mine as his hand lowered into the bikini. His eyes didn't waver when he slid one finger inside me.

I hissed. Throwing my head back, I started to rock on his finger as he thrust it rhythmically inside of me.

"No, look at me," he commanded.

When I looked back down, he slid a second finger in me. I had to bite my bottom lip to stop the shameless sounds that were building in my throat.

"The condoms are in the bag," he exhaled, a quiet desperation in his voice. It was as if watching me come undone was undoing him too.

I shook my head, rocking my hips, chasing my pleasure. "You don't need one," I managed to get out, panting shamelessly. "You said you love sex bare. Willis gave me the shot. We're good."

"Thank fuck!" He moved my bikini bottom to the side and entered me in one powerful thrust, causing me to arch my back. I threw my head back from the pleasure of having him buried in me, every rational thought being stripped away.

I wrapped my arms around his neck as he gripped my hips to keep me in place during each powerful trust.

"Oh, Angel," he growled. Licking a path up my neck, he nibbled on the soft skin of my jawline. "Being in you is like stepping into heaven. I never want to leave your body."

"I'm close. Jesus, I'm so close."

He sucked one of my nipples into his mouth, biting just hard enough to bring a zing of pleasure down my spine and into my core.

"Caleb… Caleb." I rocked my hips faster, meeting him thrust for thrust until he let go of my hip and pressed his thumb against my bundle of nerves, sending me over the edge so deeply, I saw stars.

I buried my face in his neck as his thrusts turned erratic, his own release close. I sucked on his earlobe and he came in an earth-shattering roar.

"I never want to let you go," he whispered, wrapping his arms around me, him still inside.

I wasn't sure if he meant now or ever, but if I was honest, both were fine by me. Because as terrified as it made me feel, I'd never felt as happy – as safe and happy – as I was when I was in his arms.

Chapter 19 – Caleb

Come to the Council Room alone. That was one hell of a text. I had to admit that being summoned by Archibald in such a way was aggravating and only served to get on my nerves.

It didn't matter how well my morning had started - when Esmeralda had woken me up the best way she could, with her lips around my cock. Who the hell did he think he was? I was the King.

"Why the frown?" Esmeralda asked as we walked down the corridor, her hand tightly in mine. Now that she was truly mine, I wanted to show it to the whole school, code be damned. If that made me look like a lovesick fool, just one look into her bright eyes was enough to dismiss any concern I could have had.

"I thought what we did this morning would have been enough to cheer you up for this first day back at school," she whispered.

I raised an eyebrow. "Maybe I just need a top-up?" I pointed at a broom closet down the corridor. "Are you game?"

She swatted at my chest with a startled laugh. "Absolutely not! I'm in enough trouble as it is!"

I trailed the back of my hand over her lower abdomen. "Come on. I just want to see your tattoo again."

I'd gotten a small Iron Man mask on the left side of my chest for Theo, an homage to his favorite superhero. When she'd shown hers to me after the tattoo session, I'd felt like I had a vice constricting my heart and lungs.

She had mirrored my heart tattoo with the addition of angel wings. It was situated in a place I hoped no other man would ever see. It should only be mine to see, to touch, to kiss… If only she knew what that tattoo meant to me. The irony of it. It was an ode to her and now she was wearing it too.

She stood on her tiptoes and gave me a quick kiss on the lips. "It's scabbed and gross, and you saw it this morning. Plus -" she pointed at a door down the corridor - "I'm going to be late."

I let go of her hand with a sigh. I didn't have to fake that. I was a sucker for this girl and it was always difficult for me to part from her. I was wondering if it was because my heart lived in her chest or because part of me still feared she would disappear again.

"See you later, Angel." I bent down to kiss the crown of her head.

She walked backward, resting her hand on her chest with the brightest smile. She always lit up when I called her Angel.

Once she disappeared into her room, I sighed again, then made my way to the Council Room.

Archibald was leaning against the table, his arms crossed on his chest.

"You called?" I sneered, waving my phone in his face before sliding it back into my pocket. "Since when do we have clandestine meetings, you and I? I don't remember becoming best friends…or even friends at all."

He rolled his eyes. "I'm here to talk about Esmeralda. I believe it's the only thing we have in common - this desire to keep her safe and happy."

I was glad he knew my desire to protect her was paramount, but I was still suspicious.

"I believe matters involving Esmeralda should be discussed with Esmeralda present."

"Esmeralda is sometimes not the most logical when she has a decision to make involving feelings. She thinks with her heart, not her head."

I crossed my arms over my chest. "Okay…" I was not committing to an answer even if I couldn't agree more. Archibald and I were raised to be cold thinkers even if my impulses toward Esmeralda were much more directed by my heart than my brain. But she was all feelings and impulsive reactions. It was a blessing as much as a curse.

"I mean, her getting a tattoo was the stupidest thing ever and you, letting her do it…"

"Have you seen her tattoo?" I asked. Even if he was her brother, I couldn't stop the dark edge in my voice. It was no place for a brother to see.

"No, God, no!" The horror on his face was almost comical. "She was giggling about it with Taylor like an enamored schoolgirl." He cocked his head to the side. "Which, in retrospect, is exactly what she is."

I couldn't deny that I was more than pleased at the idea of an enamored Esmeralda.

"I didn't let her do anything. She's a grown woman, Archibald. If she wants a tattoo, she should be able to have a tattoo." I didn't need to admit that it appealed to my male ego, my inner caveman, to have my brand on her skin.

"Fine." He threw his hands up in exasperation. "But it's just that she was talking about coming to Brown with me."

I tensed. "When?"

"Before New York."

Was that why she'd asked where we were going? I hated the idea of her going to Providence, away from me. "Okay, and what happened?"

"I sent her the brochure and the application form. A formality, really. The Dean said he just needed it for a paper trail. She said she wanted to wait a bit, that she wanted to, and I quote, 'weigh up her options'. I can't help but wonder if what she is weighing is about a hundred and sixty pounds of blond assholry."

"One hundred and seventy-two please, and what if it is the case? We're together."

"For how long?"

As long as she wants me, I almost replied but sudden voices behind the door made Archibald grab my arm and pull me into the file storage room.

"What the fuck?!" I whispered, turning on the light on my phone.

"Us together in a room would be suspicious. I panicked," he whispered back.

I rolled my eyes. "Oh, yeah, and us together in a dark storage room would be a picture of innocence by comparison."

He shrugged with a sheepish smile.

"You know I love you, Tay, the best way I can love a woman – the deepest way, but it's not enough," St. Vincent said as he walked into the room.

Of course it had to be St. Vincent and Oppenheimer. Now I knew Forbes would tackle me before I even tried to open the door. He was leaning closer to the door, eager to hear this conversation.

"Why not?"

You know why, you idiot. He likes penises, I thought with irritation.

"Because you deserve better, sweetheart, and you know that."

"Is it because of Philip?" she asked with uncertainty.

She didn't think she was really dating him, right? No, she couldn't be that clueless.

"No, Philip and I were never serious. I can't have a relationship here, in this town, in this country."

Archibald turned sharply toward me, his eyes widening in realization. 'Gay?!' he mouthed to me.

I rolled my eyes again. Fuck, this guy could be so clueless.

"You're leaving, aren't you?" Her voice was small.

"Yes, I'm sorry. I don't want to leave you behind, but I've been accepted to La Sorbonne."

"Oh, that's amazing! Oh, Antoine, I'm so happy for you!"

He chuckled. "Yes, and I think our fake relationship won't last the distance. Have you told Esmeralda yet?"

"About college?"

"Yes."

"In a way. In passing." She sighed.

"So, no."

"I will…soon. What are you doing?"

"Texting them. I have news to share."

It took me a second to realize what that meant, but it was a second too long as both mine and Archibald's phones pinged at the reception of the text.

We both froze, looking at each other, each hoping that maybe they hadn't heard it, but I should have known better. When was the last time life had given me a break?

The door opened and I faced a smirking St. Vincent and a glaring Oppenheimer.

"Well, well, well. Here are two guys I never thought would come out of the closet," Antoine challenged, his grin widening.

"Maybe we should switch places. It's clearly where you belong," Archibald snapped. "Isn't that right, hypocrite?"

I frowned at him. Archibald was an asshole, but he was not a bigot. "What's got into you?" I asked after we exited the closet.

"I hate being taken for a fool. I thought you would understand."

Bullseye. He'd gone straight for blood, but he was right.

"It's not about you, Archibald," Taylor spat. "Contrary to popular belief, you are not the center of the universe."

"Seriously guys, we need to stop that! I can't keep getting out of class by pretending I need to pee! The teachers will start to think I have a weak bladder," Esmeralda scowled with exasperation as she entered the room. I was grateful for the distraction.

"Or prone to a UTI with all the sex you're having with Mr. Hotshot!" Antoine pointed at me.

I cocked my head to the side. It was not a completely crazy assumption.

"Caleb!" she exclaimed. "Don't agree with him!"

"You're gay?" Archibald asked Antoine. Ah, yep, we were still on that.

Esmeralda threw me a side look and I shook my head. She really didn't want to know.

Archibald looked at her and his scowl deepened. "You knew too?!"

She returned his gaze with wide eyes, like a deer caught in the headlights. I tensed immediately, my instinct to protect her overwhelming.

"You knew how miserable I was and you didn't think about sharing?"

"Archie, it wasn't my secret to share."

"I am your brother Esme, not him." He pointed to Antoine. "Not her." He pointed to Taylor. "But me. I'm your blood. Your loyalty should be to me!" he barked, taking another step closer.

I stood in front of her. "And I think you should chill the fuck out. Right now."

Archibald's eyes flared with anger. "Are you protecting her from me?" He gestured from his chest to mine as if it was the most ludicrous thing in the world. In retrospect, it was.

Esmeralda placed her hand on my arm, trying to push me out of the way – as if there was even the slightest chance she could make me move.

"I'm just asking you to chill out. I don't like your threatening vibes."

"Why? Do you think I'll strike her?"hHe asked through gritted teeth. "Don't mistake me for you."

"It's in your blood. Like father like son." That was a cheap blow and I knew it the moment it came out.

Archie paled. It was a secret that he had shared with me when we were young, when we'd believed we would be on the same side forever. When we still thought we wouldn't have to compete. He had admitted that he had seen his father strike his mother when he'd been a toddler, and that had stayed with him.

Before, I wouldn't have regretted saying this to him, but it seemed that Esmeralda's goodness had tainted my soul because I regretted my words as soon as they'd passed my lips. I was not foolish enough to apologize though.

Esmeralda dodged in front of me and pushed me with all her might. She barely made me stumble a step.

"Caleb, enough!" She was a fierce kitten – defensive of her own, but as threatening as said kitten.

She turned to Archibald. "Please, Archie, you know I'm right. You know I couldn't just do that. There's so much history I'm not privy to. I couldn't meddle."

Archibald looked down at her, his lips pursed. He sighed before turning to Antoine. "So you wanted to talk?"

I felt Esmeralda's pain as she recoiled under her brother's dismissal. It took all of my willpower not to punch him unconscious, but Esmeralda wouldn't want me to pick that battle, that much was certain. With her already angry with me, I couldn't afford to make it worse.

Her rejection was my rejection. Her pain, my pain. Was this what love did to you?

I brushed my fingers against the back of her arm. She moved away, but I decided not to press the issue. She was hurt and angry.

Antoine looked from Archibald to Esmeralda with regret on his face. Did he regret driving a wedge between siblings who had only just found their connection? He should. Secrets and lies only served to poison anything good. There were no white lies, not really. The ultimate goal was always selfish.

He shook his head. "Yeah, we finally managed to track the number Phang called. He called it twelve times that evening. It was more difficult to track than I'd expected. It went from a pizza chain to a private investor firm to some construction company to–."

"Can we just wrap it up? The suspense is unnecessary," Archibald interrupted. He wanted to get away and lick his wounds in private. It was something I could understand better than anyone.

"Anyway," Antoine shrugged. "The ultimate owner is Matracon Corp."

Esmeralda was puzzled by the revelation. She didn't know about our businesses.

"It is my father's company," I clarified for her benefit. "But it makes no sense. He was genuinely worried about Esmeralda when he'd found out about the car. He hired extra security. Granted, I think he knows more than he is saying and something is on his mind, but he wouldn't have tried to kill her."

"He is your father, so I–" Antoine started.

"No," I shook my head. "This is not some kind of family loyalty. He is scum and a borderline pedo. I know what he is. I have no illusions. I am sure he would have it in him to kill someone or at least have someone do it, but this is not him."

Archibald sighed heavily. At least he believed me. "Okay, so we're back to square one?"

I shook my head. "Not necessarily."

"So what now?" Archibald asked.

"Now -" I turned to Esmeralda - "we get married."

The room turned silent, but I was pleased to see that Esmeralda looked intrigued more than anything. It was not the outright rejection of the idea that she used to show me.

"Are you out of your mind?" Archibald hissed after he recovered from the initial shock. "Are you really trying to get her killed? Marriage is not the solution, especially if you're going to divorce a week later."

I tensed at his words because they'd hit home. Esmeralda cared about me. I couldn't deny that, but she had run the first chance she'd gotten and that was not something I could forget even if I wanted to. And there was always that question: given the right circumstances, would she leave again? We couldn't get married until I had certainty in my answers. I would not allow it.

"Not for real, Archibald!" I snapped at him.

"Oh, you'll hire a fake pastor? Like in the movies?" Antoine asked, beaming. That man really had a taste for theatrics.

"Ant?" Taylor shook her head. "Not right now."

I threw him a look which I hoped conveyed all my annoyance. When he looked away, I knew I'd succeeded.

"We have the pre-wedding party next week. Let's go through with it. Everybody will be in the same house." I pointed at Archibald. "It will allow you to sneak back to your place and look around in peace. Because our house will be full of people, all of the alarms will have to be disconnected, including the one linked to my mother's quarters."

"So I can sneak in there and try to find clues," Esmeralda offered.

"Yes, you or someone else," I offered. I hated the idea of putting her in danger, but she was still annoyed about my altercation with Archibald. "We'll all be there, making it easier to monitor and keep an eye on things without looking suspicious."

Archibald cocked his head to the side, pondering my plan. I could see he hated that it made sense, that he hadn't thought of it before me. "It could work," he admitted reluctantly.

"It will work," I pressed confidently.

Archibald sneered. "It'd better work because if it doesn't, my sister will become an Astor a week later whether she wants to or not."

"Archie, I'm sure we–"

"Are we done here?" he asked, cutting her off.

She winced at the rebuff and looked down in frustration. Lord, did I want to end his life.

"I think so, yes," I replied instead.

He gave us a sharp nod and turned around briskly, leaving the room with his back straight with tension.

I nudged Esmeralda. "Go after him."

She looked up at me with confusion.

I gave her a small smile, gently brushing my knuckles on her cheek. "Trust me on this. He might not know it, but he wants you to follow him, to be there in his distress even if he mistakenly thinks you've got a part to play in it. He wants you to fight for him."

I knew that because that had been me once. I'd wanted someone to care enough to keep on coming, no matter how much I'd pushed them away.

"Thank you."

I kissed the top of her head. "Anytime. He is probably behind the pool."

She smiled at me once more. I watched her as she left the room and took my human part with her.

Antoine scoffed, "I never thought I'd see the day Caleb Astor would be pussy-whipped."

"Nope," Taylor said, taking a step away from him as I turned around slowly.

"And why don't you two go get fucked?" I growled. "You've put her in a very bad situation with Archibald."

"I didn't–" Taylor started.

I raised my hand to stop her. "Yes, you did! You never should have put her in the middle of all this. You're her best friend; he's her brother. There was no winning for her. You knew it couldn't end well."

"Okay, you shouldn't be all self-righteous either. You've been the worst of all of us."

I nodded. "True. I am not denying that, but I need you to fix it with Archibald. I don't care what you do or how you do it. Things need to be fixed by the party next weekend. Are we clear?"

"Crystal."

"Perfect." I walked to the door. "Oh, and St. Vincent?"

"Yeah?"

"Our parents won't be in charge forever. Be who the fuck you want to be because nobody really cares," I added before leaving to see if Esmeralda was okay.

Chapter 20 - Esme

The night of the party arrived much faster than I'd expected. The stress was so high I wasn't sure I would get through the evening and the plan without a fault. All eyes would be on us tonight. We were the golden couple. Vanishing, as we'd planned to do, would be really difficult.

"Up or down?"

I turned my head to look at the stylist. "Excuse me?"

She sighed. "Have you listened to anything I've said?"

No." I threw her a chilly look I hoped was as good as Caleb's. Apparently, she was a big deal and hard to get, but I really didn't appreciate her talking to me as if I was a difficult child.

A knock on my door distracted me. I laughed with relief when Sophia entered the room.

"Oh, Esmeralda, honey, you are so beautiful!" She smiled at me and the tenderness in her eyes thawed me a little. "I hope I'm not bothering."

I smiled gratefully at her. "No, I'm so happy you're here."

"Would you mind leaving us?" Sophia asked the stylist.

"I'm not done!"

"Her makeup is done and her dress is laced. I can do her hair. I need time with the future bride."

"But–"

"Thank you," I announced, not leaving any room for discussion.

She shook her head and grumbled, "Unbelievable."

"I don't like her," I admitted as soon as the door closed behind her.

Sophia waved her hand dismissively. "Nobody does, dear. We just accept her because she's good. I hope you don't mind me coming to see you? I've barely seen you since you came back."

"I'm sorry," I said and I meant it. I did like Sophia a lot, but I'd had too many things to deal with and the last week had been spent trying to mend things with my brother. Our relationship was still tense, but he'd started to understand that I hadn't been trying to betray him. Caleb's advice to go after him had been perfect. I always knew those two were much more similar than they wanted to admit. But maybe that was why things were always so difficult between them...

"It's alright. I'm glad your father's plan to destroy you, failed. Sit. Let me do your hair. Everybody is here. It will soon be time for the couple of the day to make an appearance."

I nodded and sat silently as she braided my hair.

"Oh, also I received your wedding dress yesterday," she let out as if it was nothing.

As she brought my braids up in a type of crown, I met her eyes in the mirror. We both knew I hadn't ordered a dress.

"That's…great."

"Uh huh. I don't know what you kids are planning, but it looked far too suspicious that a couple of weeks before the wedding, there was no dress. Your father is not stupid, Esme. He was getting suspicious. And please tell your brother to be more discreet when he is snooping around the house. I am not sure how long I can keep distracting your father."

I didn't know what to say, once again touched by her help without even asking for it.

"I can see you are genuinely fond of Caleb Astor, but you're only eighteen. You've barely lived. Nobody should be forced into something they don't want. You shouldn't be making big choices now. You need to experience life before settling down."

"Are you talking from experience?" I asked, standing up, knowing she had barely been an adult when she'd been thrown into my father's net.

"I am," she confirmed as she helped me straighten the lavender silk of my floor-length dress.

"Tell Archie that your father changed the safe code. It's your mother's date of birth now. Tell him he has another safe in the basement behind the bar; the code is 1929. Also let him know that there is a security system he doesn't know about. Once he gets into the house and disables the alarm, he will need to disable the secret alarm your father has for his office and the basement. The control is in our room, behind the Venice painting."

"How–"

"How do I know all this?" She laughed. "Being the idiot wife helped me, Esme – being underestimated was my strength. Use this information wisely. I believe in you."

We were leaving our room when Caleb exited his with Archie on his tail. They were both stunning in their custom-made tuxedos. There was so much power in these two guys. They were forces to be reckoned with.

I reached up and touched the wings necklace Caleb had bought me. For some reason it made me feel safer to wear it.

His eyes followed my hand. He flashed me a little smile as he moved his arms a little to show me the cufflinks I'd bought him.

Wanting to be close to him, I took a couple of steps toward him. When I extended my hand, he eagerly took it and kissed the back of it.

"Angel, you're stunning," he whispered, his eyes shining with love and adoration.

I took a step closer, leaning against him. "You look super-hot. Tonight I'll make you strip," I whispered. I kissed his cheek gently, making sure not to leave any lipstick on his skin.

"Oh God, you two are adorable!" Sophia beamed, resting her hands on her heart. "Archibald, let's go down and let everyone know the lovely couple is on their way."

She turned to me and gave me a look full of meaning. Be careful, be discreet and be smart – I could see it all on her face.

"What was that all about?" Caleb asked when they disappeared down the corridor.

"She's on our side. We made mistakes and she fixed them. I–" I turned toward Caleb. "She is our ally."

Caleb looked down at me, detailing my face. "Maybe, but she is in it for something."

I shook my head. "I don't think so."

He chuckled. "She knows we're after your father?"

I nodded.

"Yeah," he said as we started down the corridor slowly. "Imagine what her life would be like if your father was gone? Rich and no strings attached. Please, Esmeralda, I'm not saying she won't be a decent help, I'm just saying there's no help without ulterior motives."

"Oh yeah? If it's true, then you've got an ulterior motive too."

"Of course!" he scoffed as we started down the stairs where our families were waiting for us.

"And what is it?"

"You, Esmeralda Forbes, always you."

Butterflies invaded my stomach and I squeezed his arm tighter.

As soon as we reached the foot of the stairs, I was swept into a hug by James. He hugged me longer and tighter than necessary. We were then led into the main room where we were welcomed by applause. After thirty minutes of congratulations, people finally concentrated on their own groups and discussions again.

Archie came toward us, a sly smile on his face. "So, future brother-in-law, may I challenge you to a game of pool?" he asked, slapping Caleb on the back.

"Can I join?" Antoine asked, clapping his hands together.

"Of course!" Archie took a sip of his drink. "I'll enjoy destroying you both."

I laughed. I knew it was all a ploy; there would not be any game. Archie would slip out by the games room window and go home, while Caleb looked through his father's things, and Antoine monitored the situation from the feeds on his phone.

"Brother, let me give you a hug for good luck." I pulled him to me and whispered in his ear everything Sophia had told me.

He pulled back, his hands on my shoulders, his eyes full of wonder and incredulity.

I nodded with a small smile. "Trust me, please," I whispered.

He kissed my forehead. "Always," he whispered. I knew then that we were going to be okay.

I looked at Taylor standing by her parents. She would be my decoy after a few minutes. I was supposed to take her upstairs to show her some wedding preps. She would then stay in my room, whilst I went into Jacklyn's room to see what I could find.

Neither Caleb nor Archie were thrilled about getting me involved in the plan, but I was the main reason for all this. It would have taken everything they had to keep me away.

"I need to ask Sophia to take care of Jacklyn."" I turned around and froze. "No, this has to be a mistake. Ben?" I whispered with incredulity as he turned from his spot. There was no denying Ben was here.

I looked up at Caleb with horror. "Caleb, no, I swear it wasn't me."

He cupped my cheek, redirecting my attention toward him. "No, I know. I asked him here."

I frowned. That was a cruel thing to do. Not that Ben and I were ever that close, but flaunting it in his face was still so unkind. "It's bad, that, Caleb."

He shook his head. "I didn't ask him here to be bad. He did something for me and we need to discuss it with you. And look -" he jerked his head toward our fathers, who were not fixed on Ben - "it's bound to keep them occupied."

"But–"

He nudged me toward Sophia. "We need to move. Go tell your stepmother to distract Jacklyn and get Oppenheimer. Keep your phone on you at all times, okay?"

I walked to Sophia. "Thank you so much for coming." I pulled her into a hug. "Keep Jacklyn busy and text me if she leaves the room," I whispered into her ear before stepping back.

She smiled back at me, but the confusion was clear in her eyes. "Of course, anything for my beautiful stepdaughter."

I nodded, the fake smile starting to hurt my cheeks. "I just need to borrow Tay for a few minutes." I pointed to where the

Oppenheimers were. Taylor was talking to a couple I'd never seen before.

"Sometimes I forget that these types of weddings are not for the actual bride and groom.

"Tay!" I exclaimed a bit too cheerfully. I needed to rein it in.

"Esmeralda! I was just about to come find you."

I greeted her parents before interlacing her arm with mine. "Do you mind if I borrow my maid of honor from you? I have a couple of orders to make tomorrow and would like some help with color schemes."

Taylor's mother nodded. "Of course. Please do. My daughter has impeccable taste."

That I could not deny. Taylor was always the epitome of fashion.

"We'll be back soon," Taylor chirped.

"Take your time, sweetheart." Her father kissed her forehead. "We'll be here."

"Your family is amazing, you know," I whispered. We made our way out of the room as nonchalantly as we could. I couldn't help but wonder if my brother was already gone or if Caleb was already sniffing around. Most of all, I worried about poor Ben. He thought he was stepping into a high-society party. He didn't know he was surrounded by sharks wanting to shred him to pieces.

"Don't worry about your friend Ben," Taylor said, almost reading my thoughts. "He knows what to expect. He's been briefed."

"How do you know?" I asked curiously.

"He told me."

I almost missed a step up. "You talked to him? Why?"

She shrugged. "I've got your back. I thought he was crashing. I wanted to kick him to the curb, but he is here on a mission."

"What mission?"

She shook her head. "He didn't say and I didn't ask. We have other things to worry about now."

I nodded. She was right. I needed to keep my head in the game, find something to save us. We had three chances to get it right tonight. I couldn't mess up my part.

"Okay, so what now?" She asked when we entered my bedroom.

I opened my laptop. "I've recorded myself saying things." I pointed at the screen, which displayed a selection of clips including 'just a minute', 'what is it?', 'I'm trying something', 'I'm not decent', and other sentences I had prerecorded.

"Are you sure you want to do that?" she asked, chewing on her bottom lip, a frown deep between her eyebrows.

"I'll be okay. I need thirty minutes, forty-five tops. They won't even notice we're gone."

"Okay…" She trailed off, the uncertainty clear in her voice.

"And what are they going to do, kill me?" I tried in an attempt at humor.

Her scowl deepened. "That's not funny!" she hissed.

"Oh, come on, it's a little funny."

"No, it's not." She pointed at the door. "Now go before you say something even stupider."

I chuckled and exited the room, finally letting go of the fake bravado I'd been showing to my friend. I walked down the corridor to Jacklyn's room and used the master key Caleb had given me. Nobody knew he had that. He'd made a copy when he was fourteen when his father had left his keys out in the open. Caleb had known they would be useful one day and today was that day.

Jacklyn's room was enormous and so not what I'd expected. It was strange for someone who'd lived in the same space for the past twenty-odd years.

All of the furniture looked plush and practical with not much extra. It looked a lot like a French country bedroom I'd seen in one of Sophia's decoration magazines. Her king bed was covered in floral print bedding, fluffy pillows, and a couple of colorful throws. A tufted cream headboard was at one end, a cushioned ottoman at the other. A comfy-looking armchair with a flowery blanket on top of it sat beside the wide French doors, which I suspected led out on to a balcony.

The cream walls sported some bird cage reproductions, making me wonder if it was supposed to be a giant 'fuck you' to the life we led. There was an enormous three-way antique mirror by the walk-in closet and a vintage set of drawers on which sat the only things that made the room personal – three photos of her and Theo. It made me angry and sad at the same time how dismissive of Caleb she'd always been. It was not his fault if he was not conceived the way he should have been. He'd still been an innocent baby, nothing more.

I sighed. Shaking my head, I concentrated on the task at hand. I'd have to have a conversation with Jacklyn about the photos though. Well, if she wasn't my mother's murderer.

My frustration was reaching a new high the more I looked. Her room was the most boring place I'd ever been in. There was nothing of interest here.

In my last attempt to find something, anything really, I rounded the bed and lifted the mattress. Who knew? She might have had the soul of a fifteen-year-old boy hiding porn. But yet again, there was nothing to be found.

"Oh, for the love of God!" I growled in frustration. I laid on the floor for a minute, just letting the desperation get to me.

I rolled over onto my front to stand up. In doing so I looked under the night table and saw there was something there…definitely. I slid my hand under and it grazed against the smooth surface of a box.

Hope and excitement resurfaced as I pulled the table up a little to get the box out. I knelt by the bed and opened the box. There were some photos in it, some of Theo with Caleb, and a brown envelope with my name on it. My hands shook. The handwriting was so familiar and inside were the pages of the journal I'd sent Caleb. It was her. It had been her all along.

"Can I help you with anything?

I looked up, startled to find Jacklyn glaring at me from her position in front of the closed door.

"You sent me the journal?" I asked, extending the envelope toward her. How could it be her? After everything, how could she have been my mother's ally?

"You're J. Astor?! Luke had asked the wrong Astor for help."

She glowered even more now. "This is none of your business."

I jerked up, offended by her quick dismissal. "Like hell it's not my business! I thought you were trying to kill me, but you were trying to help me?" Saying it out loud didn't help it make any more sense.

"Kill you?" She laughed. "Why on earth would I want to kill you?"

"Why on earth would you want to kill your son?" I knew it was the wrong thing to say, but I couldn't help myself.

"Get out of my room. Now!" she commanded.

I took a step back, closer to the window, but keeping the envelope in my hand. "No." I shook my head. "I won't leave before you explain everything to me."

Jacklyn paled. I didn't understand why until I felt cold metal press against my temple and the distinctive sound of the hammer of a gun being cocked.

"Hello, Esmeralda," said a voice behind me.

"Miss White?" I asked in shock. No, it wasn't possible; this had to be a mistake. She'd been so nice to me, so welcoming and supportive. Why would she want me dead?

She slipped behind me, wrapping her free arm around my neck. "I'm sorry it had to come to this, Esme, but you are too stubborn for your own good."

I tried to move within her grasp, but she tightened her arm around my neck. She was much stronger than she seemed. "But you were my friend. I liked you!" I was hoping that I could talk her down. It didn't have to come to this. "Whatever it is, I'm sure we can fix it."

Jacklyn was staring at us, her back against the wall by the door, her hands clasped against her heart. I wouldn't blame her if she bolted. Hell, I would even approve.

Anne White pressed the gun a bit more firmly against my temple. "I told you to stop looking. I told you nothing good would come from it, but you didn't listen." Her voice was quivering, with anger or fear I wasn't sure, but it didn't fit the 'stone-cold killer' persona she was trying to invoke.

"I did listen. I stopped!" And I'd done it only because I'd believed her. Why had I been that stupid?

"Don't lie to me. Everybody lies. I can't take it anymore," she growled.

"I'm not lying. We started the whole investigation when you tried to kill me with the wine. That is what made us speed up."

"The wine was not for you; it was for her!" She jerked her head toward Jacklyn, who took an involuntary step toward us. "Don't move or I swear you'll have to scrape her brains from your wall," Anne barked at Jacklyn before turning back to me. "James always told me how high she was on her meds. An overdose wouldn't have been suspicious. It would have been kind really."

The gun shook against my head, making it all even more terrifying. She was unstable enough to just pull the trigger by accident at this point.

"You were supposed to be back! I heard them talk in the corridor. Your son said you would be back and I knew what a train wreck you are. You can't resist Gewurst! You were supposed to drink the wine and die. Why didn't you die?!" she cried out. "If you did, James would have been free and he would have married me like he promised."

Jacklyn threw me a worried look, bringing her hands up in surrender. "James made me the train wreck I am, just as he made you the woman holding a gun at an innocent child's head. With or without me, James wouldn't have picked you. He would not leave me for anyone. Killing Esmeralda won't help you with that."

"Esmeralda brought this on herself," she spat.

I prayed Caleb would realize I was missing. I hoped Taylor would call someone, anyone. I'd been gone longer than planned.

My heart was in my throat. I didn't want to die. Why was life so determined to kill me? I started to sweat. I had so much more to do, so much more to say. I couldn't go now. Caleb needed to know how I felt.

"Please, Miss White, I swear I don't know anything. Just let us go."

She laughed. "I'm not stupid. I would not make it as far as the property boundary before being gunned down like a dog. You should never have sent someone to Oklahoma. This was none of your business."

"Is that why you cut the brakes on my car? Because you thought I sent someone to investigate you?"

"No, I cut the brakes of your car because of the yearbook, because you kept looking into me when I told you to stop. I thought you would die and when that stupid bitch Aleksandra died in your stead, I thought you would be scared and smart enough to let it go. I liked you enough to give you another chance to reconsider and make the right choice, but you had to keep on going! Because of you, he doesn't want me anymore! He said I'd gone too far and then told me to leave and never come back. He said we were through for good just because of precious little Esmeralda Forbes." She sneered. "Perfect. Little. Esmeralda. Forbes." She tapped the barrel against my temple with each word.

"No, we didn't send anyone there. We didn't want to waste resources on someone we didn't think was relevant. I didn't send anyone to Oklahoma, I swear."

"You did," she insisted. "Your little boyfriend from Missouri, he talked to the wrong people, Esmeralda."

"No, she didn't send him. I did," Caleb announced, sidling into the room followed by his father, who was looking at White with murder in his eyes.

I felt both strangely at peace and terrified to have him in the room with me and the unstable woman with a gun.

"Anna, what do you think you're doing?" James asked coldly, his eyes on the weapon.

Ah, he knew who she really was. I glanced at Caleb. He was looking around the room trying to assess the situation, but his eyes always came back to the gun against my head.

"Anna, come on. I'll take you home."

"This is all on you! You will not mess with my head again. I don't believe you anymore. You played me for twenty years! No more!" She spat at James, some of her spittle covering my cheek.

"Just put the gun down, Anna, and let's talk," James tried again, bringing a hand forward in a pacifying gesture.

She shook her head. "I hate you! I finally hate you…" she sobbed, the gun shaking against my head again.

I took a deep, shaky breath as my eyes locked with Caleb's. Despite the fear I saw in his, I felt a certain comfort. 'I love you,' I mouthed to him.

His jaw locked, his eyes morphing from fear to determination. "Take me instead," he told her. "I'm his heir."

"Caleb, have you lost your damn mind?!" James barked at him and for the first time, I saw genuine concern in his eyes.

"Why not?" White asked, taking the bait. "You took our baby away. Maybe it will be retribution. I was eighteen, James! Eighteen! 'It's not the right time for a child, Anna; Jacklyn is pregnant, Anna; we'll have a family soon, you and I, but I need time to make things right for us. We need to deal with your commitment to William first. You can't have my child now, but later. I swear, Anna,' and I'd listened! I. LISTENED!"

I froze. Despite having a gun to my head, I couldn't help but feel bad for her. This was the man she'd told me she was in love with. She'd been so into him that she had done all of his biddings.

"Anna, doing this will get you nowhere," James pleaded.

Jacklyn snorted. "You're really good at destroying a woman's sanity, James. I have to give you that." Her bravado was back. She was standing straighter, her arms crossed on her chest. The hate she felt for her husband finally had purpose.

"Not now, Jacklyn. Not now."

I had to hand it to her. She was a cold bitch, but I couldn't help but be impressed. She was a force to be reckoned with.

"When you told me that you couldn't get over your obsession with Victoria, I understood what you wanted!" White pressed on. "When you told me you would be able to move on and be with me if she was gone, I did it for you! Always for you! You made me a murderer and gave me nothing more than empty promises."

"Don't listen to her. She is obviously lying," James scoffed.

I glared at him. Sure, why not antagonize the scorned woman with a gun.

"Actually, I don't think she is," Caleb piped in, taking a step closer. Anne missed it, but I didn't. I silently begged him to stay back. "She might have done it, but she didn't have the means or the power to get Phang on board, to hide evidence and create fake reports. Only you did," he added, looking at his father. His voice was eerily calm like he was planning something.

"Caleb, you don't know what you're talking about. You'd better shut up," James barked, letting go of his mask and showing us the monster he truly was.

"Phang called you, didn't he? He told you we went poking around. We were tracking his phone by the way. You walked right into that one."

"Victoria didn't want him. That was inconceivable for James Astor, but he was much too proud to just take her out," Jacklyn said. She waved her hand toward Ms. White. "He used the idiot here to do it for him. Don't blame yourself, honey, you're not the first one to do idiotic things for this man, me included."

I looked at her with confusion. Then anger overtook my fear. Was she trying to get me killed? How could she look so cool and composed?

Jacklyn waved her hand dismissively. "Let the little girl go. Kill him instead. It'll teach him."

Ah, I see. Redirecting the gun was her tactic and it wasn't a bad one for anyone who wanted to take her husband out.

"He is obsessed with her," Anne countered. "She looks just like Victoria."

Jacklyn shook her head. "He is just obsessed with her because she is Caleb's and the boy was foolish enough to fall in love with her. James thrives on misery. Caleb is not allowed to succeed where he failed. Isn't that right James? Whoever your son will ever love, you'll take away? To make him the perfect, cold, and bitter heir you want him to be?"

"You're right," White whispered so softly that I was convinced it was not meant for anyone's ears. "The only thing that matters to him is his heir."

The gun moved from the side of my head, but I didn't feel any relief as she pointed it at Caleb's instead. "The only thing you care about is your legacy. I'm going to take it from you, even if it's the last thing I do! You took my child, I'm taking yours!"

Caleb looked at me, his eyes glistening with unshed tears. He gave me a small smile as if to say 'it's okay. I'll happily die for you. I love you.'

"ANNA, DON'T!" James roared as Jacklyn's face morphed into pure horror.

I felt it before she did it. White's body tensed, bracing for the recoil of the gun, and I just reacted. I couldn't let Caleb die, not for me, not for anyone. I pushed backward with all my strength, with all that I felt, the fear of Caleb being gone. The power these feelings, this surge of adrenaline, gave me, surprised me as we went through the French doors in an audible crash.

I heard her scream at the same time as pain slashed through me. The remains of broken glass had broken through my skin. Then suddenly White was not behind me anymore and I fell freely. The last thing I saw before my head connected with the hard floor of the balcony was James holding his throat. Blood poured through his fingers. His face was frozen in sheer shock. I felt the crack of my skull all the way to the bottom of my spine. Everything became blurry, the voices muffled. But I knew Caleb was safe and so I sank into oblivion in relative peace.

Chapter 21- Caleb

I fell in and out of sleep to the rhythmic beat of the hospital heart monitor – the proof that my Esmeralda was still with us. I moved in my seat, wincing as my neck cracked. I was going to pay for these last two nights spent on this uncomfortable chair, but there was no way in hell I was going to leave Esme after she'd risked her life for me.

That crazy bitch had really planned on killing me. If it hadn't been for Esmeralda, I would have been gone.

"That really doesn't look comfortable."

I opened my eyes wide and looked at the most beautiful eyes in the world. My heart finally started to beat normally again.

"Then please stop trying to die on me – three times is the maximum I can endure losing you for a lifetime." I stood up and winced at the pain shooting through my back and legs. "Are you thirsty?" I asked.

She looked at the pitcher of water like it was the gift of life and nodded eagerly. Her voice had been thick and gravelly, most likely due to both the prolonged sleep and dry throat.

I poured her a glass and sat gently on the bed by her head. Sliding my arm under her back, I helped her rest her head against my shoulder. Lord, how would I ever be able to live without her by my side?

You might have to. You might have to be the bigger person and let her go, my conscience claimed. It was a voice I'd always ignored before. I'd had it smothered, but she had revived it. Oh, the irony of it all…

"How long have I been out?" she asked after taking a long drink.

"Two days," I replied, kissing her forehead.

"Your father? Oh God, Caleb." She shook her head against my arm. "I killed him, didn't I?"

Was she crazy? I looked down at her. The man had organized her mother's murder and she felt bad? I frowned. "Do you remember what happened?"

She blinked back her tears. "Mostly."

I sighed, kissing the crown of her head. "You didn't kill him; White did. And she would have killed me if it wasn't for you Esmeralda. In retrospect I think it was a good trade-off."

"No, I know that. It's just–"

"Listen, Angel, listen to me carefully. He was a very bad man who did terrible things. He was happy only when he destroyed and hurt others. He had your mother killed, Esmeralda, and Lord knows who else." I tightened my hold around her shoulders, resting my cheek on top of her head. "He had it coming and it was what he deserved. You saved my life, but you can't ever do that again, okay? Never put yourself in danger for me or anyone else. I don't think I could live in a world you're not in."

She nuzzled into my neck silently and I loved that. I loved that she was seeking me for comfort. "What about White?"

"She got arrested, but she killed herself in the cell. She'd lost the source of her obsession by her own hand. She wasn't equipped to deal with that." I didn't specify that I was almost certain her suicide had been a cover-up. She'd known too much, but Esmeralda didn't need the added burden – not all truths had to be revealed.

"Let's just ring for the doctor, okay? Just to make sure everything is fine." I reluctantly removed myself from the bed and pressed the buzzer.

"What are you doing?" she asked when I reached for my phone.

"Texting your brother." I sighed. "He's going to be so pissed at me." Well more than he'd previously been. I'd thought he was going to kill me when Esmeralda was put into an ambulance. I rubbed at my jaw, wincing at the phantom pain of his fist.

I hadn't defended myself. I'd deserved it. I was the one who used Esmeralda for this investigation. Willingly or not, I'd put her in danger.

"Why would Archibald be mad at you?"

Take your pick. "Because I'd only just convinced him to go home and rest. Oh well."

"He'll be okay." She smiled reassuringly.

Dr. Willis walked in with a nurse. "Miss Forbes, we really need to stop meeting like this."

She nodded with a small smile. "It's the last time, I promise."

He looked at me expectantly and I sat on the chair. Crossing my arms on my chest, I made my intentions clear.

"He can stay," Esmeralda offered as the doctor started his assessment.

"You got lucky, Miss Forbes. Once again you defied the odds," he said, draping his stethoscope over his shoulders.

And thank fuck for that! I wanted to say. At least life was not fucked up enough to take away the only good thing left in it.

"You suffered a closed skull fracture due to your fall. It was luckily minimal enough to avoid surgery, but you may still suffer from side effects given the two-day coma you were in."

"Okay?" She sounded frightened and started chewing on her bottom lip as she often did when she was anxious. I was somehow pleased by it. I hoped he would scare her enough to stop her from doing something this stupid in the future.

"We're going to keep you here for the next seventy-two hours. I'm sure you will be fine, but it will just be an extra precaution."

"Whatever you think is best," I responded in her stead.

She threw me an annoyed look that I held steadily. She could fight me on this all she wanted. She was going to stay in this bed even if I had to tie her to it.

"Very good. Just don't hesitate to beep should you need anything." He took a few steps and stopped in front of me. "I'm sorry for your loss."

"Thank you." I pretended to believe it and he pretended I cared.

"When is the funeral?" she asked with a small voice after the doctor had left.

"Tomorrow."

Her eyes widened. "That fast? Oh, I'm sorry, Caleb. I won't be there to support you."

"My mother wants it all to be done and dusted as quickly as possible." I waved my hand dismissively from my spot on the chair. "I don't need support. You know what I felt when he was declared dead on the scene? Relief, a relief that would have made me laugh on the spot if I was not sick with worry for you." I sighed. "I just need you to get better."

She frowned. "When you came into the room that day, you said you'd sent someone to Oklahoma. Was that true?"

I nodded, pulling the chair closer to her to take her hand. I feared she might get angry with me.

I pulled her hand to my mouth and kissed it. "Yes, none of you wanted to listen to me. I knew there was more to her." I shook my head. "So just before New York, I called someone to help. He was reluctant at first–" I cocked my head to the side. "I mean, his pet name for me is 'sociopath,' but he did it for you."

"Ben?" she cried with incredulity.

I nodded. Ben Deluca, my ally and enemy in so many ways. My rival who was now sitting in the waiting room to talk to my girl, my heart. One I needed to offer an out. "He went under the pretense of a campus visit and managed to talk to some of White's old friends." I rolled my eyes. "He didn't do it for free though. He stayed in the most luxurious hotel and is now the proud owner of a Ducati Panigale V4R."

She chuckled. "Good for him."

"Yeah."" I nodded. "Talking about Ben, he is not a bad choice, you know." Fuck, why was this so hard? I had all the best intentions, but I felt like my heart was being shredded into pieces. "He is annoyingly good with his 'knight in shining armor' complex, but you could pick worse."

"Caleb, I don't understand." She gripped my hand tighter.

I removed my hand from hers and leaned back in my chair. I couldn't do it if I kept touching her. It would be impossible.

"I'm saying that with my father gone, I've been put in charge now and I can grant you your freedom. You can go and be who you want to be, study wherever you want to, and…be with Ben if you want to".

"What about us? You said you loved me." The hurt in her voice made me ache, but I had to give her a real choice.

"I did, I do, but if you were to choose Ben, I'd be okay– Knowing that you're happy and well somewhere, I'd be fine." I gave her a smile even though I was dying inside. With her gone I'd keep on breathing, functioning, but I would not be alive, not anymore – not like when she was in my arms.

"You want me to leave you?" Her voice was so small, so feeble I almost changed my mind.

I'd rather die. I reached in my pocket and got her engagement ring out. "No, I want you to do what you want to do. Not what you are expected to do or what you think you should do. There doesn't need to be a wedding next week. We can cancel saying that we're in mourning or we can go ahead with it, saying it would honor my father's memory." I shrugged. "We can- *You* can do literally whatever you want." I jerked my head toward the door. "Ben is waiting to see you. I'll let him in and you guys talk. Whatever you decide to do is fair, Esmeralda. You never committed to these choices, not really." I stood up.

"Caleb, no wait. Let's talk some more," she begged and I stopped by the door, considering it before shaking my head.

"See you in a bit," I said, stepping into the corridor and closing the door behind me.

"How is she?" Deluca asked from his chair outside the room, a half-drunk cup of coffee and some sports magazine at his side.

"She's good. We got lucky." I gestured to the door. "She's ready to see you."

He stood up and gave me a nod. "You're not too bad, all things considered."

"For a sociopath?" I joked.

He gave me a half-grin. "Yeah, and for a rich asshole."

I took his seat and bowed my head. "Thank you for watching out for her."

"Always," he replied, walking into her room.

I settled a bit more in the chair. Grabbing the magazine he'd left behind, I did my best to concentrate on something, anything, other than what was happening on the other side of the wall.

I rolled my eyes. Who even cared about fantasy league? I threw the magazine onto the seat beside me. I looked at my watch. Maybe a coffee would help.

I was about to go down to the hot drinks machine when Archibald stormed up the corridor, half-dressed, his hair in complete disarray.

"Sorry!" He was breathless. "I was sleeping and not sure why I didn't hear your messages."

"You were exhausted, Archibald; no surprise there. But I told you in the text that she was fine."

He frowned. "Why are you out here? Did she kick you out already?"

I chuckled, but it lacked humor. "No. Ben Deluca is in there, possibly declaring his flame to her."

"And you are letting him live?"

"I let her go," I admitted. "I told her to choose whatever she wants, that I'll be fine." I sat back in my seat.

"But I thought you loved her?" he asked with confusion.

"More than anything."

"Then why?" He shook his head.

I sighed, resting my forearms on my thighs, looking down at the overused linoleum of the corridor. "Love takes so many forms, so many. Did you know the Greeks have four primary words for love?" I nodded as if I was having an actual conversation. "Philia, Storge, Eros and Agape. Agape is the strongest of all. It's showed by actions and Esme did that when she risked her life to save me. And I've just done that when I let her go, pretending I'd be okay." I looked at the door, the pain I was feeling almost visceral. "I used to think she weakened me, but she doesn't. She makes me invincible. I will never be the same without her. She changed me in ways I could never express." I tapped the center of my chest. "I can't do it without her."

Archibald rested his hand on my shoulder. A very small gesture of comfort, but it meant so much for both of us. Could we ever fix what we'd broken?

"Then why say otherwise? Why let her go?"

I turned to look at him, uncaring that he could see the beginning of tears in my eyes. "Because she is the love of my life and I can't settle for less than the same, not with her. It would kill me."

Deluca exited the room. "I'll see you soon, man."

"What did you think he meant?" Archibald asked as we watched him walk down the corridor to the elevator.

"I'm not sure," I replied. My heart hammering so hard in my chest I felt grateful to be in a hospital because I was sure it would give out.

"I need breakfast," Archie said. "Go in and speak with her. I've got time." He slapped me on my back.

I realized I must look like shit if he was ready to do that for me, knowing how much he wanted to see his sister.

"Thank you."

He nodded. "I'll bring you a coffee."

"Yeah and some cyanide – it all depends how this conversation goes."

"Cyanide. Got it."

I knocked softly and took a deep breath, trying to place my cool mask into position as I walked into the room.

She was looking down at the engagement ring, toying with it.

When I approached her bed, she extended it to me. "I can't marry you this week," she said gently.

I extended my hand and she dropped the ring in my palm.

My stomach squeezed at my need to heave. I was losing her, I was really losing her. Once again, I was not the first choice.

"Caleb?"

I looked up from the ring, feeling numb. "What?"

"Did you hear me?"

I nodded. She was making me say it – she was being cruel. "You don't want to marry me," I repeated, and I couldn't believe my voice sounded so calm, so dispassionate when I was in fact dying.

"No."" She shook her head. "I said I can't, not that I wouldn't."

I sat down heavily on the chair beside her bed. "So, what are you saying?"

"I'm saying that I'm not the same girl that came to Stonewood last year, I grew, I learned, and I felt. No matter what you say Caleb, I know you love me deeply, probably just as much as I love you." She extended her hand toward me; I knew I was supposed to take it, but I was just so overwhelmed by everything she was saying I couldn't move.

"How could you even think I would consider another man? I would have literally died for you, Caleb, but I don't want that ugly ring I picked out of spite, or that fancy wedding that neither of us really wanted."

"So, you want to be with me?" I hate how insecure I sounded.

She chuckled, extending her hand again and this time I grabbed it like it was a lifeline. "More than anything. You're it for me, Caleb, and I want a ring and a wedding but not now. Let me go to university with you, let's move in together, build a life and then get married."

"Oh, thank fuck!" I stood up and peppered her face with dozens of kisses. "Yes, a million times yes! Let's be engaged forever if that's what you want. I called you a pawn once, but Esmeralda, you're not a pawn. You've never been a pawn." I kissed her and sat beside her on the bed. "You are the queen of the chessboard of my life, Esmeralda Forbes. You have all the power because you own your king. You are protecting me and without my queen I'd lose the game. I'd be checkmated because there would be no reason for me to keep on trying, not without you."

"And yet you were ready to let me go?" she asked, her gray eyes shining with tears.

"I love you enough to do that. Love is selfless, right? Or at least it's supposed to be?"

She looked down at her ring finger. "Do you think you could get it back? The angel-wing ring?"

I smiled. "Are you sure it's the one you want? We can go get another one, start fresh."

"Sure."" She rubbed her ring finger. "I just loved how I felt then with you. It was such a perfect ring."

"I'm sorry, sweetheart. I can't get it back because I never gave it away to start with."

She looked up at me with incredulity. "You didn't?"

I shook my head, reaching into my jacket and pulling out the ring box.

"You had it on you?" she asked with incredulity.

I shrugged. "I was planning to have this discussion after the party. I always wanted our relationship to become this."

She looked down at the ring as I took it out and slid it onto her finger. "My fiancée." I loved saying that now that it was true. "Are you sure you want to commit to me?"

"I could ask you the same," she replied. "You're a smoking-hot millionaire about to go to university. Are you sure you want to be tied down with poor old me?"

I laughed at that, just thinking about any other woman is ludicrous. "100%, you're it for me. You're tattooed on me, both figuratively and literally."

"The tattoo?" she asked with incredulity, sliding her hand in my shirt to rub it softly, making me shiver. "You got it for me?"

I smiled. "Yes, the tattoo was for you. It was always for you. You rule my heart and my forever, Esmeralda. You are not just part of my life; you are my life."

"I love you Caleb, so much."

I kissed her. "Say it again."

She cupped my cheek. "I love you."

I rested my forehead against hers. "I love you too." I sighed, finally feeling at peace. No matter what I would face, the challenge of taking over my father's empire at eighteen years of age – everything. I could face everything with that woman by my side.

Chapter 22 - Esme

Caleb laid beside me, his head on top of mine, my hand in his. He had me wrapped in a cocoon of warmth and I loved it.

I sighed, looking at my ring again.

"Are you happy?" he asked, taking my hand and running his thumb over the ring.

"That you're here with me, that we're engaged and in love? Yes of course."

"But?"

I sighed. "Things are a mess."

He nodded. "I know." He pulled me closer to him. "But when you're in my arms I don't seem to care."

Who would have thought that my man could be so romantic?

I cursed inwardly when somebody knocked. Archie's head appeared.

"Seriously? I'm outside waiting to see you and you're cuddling?" he asked, but his voice lacked heat.

Caleb just looked his way before settling back on the bed.

I raised my left hand and showed it to Archie. "We're engaged!"

"Congratulations! I don't think Caleb could ever do better and if you're ready to settle..." He shrugged.

Caleb snorted and flipped him off.

I was glad Archie didn't point out that we'd been engaged before because this was different. This was real and wanted and born from love not hate.

"I brought you your coffee, Astor, but I think it's time for you to go home and shower. You're really making the hobo chic your look, man, but two days without a shower should be your limit."

"You want me to give you some alone time?"

Archie smiled. "And some people say you're stupid."

Caleb sighed, clearly reluctant to let go of his spot beside me. "I'm not the one they called Shaggy."

"I–" Archie's nostrils flared in anger. "No, I won't take the bait. Just take your coffee and go. We need some sibling time."

Caleb smiled yet again and I loved it. I wanted to keep all of his smiles and would make it my life's mission to make him smile as much as I could.

He bent down and gave me a soft kiss. "I'll be back later. I love you."

"I love you too."

Archie gagged as Caleb shook his head and exited the room.

I looked at my brother, my eyes narrowing. "I swear if you make a gagging sound one more time, I will gut you."

Archie raised an eyebrow. "Fuck, don't be so defensive. I'm glad you worked it out. You're good for him and he adores you."

"We're not getting married next week though."

"No?"

I shook my head. "I'm not ready for this. We need to get to know each other more. Be ourselves."

Archie nodded. "So, you're not coming with me to Brown anymore, are you?"

I felt guilty, but at the same time I didn't. He was my brother and I loved him, but I had a life to build.

I shook my head. "No, I'll be going to Cornell with Caleb. I'm sorry, Archie."

"Don't be sorry. I understand. He's your future. Well...if he can still go there."

"What do you mean?

"I don't think it has sunk in since he refused to leave your side after what had happened. Your recovery was all he could think of, but with his father gone, he is in charge. He is now the CEO of a portfolio worth billions."

I shrugged. "It doesn't matter. I'll go where he will go and if he needs to stay here, I'll stay here."

"Okay."

I narrowed my eyes in suspicion. "Okay? Just…okay?"

"Yes," he shrugged. "Who am I to stand in the way of love?"

I scoffed. "Now that's just a bucket full of shit. Spill it, Archie."

He rolled his eyes. "I've got my own plans – with Taylor." He winked. "Talking about her, you know you don't have to pretend to die on me to have me forgive you. I'm not even that mad about the whole Antoine thing anymore. It is actually a good thing."

"Is it? You're finally letting go?" I knew it would be hard for him, but it needed to be done. I was sure that university, the much-needed distance, would help.

"No, I'm going to fight harder."

I sighed. I would not play dumb again. "Archie, I really think you need to let it go. Have you seen the extent of what she was ready to do to keep you at bay?"

"Yes, but don't you see? It means there's still hope. She was so worried about her own feelings for me that she pulled this."

I grimaced. "I'm not sure you should see it like that."

He waved his hand to stop me. "I supported your choices even when I disagreed. Can't you just do the same for me?"

I looked down at my hands in shame. He was right. He'd supported my choices even when he clearly hadn't approved of my attachment to Caleb. "I just don't want you to be disappointed and suffer."

"I don't think I can suffer any more than I do now." He gave me a sad smile. "Having her close enough to touch and being denied, it's like torture."

"What about father?" I tried a different tactic. "She is not exactly what he would approve of in a match."

Archie chuckled and shook his head, "Father can go fuck himself. My research at the house turned out to be quite fruitful, you know. Father will never bother us again. Information is power, Esmeralda, and you and I – we have it all."

I sat up straighter in bed. "What do you have?" I whispered as if we could be heard.

"Father's business – the non-legal one. Evidence of a collusion, multiple briberies... Everything. If anything went to the FBI, he would spend the next twenty years in a cell."

"Does he know what you have?"

Archie smiled and nodded once. "He knows what we have. He knows it's hidden. I've got your back."

"And I have yours."

He nodded. "I know you do, but no more danger now that we're done, okay?"

"Scout's honor!"

He rolled his eyes, leaning back on his chair. "I really thought it was him, you know."

I didn't need to ask who he meant; I knew because I thought the same. Our father was narcissistic enough to want to kill anyone who chose 'wrong' in his eyes.

"I know. I thought so too."

He shook his head. "I was dreading finding anything like that because even though I despise the man…" He trailed off, looking away.

"I get it. It would have been a heavy load to carry for you, for us." I extended my hand to his and he took it tightly. "We'll be okay now. We're a family and we can rebuild our life, all of us." And I would need to help Caleb heal from the added burden, an addition to his father's sin – the cold planning of my mother's murder.

"I called Luke. He is on his way to see you."

"You did?" I was surprised because last time they were together, I couldn't really say my brother had been a fan.

He nodded. "He is family – *our* family – and I want to get to know him too. He is linked to mom and now that I know she never wanted to leave me behind, I want him in our lives."

I smiled. Even if the events we had just lived through were horrific, we were all starting to heal. If we could stay united, I knew we could leave the darkness behind – at least most of it.

He rested his head on the bed. "I got so scared. Don't do that to me again, please. I love you more than I can say."

"I promise, brother. I'll be careful from now on." I patted his head. "I'm here to stay and kick your butt every time you do something stupid."

"That's going to be a full-time job," he jested.

I snorted. "You don't say." Life might become calmer from now on, but I knew it would never get boring, not with Archie and Caleb to keep in line.

****

The next couple of days dragged despite the visits. Even my father came and stayed for a few minutes. It was obviously only for appearance's sake and I loved knowing we had power over him.

The only one who didn't come was Taylor. She facetimed me though to apologize, saying she had something she could not miss. She told me she would explain when she was back, but I already suspected she was planning on attending university far away. It was the only way to get away from Archie. I would've done the same if I were her.

Bored, I turned on the news. They were taking about what had happened that night. It was so ridiculously wrong though, I couldn't help but be frustrated...and a little impressed. Based on the news, Anne White had been an unstable woman obsessed with the rich of this town. She'd had a neurotic breakdown where she'd tried to kill me. In a heroic gesture, my future father-in-law, James Astor, had sacrificed himself to save me.

I snorted. "Loads of shit," I muttered.

"This is how news works in our world, Esmeralda. Rich demons are too powerful not to die as heroes."

My head jerked up. Jacklyn was standing by my door in all her glory. She was in a sober black designer dress I assumed she'd worn to the funeral today, and carrying a pair of oversized sunglasses in a gloved hand.

"Caleb is still busy with the board members," she said as if to justify her presence in my hospital room.

She walked to my bed as I adjusted the covers almost subconsciously. This woman had a way of making me feel inadequate just by looking at me.

"They are nervous to have a man so young take over. They shouldn't be; he is as smart and as cunning as any of them."

"I'm sorry about your husband," I said.

"I'm not and neither should you be, dear. That man belonged in a grave or a prison cell. Personally I'm quite fond of the option that was picked."

"Okay… What can I do for you?"

"May I?" She pointed to the chair by my bed and I blushed at my lack of decorum, as they would say.

"Yes, of course."

"I came to discuss the subject we'd started the other night."

"You told me to get out and that it was none of my business."

She sat partly on the chair, her back straight, legs folded to the side. It was like Princess Kate or something. Would I be expected to do that too after I married Caleb?

"And frankly, it isn't, but I believe you deserve some explanation. I've sprung that upon you by giving you the journal and my note started all of this." She took a deep breath. "I presume, based on your abrasive comment, that Caleb told you what happened with his back."

Even under her mask of coolness there was shame there. I saw it. "Yes, he did."

She nodded. "I was different then and despite what my son seems to think happened that night, what I did... It is one of my life's biggest regrets."

I remained silent, just looking at the ice queen in front of me. I suspected she was just like her son - feeling everything, only so deep inside that nobody knew.

She took a deep breath. "While I was away in Europe after...the incident…"

Ah, 'incident' – so this is what we are calling it.

"…your mother started to write me letters. I never answered and I'm not even sure how she knew where I was.

Maybe it was James trying to play the sympathy card to get in her pants or…" She waved her hand. "It doesn't matter how, but she wrote about life at home and everything and nothing, never once mentioning the incident itself. She talked about Caleb's recovery and how he was often at her house with Archibald. Those two were as thick as thieves for a while."

"They are getting closer again now," I told her, one positive from this whole mess.

She nodded. "Yes, because of you. So the more she wrote, the more I saw the woman she really was, not the evil homewrecker I'd taken her for. James was sneaking around a lot and I did not care. If he had sex with other women at least he wasn't touching me." Her mouth tipped down in disgust. "But he was taking this obsession with your mother to a level that was shaming me. Everything was Victoria. He was sick enough to ask me to dress like her and have my hair done like hers, which I, of course, refused to."

How sad was it to be disgusted by the touch of your life partner?

"But under the cover of my pills and alcohol, I saw it all. I'm perceptive and I knew your mother had a secret. I just thought for a while it was an indiscretion with my husband."

"How?"

She chuckled. "Like I knew you were sneaking around that night at the party, dear. I knew you and my boy had something planned the moment you'd stepped into the room." She rolled her eyes. "And Sophia, Lord was she obvious – slipping away was child's play."

"I see," I said, slightly chastened.

"I never would have expected your mother to hide such a secret. I followed her to an internet cafe in Port Harbor and slid behind her. I saw photos of a little girl and I knew. From the moment I saw the photos I knew."

I blinked back the tears, imagining the pain my mother had gone through to ensure my freedom.

"She was terrified when she realized I knew her secret, but how could I betray her? I understood her love and her feeling of loss – William had sent Theo to an institution. My son had been taken away from me and it was a loss you never really heal from."

I wanted to shout at her, tell her she had another son that needed her love, a son who never thought he was good enough because he'd never been able to gain his mother's love. A son that I loved with everything I was.

"Do not judge me, Esmeralda. I love Caleb even if it is not something either of you believe. But he was strong and becoming what his father wanted him to be. He didn't need me."

"Yes, he did. He does."

She looked stricken for a moment, at a loss for words which I expected wasn't a common occurrence.

"I owed your mother for the kindness and solicitude she showed me when all I'd ever shown her was contempt and hate. She told me about what she did with you and I promised to help as much as I could. She feared for herself…" She looked away. "In retrospect I think she feared William would lock her away somewhere. Not that it matters. Your mother told me to keep her journal. It was a letter to you, something she hoped would help you should you be brought back into this life." She sighed. "Something I knew was inevitable."

"Why tell me about the murder? How did you even know?"

She folded her hands on her lap. "Because nobody's ever careful in front of the pill-popping wife. The one too high and too stupid to see, to hear, to understand."

I narrowed my eyes in suspicion. "You're not taking those pills are you, not really."

Her face morphed into a grin as she shook her head. "Not most of them, no. I haven't for years, but being underestimated, looking weak was my greatest strength. As for telling you. I did that so you would run and never look back. My husband was much too happy to have you in Stonewood. I could see the cogs of his sick mind at work and I knew he was sick enough to want from you what your mother had never given him."

Bile rose in my throat. James had been a sick man.

"I had the journal delivered by the janitor. The cleaning crew is always invisible everywhere you go. I did that before I'd known my husband would try to marry you into the family. Once Caleb started to show an interest in you, and I saw it at the engagement party during your dance, I knew he would go to the end of the world to bring you back. There was no saving you. It was too late. I never expected you to be reckless enough to try to solve this murder, though."

"I'm deeply in love with him. I'll make him happy – as happy as he'll allow himself to be," I admitted, running my hand over the engagement ring.

She looked down at the ring and nodded thoughtfully. "You are obviously quite enamored with my son and he is quite passionate about you as well. It gives me hope that you will be his beacon of sanity, his safety net in the world he is about to navigate. He doesn't yet comprehend the weight of responsibility and obligations thrust upon his shoulders, but he can do it. He is strong enough to do it and with you by his side, maybe he will prevail." She moved her hand and let it hover over mine, unsure. Or maybe it was simply unfamiliar for her to offer kinship.

She finally decided and rested her hand on mine. "You're kind. You befriended and cared for Theo. You love my son despite his shortcomings and for that I'll forever be grateful. This is the last we'll speak of the past and of my doubts and apprehension for the future ahead. Caleb is strong and overwhelming in so many ways. He will undoubtedly become a force to be reckoned with. He will be what his father never could - all-powerful, but without letting it swallow him in the process." She squeezed my hand. "I know he would never do it willingly, but this life has a tendency to dim the light in people. Don't let it happen to you because your love for my son will know some dark days. He will not always be easy to love, but you will shine through."

I turned my hand to squeeze hers back. "I will. I promise I will. I have enough love and hope in me. I know he loves me.

I have no doubt, but thank you for helping me, for telling me the truth about my mother. I'm glad that, despite all of it, she had an ally she could trust."

As if on cue, Caleb walked in. He still had his dark funeral suit on, but his tie was undone, dangling on the side of his neck.

The beautiful smile that was on his face disappeared the moment he saw his mother. His eyes narrowed at the sight of our hands clasped together.

"Mother, I thought you would be back at home entertaining our guests during the wake."

She stood, smoothing her dress and nodded toward me. "Esmeralda, if you'll excuse me I have the simulacrum of the grieving widow to play. I shall see you very soon."

"You will. And thank you again for everything."

"What did she want?" Caleb asked. His voice had a coldness that he had not used with me for a long time.

"Caleb." I extended my hand toward him. "She is trying. Let her. For me."

He sighed. "For you." He kissed me. "I have good news. I met Dr. Willis in the corridor. He is preparing your discharge papers."

I smiled, so happy to go back home, to my shower, to our bed. "How was your chat with the board?"

He shrugged. "We will know more in a few days. They are giving me a little while to mourn. You know...respect and all." He snorted. "But I'll face every challenge."

"Yes, you will. *We* will, together, because I'll be by your side every step of the way."

"Where you belong," he added.

"Where I belong."

Chapter 23 – Caleb

The days following my father's funeral were anything but fun. They were a succession of classes followed by lengthy board meetings that set up my role and established my legitimacy.

I had to make hard choices to ensure I would not be challenged – not that I could lose the empire my family had built. I could though lose the role of CEO, at least temporarily, and this was not something I could ever allow. Astors had been in control of our conglomerate for over a hundred and seventy years – this was not about to change today.

Some choices had been harder than others, but one thing was certain – coming home to Esmeralda made the weight lighter. But tonight was a bit more difficult because I was about to impose a directive on her. I'd always tried to give her options, but this time choice was not possible. I hoped she would see that.

I walked into my room just in time to see my beautiful fiancée stepping out of the bathroom, fresh out of the shower, a thick towel wrapped around her goddess-like body. I would have never thought I could ever be jealous of an inanimate object and yet here we were.

My hands twitched at the impulse to rip the towel from her body. I wanted to make love to her for the next few hours, worshipping every inch of her skin.

"What are you thinking about?" she asked, her voice a little deeper than usual. She wanted me just as much as I wanted her right now.

"I'm thinking about how much I want to bend you over the bathroom cabinet and show you how much I miss touching you," I growled. She crossed her legs under due to the heat of my gaze and the dirtiness of my words. She wanted that too.

"Abstinence is getting hard," she agreed, her gray eyes turning steelier. I recognized that color perfectly. Her eyes always looked like that when she was angry or aroused.

Doctor Willis had discharged her on the condition that she would limit any physical exertion for the next few weeks. Esmeralda had offered to go back to her own bedroom for the time needed. I had scoffed at the sheer stupidity of the proposal – as if I ever wanted her to sleep anywhere other than in my arms. I was never going to let her go.

"We're not animals," I'd replied. "We can sleep together without sex. I just want you with me. You keep the nightmares at bay."

And it had been true. I'd never slept better than with her in my arms.

But it had been difficult, more than we'd thought it would be. So we made sure to always stay clothed whenever we were together just to avoid pushing things too far. There was only so much a man could take.

Seeing her like this – bare feet and bare skin, wet tendrils of hair sticking to her neck, some droplets of water still peppering her shoulders... My body reacted and there was nothing I could do to rein it in, even if I wanted to.

She looked down. Staring shamelessly at my straining pants, she bit her bottom lip. I knew that her thoughts were just as decadent as mine.

"As much as I would love to take care of this problem, we're late. Your mother has already checked on you twice."

I rolled my eyes. It had not even been our idea to arrange this little gathering. A sort of 'In Memoriam' mixed with a 'Welcome Home Esme' as well as a 'Goodbye Antoine, we hope you enjoy Paris'.

"Can't your Uncle Luke distract her?" I sighed, undoing my tie and dropping my suit jacket on the chair beside the door.

Luke had been with us for a week now. I was not sure what Archibald had found on his father, but no word of protest had been uttered.

I loved seeing Esmeralda with him. She was so carefree. The smile she had given when I'd offered for him to stay a while had been worth any hassle his presence could have caused. I'd loved it so much that I'd even sat down and listened to the 'talk' about respecting Esmeralda and treating her right. The man didn't know I'd rip my own heart out if she asked me.

"I think if those two spend any more time together, it will end up in a murder-suicide."

I cocked my head to the side pretending to ponder the option. I threw my hands up in surrender. "I just need a quick shower. It's been a long day."

She detailed me, her eyes seeing right through me as usual. "Is everything alright? You look tired."

I grabbed a change of clothes and walked into the bathroom. "The board's not going easy on me," I admitted. I could let the walls down when I was in my room. With my Angel, I could share my doubts, my fears, my weaknesses without any fear of being hurt in the process. It was a treasure I thought I would never get.

"Want to talk about it?" she asked as she settled on the vanity we had moved from her room to mine in order to do her makeup.

"It's more than that. I need to," I replied, getting into the walk-in shower and watching her do her makeup through the steamed-up glass of the cubicle. It was all so domestic and I loved every second of it.

"We've got a problem." Better rip the Band-Aid off now and see how it goes.

"Okay?" she called back cautiously.

I sighed, resting my forehead against the black tiles of the shower wall. The hot water felt wonderful on my tensed back muscles.

"The board said that if I want to assume the role of CEO, I have to fulfil all the functions, no exception." I was so angry. I could see my father's former right-hand man salivating at the idea of having the top job. The more eager he was, the more adamant I was to take it from him.

"What do they mean by that?" dhe asked from the walk-in closet as I stepped out of the shower.

"It means that I'll need to be in the office at least twice a week and attend the fortnightly early morning calls with London and the monthly very late calls with Shanghai."

She walked into the bathroom dressed in a simple pair of dark jeans and a red V-neck blouse.

"You look stunning," I offered, buttoning my shirt.

She rolled her eyes, her high ponytail waving from right to left as she bounced toward me. Standing on her dainty red-painted toes, she gave me a chaste kiss. "You always say that! Even last night when I wore my sushi printed flannel pajamas."

"And it was true then too. You're always beautiful." I lifted her and sat her on the counter beside me before I started to shave.

"I guess we always knew that taking over would be a lot of responsibility, Caleb. It's alright. There is nothing you can't do."

I sighed. "Your faith in me is commendable." I met her eyes in the mirror. "But it also means we can't go to Cornell, Angel. It is too far. It's not practicable."

She shrugged. "Okay, there are a few colleges around here. It's not a big deal."

I stopped shaving and turned toward her. Had my girl lost her mind? "No, I was not thinking of community college, Esmeralda… I was saying we can't go to Cornell; we need to go to Yale. It's only an hour away, so it will be easier on me, on *us*."

She started to laugh, full belly laughs, tears-in-her-eyes kind of laughs.

"What?" I asked self-consciously.

She kissed the tip of my nose. "Oh, I love you."

I glared, but my heart was elated - as it was every time she reaffirmed her love for me.

"What?"

"You are acting like it's an issue – Cornell or Yale or whichever college. I. Don't. Care. All I want is to be there with you."

"How did I get so lucky?" I asked as a weight eased in my chest.

She shrugged. "You're lucky you're hot."

I finished my shaving under her inquisitive eyes.

"Something else is bothering you," she stated. Reaching for the face cloth on the counter, she wiped at shaving cream on the side of my jaw.

I grabbed her hand and kissed the underside of her wrist. "How is it you know me so well?"

She smiled. "Because I'm attuned to you, because I care."

I helped her down from the counter, but kept her in my arms, molding her body to mine.

"It's going to be hard, going to class and managing everything. They will not cut me any slack. I'll be so busy, I won't see you much. I'll be exhausted all the time." I rested my forehead against hers. "It's going to be trying so early in our relationship and I miss you already."

She rested her hands on my cheeks, keeping my forehead against hers. "We'll make it. We didn't have the best start, but we've bloomed despite all odds. It might be difficult, but it wouldn't be us if it was easy. I have no doubt we'll make it. We can make it work. I can attend your classes if you can't."

My woman was so positive. Just a few words and all the weariness and anxiety caused by today's decisions, evaporated until only hope remained.

She let go of my cheeks and took my hand. "Come on, let's go party."

I took her hand and let her lead me down the hall like a lovesick puppy. I didn't even care that anybody could see us.

"Oh, I forgot to tell you. I saw Doctor Willis today. He gave me the all-clear to resume all my normal activities," she announced as if it was not a big deal.

I stopped walking just before we reached the stairs and pulled her back toward me.

"What?" she asked with a cheeky smile that made me want to bite her just how she liked it.

"You didn't think about telling me that *before* we left our bedroom?"

"Well, if I did, we wouldn't have made it out."

I raised an eyebrow, brushing my knuckles against her stomach. "That's the idea."

She swatted my hand away. "Later. We have all night. Let's go before your mother bursts a vein and sends Luke to get us."

"Fine!" I replied, pouting like a petulant child.

She chuckled again and pulled me down the stairs.

I was grateful to see that this party was much smaller and simpler in tone than the last one. I didn't hate most of the people here either.

We stood side by side as she accepted all of the well-wishes given in varying tones of sincerity.

"Should we worry?" I asked, jerking my head toward William. He was scowling toward Luke who was deep in conversation with Taylor's parents.

"Nah." She waved her hand dismissively. "William is harmless now, at least to us."

"You're welcome," Archibald whispered from behind us.

He hugged Esmeralda and gave me a nod. His eyes trailed in the room to find Taylor Oppenheimer alone by the drinks station.

"I'll be right back," he said. He kept his eyes on her like a predator on his prey.

"I smell drama," Esmeralda whispered reluctantly, following him with her eyes as she chewed on her bottom lip.

She took a step toward them, but was stopped when Antoine came to stand in front of us.

"Esme, thanks for the little party."

Esmeralda smiled, giving him a hug. "You're welcome! You're going to be missed."

"I'll miss you too. I'll come back to visit, see the family." He put his hands in a prayer gesture. "I'll miss the drama too. Can you just film whatever shit eventually hits the fan?"

"Here we go," I muttered. Antoine couldn't be serious for more than five minutes or he would die.

Antoine chuckled before sighing. "I'm glad you took over. It gives me hope that when I come back I can be me."

I nodded. Resting my hand on his shoulder, I squeezed it in comfort, something I would never have considered doing before meeting my fiancée. "You can be yourself St. Vincent, I'll – No, *we'll* fight by your side."

His eyes turned misty. This was probably the first time I'd ever really saw something other than his usual clownish persona.

"Well, fuck," he sniffled with a chuckle. "I need a drink. A plus tard, les amoureux."

"What did he say?" Esmeralda asked.

"He said 'see you later, lovebirds'." I turned toward her. "Talking about lovebirds, we have some matters to take care of. I've been nice by staying here for an hour, but now..." I jerked my head toward the stairs.

Esmeralda leaned toward me. "And the matter I need to take care of is your penis, I suppose? Is the little guy feeling neglected?" she whispered softly.

I gasped in mock offence. "*Nothing* is little about my guy, thank you very much!" I cocked my head to the side. "But yes, he is feeling unloved."

She chuckled, shaking her head.

"But the business I was talking about was more about mutual, overwhelming, and if possible, multiple orgasms."

She looked at me with hooded eyes, her desire just as flagrant as mine. "Okay, just let me say goodbye to a few people and we'll sneak away."

I looked around the room to find Archibald, but he and Oppenheimer were glaringly missing. A wave of irritation engulfed me. If one of them cockblocked me tonight, I swore they'd regret it.

"I'll give you ten minutes to say your goodbyes. Then I'll come find you and carry you to the bedroom kicking and screaming."

"There won't be any kicking… But I sure as hell hope there'll be screaming," she teased, walking toward Luke.

I looked at her go, hypnotized by the sway of her hips. She didn't flirt like that often, but when she did… Fuck, it did things to my body I couldn't control even in a room full of people...which included my mother.

"I couldn't find Archie and Taylor," Esme sighed once she was back by my side.

I growled at the concern in her voice. I was going to murder them for killing the mood.

"They're fine – grown-ass adults and all that." I took her hand and pulled her down the corridor and up the stairs. I was glad she didn't put up any resistance because if she had, I would have done what I said and carried her.

She dragged her heels when we reached her old room.

"They're fighting," she whispered, stepping closer to the door.

There was no need to get that close. The screaming match between Archibald and Taylor could be heard just fine from here.

She put her hand on the doorknob. "Maybe we should–"

"Oh, no you don't!" I grabbed her hand to stop her from opening the door. "This is definitely not something either of us want to be meddling in."

"But–"

"Trust me, I know your brother. They need to let it out. Shout and release all their pent-up anger." I shrugged. "It's been a long time coming."

She sighed, throwing a last look to the door. "Fine, I just hope you're right."

"I am," I affirmed much more confidently than I felt. "Let's concentrate on us now, okay?" I asked as we walked into our room.

"Okay, fine." She stood in front of the door. "Now strip," she commanded.

I raised an eyebrow. "And why would I do that?" I asked teasingly, already starting to undo my shirt.

"Because you owe me one for the pre-wedding party," she grinned.

I pretended to ponder that. "I suppose you're right. A promise is a promise."

I removed my shirt. As expected, she noticed the new tattoo straight away. She was so aware of me, inside and out. She knew me like no one else - my dark corners, weaknesses, exposed nerves and all. Yet, she still loved me without restriction. How did I get so lucky? I wasn't sure.

"New one?" she asked, coming to stand closer to me. She rested her slender, delicate hand over my racing heart and the still-raw new tattoo.

"Yes, I had it done last week."

I rested my hand over hers. It felt like every time she was near me, I had to touch her one way or another. I realized it had started way before I'd realized it. She was a magnet, the sun I was orbiting around.

"Why a compass?" she asked, cocking her head to the side. "And I'm sorry to say, but the tattoo artist made a mistake."

"How is that?" I asked, not able to contain my smile. My girl was all in the details.

She moved her hand and brushed the top. "This is North, but he put East instead."

"Did he?" I asked, playing along.

She nodded. "Yes there is an 'E' instead of an 'N'." She looked up and smiled. "Don't worry. It can be fixed. And it's so tiny, nobody else will notice it because if anyone tries to look that closely at your chest, I'll knock them out."

I chuckled, grabbing the back of her neck and pulling her into a kiss. My girl had a possessive, jealous streak and I loved it. She was silly to think I could even be interested in anyone else, but it felt nice to see my kitten - No, my lioness, get her claws out.

"It was not a mistake, Esmeralda, my love. E is my north. *You* are my north, my moral compass, my northern star in the dark sky. You're the only one able to bring me back from whatever dark corner I sink into."

"And when I thought you could not get any more romantic," she sighed, brushing her lips on my tattoo. "I love you so much, it's surreal." She reached for my belt and I thanked God she was taking the lead. But then the door slammed open to reveal a furious Archibald.

His pants were not fully buttoned. His shirt was open. His hair was in complete disarray. *At least someone got laid,* I thought darkly.

"She is leaving?!" he asked Esmeralda as she took in his attire with concern and a hint of disgust.

"You just had sex?" she asked horrified, her mouth tipping downward now.

"Gross to think about your sibling getting laid, isn't it?" He scoffed. "Well imagine how I feel every day looking at you two."

"Archibald, maybe this can wait 'til tomorrow? Please?" I was not above begging at this point.

He took a look at my state of undress. Turning to Esmeralda again, his anger faded, replaced by weariness. "She is leaving," he repeated to her. "Did you know?"

Esmeralda took a step back, resting her back against my chest. "No, I knew she was in the selection process, but nothing was sure and she didn't know yet what she would do."

He ran a hand through his hair. "England, she's going to England." He shook his head. "She gave me her virginity tonight and now she is leaving me."

Kill me now.

"You and me both," Esmeralda whispered and I realized I'd spoken out loud.

"How?" He sat on the chair by the door, clearly here to stay.

Esmeralda went to him and kneeled by his side. "How what?" she asked kindly, taking his hand in hers.

"How am I supposed to let her go? How am I supposed to let her forget when all I want is for her to be mine?" His voice was thick with emotion. His pain was so close to the one I'd felt, it still resonated in my chest. "I love her, Esme. I think I always did and I fear I always will."

Esmeralda threw me a helpless look and I sighed, looking heavenward.

"You'll be fine, brother," I said. It had been years since I'd called him that, but yet it still felt right. "It will hurt like a bitch. I won't deny that, but you won't be alone. You're going to come with Esmeralda and me to Yale. We'll do the whole college experience and who knows what will happen. Maybe you'll move on, but maybe she'll realize you are it for her too and she'll come back." I took a step closer. "But you've got a support system, man. You have your sister and you have me."

"You want me to...come with you?"

I looked at Esmeralda and the look of gratitude she gave me took my breath away. She made all sacrifices, all hard choices, worth it.

"Of course!" I scoffed. "They'll need kings to rule over them and two is better than one. Plus, you'll need to help me keep your sister in check and stop her from being the campus saint or she'll bring home all the strays she can find."

She glared at that, but it lacked heat.

Archibald nodded. "Yes, I'll come with you guys." He leaned toward Esmeralda and kissed her forehead. "Being with you will help me hurt less. I'll feel less alone. And maybe you're right, maybe it's what we both need – some distance."

I nodded and sighed with relief when he finally stood up. I needed my alone time with my future wife.

"Okay, well, I'll go home now. I think it's for the best and you can go back to…" He gestured toward us with a grimace. "Whatever. I'll see you tomorrow."

"You think he'll be okay?" Esmeralda asked as soon as I'd closed and locked the door. I wouldn't be foolish and make the same mistake twice.

"I think so. It's going to be hard, but he won't be alone. He'll have you, the brightest, most loving woman in the world, to help him." I took her in my arms and kissed her deeply.

"Thank you," she whispered against my lips.

"What for?"

"For taking him with us, for knowing that I needed him close." She wrapped her arms around my neck. "I'll love you forever, Caleb Astor."

"I love you always," I answered before laying her gently on the bed.

I made love to her that night, slowly, sweetly, reverently. Archie's pain had awoken the memories I had of losing her, of the uncertainty over whether she'd ever be fully mine.

But she was mine, fully, completely… Just like I was hers. Forever - until our last breath and even beyond if I had any say in the matter.

Epilogue – Caleb

Six months later

Life was good, really good – in ways I'd never thought it could be, in more ways than I deserved it to be. But my heart was lighter than ever and so full of love for the petite woman now standing in the kitchen of the three-bedroom apartment we shared with Archibald. I had not been particularly excited to share our love nest with her brother, but he had taken me up on our offer to join us at Yale. I had thought he would take his own place, somewhere not too far away, but I didn't have it in me to separate them. If he wanted to torture himself with all our PDA and our nightly lovemaking, that was his problem, not ours.

I was tired. Recent days had been hard, what with finals and the demands of the board. But it was going to get better now; I had officially been named CEO.

I regained some energy as I watched Esme without being seen. She looked so endearingly ridiculous with her messy bun, black leggings, multicolor woolen socks, and duck-covered apron, along with flour on her cheek and a trace of chocolate on her neck.

I approached her slowly, then wrapped my arms around her, making her jump.

"Oh, you're home early," she huffed.

"Uh huh, my exam was done and I wanted to come back to you." I always wanted to be with her. You would have thought that living as a real couple for the past few months would have dimmed some of my obsession with her, but no. If anything it was running deeper. "You've got chocolate on your neck... I'll take care of it." I licked her neck, making her shiver.

"Caleb, not now," she chastised, but the little movement of her hips, the brushing of her beautiful butt against my growing erection, seemed to say otherwise.

"What are you doing, Angel?"

"Experimenting for Thanksgiving dinner. I think this cake will be good."

I looked over her shoulder to the cake she was cutting.

"Here, taste." She took a small piece between her fingers and extended it to me. When I took the piece, I sucked her fingers into my mouth, making her gasp.

"I like it." And it was true. My woman was proficient in the kitchen. She was actually proficient in everything she set her mind to and I was not surprised. She was beyond amazing.

She nodded. "Good. Tomorrow I'll experiment with the stuffing and gravy."

"Why don't we order dinner?"

She shook her head. "I want us to be normal during college. It's only five of us. I'll cook."

I kissed her neck again. I didn't have it in me to remind her that going to Yale debt-free and living five minutes from campus in a high-rise apartment which had cost me over one million dollars was not 'normal college experience.' This woman was my heart and I had no shame in admitting that I was completely whipped by her. She was the boss of me and I had made my peace with that.

"Okay, but you know your brother will eat basically anything and my mother and Sophia can't boil an egg, so whatever you put out will be amazing. I'm proud of you, Angel."

She sighed, leaning against me and I knew I had won.

I untied her apron. Turning her in my arms, I kissed her deeply. After pulling her to the leather sofa in the living room, I settled between her thighs and felt her heat through her leggings.

I thrusted forward. "I can't wait to put babies inside you."

She smiled. "After college. We'll have a little Theo."

"And a little Victoria," I added, kissing her more deeply.

"Fucking hell, you two!" Archibald barked.

I sighed, turning my head to see him glaring from the entrance.

"If you're not happy, you can always move out," I barked. That man caused me more cases of blue balls than he was worth.

Esmeralda slapped my arm, but at least she didn't make me move for which I was grateful. I didn't want Archibald to see my giant boner.

"Well, you better get it out of your system and do it everywhere during the break. I'll be away then."

Esmeralda tensed under me. "It's Thanksgiving, Archie."

"I know, but I've decided to go visit Europe."

Oh, for fuck's sake! "Let me guess, England? And more specifically, Oxford?"

Archibald shrugged. "Maybe." He gestured toward us. "I'll be in my room. Just– Just don't be too loud and throw the couch out afterwards, okay? I'll even pay for a new one."

I rolled my eyes, but concentrated on my fiancée again. She was certainly not in the mood anymore, looking worried more than anything.

"I thought he was moving on," she whispered, looking into my eyes.

"Let him try again. He needs to try everything he can so he can say he fought to the end. Losing a piece of you is hard."

"You understand him?"

I nodded. "I would have gone to the end of the world for you, Esmeralda. I never feel complete away from you. If he feels he needs to try again, we should support him."

She sighed. "I don't like when you're the reasonable one."

I grinned. "Me neither. I'd rather be your alpha asshole who loves to worship your heart and your body."

She chuckled. "I love you, idiot."

"But I'm your idiot."

"Forever?"

I smiled. "Always."

Epilogue – Esme

Ten years later

I stood by the bay window, holding Vickie's brown teddy in my arm. I looked down at the beach where my husband was engrossed in the majestic sandcastle he was making with our four-year-old daughter.

It was a beautiful sunny day and unseasonably warm for November in Connecticut. Vickie had wanted to make a sandcastle and there wasn't much Caleb would deny her.

He adjusted her coat, then her hat which sat on her beautiful blonde curls. My heart squeezed in my chest. I couldn't believe he had ever thought he would be a bad father.

He was the most attentive dad in the world. He used to take turns at night to help with the feedings and diaper-changes. And now, even when he was extremely busy with work, he always put us first, never missing a birthday, soccer game, or ballet recital.

This man was still the love of my life. I didn't think I could love him anymore than I had when we'd gotten together, but I did. Every time he made it home early enough to read a story to the children. Every time he made love to me like it was the first time, even though we knew each other's bodies by heart now. I loved him more.

This man and our children were my life.

"Mummy?" I turned toward my six-year-old son who was dressed as Iron Man. Oh, the irony.

"Yes Theo?" I smiled at him. He looked a lot like Archie, something he enjoyed teasing Caleb about.

"Is grandpa Luke coming today?"

"Yes, of course he is, baby."

Grandpa Luke, my uncle Luke, was now Jacklyn's husband – something that had almost caused Caleb to have an aneurysm. But they were both really happy against all odds.

"Why is that?"

"Because he is the best at making voices in stories!" He beamed. "And I have the new book daddy bought me for him to read tonight."

"Ah," I chuckled. "We won't tell Uncle Archie or Daddy though, alright? It would make them sad."

It would also make them super-competitive and as usual, they would go to extreme lengths to get the number one spot, no matter how trivial it was.

"Tell me what?" Caleb asked, his gravelly voice still making my heart squeeze in my chest all these years later.

I turned to find him carrying Vickie in one arm, her hat and coat discarded. She was the spitting image of her father – down to the sternness of her look. I felt bad for any boy who would ever show her some interest. Between her attitude and Caleb's overprotectiveness, I feared for the poor guy's life.

Theo hugged his father's leg. "Grandpa Luke's coming tonight."

"Yes, he is." Caleb looked up to me with his half-grin. Standing like that, holding our daughter, it made me melt into a puddle.

I bit my bottom lip and his eyes darkened a little.

"Theo, are you done with the Thanksgiving decoration for the table tomorrow?"

Theo nodded. "I only have the pinecones to do, daddy."

"Victoria, do you want to go help your brother?" he asked, setting our little girl on the floor.

She nodded. "Tell mommy about the castle," she said before extending her hand toward her brother. "Theo, hand," she commanded.

I chuckled. She really was her father's daughter.

We both watched them go down the corridor to their playroom. It was now a family tradition, something I started all those years ago – Thanksgiving with the Astors.

Caleb pulled me to him, kissing the top of my head. "We did good."

I nodded, leaning into him. "We did..." I sighed with happiness.

"Maybe we can make another one?" He tried.

My heart accelerated in my chest. "Yeah?" He knew I wanted a big family. And I would love another child. Another piece of us in the world.

"My mom and Luke will be here tonight. They love taking care of the kids..." He shrugged, leaning down to give me a chaste kiss. "I booked us the bridal suite at the Seahorse Hotel..."

"Someone is confident," I teased. Turning in his arms, I wrapped my own around his neck. "So what is this story about the castle?"

"Ah, yes. I'm happy you asked. Our daughter and I built the castle where we will move. I will reign as the almighty kind King along with you, the most beautiful Queen the land has ever seen, and our adorable little prince and princess."

"That's a lovely thought."

"Have you ever regretted it? Taking me as your king?"

"Not one day in my life. You're my happily ever after."

"You are too, my queen. I love you forever."

"I love you, always." I pulled him into a kiss, getting lost for just a few minutes in our little piece of heaven.

The Patricians continues

So, whilst I was writing this opus, I realized I couldn't close Archie and Taylor's story in this book. There was too much to say and they deserved their own book.
Their story, and Enemy-to-Lover second chance romance, will be told in a standalone set five years in the future (with flashbacks on what really happened when they were teens). It is tentatively set to be released mid-2021 and is titled "**Bittersweet Love**".
Now our favorite King of Mischief Antoine St-Vincent – He also has a story to be told. He will get his novella I'm hoping end of this year/ early next year. It will be a book 2.5 happening during university. It is tentatively titled "**Bittersweet Truth**".

About the Author

R.G Angel is a trained lawyer, world traveler, coffee addict, cheese aficionado, avid book reviewer and blogger.

She considers herself as an 'eclectic romantic' and wants to write romance in any sub-genre she can think of.

When she is not busy doing all her lawyerly mayhem, and because she is living in rainy Britain, she mostly enjoys indoor activities such as reading, watching TV, playing with her crazy puppies and writing stories she hopes will make you dream.

If you want to know when R.G.'s next book will come out, or what signing she will be attending please follow her Facebook page, join her Readers' Group "RG's Angels" or email her as rgangelbooks@gmail.com.

Printed in Poland
by Amazon Fulfillment
Poland Sp. z o.o., Wrocław